BREATHING—
DARK AND HAIRY

GARY RIDOUT

Dedicated to The Carpool Gang:
Paige "Turner," Rob "Inson," and Graham "Cracker"

BREATHING—
DARK AND HAIRY

1

LEAVING THE FLATLANDS

June-July, 2000

IN A NORMAL BASEMENT IN A NORMAL HOUSE, A NORMAL girl named Amanda Wilson was moving a mountain of clothes from the washer to the dryer. All was quiet, but she was not alone. Behind some boxes, something was breathing quietly. Waiting. It was furry but small, and it was patient. Waiting for the perfect time to strike. Amanda hummed as she mindlessly threw damp clothes into the belly of the dryer. Setting the dial, she sensed something abnormal in the quietness. She could hear the TV upstairs, and she knew her dad was there, but still. Something. Suddenly blackness hit as every light went out.

"Get me outta here!" screamed Amanda as she leaped over a pile of magazines toward the basement steps. What is it? she thought as she struggled in the blackness and felt her body start to shiver. She began to feel the wall, knowing it led to the wooden steps. Fumbling for the light switch, she felt heavy breathing on her neck. She grabbed for the switch, but missed, and a bear claw hit her hand. "Aahhhh!" she screamed. She fell on the bottom step. A furry form leaped on top of her, knocking the breath out of her. Amanda groaned in the blackness. She realized the size and shape of the thing and shouted, "Get off me now, Bill-Lee! And get that

1

silly bear suit off; you know I'll have nightmares for the next week! You know about me and the dark. I have a phobia." The basement quickly illuminated as Amanda hit the light switch.

The eight-year-old's voice rang out. "Phooey on your phobia, Amanda. This is our basement, and you knew it was me in the bear costume."

"Not at first, but then I could smell Reese's Peanut Butter Cups on your breath! Yuck! And guess what, big guy, that bear costume is history. I am hiding it from you, and you'll never see it again."

The two untangled themselves and brushed off the basement dirt. As brother and sister were standing at the basement steps, Amanda said, "Besides, we need to be getting ready for our move to the mountains; I hear there's a bear around every corner where we're going."

Bill-Lee threw the bear costume on the bottom step and raced his sister to the top. Trying to be a sophisticated thirteen-year-old, almost-eighth-grader with a pain-in-the-neck little brother was stressful sometimes. Amanda grabbed his shoelace and made him trip so she could win.

"Ya stinkin' cheater!" Bill-Lee screamed as he lay crumpled on the steps.

Ah, the satisfaction, thought Amanda.

Almost breathless, the two combatant siblings made it out of the basement and into the living room.

What a crew! thought their father, whom they called "Big Dad." He looked comfortable but frowned as he sat nestled in his recliner. Big Dad was big. At six feet four inches, he towered over his offspring. Big Dad was their rock and security. Amanda was about a foot and a half shorter and mainly looked like a little girl, but sometimes Big Dad could see flashes of a young woman shining through. Bill-Lee would never make the center on any basketball team. He was a solid three feet eleven inches and weighed in at sixty-two pounds. "I don't know what you two have been up to," said Big Dad, "and I don't think I want to know. Amanda, what about the sheets?"

"They are in the dryer."

"That's great," he said. "Now, Mr. William Lee Wilson, have you brushed your teeth today? I can smell a heavy scent of Reese's Peanut Butter Cups."

In a flash, Bill-Lee was gone.

Big Dad looked at Amanda. "That boy will be the first in our family to have dentures; it's like he's allergic to toothpaste." He called after his son, "Hey, remember to hum the entire Happy Birthday song before you stop brushing!"

When Bill-Lee returned with much fresher breath, Big Dad called for a family council meeting. They had several of these meetings each month because a single father with two active children had to work hard to keep everybody talking and understanding. All three walked into the kitchen and pulled chairs from the table to meet. One other family member attended but didn't say anything. That's because Bunster, a seventy-five-pound golden retriever, couldn't speak English.

As they were getting organized, Amanda stood up and looked at the photos on the refrigerator. She recalled the conversation she had had earlier in the day with her friend Nan.

"Hey, girl," Nan had said, "we will always be friends."

"Let's pinkie swear," said Amanda, and they locked pinkies to signify the promise.

"Amanda, are you daydreaming again? This meeting is about our move to the mountains. Mr. Fresh Breath and I invite you to join us."

Amanda smiled and settled into a chair at the table.

Big Dad went over the logistics and schedule for the move. As he talked, Amanda thought about how happy she was for her dad. She knew it was special for him to get a promotion and move to the mountains he loved. Little Bill-Lee didn't say much. His chin quivered when he realized they were moving a long way from his most favorite spot in the world, the park over on Anderson Drive. Amanda was looking on the bright side. She was adventurous and grew very excited about the idea of hikes down paths with crayfish-filled creeks, trout-filled rivers, and all sorts of wild creatures and sights.

When the meeting adjourned, Big Dad put his arm around Amanda and said, "I'll do my best to make sure this move helps you overcome your fear of the dark."

"I think it's getting better, Dad; I don't even think I'll have any nightmares after stupid Bill-Lee jumped on me with his bear suit on."

Big Dad hugged her and walked outside to feed Bunster. The big yellow dog gobbled down his food in the dark. "Honey, I wish you were here to help me," Big Dad said as he looked up at the stars. "I know Amanda's fears of the dark are because of that night. I'll work hard with Amanda to help her grow up as strong and brave as you were." He breathed deeply and noticed that the coolness of May evenings had changed into more humid and warmer June nights.

Two weeks later, Big Dad told the children about a house he had bought in the mountains. "You should have let me pick the house," said Amanda. "You know I have an eye for cool houses; I watch HGTV all the time."

"Well, you are certainly correct, *Realtor Wilson!*" said Big Dad. "But I was up there for an engineering orientation, and a buddy of mine told me it was too good a deal to pass up. The house sits near the top of a small mountain. It is also in walking distance to the town of Smith's Gap with many hiking trails into the deep woods. There are ponds and caves nearby. The house looks like nature has tucked it into the ground. It has trees, vines, and rhododendrons all around it. Vines encircle the bottom of the house. You guys will like it; it's a real mountain experience!"

Bill-Lee threw up his hands and looked at Amanda; she could tell her little brother did not understand what he meant. As she searched her dad's eyes, she realized she wasn't so sure either.

Five weeks later, in late July, with the SUV and trailer loaded, and Bunster panting in the back, the Wilson family wound their way west, past Asheville and Weaverville, and finally up Highway 32 to Smith's Gap. After driving through the town and taking a few turns, Big Dad bellowed, "I see the moving truck is already here. Hopefully, the crew is about finished unloading."

"This is it!" said Amanda as she looked at the new house in the mountains. Jumping from the SUV in excitement, Amanda and Bill-Lee admired the vines and bushes surrounding the house. The summer sun and rains had made everything green and beautiful. There was one circular spot in the yard that had a different color grass. It was brown and ugly. Bunster immediately went to the spot and began sniffing.

"Oh no! Don't do it!" screamed Big Dad. But it was too late. The big dog began rolling in the brown grass, over and over again.

"That would be bear doo. See the berries?" said the voice from a boy at the edge of the yard. The Wilsons stared in the direction of the voice, but they could see nothing through the thick underbrush. "Hope y'all got some good dog shampoo!" With a quick giggle, the boy ran off.

"Whoa, that stinks! And who the heck was that? Oh well, let's find some shampoo and quick!" said Amanda.

Big Dad rifled through his suitcase and came up with a tiny container of shampoo. "This is all I could find," he said, as he handed it to Amanda."I'm going into the house to see what else I can find."

Amanda spied a moldy water hose attached to a spigot in some bushes at the side of the house. "This will work!" she shouted as she grabbed the end and turned the water on. In just a second, Bunster stood staring into space as Amanda and Bill-Lee sprayed the big dog and covered him with soap suds. "Make sure you get his jaw, and his back, that had a lot of bear doo on it. Oh gross, look at his dog collar; it's brown!" said Big Dad. Bunster looked up mournfully when he heard Big Dad's voice. "Big guy, you will smell much better after this, and don't look at me like you're being executed!"

"Almost got all the soap," said Bill-Lee as he hosed down the yellow dog.

After the wash, Bunster shook all the water everywhere. Big Dad temporarily chained the clean dog to a tree. "We'll be back before you know it, buddy. Now lick yourself dry."

The trio turned and noticed four men standing near the moving truck. "You guys sit tight while I thank the movers." Big Dad walked over, opened his wallet and tipped the head mover. They smiled, shook his hand, and jumped into the truck.While this was going on, the slightly damp brother and sister stared at their new home. "OK, let's see what you think!"said Big Dad as he started up the steps. Immediately, Amanda and Bill-Lee realized what Big Dad had meant when he called the house "a real mountain experience." Between the kitchen and den were smooth tree trunk columns.

"It's like we're really in the forest when we go inside," said Amanda.

Little Bill-Lee squealed as he ran laps on the main floor. Nooks and closets served as hiding places for Amanda and Bill-Lee as they started a quick game of hide-and-go-seek. Since Amanda was such a good hider, Bill-Lee could not find her and went upstairs to his new bedroom. He admired the knotty pine paneling that had been lovingly cared for by the previous owners.

Amanda bounded upstairs to check on the stuff in her room. At the top step, she met Bill-Lee.

"That's the last time I play hide-and-seek with you! I could never find you! It made me hungry, though. Where are the Pop-Tarts?"

Amanda laughed and walked into her new bedroom. She began emptying boxes and saw all the familiar things: her seventh grade Daniels Middle School yearbook (she had been a representative on the student council), her love notes from Thomas and Ben (eighth graders!), her awards (not too many), her last-day note from math teacher Ms. Wheeler (her second mom), and completed assignments from the last week of school (throw away now, I have a stomach ache). Down at the bottom of a box was one last item, wrapped in newspaper. When she unwrapped it, a lump came in her throat. It was a picture of seven-year-old Amanda running to her mom. Her mom was so pretty and so happy. Amanda's eyes filled with tears as she saw that the picture glass was cracked. "No stinkin' mover will mess up this picture! This is priority one—getting some new glass! And that's just what I'll do. Tomorrow. OK, Mom?" she said as she gently set the picture by her bed.

Since Bill-Lee was downstairs, Amanda had the chance to do some real unimpeded exploring. Slowly wandering around the bedroom, she trailed her hand along the walls. Stopping at the open closet door, she looked inside. Moving a box into the closet, she spied a three-foot-tall door in the back corner of her closet. Hearing Bill-Lee clumping up the stairs, she pulled on the old knob and peered in. Inside was a wonderful storage room. It was just the right size to be alone sometimes, and it had a great musty kind of secret smell to it. Quickly she pulled a yellowed string, and a light came into the little space. Hearing Bill-Lee singing in his bedroom, she peered deeply into the storage space and crawled in. Her eyes adjusted enough so that she could dimly see another small door about ten feet away. "Hmmm," she said as she crawled on her hands and knees to the door. She pushed it open. "Big Dad's closet." Considering how the three bedrooms were in a row upstairs, she had a devilish thought: these bedroom closets are all connected by this long storage space, which means there's another door to Bill-Lee's closet. Seeing another string, she pulled it. A light came on, revealing a third small door. She began to push it open but heard the squeaky little voice of her brother. "This is going to be fun!" she said. "Real fun!" Through a crack in the door, she could see Bill-Lee as he jammed his clothes in a drawer and then pushed a model car on the floor. He then started humming as he jumped on the bed and lay staring at the ceiling.

You little dork! That bear costume wasn't so scary! she thought. With her fists, she slowly tapped the walls and the joists in the storage area.

"What? Who's...who's there?" said Bill-Lee quietly.

Amanda tapped the walls a little harder.

"Whoa! Big Dad, where are you?" Bill-Lee ran out of the room and down the stairs, skipping every other step for more speed.

Amanda scampered back toward her room, wiggled out of the storage room door, and jumped on her bed just in time to see her dad come to the door.

"Did you hear something?" he asked.

"I think I did, but I'm not sure," she responded.

"Oh well, something scared the wickies out of your little brother; I guess he'll sleep with me tonight. What do you think about our house?"

"It's great!" said Amanda.

"Looks like we'll all love it," said Big Dad. "But I just wonder, why does it seem to jut up so high on the sides? It's almost like there could be another floor down below."

Big Dad vanished down the steps and in just a few minutes unearthed some macaroni and cheese and a cooking pot from the boxes all over the floor. "Hey, guys, come on down for our first meal. You're going to love it."

After dinner in the new house and a night of restless sleep, Big Dad assembled the family the next morning at the breakfast table. "Today we are going to see your new schools," he said. Several groans came out of young mouths.

"School doesn't start for three weeks, why do you want to ruin the day?" complained Bill-Lee.

"This won't take long, and it will help, you'll see," he said.

After an eighteen-minute ride down the mountain, Big Dad located the first school. "OK, here's the middle school, and you, Miss Amanda, will be a big eighth grader at Jackson Middle School."

Amanda peered out the window, trying to look uninterested.

"Got any questions, Amanda? I believe your new school team name is unique: 'the Snarlin' Possums.'"

9

"What was that?" asked Amanda, suddenly showing more interest. "I have heard of a lot of team names, but that is the most *rural* I have ever known."

"What's roo-al?" asked Bill-Lee. "I can't even say it."

"I guess she means 'backwoods,'" said Big Dad.

Amanda looked at the football field and saw a scoreboard with a giant opossum at the top. The animal crouched with mean red eyes and a big tongue hanging out of its mouth.

"I think possums are bottom-feeders in the animal world," Big Dad laughed. "Hopefully your teams will be better than that."

"I wonder if they have a volleyball team?" she asked.

"That would be a great way for you to make friends," said Big Dad. "Let's pull in and find out."

The school was way older than Daniels Middle School in Raleigh. It had a combination of old carpet and ancient tile on the floor. It even smelled different, kind of like an old lady's perfume or an old man's aftershave. It reminded her of Great-Aunt Sophie's living room. As the Wilson family entered the front hall, a loud voice greeted them.

"Good morning, campers! You don't get extra credit for coming to school three weeks early, but we are glad to see you. I'm Jim Rifkin, principal." With that, he bypassed Big Dad's outstretched hand and went straight to shake Bill-Lee's hand. After a few shakes, Bill-Lee found he could not get free. "OK, you can let go." Bill-Lee's face turned red as Mr. Rifkin grinned and finally released the sweaty little appendage. He quickly bowed in front of Amanda and grabbed Big Dad's hand for a friendly handshake. "We are glad to see you at Jackson Middle School, the pride of Smith's Gap, North Carolina. What can I do for you folks today?"

"I am glad to meet you, Mr. Rifkin. I'm Bill Wilson, and we have come to enroll my daughter, Amanda, into Snarlin' Possum Mid...I mean, Jackson Middle School."

"Hey, honest mistake, sir," said Mr. Rifkin. "I have researched this, and we are the only public school in the nation with a team mascot called the Snarlin' Possums. There are so many of the little critters around here, we said 'Why not?' Did you know that opossums are this continent's only marsupials? They eat insects, snails, small rodents, and dead stuff. Just one possum eats up to five thousand ticks a year, yet they don't ever contract Lyme disease. Ninety-five percent of possums are naturally immune to rabies. They may be ugly, but possums are more scared of you than you are of them. Enough about our incredible mascot. Now, let's get you over here to see Miss Yardley and her lovely assistant, Cara Parrish."

As they walked down the hallway toward the next office, Amanda thought about all she had learned about opossums in the last ten seconds. This place is so oriented toward animals, she thought, it's like people and animals do live together nicely in this area.

"Here it is, and here they are," said Mr. Rifkin as he pointed into the secretary's office. Amanda looked into the small office and saw Miss Yardley and a girl about her age. The girl had dirty blond hair and was slightly overweight. You might call her "chubby"; others might say "big-boned," Amanda thought.

As they made introductions, Big Dad told them about Amanda's question about volleyball.

"Hey, I am captain of the volleyball team," said Cara. "While your dad signs you up for school, let me walk you and the little guy down to the gym."

Amanda looked into the darkened classrooms as they walked down the hallway. Each of the classrooms had huge, tall windows that opened in several places. Mint green walls and shiny, dark wood floors showed the age of the school. Tile and carpet were on the floors at Daniels Middle School in Raleigh, but these floors were different. They were shiny from decades of wax and lacquer. As Amanda stared, she did not speak; she knew she was getting overwhelmed. All these changes, she thought. Can I handle it?

Cara broke the silence. "Where are you from?" she asked.

"East of here…Raleigh," replied Amanda.

"I've only been to Raleigh once, on a school trip to the capital. We saw some museums, statues, and this cool park; I think it was called Pullen Park. Raleigh is a pretty cool place, though."

"Oh, I love Pullen Park. Bill-Lee, you remember we had a picnic there last summer. Yeah, Raleigh is nice, but it's so beautiful here. Do you see much wildlife?"

"You mean boys? Oh, not much."

Both girls laughed.

"How about bears, mountain lions, deer, elk, or possums?" asked Amanda.

Cara was quiet for a moment. "You know, that is a stupid name—Snarlin' Possums. Oh, back to your question, yes, there is wildlife. A bear cub and his mother ran across the playground when I was in the fourth grade."

Amanda's eyes got big. "Was anyone hurt? Did they put the school on lockdown?"

"What the heck is lockdown? No, but I need to tell you, this is what I heard on the PA from Mr. Rifkin: 'All students and female staff stay in the school; all male staff meet me at the flagpole and help me search for the bear. Mr. Leonard, bring your gun.'"

"Wait, wasn't that a different school? Has Mr. Rifkin always been your principal? But more importantly, why did he only call on the men?" asked Amanda.

"Yeah, Mr. Rifkin was the elementary school principal then. And, yes, in Rifkin's eyes, men are strong. Men should protect women and children. That has never set well with my friend Mary Frances Bradshaw."

Amanda was laughing so hard she started choking.

"What's wrong with you, girl?" asked Cara.

"I have moved to another world! Don't know who this Mary Frances is, but I would like to meet her. Who is she?"

"We certainly don't have time to get into that subject. Hey, there's the gym." The group walked outside to a large building attached by a covered walkway.

As Cara opened the doors, Amanda peered into the darkness. Seeing the blackness, Amanda felt a cold tingle swoop over her body. Her eyes grew wide. She said nothing.

Bill-Lee nudged Cara and whispered, "She's afraid. She has a ..."

Trying to be a fabulous tour guide, Cara turned her focus from Bill-Lee, found the light switch and illuminated the gym.

In a flash, Bill-Lee spied a loose basketball and started trying to shoot at one of the wooden backboards.

"Oh my gosh!" exclaimed Amanda loudly. Cara examined Amanda's face, as she stared into the gym. All Amanda could think about was watching boys playing basketball in an old 1940s-style gym on *The Andy Griffith Show* when she was watching TV Land on cable a few months back. The walls of the gym were dark, the ceiling had dark wooden beams, and the floors were tile. In the center of the gym on the floor was a crudely painted Snarlin' Possums logo. Some of the "S" in "Snarlin'" was gone. A partially rusted cage surrounded the metal clock at one end of the gym. The smell was like an old barn, actually kind of nice.

"Uh, earth to Amanda, are you there? What do you think?"

"We are going to win some volleyball games in here," said Amanda. "I can't wait."

The girls slapped hands and turned to leave.

"Hey, wait, don't leave me in this cave!" shouted Bill-Lee.

Cara quickly switched off the lights, and the threesome walked back up the hall to the office.

"Congratulations!" shouted Mr. Rifkin. "You are the world's newest Jackson Middle School eighth-grader, Miss Amanda Wilson. I look forward to seeing you in three weeks!"

As they walked to the car, Big Dad put his arm around Amanda. "Well, how did your school tour go?"

"It was fine," she whispered. "The darkness phobia got to me when I looked into the gym with no lights on. But I got better."

When they got to the car, Bill-Lee quickly changed the somber mood about darkness and sadness as he shouted, "I want to go to that school; it seems great. Just think, if they have a beauty contest, you could be the Snarlin' Possum Queen!"

"That's enough!" said Big Dad as they started down the road with Bill-Lee snickering in the back seat. Toward the end of the parking lot, there was a sign that read, "You are now leaving Snarlin' Possum territory, Our Students NEVER Play Dead!" At the top of the sign was a huge gray animal with a big smile on it.

"Don't even start," growled Amanda as she stared in the back seat at Bill-Lee. Unbelievably he stayed quiet. Big Dad grimaced, though, as he spotted an evil grin from Bill-Lee in the rearview mirror.

"Right around the corner here is your school, Bill-Lee. It's called Winston Elementary."

"When my brother goes there it will be called Weenie Elementary!" shouted Amanda.

"Oh Lordy," said Big Dad, "I declare this school tour to be over. We'll get you enrolled next week, little guy."

2

THE PRISONERS

July, 2000

Sadness and darkness extended from Smith's Gap and the dark gym at Jackson Middle School to a remote prison farm about two hundred twenty-five miles away, near Greensburg, South Carolina.

"Everyone up! Get up!" The guard jogged down the hall with his black baton clanging against each rusty bar of the thirty-nine cell prison farm camp. "This ain't no country club, this ain't no Ritz-Carlton! It's five fifty-nine a.m., now get up!"

A very skinny and hairy ankle moved out of the sheets in cell number twelve. The cell belonged to forty-five-year-old Muzzie Spicer, a five-foot-five-inch man of below average intelligence who was almost always in the wrong place at the wrong time. When Muzzie turned sixteen in the ninth grade, he turned his back on any more people telling him he needed to learn to read. He hated reading. Little did he know that the real world required a lot of reading skills. He had no preparation for it. Breaking into people's houses and drinking to excess became a lifestyle for the short man until he realized he had a knack for fixing things. The long arm of the law disrupted his life when he got caught in Columbia, South Carolina, trying to break into his neighbor's trailer. Over the last three years at the prison farm, Muzzie had made only one friend, and that was the notorious Lebie Jenkins. Jenkins was notorious because he was a forty-year-old Southern boy who did not take anything from anybody. "I think he was born fighting!" said his exasperated principal who finally expelled him from school forever when he was a tenth grader in Hopewell, South Carolina.

"Yo, Spicer, it's your turn to lead the jumpin' jacks," shouted the guard. Thirty-eight men of all ages and races half-marched into the still-dawning July sun from the inmate housing building toward the exercise yard. "Hey! Quiet in the line!" the guard yelled. "Spicer, get up here! What did you say?"

"I said nothing," said Spicer, almost whispering. Another prisoner pushed Muzzie Spicer in the back, causing him to trip and almost fall.

"I saw that, Lebie Jenkins!" said the guard. "You must think I'm as dumb as old Ricky Zinn over there in the corner. Hey, Zinn, it's time to wake up! Somebody grab Zinn's wheelchair!"

Just past the bunkhouse doorway sat a slightly overweight disabled man. He was dressed neatly in blue jean shorts and a seersucker button-down shirt. His eyes rolled back and forth, and some drool dripped out of his mouth. He wore almost brand-new athletic shoes that got zero wear because he could not walk in them.

"Now back to you, Jenkins, keep pushing other convicts and I'll see to it that your stay here at the 'Hilton' gets extended another couple of months. How would you like that?"

"I didn't mean anything, boss man," said Lebie Jenkins. "You know me and Spicer are tight. And now, sir, can I go help poor dumb Ricky Zinn?" Lebie Jenkins grabbed the handles to the wheelchair and pushed Ricky Zinn down the path toward the exercise yard. The sudden push startled the invalid young man as his eyes became wide and his head jerked back.

"Jenkins, you are the king of suck-ups! Why, I think you invented sucking up. Go ahead and push Zinn in the shade near that oak tree, but slow down. If he gets hurt, it's on you."

"What's going on out here?" said a moderately well-dressed woman in her mid-sixties. "You guys better be taking good care of my son, Ricky."

"Yes, ma'am," said the guard. "One thing I know for sure, Mrs. Zinn, you are the superintendent of this prison farm camp and your son is a good guy in need of good care, that's what you told me. I won't forget it."

"Good deal," said the woman. "Tell you what, have someone push Ricky into my office: it's hot out here already, he's probably ready for some air-conditioning." Mrs. Zinn turned and walked toward the white building that housed her office.

"Yo, Spicer, push Ricky over to the main house. His mother is ready to see him for a while." With that, the short man with the grayish beard hustled over to the wheelchair and proceeded to push Ricky to the main house. Soon Muzzie felt a rush of cool air as he went into the main office of the prison farm camp.

"Morning, Mrs., here, uh, he bring Ricky."

"Just leave him there, I will be out in a minute," she said from a back room.

"OK," said Muzzie. He decided to take advantage of a few moments of cool air and quietness. He walked around in front of Ricky Zinn and looked at him. Ricky was a thirty-four-year-old disabled man with very expressive eyes. For a moment the two stared at each other. "Ricky, I hope you get better one day," said Muzzie. He was shocked to see the ends of Ricky's mouth turn up as if to smile. "Gotta go," Muzzie added, and he turned to go to the door.

"You still here?" shouted Mrs. Zinn as she emerged from the back room. "Git, git! I swear you guys will take advantage of anything! Get out of here and get in the mess hall; your breakfast is probably getting cold!"

"Yes, ma'am," said Muzzie. Breakfast always is cold, Muzzie thought as he went out the door. He quickly made it to the exercise yard and was thrilled to see his fellow inmates just finishing up their exercises. Wow, got out of that; this worked out great, he thought as he jumped into the line of men plodding slowly forward.

"All right!" said the guard. "Let's move toward the mess hall!"

As they walked on the dirt exercise yard toward the mess hall, Lebie Jenkins came up next to Muzzie. "Hey, buddy, let's sit together today. I got some stuff I want to tell you."

Muzzie nodded, grabbed a tray, and sat right next to Lebie. As they took in the first few breakfast bites, Lebie whispered to Muzzie. Suddenly, Muzzie's eyes grew large, and he stared at Lebie as he was chewing.

"Can't believe it," whispered Muzzie to Lebie.

Just then, Mrs. Zinn pushed Ricky's wheelchair into the mess hall.

"Hey, boss lady, bring my friend Ricky over here; he can sit with me and the Muzz," said Lebie. A crack of a guard's baton on the table startled everyone. "You show respect to our superintendent, or else, Jenkins! Her name is Mrs. Zinn, not 'boss lady'!" shouted the guard.

Mrs. Zinn allowed the ruckus to calm down and wheeled Ricky over to the table.

"Hey, buddy," said Muzzie, pulling the wheelchair toward him, "come on over." Ricky's eyes moved back and forth as a faint grin came on his face.

Lebie stuck a fork into some type of breakfast meat. He popped some meat in his mouth and then fed Ricky a forkful. Lebie's and Muzzie's heads ducked down, and they continued whispering to each other.

Ricky Zinn stopped chewing and sat staring and listening. No one noticed his eyes becoming wide open as Muzzie and Lebie whispered. Ricky stared at the duo with his mouth open. A tear rolled out of his eye as they ducked their heads and continued whispering.

"Look at that trio," said one guard to another.

"Wonder what in the world is going on there," said the second guard. "Hey, guys, better stop talking and eat up; KP starts in five point three minutes."

Lebie continued feeding Ricky some of the unknown breakfast meat. As Ricky chewed, a guard noticed a tear on his cheek and wiped it off.

Almost simultaneously, someone in Smith's Gap felt a headache coming on. Amanda Wilson was folding clothes in her new bedroom when the pain hit her. She frowned as she felt her temples. What is this feeling? Have I been clenching my teeth? I don't get headaches! she thought.

Back at the prison, a guard came into the mess hall, surveyed the scene and yelled out, "Can't you guys even look after Ricky? He can't do all this for himself. Something has made him cry. Must be the spicy livermush. Hey, Jenkins! The superintendent wants to see you in her office, pronto."

Lebie Jenkins shot a questioning look at Muzzie and took off toward air-conditioned heaven in the superintendent's office. As he opened the door to the office, Mrs. Zinn ushered him to a chair in front of her desk.

"Jenkins, I have just received word of your release for time served. You will be finishing seventy percent of your three-year sentence for assault in the next few months. With the new regulations and your reasonably good behavior, you will be released in eighty days, which is the tenth of October."

Lebie Jenkins leaned back in the chair, smiled broadly, and crossed his arms, ready to make a statement. His "victory" speech was interrupted abruptly by a knock on the door. The hinges squeaked as the door came open. "Sorry to interrupt, Mrs. Zinn," said a guard, "but one of the state prison guys is here. What do we do with Ricky?"

Mrs. Zinn grimaced as she looked at the guard and then cut her eyes over to Lebie Jenkins. "Could you escort Jenkins back to the mess hall? Keep Ricky there and deliver Jenkins back to his group. On your way, ask our guest to wait in the outer area." Mrs. Zinn stood up and motioned for the guard to step over to the corner of her office, away from Lebie Jenkins. Always interested in prison gossip, Lebie strained to hear the conversation.

Mrs. Zinn and the guard whispered at first, but as they spoke, Mrs. Zinn became more agitated. "Look, you know I can't afford to pay someone to watch my son. Just keep this arrangement on the down-low as always."

The guard nodded and motioned for Lebie to go with him. In just a few moments, Lebie and the guard walked up to a group of men who were hoeing one of the three fields of vegetables. After working two rows of cucumbers, a voice rang out from the superintendent's building. Mrs. Zinn was calling Lebie and Muzzie into her office.

"What da heck is this about?" asked Lebie as he walked across the yard with Muzzie.

"Don't know!" said Muzzie.

"I knew you didn't know; that was a rhetorical question!"

"Oh, a what?" asked Muzzie.

Lebie just frowned as the two arrived at the superintendent's building and knocked on the door. Mrs. Zinn opened the door and pointed to a conference table where a stranger in a suit was sitting.

"Gentlemen, uh, men, this is Jesse Taylor with the Division of State Prisons. Since we are the smallest prison in South Carolina, we are thrilled to get a visit from Columbia. Today is a great day." They kept straight faces and feigned rapt attention toward Mrs. Zinn.

"What's Columbia?" Muzzie whispered in Lebie's ear.

Lebie elbowed Muzzie and stared at Mrs. Zinn.

"Mr. Taylor has given me some interesting news. Both of you are due to be released soon—Lebie Jenkins on October 10 and Muzzie Spicer on October 26. The research boys in Columbia have found that releasing two prisoners together can have positive effects. Released pairs have a higher success rate in the outside world." Mrs Zinn crossed her arms and stared at Lebie. "Mr. Jenkins, with that in mind, we will be delaying your release until October 26, and you both will get out that day."

"But, Mrs. Zinn, what did I do? Why is my association with Spicer costing me another sixteen days in this place?"

"This is *not* a negotiation. Jenkins, you actually should be serving another three hundred twenty-nine days. You and Spicer will leave here on October 26. Now sign your name to these documents. You will get a copy later. Case closed! Now you two get back to the cucumber field!"

The room erupted with the sound of metal chairs scraping on wood floors as Lebie and Muzzie trudged out of the building and toward the hot field filled with cucumbers and prisoners.

The normal hum-drum of prison life was replaced with great anticipation as Lebie and Muzzie began to think about being released in October. One night when they were getting ready to leave the TV room, Muzzie grabbed a calendar off the wall and walked up to Lebie. "Lebie, show me when we out of here?" Muzzie grunted as he shoved the very dog-eared and soiled calendar into Lebie's face.

Lebie grabbed the calendar and put a red X on October 26. "Buddy, that looks like a Thursday to me. It's going to be a super-great Thursday!"

Lebie carefully returned the calendar to a nail on the gray wall and the two inmates walked toward their cells.

"Me want to hear more story, Lebie story. You know, Ricky Zinn, the wreck, you know. You and Ricky friends? How you know him?"

"Muzz man, I am really tired right now, but don't worry, over the next few weeks I will tell you more of my life story and the story of Ricky Zinn."

"Lights out!" shouted the guard as he watched each inmate go into their cell. "Everybody at this country club needs to be snoring in ten minutes!"

At the flip of a light switch, Muzzie stood in cell number twelve, looking across the corridor into Lebie's cell. "Hey, Lebie, tell more!" said Muzzie in a loud whisper.

"Good night!" shouted Lebie back across the hallway.

"Quiet!" said the guard. Muzzie stood for a moment and then lay down on his bunk, staring at the ceiling.

Wonder what he knows about Ricky Zinn, thought Muzzie. I wonder.

3

THE HISTORY OF RICKY ZINN, LEBIE JENKINS AND MEAN GRANDMA ZULU

LIKE THE INTERTWINING OF TREE ROOTS ON A RIVERBANK, the lives of Ricky Zinn and Lebie Jenkins were mixed together since they were young. Shortly after Lebie was expelled from high school in Smith's Gap, his exasperated parents sent him to live with his aunt and uncle in Hopewell, South Carolina. The Jenkins family said they could not get him to behave and they felt that a change would do him good. Lebie always said that the change from Smith's Gap to Hopewell had no positive effect on him. He was as mean and conniving as ever. Lebie lived with his aunt and uncle in a blue and white single-wide trailer in Bliche's Trailer Park just outside of town. The trailer was just down the hill and through the woods from Ricky Zinn's neighborhood. Each day Lebie would walk to school and see a short little sixth-grader walking ahead of him. They never spoke. "I guess he thinks he's better than me," Lebie always said. Lebie and Ricky attended the Hopewell Union School. A union school is one that includes grades K-12. Lebie was already angry about being sent away from his family, but he became angrier when one day at school he was forced to sit through a boring sixth grade Honor Society induction. He grimaced when he watched Ricky get his Honor Society pin and wave back to his mother. Shortly after the induction, Lebie decided he would take Ricky down a notch or two.

"Hey, kid, what's your name?" asked Lebie as they walked down the road from school.

"I'm Ricky Zinn," Ricky said in a shy whisper.

Lebie walked right up to Ricky and pushed him into the bushes. He stood with his fists raised waiting for a fight. Ricky's response gave him a delightful surprise.

"Please don't do that anymore. What do you want from me anyway?" asked Ricky weakly.

"I want your loyalty; just do what I say, OK?"

Ricky ducked his head, looked down at the ground and said, "OK."

Lebie knew he had the first member of his "gang."

As a young child, Ricky got no real direction from his mother. She worked all the time in her jobs as a house cleaner and sometime caregiver for the elderly. In the evening she sat at the kitchen table and studied for her Associate of Arts degree at the local community college. After six years of tumultuous family life, Ricky's father left the family and moved south of Hopewell, three counties over. Ricky was three when his dad moved out. That's when Ricky's mother went to the courthouse and changed Ricky's and her name back to her maiden name: "Zinn."

It was Ricky's grandmother, Zulu Zinn, who caused him to be so compliant, or in Lebie's words, "a real weenie." Grandma Zulu cared for Ricky during the day when his mother was working. "Cared for" was a term used very loosely. Generally, "caring" means there is some love and affection involved. Zulu Zinn did not understand love. She understood control and punishment. Most Hopewell people called her "that mean old biddy." Her favorite punishment for Ricky was to lock him in the dog house in the backyard when he was bad. To Zulu, "being bad" described a whole host of behaviors. It could range anywhere from total defiance to a smirky look.

Ricky longed to tell his mother about the doghouse but was afraid if he did, the punishments would only get worse.

The summer when Ricky turned ten, the punishment took a turn for the worse anyway. One day as Zulu was locking Ricky in the dog house, she noticed a tiny wasp nest growing in the far end of the dog house near the roof. A mean grin came on her face as she studied the two wasp guardians staring at her. A month later, she looked at the nest. It was now seven inches across and covered with large dark brown wasps, ready to sting. She got to work immediately, sawing a small hole on the outside of the dog-house near the nest.

Then it happened. Several weeks later, Ricky talked back to his grandmother after she screamed at him that the breakfast dishes were not clean enough. Grandma Zulu grabbed his hand and took him straight to the doghouse. She shoved him in, and slammed the little door. Crying quietly, he settled in the corner. Usually, he would try to take a short nap while he waited for Zulu to cool off and release him.

This time was very different. In the quietness of the dog-house, Ricky heard a sound. Through the low sunlight, he noticed a thin stick inching through the newly bored hole. He could see his grandmother's wrinkly hand as he peeked through a crack in the side of the dog house.

"What cha doing, Grandma?"

"You just wait, this is something you won't forget, and you will behave from now on!"

All of a sudden, the blood rushed out of Ricky's face, as he saw the stick jab at the seven-inch-wide wasp nest.

"No, Grandma, no," screamed Ricky as the mad wasps scattered around the doghouse. Then it started, two wasps landed on Ricky and instinctively stung their idea of the intruder. Then three more. "Please, Grandma Zulu, please!" Ricky pushed hard on the doghouse door. Nothing happened. One more wasp landed on his leg and stung him. He pushed even harder on the doghouse door, and to his surprise, it popped open! Ricky crawled out of the doghouse, stood up and ran to the back porch, feeling dizzy. Then he fainted and fell to the ground. All was quiet. Zulu had left the backyard and was in the house straightening up the kitchen.

Ten minutes later, the back door came open, and Zulu's eyes grew wide. She looked at the yard near the back steps and saw a very different grandson. Ricky was lying in the dirt, motionless. His skin had turned red, and he seemed to have trouble breathing. What she saw was a preview of the way Ricky Zinn is today. Immobile, almost comatose. "Ricky!" she screamed as she looked at his body lying in the grass. Quickly she called her doctor, and an ambulance roared up promptly.

The EMTs went right to work giving Ricky a shot of epinephrine. "He needs to keep a preloaded syringe with two doses of this stuff from now on. A bee sting for someone with allergies like his could be deadly."

Zulu watched as Ricky miraculously began to recover and sit up in the yard. She turned and thanked the EMTs. "Ouch!" screamed Zulu as one last angry wasp stung her. She brushed the dark brown insect off her arm and crushed it under her worn-out sneaker. "Boy, that does burn," she said as she looked at her grandson's red and swollen body. "We got to get you in the house to lie down for a while. I'll even let you watch your favorite TV shows for a while." Just then a quiet thought gave her pause: what is my daughter going to say about this? "For gracious sakes," she said, "they could question me for child abuse!" She began to scheme as she helped Ricky up the stairs and into the house. He can never tell what happened. "I know what I'll say," she said out loud to herself, "I'll say I rescued him when he got into the doghouse playing! I saved him from a lot of pain! That's what everyone has to think, or I am in big trouble!"

Zulu didn't know it, but Ricky had heard her last statement. Even in his pain, he offered a quiet smile, knowing the power tables had turned in his favor. As he lay on the sofa watching TV, he slowly drifted off to sleep.

"Well, how is everyone today?" said a loud voice that awoke Ricky. He smiled because he knew his mother was there. Zulu ran out of the kitchen with a dish towel, drying her hands.

"Your boy is looking bad, Nora; he tangled with a wasp nest and lost!"

"Help!" came Ricky's voice from the sofa.

Ricky's mother stopped short as she entered the living room. Her hand went to her mouth. "What," she shouted, "in heaven's name? Mother!" Ricky's mother knelt next to the sofa and hugged her ten-year-old son tightly. After a minute of comforting, she wheeled around to her mother. "You tell me every detail of what happened to Ricky!"

Ricky listened intently for the next fifteen minutes as the most outlandish tale spilled out from his grandmother to his mother. "I tried to hold him back from getting in the doghouse near the wasp nest. He would not listen."

"Are you going to be OK, sweetheart?" Ricky's mother asked as she stroked his jet-black hair.

"I can breathe better now, and my arms aren't as swollen. I sure have learned about how mean wasps can be!"

Even Zulu was taken aback by Ricky's last statement. He was really good about this. Hopefully, her meanness would go unpunished one more time, she thought.

The next morning, Ricky's mother put lotion on his stings, took him to Zulu's house, kissed him goodbye, and left for work. Ricky went into the living room hoping to watch cartoons after breakfast. Zulu was watching her favorite TV show and holding her second cup of coffee. After surveying the scene, Ricky did the unthinkable. He walked up to the TV, glared at Zulu, and switched the channel to his favorite cartoons.

"Switch that channel back now, boy!" screamed Zulu.

Ricky stared at his grandmother with a slight smile and left the room. Zulu heard the back door slam.

Wonder what he's up to, she thought, as she rose to change the channel back. In just a moment she heard Ricky's voice.

"Grandma," he called, "I need help!"

"What is it?" she said as she leaned against the doorframe in the kitchen.

Ricky's voice became very stern. "I think we should have an agreement. You told a pack of lies to my mother yesterday. I will keep it our secret. But if you get mean again, it will not be a secret, and I will tell every detail. I have hidden the wasp nest and the stick you used to stir up the wasps. Today is a new day! No more meanness! Got it?"

Zulu looked at her conniving grandson and replied, "Message received."

For Ricky, "caregiving" had just taken a very good turn for the better.

Two years later, Ricky told Lebie Jenkins the story of his grandmother, Zulu. "Where is that witch now?" asked Lebie.

"Oh, she just celebrated her seventy-fifth birthday, has had a slight stroke and can't do much, but she still lives in the same little house six doors down from us."

"I am thinking, man, I am thinking, this can't go on. Hey, Zinn, I got an idea about a great word called 'revenge.'"

"Oh, I don't know, Lebie. Zulu is pretty old and weak."

"Zinn, you are in my gang; this is now gang business and the gang sticks up for each other."

About a week later, Lebie had finalized his revenge plan and revealed it to Ricky Zinn. "Hey, that old lady will be sorry she ever messed with you! Now let's get over to her house, and I will show you what the word 'revenge' means!"

In less than fifteen minutes, the Lebie Jenkins gang (Lebie Jenkins and Ricky Zinn) was standing behind some bushes across the street from Zulu Zinn's house. The sun was slowly going down as they stared at a large "keep out" sign near the welcome mat at the front door. Shaggy, untrimmed bushes covered the windows on the front and sides of the house. The vinyl siding was green with mold, and the roof had large splotches of moss growing on the shingles, a testament to the humid South Carolina weather. In the darkening of the day, neither of the boys noticed something that was very new. It was a silvery, shiny corkscrew device to tie up a dog. Ricky and Lebie did not know that Zulu had gotten scared a few months ago and purchased a very loyal, very large, and very mean Doberman pinscher named Zool. He was trained as a watchdog because Zulu watched TV news for eighteen hours every day in her living room and was sure there was a burglar, rapist, or murderer around every corner. She liked the dog and especially his name because it sounded like hers and she knew he could be as mean as she was.

The trainer had said that he would be extremely obedient and knew all the commands. Zool responded immediately to "sit," "stay," "come," "crate," and "heel." There was another command Zool knew and would respond to, and the trainer grew very serious when he described it. This command was "kill."

"I hope you never use this command," said the trainer. "Most people will change their minds about whatever bad thing they were thinking when they see a ninety-pound growling Doberman pinscher. You won't like what happens if you use the command 'kill.'" Zulu just grinned when she heard that statement.

"At least I will feel very secure," she said as she stroked Zool's shiny black and tan coat.

Motivation and logistics were the name of the game as Lebie and Ricky stood looking at Zulu's house. "This old biddy will wish she never heard the word 'wasp,'" said Lebie as they watched the house. "I will take this rock and toss it through the picture window; that's the room where she is watching TV. You sneak around to the back door and use this screwdriver to get in, then run through the house with this tar stuff, and when you see the old bag, throw it at her. While you are doing that, I will be banging on the side walls with this garbage can lid. It's beginning to get dark so I hope no one sees us making all this racket, but she will have the bejeebers scared out of her."

"Sounds like a plan. If that's what you want to do, I'm your man," responded Ricky.

"All right, let's do it." With that statement, the "gang" went into action. Ricky took a can of black tar paint to the back door and waited.

In the front room of the house, the loud TV blared away and Zool's ears perked up. On the recliner next to Zool sat Zulu, snoring into her third nap of the day. Zool growled quietly, trotted to the kitchen and waited. Just then a rock crashed through the picture window and landed on the old carpet. Zool left the kitchen and ran to the front room. With glass pieces everywhere, Zulu woke up and grabbed her cane. She looked out the front window and saw Lebie Jenkins standing in the front yard. "I'll get you! I know you, Jenkins!" she screamed as he ran across the street. Zool perked his ears up and whirled around when he heard noises at the back door. Ricky was concentrating on the lock and did not hear the big dog's footsteps. A quick push with the screwdriver dislodged the latch. Ricky grabbed the tar paint and burst into the kitchen. He slung the gummy substance all over the place. In the hallway past the kitchen, Ricky stopped short. He was astonished to see a huge dark form growling deeply in the partial darkness. Screaming, he dropped the tar paint can and ran toward the door. Zulu knew that her end was near. She was sure this commotion was caused by a murdering rapist from some other country, just like she had seen on the news so many times. The scream did not sound familiar at all, even though it came from her flesh-and-blood grandson.

Sitting up in the recliner, she screamed, "Kill!" That was all Zool needed. In the blackness of the kitchen, Ricky saw a beast leaping toward him. That was the last thing he remembered. His body became limp as the ninety-pound black monster bit his arm, neck, and head. Zulu gasped as she turned the light on in the kitchen. Looking at the twisted and mangled body on the floor, she screamed, "Sit, stay." Fumbling for the phone, she dialed 911. "Yes, this is Zulu Zinn, I have had a break-in and an injury. I need an ambulance and police now!"

In the front yard, Lebie could tell that something had gone wrong. He was already across the street behind the bushes when the ambulance and police car arrived with their sirens wailing. "That's enough excitement for me. Hope the old lady got what was coming to her. I'll catch up with Ricky tomorrow."

As two male EMTs rushed into the kitchen, they were stunned. "Get this dog out of here!" one of them screamed.

"Crate!" said Zulu, and the big canine rushed to his wire cage and lay down. Zulu locked the crate door.

All the training the EMTs had faded out when they looked at the bloody scene in front of them. Finally, a female EMT brushed past the two men and said, "Don't just stare, let's get him stabilized! Don't just *stare!* He needs help!" Soon they all were working on the mangled twelve-year-old figure of Ricky Zinn.

Two police officers appeared at the front door to speak to Zulu. "What is going on?" said one officer.

"Well, sir, I was watching TV—you know that news show that comes on at six thirty with that blond-haired woman?"

"Ma'am, please move along with the story," said the second officer.

Giving that officer a mean look, Zulu continued, "All of a sudden, this rock came through the front window and…"

"Coming through," said an EMT.

"Is the little scoundrel going to be all right?" asked Zulu.

"A lot of bites, but it appears that he passed out from fright rather than loss of blood."

"Let me get a look at the little ruffian; don't know what the world is coming to!" Just then she drew back. "That's Ricky!"

"Who?" said the EMTs and the two police officers almost in unison.

"That's my grandson!"

In all the confusion and a large amount of blood, the EMTs and Zulu did not notice the large wound hidden in the thickness of Ricky's hair. They did not notice the first bite from Zool. It was the largest one, a bite near the top of Ricky's head.

In about five minutes, Nora Zinn answered a phone call from her mother about Ricky. Hanging the phone up abruptly, she rushed to the hospital. After sitting in the emergency room waiting area for two and a half hours, she began to drift off to sleep.

"Are you the child's mother?" said a man in blood-stained blue scrubs.

"Yes, sir," said a startled Mrs. Zinn as she stood up rubbing her eyes.

"Hello, I am Dr. Eibner, emergency room doctor here at Spartanburg Medical Center. Your son is now stable and has received both a skull X-ray and a CAT scan. Ricky is in a room in the neurology ward where a neurosurgeon will examine him in the morning. He is sleeping now and is under some sedation; I would suggest that you go home and get some sleep. The neurosurgeon can meet with you tomorrow morning after his examination. Rabies is not a threat because the dog is up-to-date on his shots. The owner has documentation. Have a nice night."

Mrs. Zinn mournfully stood watching the "very efficient" doctor walk away. He soon vanished into a door marked "No Admittance." Grabbing her Diet Coke, Mrs. Zinn walked slowly toward the exit of the hospital and made the trip home.

The next morning, Mrs. Zinn got to the hospital and found Ricky's room. Her mother was already sitting by the bed. "I don't know what the world is coming to, Nora," said Zulu. "But I did get a look at the boy that was with Ricky. It was that Lebie Jenkins kid from the trailer park. I notified the police but they can't find him."

"I knew that kid was no good. Hopefully, he is out of Ricky's life," said Mrs. Zinn.

The two were interrupted as Ricky's attending physician,

33

Dr. Brinson, a highly regarded neurosurgeon schooled at Duke University, entered the room, introduced himself, and sat down. "As you can see, your son has still not regained consciousness, and this is causing great concern. We are studying his blood work and examining the damage done by the dog," Dr. Brinson said as he cut a side-glance at Zulu.

"The dog is no more. I am getting an electronic security system," said Zulu as she looked down at the floor.

"You better duck your head; that monster almost killed my son—your grandson!" screamed Ricky's mother tearfully.

"What in the heck was he doing busting in my house? And why did that Jenkins kid throw a rock through my nice picture window?"

"Ladies, please," said Dr. Brinson, "keep your voices down; we may have to limit his visitors to only one at a time!" The doctor looked down at his chart and the room got quiet. "Mrs. Zinn, your son has sustained some brain damage. The dog's teeth went through the cranium. This deep wound is the reason he has not regained consciousness."

Ricky's mother gasped and reached for her handkerchief. Ricky's grandmother tried to put her arm around her distressed daughter.

"Don't touch me, you, you monster. You don't deserve to live!"

Both women wept silently. Finally, Zulu got up and trudged out of the room.

That afternoon Dr. Brinson met again with Ricky's mother.

"I am distressed to tell you that the dog bite occurred at a very vulnerable place in your son's brain. The next few days will be crucial, but there is a real chance that Ricky will not speak or walk again."

Mrs. Zinn sat very still and cried quietly. She knew those words would change things forever. That afternoon, she called her mother to tell her the bad news about Ricky. The phone call was brief and sad. "I don't know what else to tell you, Mom," said Mrs. Zinn. "There will be a hard road ahead for Ricky." She waited for her mother's response, but there was none.

"Click" went the phone.

One week later, neighbors reported they had not seen Zulu in several days. The police chief, Ruel Twiggs, called Mrs. Zinn and together they entered the front door of the small home with now dried-up impatiens on either side of the door. As they opened the front door, both were taken aback by an unforgettable odor. "Mom!" yelled Mrs. Zinn. The pair split up to search the house.

"She's in here!" yelled Officer Twiggs from the living room.

That last sight of Zulu Zinn's five-day-old dead body was one her daughter would never forget. Two bottles of sleeping pills sat neatly on the side table. Her eyes were still open. Mrs. Zinn touched her face to try and close her eyes.

"She's been gone too long," said the police chief. "You cannot get her eyes shut, but look at this."

On the floor near the chair where the body was seated was a white sheet of paper. On the paper, in felt-tip marker, was neatly printed, "Please forgive me."

4

FIRST PRIORITIES

August, 2000

THE DAYS WENT BY QUICKLY AS THE WILSON FAMILY
began to get used to Smith's Gap, North Carolina. "School
will be starting in three days, and we'll need to be going into
town to get some school supplies," said Big Dad. "You may have
homework from the first day. Let's take a short walk into town
and get what you need." Amanda quickly ran upstairs to get her
mom's picture.

"Where did she go?" asked Bill-Lee.

"We'll soon see," answered Big Dad.

In a second, Amanda came bounding down the steps with a
small bag.

"You bringing candy? I want some!" shouted Bill-Lee.

"This is Mom's picture. I need to get it fixed," answered
Amanda curtly.

Realizing he wasn't getting candy, Bill-Lee took off yelling,
"I'm the fastest," as he disappeared down the path into the forest.

The family was soon walking along the main downtown
street of Smith's Gap. After buying all the necessities in Creech's
Drug store, the trio each got an ice-cream cone and sat on a sidewalk bench. In mid-lick, Amanda spotted Hester's Hardware

Store across the street. She remembered the bag in her lap and the promise made several weeks ago to her mother. "I need a five-by-seven-inch piece of glass," she announced to Big Dad and Bill-Lee.

"What'd you do," asked Bill-Lee, "break a window?"

"Yeah, like I'm gonna break your face... It's personal," she said.

"You go ahead," said Big Dad. "Bill-Lee and I will walk over to The Pet Emporium down the block and see about some stuff for Bunster."

As they finished their cones and parted ways, Amanda walked across the street to Hester's Hardware. Inside, Amanda realized the real neatness of moving to Smith's Gap. Here was an old-fashioned store like nothing she had seen back in Raleigh. A bell affixed to the top of the door rang when she entered the store. There were rows of shelves and a loft at the back of the store with some steep steps to it. The smell of the store was intriguing, like an old book. Looking at the blackness at the top of the steep steps, Amanda thought she saw movement and quickly averted her eyes. A woman's voice interrupted the sudden chill she felt.

"Well, laws have mercy, look at you! And how can I help someone as pretty as you?" Amanda was taken aback. In front of her stood a thin older lady with wild frizzy hair and no makeup. Amanda noticed a tattoo on her wrist with the letters "MFJ." She wore a red plaid hunting shirt and dark brown khaki pants. Even her shoes were tough-looking. Instead of cute flats, she wore scuffed-up hiking boots. In one hand was a half-eaten granola bar, and a thick leather glove covered the other hand.

Amanda realized why that statement hit her so hard. No one had said much about her being pretty since her mom had

37

died. "You are the prettiest," her mom would always say. "Come give me a hug and don't let go." Amanda sighed. "Oh, I need a piece of glass cut for a five-by-seven-inch frame. Here's the picture," she said.

"Oh, this is you and your mom. Are you getting this fixed up for her birthday?"

Amanda looked the woman in the eyes and said, "I wish I could."

"H.S.! Come here! Cut this pretty girl some glass." And just as quickly she said, "My name is Mary Frances Bradshaw and here's my number one employee, H.S. Stevens."

Coming from behind a counter like a magician, a dashing young man with a blond ponytail and pacific blue eyes appeared. He gave Amanda a quick once-over and glanced away.

"Five by seven and cut it the best way—no chips!"

"I got it," said H.S., and Amanda noticed that his voice had the screechy quality of one just beginning to change.

"It's nice to meet you. My name is Amanda Wilson, and I can't believe I am meeting Mary Frances Bradshaw! I heard about you from a girl I met a few weeks ago. Her name is Cara."

"Wow, you are making me feel like a real celebrity. All I know is, we are happy to have you in Smith's Gap. Where are you from?"

"Raleigh, about five hours east of here," replied Amanda. "By the way, what does that tattoo mean?"

"No need to get into *that* thing right now," replied Mary Frances. "Yeah, Cara is my friend and soul mate; she is a hard-working young lady. I would nominate her as your new best friend. But let's talk about you. Why did you say you wished you could give the picture to your mom? Your folks split up or something?"

"No," said Amanda, "my mom was killed by a drunk driver four years ago."

"Laws, that's awful," said Mary Frances. "Looks like you're going to need a mom and I may just be it."

Amanda swallowed hard and was speechless. What sort of a person was this? One of the stranger residents of Smith's Gap for sure. But kind of cool.

"I am cool," said Mary Frances, "super cool!"

Wait a minute, can she...? Amanda thought. Just then noises came from the old gray rafters near the back of the cavernous store.

"Hey, I need you to meet my other employees!" Mary Frances put two fingers in her mouth and let out a huge whistle. Suddenly, the scratchiest screeches Amanda had ever heard began, and three ravens floated down to a four-foot-long shovel handle fashioned into a perch. Amanda noticed newspapers neatly placed underneath to catch raven droppings. "This is Edgar, Allan, and Poe."

"I would have named them Blacky I, II, and III," laughed Amanda. Then she heard a splat on the newspaper.

"Edgar! Just what have you been eating? Been hurting your stomach, I see. I saw you guys flying around Benji Parker's persimmon tree. You know what persimmons do to your little raven stomachs!" Allan, the largest raven, flew over to Mary Frances' head and just sat there. "You know I can't keep my balance with you up there! Git, git,git!" The big bird lifted off effortlessly and landed on the front counter. He stepped around, looking at the items on the counter. Amanda watched him as he stared at a bowl of very shiny bear charms. "No, no, don't even think about it!" screamed Mary Frances. In a flash, Allan grabbed a shiny bear charm and started to take off. Faster than lightning, Mary

Frances leaped on the counter and tackled the raven. "Squawk!" A bird holler echoed through the store. Just as quickly, the shiny little bear was rescued from his beak and Allan flew back up to the perch. "Yeah, about three years ago, I was walking in the woods about a mile from here, over near Luke's Pond, and laws-a-mercy, I heard the screechiest mess you could hear. I went into the woods about one hundred feet off the trail, and there was a red-tail trying to kill three little raven chicks."

"What's a red-tail?" asked Amanda.

"Girl, a red-tail is a red-tailed hawk, one of our beautiful birds of prey. But I just had to save the little chicks. And now look." Both of them stared at the three ravens who were preening each other and looking like they were ready for a mid-morning nap. Breaking the silence and pointing her finger at Allan, Mary Frances screamed, "You are banned from the store for a week." With that, Allan squawked and flew out an open window in the top part of the store. "He knows he's been bad, but he can't help it. He also knows I'm just kidding. All ravens like shiny things, like some people, I guess." Just then a second raven flew down to the counter from the perch. "Hey, Amanda, say hello to Poe. Here, give him this piece of granola bar. He'll be your friend for life."

Amanda held out a piece of the bar, and the raven examined it and gulped it down. After he stared at Amanda for a true five seconds, he let out a huge, "Caw, caw, caw."

"Now that's rude, birdbrain! Instead of yelling at your new friend, you should say, 'Thank you.'"

Amanda noticed Poe was staring at the wiry little lady as she spoke. Then he walked over to Amanda's hand and hopped up on her wrist. Amanda drew back; feeling the claws on her hand was something totally new.

"That's why I wear this ratty old glove, keeps the razor claws from breaking the skin. 'Course you got young thick skin; mine is getting older and thinner, gettin' to the point where these guys' claws are always making me bleed. Just be still," said Mary Frances. "Ravens like to just be; Poe here wants to just be with you right now."

Amanda stared at the raven and marveled at his large beak and dark eyes. "I've heard of strange pets," said Amanda, "but these ravens are some of the strangest." As if he was offended by the comment, the big raven flapped his shiny black wings, made a gurgling croak and flew back up to sit with the smallest raven, Edgar, on the long shovel handle.

"I know," said Mary Frances, "but these are three very important individuals. First of all, Edgar—"

"Here's the glass," interrupted H.S. "I cut it very smoothly so it will fit the frame."

Amanda slid it into the frame and once again looked at the picture behind gleaming glass.

"Just perfect, your mom deserves the best! She's smiling at you right now."

That's what I was thinking, thought Amanda as a tear came to her eye. She paid for the glass, turned and left without speaking.

"She needs help," said Mary Frances, "and she knows it."

The walk back from downtown Smith's Gap was much quieter. "What's on your mind?" Big Dad asked Amanda, who looked deep in thought. They both watched Bill-Lee run down the path that led to the house.

"Oh, nothing really; just got a lot to think about."

Big Dad noticed her sad face but had no idea what to say next.

Four days later and midway through the second day of school, Amanda was sitting with Cara in the cafeteria. "I'm feeling better about school today. I have figured out how to get to the different classes, and I know where the bathrooms are."

"Jackson Middle School is not a very big place," said Cara as she grabbed some potato chips. "I know it's not Raleigh, though, and it takes some getting used too."

"Hey, guess who I met! Mary Frances Bradshaw...and her ravens."

"How about the dreamy guy in the store, H.S. Stevens?" asked Cara. "I hate that he has moved to the ninth grade at the high school. I loved, loved, loved seeing him in school each day last year."

"Yeah, he was cute. Hey, I know you'll think I'm crazy, but I think Mary Frances Bradshaw can read our minds. I mean, she sees things we don't see."

"You just wait," answered Cara. "She is a psychic; my mom gets spooked out by her. My mom only shops at the big hardware store in the next town now. She says she goes into a hardware store to buy stuff, not to be stared at and analyzed. We are positive Mary Frances can read minds."

"You think she sees dead people?" asked Amanda. "Like in the movie *The Sixth Sense*?"

"I don't know, but my mom says that Mary Frances hears and sees things that normal people can't see or hear," replied Cara.

Cara knew it was time to go ahead and blow her new friend's mind. "But, hey, Amanda, it gets weirder—is 'weirder'a word? Anyway, she can hear animals talking. She told me that spiders have an English accent and snakes have a Southern drawl."

"What? She's crazy!" Amanda shouted. "You mean she can hear a spider say, 'OK, I'm going to spin this web after tea-time'? I'll never look at a spider or snake the same way."

"Yeah," laughed Cara, "if I see some snakes in the future, I'll say, 'Ya'll get out of here!' Hey, girl, the other day I was walking on the back path toward town. I saw Mary Frances talking to a tree; you know the tree that somebody put the face on. I thought she was having a freaking conversation with the tree! I snuck into the bushes and realized that she was not talking to a tree but a large praying mantis."

"Get outta here!" said Amanda.

"No, seriously, the praying mantis spoke perfect English, only with a Lithuanian twang."

"A what? What is a Lithuanian twang?"

"Just forget it," said Cara. "One day you will hear and see."

5

EDDIE AND THE LEGEND OF THE BOX

October, 2000

I T WAS A CHILLY FRIDAY EVENING IN OCTOBER, AND WHILE the Wilsons were eating supper, Big Dad asked Bill-Lee about his new friend, Eddie. "I'm glad you've found someone to be your buddy. It's lonely enough up here. Tell us about him."

"Well," said Bill-Lee a little slowly, "I met him in my class the third day of school. He's a neat guy and knows a lot about the mountains. He has shown me some big waterfalls and some creeks where we catch salamanders and crayfish."

"What does he look like?" asked Amanda. "Maybe Cara and I have seen him before."

"He's a little taller than me, and he has thick black hair—like a bear," said Bill-Lee.

"I know that kid," interrupted Amanda. "He sometimes hangs around Creech's Drug store in town. He's a super geek!"

"Shut up, just shut up! He's not a geek, he's my friend, and he doesn't just hang around the drug store, he works there because his family owns it!" screamed Bill-Lee.

"Dad, you should see this guy," said Amanda. "He's got braces, and every time I've seen him, he's had food in his teeth. His mouth is a real trip. I mean, he has this bump right between his front teeth, right here!" She stuck her finger near Bill-Lee's front tooth, and he tried to bite her.

"I'll bite your finger off if you do that again," screamed Bill-Lee, and he ran to his room crying.

"And, Dad, he's got this big upper lip, and his lips curl up when he talks, and gross, he sometimes drools and spits when he talks! Cara says he is a crazy guy. He always tries to get the sixth-grade girls to talk to him. He even tried to jump off the back of his roof one time. Oh yeah, and he's a pyromaniac; he loves fireworks and set part of the woods on fire down near Luke's Pond. He took a lighter to school on a field trip and burned a girl's pants with it. But the craziest thing about him is what he eats occasionally."

"What's that?" asked Big Dad.

"He eats dirt. He eats dirt, Dad. Cara told me he was sitting at the drug store counter eating a bowl of dirt with honey on it."

"I've heard of that," said Big Dad. "I wrote a paper about it back in college. As I remember, dirt-eating is a very peculiar habit, mainly of very poor people in the Deep South. It is called geophagy. The ancient Greeks did it and also our Native Americans. Usually, women are dirt-eaters, especially if they are pregnant. Many people in sub-Saharan Africa eat dirt. Doctors don't endorse it, but some nutritionists think eating dirt may have health benefits because the soil has nutrients."

"And you can't beat the price of a bowl of dirt—it's free," said Amanda. "But, Dad, it's dirt! Who could eat stuff that we walk on and dogs like Bunster pee on?"

"Amanda, I didn't say we were having salad and fried dirt for dinner! Maybe you shouldn't be so quick to judge people that are different and immediately think you are better. Think about it. Seriously, Amanda, Bill-Lee has finally reached out to someone to be his friend, and here you go downgrading the whole thing. I need you to think about that, too."

"I hear you, Dad," said Amanda quietly. "Bill-Lee is my brother. I need to support him, not laugh at him."

"Well said," said Big Dad.

Amanda sat quietly and smiled at her dad. Her eyes went over to a small potted plant on the windowsill, and she smiled and licked her lips at the black soil in the pot.

"I love you, crazy girl," said Big Dad with a laugh. "I guess we've learned everything we ever wanted to know about Eddie, and I, for one, can't wait to meet him. Let's go up and visit with your brother." Big Dad and Amanda walked up the steps to Bill-Lee's room to see how he was doing.

"I think your sister has something to say to you." Amanda and Big-Dad looked at the back of Bill-Lee as he lay crumpled on his bed facing the wall.

"What does she want?" he said loudly.

"Bill-Lee, I just want to say I'm sorry, and I'm glad you have a friend here."

Turning over, Bill-Lee stared at Amanda and then looked at his dad.

"What do you think, buddy? Can you forgive your sis?"

"Sure," said Bill-Lee. "As long as she knows she's on probation."

"Pro what?" said Amanda.

"For two weeks you have to be extra nice to me, no more laughing, no more name-calling."

"That may be a good rule for both of you. Now let's shake on it," said Big Dad.

The two siblings stared at the floor as they grabbed each other's hand to shake.

"Hey, you two look into each other's eyes when you shake hands. Now do it again."

Amanda and Bill-Lee stared at each other as they shook hands for a second time. After the handshake, Amanda stared at her hand.

"Young lady, don't even say it," said Big Dad.

Amanda left the room, however, and ran to the bathroom to wash her hands.

The next morning after breakfast, Big Dad asked Bill-Lee to clean up the dishes.

"I did it last time," complained Bill-Lee. "Amanda never has to do anything around here."

"Son, she cleaned up dinner dishes last night," said Big Dad.

"And there were twice as many," Amanda chimed in.

"OK," said Bill-Lee, "but could you guys sit here and listen to this story that Eddie's father told Eddie and me yesterday?"

"Well…I've got a lot to do," said Amanda as she stood up to leave.

"Sit!" said Big Dad.

"Yeah, sit like a dog!" said Bill-Lee.

"Someday you're gonna wish you did not say that."

"Hey, guys, cut it out. Don't you remember *probation?* Now tell the story, Bill-Lee," said Big Dad as he put his head in his hands.

"It's called The Legend of the Box, and it's really neat because Eddie and I are going to find it. Back about 1870, three gold miners lived in this area before it became Smith's Gap. The miners looked for gold down where Trout River runs into Luke's Pond. They found so much gold, they were rich. They kept the gold in a metal box about like a shoe-box. The box also contained maps to other areas that had gold. Soon they became nasty, and each plotted to have all the gold and the maps in the box. A gunfight broke out one night, and all three of them got killed."

"By greed," said Big Dad.

"What's greed?" asked Bill-Lee.

"It's when someone wants it all," said his dad.

The next day at school, Amanda ran up to Cara. "By the way, my geek brother was talking about The Legend of the Box. Do you know anything about it?"

"We don't have time," said Cara. "But the word around Smith's Gap is that it is real…real magic. I gotta go."

Later, at lunch, Cara and Amanda made sure they were sitting away from everyone else in the cafeteria. "OK, tell me about the magic…and the box," demanded Amanda.

"Wow, this is absolute mystery meat," said Cara as she stuck her fork in a brown gooey substance in the middle of her school lunch tray.

"I think they call it country-style steak," said Amanda.

"It's country-style something," grimaced Cara as she pushed her plastic fork into the meat. The fork promptly broke into several pieces, and Cara put her head down.

"My goodness, girl, I'll be right back! What have I got to do to hear the story of the magic and the box?" Amanda jumped up to get another plastic fork for Cara.

"Thanks for the fork. OK, here goes. The belief is that the box is the root of all the magic in this area. Old-timers say that the box contained several pounds of gold, which in those times was worth about fifty thousand dollars. In 1870, fifty thousand dollars was like a million dollars is now. That box caused the death of three miners, according to many people. Our head magician, Mary Frances Bradshaw, believes that magic has spread to

Luke's Pond and to many of the people and creatures in the area around Smith's Gap."

"What creatures are you talking about, like Eddie or that geeky guy in math class?" asked Amanda.

"Oh, that's Oliver. Yeah he slipped me a note about a week ago—yuck!"

"OK, enough about geeks, there are plenty of them in middle school. What do you mean by the word 'creatures'?"

Cara stared at Amanda as she wiped country-style steak juice off her mouth. "When I say 'creatures,' I mean animals, like birds, bears, spiders, snakes. Luke's Pond is where many people think the box is. There was an earthquake in 1880, and the legend is that the box sunk right into the pond, never to be seen again. Other people believe that the box is hidden somewhere in a cave near Luke's Pond. Regardless of where it is, people believe that the waters of Luke's Pond and the area around it are magical and many of the creatures are magical. Mary Frances believes that Luke's Pond water is enchanted. She gets bottles full of it."

"OK, so remember a few months ago, I was telling you about the spiders, the praying mantises, and the snakes?"

"Oh yeah, English accent, Lithuanian accent, and Southern accent, how could I forget?"

"Well," said Cara, "since I was little, the Smith's Gap legend has been that people who believe and hang around Luke's Pond enough can participate in that magic."

"Pretty cool," said Amanda. "Hey, don't look now, but Oliver is coming toward you. I'm taking my tray up."

As Amanda handed her tray to the ladies in the window, she looked back at Cara. In horror, she saw that Oliver was not only talking to Cara but had sat down next to her. Cara gave Amanda a sad and questioning look, like, "What do I do now?" Just then,

Amanda spied Mr. Rifkin, who was talking to several teachers near the sweet-tea dispenser. I don't want to do this, Amanda thought, but Cara is my friend, so here goes. "Uh, hi, Mr. Rifkin, yeah, do you see that boy sitting with Cara? I think his name is Oliver, and he is away from his assigned table."

Mr. Rifkin studied the cafeteria and locked onto Oliver like a laser beam. "Amanda, thank you for helping me keep this place straight. Everyone knows that we have assigned tables, and that young man, Oliver Spooner, is at the other end of the cafeteria and away from his table!"

"Hey, Spooner!" With that, Mr. Rifkin marched over to the offending ruffian and leaned over to speak to him. In just a second, Oliver was headed back to his side of the cafeteria with his head down. Cara jumped up quickly with her tray to take it to the tray window. She shot a big smile to Amanda.

"Wow, that was close," said Cara. "Guess what he was talking about?"

"No clue."

"He asked me to go to the eighth grade Snarlin' Possum Ball with him. I hated to hurt his feelings but Rifkin walked up just in time, so I didn't have to come up with an excuse. I appreciate your help, good buddy!"

"No problem," said Amanda. "Now we have got to find that box."

"Uh, earth to Amanda!" said Cara. "It's been gone over a hundred years, yet you act like it's on aisle six at the grocery store!"

"I'm feeling pretty magical about this adventure; I think we can do it!" said Amanda as the bell sounded, ending lunch.

Wow, she seems determined, thought Cara, maybe so, maybe so.

6

THE DARK STORY

October, 2000

"**H**ow many cups?" asked Amanda.

"I think it's one and one-third," answered Big Dad. "These pancakes will be world class." Big Dad smiled as he stared out of the window. He looked at the yard and the changing leaves. I love Saturday mornings, he thought. The kids seem to be adjusting. Maybe we will be alright here.

"Feed me now, feed me now!" shouted Bill-Lee as he sat at the table with a fork in one hand and a knife in the other. As usual, Bill-Lee's hair was straight up in the front and a complete tangled mess everywhere else, and also, as usual, he was wearing only socks and Superman underwear.

"What kind of customers does this place get?" asked Big Dad as he chuckled. "Your socks don't even match! How about a little help? Can you put the plates and the napkins out?"

"I'm too hungry to move!" said Bill-Lee.

"Then I know who gets the first two stacks: Dad and me!" said Amanda.

With that threat, Bill-Lee whipped his partially naked body into action and assembled the correct utensils more or less where they belonged.

The good smells of the kitchen swirled around like the cold winds of Smith's Gap. The warmth overshadowed the heavy frost outside in the October morning. But something breathed deeply in the dark and then was quiet.

"I'm glad we bought this place," said Amanda. "It's nice to have a change from everything flat. I saw three deer near the big rocks yesterday. Two does and a young fawn. The fawn is almost completely brown now: no more spots. When they saw me, the does snorted,and they all took off in a cloud of dust."

"And a hearty,'Hi-yo, Silver! Away!'" said Big Dad loudly.

"What was that all about?" shouted Bill-Lee as he was again holding a fork and a knife like a medieval knight at the table.

"Oh, it's nothing," said Big Dad quietly. "That's just what my most favorite TV western hero from the 1950s, the Lone Ranger, said when he rode his horse, Silver. Hey, Amanda, you seem to be enjoying mountain life, but you sure did love the ocean. Now it would be a day's drive to get there."

"Yes, but there was very little wildlife in Raleigh and at the beach; it's hard to go bonkers over a gray squirrel or a seagull."

Amanda looked over at the pretty fire her dad had made first thing in the morning. Just then, heavy fur pushed against a warm brick wall about twenty feet below the fireplace.

As the pancakes disappeared from the table, Amanda asked, "Dad, Cara has asked me to sleep over this Friday night; can I do it?"

A loud burp came from the end of the table. Amanda and Big Dad stared at Bill-Lee who was cutting into his last pancake.

"What was that?" asked Big Dad. "And what do you say?"

"Excuse me," answered Bill-Lee quietly.

"Well, Dad, can I go to Cara's Friday night?" asked Amanda as she glared at Bill-Lee.

"Oh, oh, sure," said Big Dad, "I like Cara and her family."

The rest of breakfast went by with little incident and only three more burps, two of which were excused.

That Friday night was a super good one for Amanda. She and Cara were busy watching three DVDs and eating most of a large half-cheese, half-pepperoni pizza. As they lay back on Cara's double bed at about one thirty in the morning, Cara asked, "What is this fear you have talked about over the last few months?"

"Well," said Amanda, kind of in a whisper, "you know my mom died almost five years ago, right?"

Cara nodded.

"Well, my fear is all wrapped up in the night she passed away. It is called nyctophobia. My brain has a messed-up perception of what could happen in the dark, so I have a severe fear of the dark. Get me some tissue because I don't talk about this much, except to my dad and the therapist."

"You go to a shrink?"

"I used to," said Amanda defiantly. "For a while, I was a real mess; I stayed home from school a lot and would cry every time it began to get dark. The therapist helped me talk it out, and now I'm halfway normal. I still don't like dark places, though. You may have noticed when we first met how I stood back when we went down to the gym at school. It was so big and dark; I wanted to turn around and run."

"Wow, I saw you move back into the hallway when we looked in the gym, but I didn't know what the heck was going on," said Cara, munching on her fifth slice of pizza.

"Well, thanks for not saying anything. My scrubby brother laughs at me about it sometimes." Amanda grabbed another slice of pizza. "This will give me strength. So girl, this is how it happened. It was early December in 1995 when the days seem so short, and it gets dark early. You know December 21 is considered the shortest day of the year. Anyway, I was helping my mom wash dishes, and she asked, 'Amanda, I'm making out a list to go to the grocery store, why don't you come with me?' And then I told her, 'Oh, Mom, there is a TV show coming on in five minutes that is good, can't I stay here? I promise I will help you bring in the bags when you get back.' She said, 'Sure,' and kissed me on the cheek.

"As she walked away, I heard her say 'OK' very quietly. The next thing I heard was the door shut. In just a second, I started to feel bad because Mom and I would talk and laugh and have fun in the grocery store, so I ran to the front yard and yelled for her. She was already in the car down the road and could not hear me. I just stood there and watched the red-taillights of the car vanish into the darkness. I must have stood there for five minutes—I couldn't move for some reason. There was a coldness that came over me. She kissed me right here, on my cheek, Cara, and I never saw her again. I started to cry; I didn't know why I was crying, but I just stood there in the dark. Finally, Bunster, who was then just a puppy, brought me a tennis ball to throw and I played with him for a while. But for some reason, I kept looking down the road in the dark. It was freaky. About an hour later, police cars came to our house. Two police officers talked to my dad. I overheard them say that a car slammed into my mom's at a traffic light. The driver of the car jumped out and ran away. The car had a case of beer cans inside, mostly empty. At that moment, my world went dark and I just lost it. I ran to my room and slammed the door. I had never slammed a door before. My neighbors, the Cooks, came over and sat with Bill-Lee and me. They tried to get us to come to their house, but I wouldn't leave. The dark fear took hold of me. I began to cry and could not stop. For seven nights, I would look down the road and cry and run to my room. I slept with the lights on and still do. My therapist would sit and talk with me. She said this darkness phobia is because of the traumatic things that happened that night after Mom's car went away into the dark."

Cara grabbed a napkin with some pizza on it to wipe her eyes. "Girl, you have been through it. I cried a little when my grandma died, but she was ninety-one and had lived a great life. That is nothing like what happened to you."

"Do you mind if we leave the lights on tonight?" asked Amanda.

"How about the lamp near you? I never sleep...Oh what the heck, yes, if you agree to be my best friend."

They hugged for a minute and then were asleep in no time— with the lights on.

7

FREEDOM

October, 2000

THE DARKNESS OF AMANDA'S STORY TURNED INTO A BRIGHT, beautiful morning several days later at the prison near Greensburg, South Carolina. As promised, two prisoners, Lebie Jenkins and Muzzie Spicer, were being escorted to the front gate to be released. The chief warden and a guard accompanied them.

"I just got to say, it's been a fun three years," said the warden. "Spicer and Jenkins, I don't know if society is ready for the two of you, but one thing's for sure: we are ready for you to leave this place. What are you going to do with yourselves?"

"Going treasure hunting off in the North Carolina mountains," said Lebie Jenkins.

"What about you, Spicer? Gonna join a speech class so you can say more than two words?" As if on cue, the guard started chuckling.

"Gonna find a dog, name him 'T,'" said Muzzie Spicer. "Find a dog, name him 'T.'"

"I don't even want to know what the heck that means," said the guard.

"OK, let's open the gates, get them out of here; we got two empty cells to clean out."

As Muzzie Spicer walked by the warden, the warden asked, "T, what in the world does T mean?"

"Stands for 'Toothless,' he got no teeth."

"He means he wants to take care of a dog who needs a lot of help," said Lebie Jenkins. "I hate to say it, but a month of 'Muzzie Care' and it might be lifeless and toothless."

"Lord have mercy, Jenkins," shouted the warden. "You know how to encourage and motivate. You are the one that needs help. You are one of the strangest."

"And the sneakiest," said the guard.

For a moment, Muzzie and Lebie just stood twelve feet outside the gate. "Hey!" said the guard. "You guys got any sense? Get outta here! Git, git, git!"

"No place to go, he don't know what to do," said Muzzie.

"Buddy, it's been nice knowing you, but my ride just showed up," said Lebie. Just then an elderly Mustang arrived, and Lebie jumped in. In a cloud of blue smoke, Muzzie stood by the side of the road. For the first time in years, he felt very alone.

"He gotta find a T," he said, and he began to walk toward the town of Greensburg.

"I hope your T is sweet!" shouted the warden to Muzzie, and with that, he slapped the guard on his back, turned and went through the gates.

Life for Muzzie Spicer was tough over the next few weeks. He spent time in and out of a homeless shelter in Greensburg. The shelter was good because it provided him with a sleeping bag, a small pillow, and a knapsack for personal items. The shelter was bad because it provided him a mentor. One day his mentor, an elderly man from the nearby Baptist church told Muzzie that God was punishing him for his sins. Muzzie just grabbed his stuff, walked out, and hitchhiked northwest toward the North Carolina mountains.

"Man, he doesn't know if he can make another step," said Muzzie as he trudged down Highway 32 Business into Smith's Gap. "He can; he just know he can." With that, he could see what he had longed for: a country store that might sell his favorite food. "Hmm, Hesta's Hawdware, maybe they sell some pok skins." Feeling tired from walking, Muzzie stashed the knapsack and the sleeping bag in the bushes and walked quickly into town. He can do it now, Muzzie thought. Cars whizzed by, going in and out of the town. One of the cars came so close it blew his soiled Green Bay Packers sock hat off. "He need his hat to live. Dat car almost got him." Climbing the two steps to the front porch of the store, Muzzie pushed the door open. "You got original pok skins? It says Hesta's Hawdware Store, but he knowed you sell some grit."

Mary Frances Bradshaw stared at Muzzie. "Where in the world did you come from? You definitely aren't from around here! Did you escape from somewhere?"

"Whoa, whoa, whoa! Maybe he is…"

"I know, and maybe he isn't," interrupted Mary Frances. "I can tell you…you isn't!"

"Whateva," said the man as he trudged over to the snack section. "He don't want no salt and vinegar, he don't want no barbecue."

"I know what he wants, buster, he wants original fried pork skins. They're right at the top of the stack. Hey, what's your name?" shouted Mary Frances. "I bet it's as spooky as you are!" she whispered to herself.

"Don't know if I tell you that name," he said as he placed two packs of pork skins on the counter.

"Oh gosh, I bet it starts with an M," said Mary Frances.

"M as in Me, and Me needs to leave," said the man as he

grabbed the pork skins, threw down two dollars, and shuffled out the door.

Mary Frances sat very still with her head in her hands in the quiet. Edgar, the fattest raven, landed on the counter. For five full seconds, the store was deadly quiet. Suddenly, Mary Frances shouted, "M-M-M Muzzie! That's it! Muzzie Spicer!" She said it so loud that the little crunched-over man froze in the dark, just steps outside the hardware store door.

That's the end of him under the radar. How she know his name? And who decided to go into dat unstable place! thought Muzzie. He needs to get off dis road and find a place to sleep; they's got to be some good caves up here. Muzzie retrieved his sleeping bag and knapsack from the bushes. "Here, self, have another pok chop. Well, it's close to a pok chop." Muzzie gobbled down the pork skin and veered into the woods onto a trail. He traveled the trail for a half-mile and then came to a cave opening. "Dis is de place!" And he ducked into the cave. "He find a little spot somewhere that's snake-free, then have a home. Gettin' a little cold out here." Using a grimy flashlight, Muzzie made his way through the passageway. "Time to do some slitherin'," said Muzzie as he got to a low spot in the cave. The cave opened up into a large room. "Over there, that be the bedroom." And he laid out his bedroll. After seven minutes of grunting and maneuvering, raspy snoring started. Muzzie's day was done.

The next morning, Muzzie was back out on Highway 32 Business again. He was startled to see a familiar woman walking toward him on the side of the road.

"Good morning," said Mary Frances. "Nice day for a brisk almost noon time walk, isn't it, Mr. Muzzie Spicer?"

Muzzie's mouth gaped open at the sound of his name in a strange town. "How you know it?" Muzzie asked.

"Know what?" inquired Mary Frances.

"His name!"

"Oh, you just might say a little bird told me. I've got ways, my friend."

"Whateva! He want a dog; where he get a dog, lady?"

"You don't want a dog, Mr. Muzzie Spicer," replied Mary Frances. "Laws, do you know how expensive it would be for you to own a dog?"

"Lady, he don't want...he need...a dog. Where he go?"

"Don't make me tell you where you can go." She chuckled at her quick wit. "Oh well, the animal shelter is two blocks south. I guess it would be better for a dog to have you than the gas chamber...maybe."

Without a word, Muzzie took off toward the shelter.

"Where's a thank-you, buddy?" shouted Mary Frances.

A short wave and Muzzie kept walking.

"The girl in the shelter is named Cara Parrish. She's nice," shouted Mary Frances. "I've got worm pills in the store when you need them."

At this point, there was no response from Muzzie, who was very excited about finding a real friend.

In the shelter, the dogs were having a barking party. Cara was going from pen to pen shoving dry food into the slits in the pens. It was Saturday, and Cara was excited about leaving because she and Amanda were going to take advantage of the warm day and go hiking on the trail past Luke's Pond. She finished feeding the animals and was ready to walk out the door. The clock struck noon. "Hurrah!" she said and walked to the door to lock it.

"You open?" asked a strange little mealy voice from the road.

Cara turned to see a very short, very dirty man walking up

the sidewalk toward the shelter entrance door. "Uh, we're closed," she said as she tried not to look the man in the face.

"No, he need a dog!"

"We'll be open Monday at nine o'clock. I am sure you, uh he, can find a dog on Monday," said Cara.

"Go ahead, let him in," said a voice from the street.

"Oh, hi, Mary Frances, this man says he wants a dog. Can you help him?"

"Give me the key; I'll help him and lock up. I'll leave the key in the security box."

"Thanks so much. Amanda and I have got a four-hour hike planned near Luke's Pond."

"You tell my sweet little 'daughter' hello!"

"Lord, woman, you too old!" said Muzzie.

"What did you say? What are you muttering about?"

"You too old for a little daughter."

"Why I ought to…Oh, forget it, let's get you a dog. Besides, she's just my daughter in my heart, not for real."

"Whateva, he want a dog," said Muzzie.

"Wow, you are just like she said," exclaimed Mary Frances.

"What you mean?"

"Don't worry your little sock-hat head; let's look at the dogs."

Inside the shelter, the barking started again when Mary Frances and Muzzie walked in. "Shut up, and you know I mean it! We can't even think with all that racket!" shouted Mary Frances. Miraculously the eighteen dogs stopped barking, but six started whimpering. "Laws, nobody wants to hear a little cry baby!" said Mary Frances to a row of six-pound Chihuahuas.

After ten minutes of poking at the dogs, talking to himself, arguing with Mary Frances, and trudging down each row, Muzzie said, "I can't believe it, T is not here."

"Wait a minute," said Mary Frances. "What is this about a 'T'?"

"T means Toothless. I knowed he was here."

A strange look came over Mary Frances as all the color in her face turned to white. "There is another room, but..."

"Get him in that room!" shouted Muzzie.

Mary Frances led Muzzie down a long hall that ended with a gleaming metal door. "This is our security ward." She reached up over the door and got a key. There was no barking as the door slowly opened. Inside was the saddest group of dogs Muzzie had ever seen.

"He knew he was here." Muzzie pointed to the sixth pen.

"These are the dogs no one wants," said Mary Frances. "We keep them comfortable until they pass away or are euthanized. The six pens are in order. Number six will be euthanized on Monday. He is a sweet dog, but..."

"But what?" whispered Muzzie.

"He has no teeth...No, he may have two."

"Come here, T. Where do he pay?"

Mary Frances opened the pen and scooped up a nine-pound, elderly Chihuahua. He growled slightly but then nestled into Muzzie's lap as he sat with him quietly.

"He found you, T. He saved you, T!"

"Let's get some paperwork done," said Mary Frances. "Now you better take good care of him; this is really against our rules and procedures. OK, what is your address?"

"No address."

"Where do you live?"

"Nowhere, Ms., he an ex-con, got out a few weeks ago, he need home, he need job, mostly he need friend, he just got his friend: 'T.'"

"Hmm," said Mary Frances to herself as she balled the paperwork up and threw it in a large trash bin. This man needs real help, she thought. But guess what? A lot of people do. You can't save the world. "Hey, it was nice to know you, Mr. Muzzie Spicer. Good luck to you!"

Muzzie hit the road with his brand-new friend tucked under his arm. "T, you gots to see his new home. Every dog loves a cave home, he hope."

With that, Mary Frances turned her back, locked the shelter door, and walked to Hester's Hardware. When she got in the store, H.S. bounded toward the door.

"Got to take an early lunch, Mary Frances, be back at one fifteen."

"No problem, see you then." Mary Frances walked back to the sales counter and straightened up a wood-glue display. When she picked up several containers that had fallen off the small shelves, a house spider ran across the counter.

"Where are you headed, Hilda?" said Mary Frances to the spider.

"Should do more. Don't sit on your bum!"

"I do plenty. I can't save the world, you know."

"Yes, missy, you do the bog-standard. Should do more. Should do more."

"You sound like a broken record. I do plenty. I do plenty."

The little spider ran off the counter and glided down to the floor on a web spiraling out of her abdomen.

"Wish I could do *spider rappelling* like you!"

"Don't go waffling on, missy. You should do more."

8

THE BIG CAMPOUT

October-November, 2000

BILL-LEE TUMBLED INTO THE KITCHEN STILL RUBBING the sleep from his eyes. "What's a spelunker?" he asked.

Big Dad poured pancake batter onto the hot skillet and turned the range dial to medium. "A spelunker is a person who explores caves. Why do you ask?"

"My friend, Eddie, was talking about a spelunker yesterday in school, and I had never heard that word before."

"It can be a dangerous hobby," said Big Dad. "People get lost in caves, they fall into unknown holes in the cave floor, and they disturb wild animals like bears, bats, and snakes."

"It would be worth the risk, as long as there were lights in the cave," said Amanda as she poured syrup on her first round of pancakes. "I've been talking with Cara about all the caves in this area. She said she knows of at least five and then there are Lee's Caverns where the tourists go."

"Lights in the caves! What a baby!" said Bill-Lee. "I think you are getting too old for that phobia or whatever it is."

Big Dad sat down and looked seriously into Bill-Lee's eyes. "That's enough of that kind of talk."

"Yes, sir," said Bill-Lee.

Amanda took a deep breath and kept eating, chewing, and thinking. Soon the room was filled with eating, chewing, and thinking.

The next day, Eddie and Bill-Lee were walking home from school. "Have you ever heard about Luke's Pond?" asked Eddie. "It's a very pretty, shallow pond near the old mill. It has little islands where wild rosebushes and water moccasins live. The reason you would like it is that these gold miners lived in a little cabin on Luke's Pond about a quarter mile from Trout River. You can still find old pots and the chimney from the log cabin's fireplace. And you remember about the legend of the box? I believe that the box is there. Some people think it is in Luke's Pond or buried in the ground, who knows? My grandpa says that the only way a fellow can get a feel for a place is to spend a night or two there." Eddie looked at Bill-Lee after he made that statement to see his reaction.

"You're right," said Bill-Lee, "but you know my dad, he'll never let me do that."

A week later, Bill-Lee talked to his dad about camping at Luke's Pond.

"No!" said Big Dad in a booming voice.

Ten days after that, Bill-Lee asked his dad again.

"You better not," said Big Dad.

Hmm, thought Bill-Lee, that was a little softer.

For the next two weeks, Bill-Lee was the most helpful little manipulator the world had ever seen. He cleaned the breakfast and dinner dishes like a machine, without being asked. He made up his bed each day and even cleaned up the bathroom he shared with Amanda. There was one thing he did that got Big Dad's attention, though. Big Dad came home at his usual time on a Tuesday evening. It was about five thirty. He heard a strange whirring sound inside the house. As he came in the kitchen door, he saw Bill-Lee vacuuming the den rug. Everything was spotless except some cracker crumbs where Amanda was sitting eating cheese and crackers.

After dinner, Big Dad sat the family down and said, "I have thought about this camp out business. I am agreeing that you and Eddie can go camping at Luke's Pond." Bill-Lee grabbed a frightened Bunster and screamed with joy.

"There's only one condition."

"Anything, Dad, anything. What's the condition?"

"I want Cara and Amanda to camp nearby."

"Oh well," he sighed, glancing at his sister. "And we'll take Bunster for protection," he said as he held up Bunster's two ears like a rabbit's.

"I have two very lightweight backpacking tents, some flashlights, and four sleeping bags that you can use," said Big Dad.

Friday was a school holiday, so Thursday, after an early dinner, the group set out to go on the big camp out. They were excited because the weather was unusually warm and pleasant for the mountains in early November. Luke's Pond was about a mile from the Wilsons' house. The march to the campsite would help tire the two crazy little scoundrels out, thought Big Dad. As they walked out the door, while Cara and Eddie watched, Bill-Lee and Amanda kissed Big Dad good-bye.

"You guys be careful, and Amanda and Cara, watch after the boys, OK?"

"Everything will be fine, Mr. Wilson," said Cara. "Remember, I am the assistant registrar at Jackson Middle School. I know about leadership and responsibility."

"There you go! You guys be leaders and take responsibility."

At that admonition, the group marched off into the twilight.

Eddie and Bill-Lee ran ahead at full speed. Because Bill-Lee's backpack had a tent in it, he didn't run far. "Hey, Eddie, let's switch backpacks—I'll give you an extra Pop-Tart!" The boys quickly switched the gear and were off again.

"Let's just walk fast," said Eddie, puffing loudly.

"You guys, we will never get there!" shouted Cara. "We need to save our strength to make the trip and set up our tents."

At that, the boys slowed down and walked slightly ahead of Cara and Amanda.

"That's telling them!" said Amanda to her friend. "These guys need leadership, and that's what you are doing—showing leadership. I was talking to my dad just the other day about the volleyball team. He told me at the beginning of the year that since I am now an eighth grader, I should be showing leadership on the team. I was so happy to report to him that just last week, I had shown leadership!"

"Oh, wait," said Cara, "I am on the team with you. Just how did you show leadership?"

"Don't you remember what I did to the seventh graders...I yelled at them!"

Both girls laughed. The laughter was short-lived, however.

"What's that?" yelled Eddie as Bunster started to bark at some noise near the trail behind the group.

"Everybody get quiet. Eddie, you and Bill-Lee stand here with us," commanded Amanda.

They all stood and looked back down the trail in the near darkness.

"Could it...it...be a...a bear?" whispered Bill-Lee to the group.

"Shhh," said Cara, "just be quiet."

Nothing.

Just then everyone saw Bunster's tail start wagging. Out of the bushes on the side walked Big Dad.

"Hey, guys!" he said to four wide-eyed faces. "I just wanted to make sure everything was fine. Things look good; I am heading back. Everyone have fun and be safe."

"You scared the wickies out of us, Dad!" said Bill-Lee.

"Good night," said Big Dad as he chuckled.

"What's a 'wickie'?" asked Cara.

Amanda and Bill-Lee laughed and bumped fists. The foursome turned back to their journey quietly and made it to the clearing near Luke's Pond.

After the tents were set up, Eddie and Bill-Lee lay down on their sleeping bags.

"Man, it gets dark and quiet out here!" said Bill-Lee.

"Yeah, we need to make good use of this night," said Eddie. "My grandpa says there's a great cave nearby. Let's get the flashlights and explore it now."

"Are you kidding!" said Bill-Lee. "I think it's too scary!"

"Oh, man, I can't wait to tell everybody at school that my friend Bill-Lee is a big scaredy-cat."

"Am not."

"Are too."

"Am not."

"Are too."

"R2-D2!"

Eddie got very quiet and cocked his head as he looked at Bill-Lee.

"OK, Eddie, we'll go as soon as Cara and Amanda are asleep," said Bill-Lee reluctantly.

In a few minutes, they decided the coast was clear. Bill-Lee, Eddie, and Bunster tip-toed past Cara and Amanda's tent. But then Eddie knew they had made a mistake. There sat the two guardians, Amanda and Cara, in front of the tent, around a small fire. Quickly Bill-Lee put his hands over his face and crept along the path. The sight of two eight-year-olds and a dog creeping in the dark caught Cara's attention. "Don't look now, but the dynamic trio is trying to escape the campsite. Your brother has his hands over his face, what da?"

"Bill-Lee!" shouted Amanda. "You guys get back in your tent right now, and stay there!"

The two boys turned with their heads down and slogged back to their tent. Bunster ran over and licked Amanda, then ran into the boys' tent. "How did you see me?" asked Bill-Lee to his sister.

"We will talk in the morning; go to bed!" shouted Amanda as she rolled her eyes at Cara.

The zipper sound soon signaled that the boys were tucked in the tent.

"Seriously, what in the world is the whole hands-over-the-face deal?" asked Cara.

"OK, are you ready?" asked Amanda. "My dopey brother thinks if he can't see you, then magically you can't see him. We thought he would grow out of it by now; he's been sneaking around for the last five years with his hands over his face, thinking he can get away with stuff."

"I guess it's good I'm an only child," said Cara. "Little brothers are strange."

The two girls poured water on the fire and got into their tent. Saying goodnight to each other, Amanda smiled at Cara and turned the lantern on a low setting.

"It's OK," said Cara, "I remember."

Soon everything was mostly dark and very quiet. Heavy breathing emanated from the girls' tent.

Little did Amanda know that Bill-Lee and Eddie had made a pact and now were determined to get out of the campsite and into the cave. In twenty minutes, the zipper on their tent went up very slowly and quietly. The boys and Bunster soon emerged and crept along the path next to Amanda and Cara's tent. As they got away, Bill-Lee's flashlight came on. "There's the path!" he whispered, and the two boys walked faster.

"This is it!" said Eddie. "My grandpa says the cave is right down this hill." With flashlights shooting light beams everywhere, they ran down the path in the dark.

Back in the other tent, Cara nudged Amanda and woke her up. "I'm more tired than I thought," said Cara, "but do you think we should check on Eddie and Bill-Lee?"

"Who, Dorko and Geeko? Oh, they've gone to sleep long ago," said Amanda as she rolled over in her sleeping bag.

"I see the entrance!" yelled Eddie. Soon they were quietly creeping along, smelling the musty wet odor of the underground wonderland. The walls were moist with dew, which made them look like a snake's hide. "Look out!" said Bill-Lee as a brown bat swooped down near them. They both stopped and sat still for a minute. "I-I-I-Is this a good idea?" stuttered Bill-Lee.

"What?" screamed Eddie with small bits of spit spewing out of his mouth. "We'll be rich! Don't you want to be rich? All we have to do is get this box."

"I guess you're right," said Bill-Lee. They continued walking for about five minutes. Just then it looked like the cave came to an end.

"We'll have to crawl now," said Eddie. "The passageway is very low."

"Great, just great, but let me get some nourishment." Out popped a chocolate cupcake that was crushed in Bill-Lee's pocket.

"I get half!" said Eddie.

"Oh, sure, you get half. Half of a half!" The cupcake was gone without chewing, and the boys began the crawl through the low section of the cave. After crawling for twenty feet, they came upon a large open area in the cave. "It's like a living room," said Bill-Lee. "This is nice." Their flashlights scanned all over the large cave room. Twice, the light beams shined on two beings who were awake and lying very still.

"We lay quiet," said Muzzie to Toothless, and the little dog did. "Oh no," whispered Muzzie as he saw a big golden retriever enter the room. Luckily Bunster was not in a sniffing mood and just stayed near the boys. Rubbing his skinned-up knees, Eddie saw two openings at the other side of the large cave room.

"Look," he said, "we are going to have to split up to find the box. You go left; I go right."

"I'm taking Bunster," said Bill-Lee as he walked off. After two minutes or so of walking, Bill-Lee realized that he was really alone. Bunster had doubled back and followed Eddie instead.

In the right-side passageway, Eddie froze as he heard footsteps coming toward him. "B-B-B-Bill-Lee, is that you?" Just then a cold nose touched his hand. "Help! Oh, it's you, you crazy dog, you scared me to death!" Three steps more and it felt to Eddie like the cave floor gave way. There was a six-foot-deep hole in the passageway, and he fell right into it. Luckily, the dirt at the bottom was soft, and it broke his fall. "Where's that sorry flashlight?" He felt around in the soft dirt until he came upon the flashlight. "I just hope it's not broken," he thought. A flip of the switch and the hole was filled with light. "Thank you, Jesus," he said as he shined the light on Bunster at the top of the hole. "Go get help!" he screamed. Bunster took off in the direction he had come from. Eddie muttered to himself, "Like he is going to do anything. He'll probably just go home and get in his dog house. I wish I was home in bed right now." Desperately, Eddie jumped to try to climb out of the hole. It didn't work. The walls of the hole were too high and smooth for his four-foot-one-inch frame. They were so smooth that his feet kept slipping. "I'll never get out," he shouted. He sat quietly. There was no sound. Eddie felt his chest getting tight. He breathed deeply. "Help!Help!" He screamed as loud as he could, then he started to cry, but held himself back. You are a third grader; you weigh sixty-three pounds, you can do it! Eddie thought as he sat down on the cave floor. In five minutes, merciful dreamland took over. Eddie laid his head on his arm and went to sleep on the soft dirt.

Meanwhile, Bill-Lee decided to go just a little further up the passageway he was following. In about thirty seconds he came upon something he couldn't believe. It was a door about three and a half feet high. It looked pretty old but was still in good shape. It was opened about halfway. Bill-Lee heard very heavy breathing and a low growl. He stared at the doorway. The growl got louder. "That's it; I'm gone!" And he took off running as hard as his filthy shoes and dirty knees could go. He didn't stop until he made it to the low part of the cave and then he crawled faster than a Komodo dragon racing to a long-awaited meal. After the low part, he jumped up and started running again. Bill-Lee was relieved when he saw that Bunster was running alongside him. Neither one of them was worried about Eddie; dog and dirty boy crawled into their warm tent and went to sleep.

The next morning, Amanda and Cara woke up and went to Bill-Lee and Eddie's tent. Unzipping the entrance, Amanda screamed, "What did you do with Eddie?"

"I don't know," said Bill-Lee, rubbing his eyes and speaking in a sobbing voice. "We both went in the cave last night. I thought he would be coming out. I got scared."

Amanda's mind went ballistic thinking about the things that could have happened to Eddie. He could have been kidnapped, injured by an animal, bitten by a snake, something could have fallen on him, he could have been abducted by aliens. OK, stop! Amanda thought. This is getting you nowhere! Do something!

"Let's go see my dad—all of us," said Amanda as she grabbed Bill-Lee's hand and marched down the trail toward home.

"Wait for me!" said Cara as she held a toothbrush in her mouth.

The three walked quietly for a while. Finally, Cara broke the silence. "You know, Amanda, we may be in as much trouble as Bill-Lee is; we were supposed to be responsible."

"What were we supposed to do? Stand guard like police officers at a prison? I am through with leadership and responsibility. It's too much of a hassle!"

When Big Dad heard the story from the girls and Bill-Lee, he immediately whipped into action, calling Eddie's father.

By nine in the morning, Eddie's father had assembled a team to look for Eddie. The county sheriff said that if Eddie was not found by noon, his staff would form a search team. In the meantime, a very strange "homegrown" search team assembled: Amanda, Bill-Lee, Big Dad, Cara, Eddie's mom and dad, Mary Frances Bradshaw, and H.S. Stevens. Mary Frances' outfit was particularly colorful. It started with a very shiny silver hardhat, an Irish plaid scarf, a Nantahala Canoe camouflage tee shirt, some khaki workpants with zippered pockets, bright red socks, and mismatched hiking boots (one brown, one black). There were also four non-human team members: Bunster, the dog, and the three ravens, Edgar, Allan, and Poe.

As they were walking toward Luke's Pond and the encampment, Bill-Lee tried to tell the group about the secret door he'd found the night before. "It was amazing," said Bill-Lee. "Everything was dirt and rock and then there was this wooden door."

"You mean earthen and rock and then the door," said Amanda.

"Shut up for the fifty-second time," said Bill-Lee.

"All I know is, you're never to go there again," said Big Dad. "This is the end of your cave exploration career."

Bill-Lee grabbed Amanda's arm and winked.

Amanda turned to her brother and smiled, then said, "Shh."

When they got to the campsite, Eddie's mother looked at the boys' tent, broke down and started sobbing. She unzipped the tent, saw six crumpled potato chip bags and some dirty socks, and cried loudly.

"This is my baby! Where is my baby? What have you people done to my baby?" She rushed at Bill-Lee.

"Whoa, whoa," said Big Dad as he stepped in front of Bill-Lee, a reminder to Bill-Lee and Amanda that having a six-foot-four strapping father was good protection. The serenity melted away, however, when they heard him speak.

"Mrs. Creech, I will be dealing with these two in a little while, don't you worry, but now we must focus on finding your son."

"It's all right, dear," said Eddie's father as he went over to hug her.

"All right, let's move out," said Mary Frances. She was a real sight with a raven on each shoulder. Poe, the third raven, sat in a tree nearby. With that shout, everyone marched down the path toward the cave. The morning was foggy and quiet. That added to the tension and fear everyone felt.

Once they got to the front of the cave, Big Dad gave

instructions. "We're gonna find Eddie in an hour. Everyone stay together. We don't need to be looking for anyone else out here."

Teenage hormones kicked in as fifteen-year-old H.S. Stevens watched Cara and Amanda walking ahead of him. His gaze became almost dreamlike. Hardly anyone noticed as he stared at the two girls.

One person did, however. Mary Frances frowned and walked over to H.S. She looked him in the eye and walked around him. H.S. was so startled he just stared back at his hardware store boss. Suddenly, she slapped him on the arm. "And I don't like what you're thinking about."

All the ravens started cawing uncontrollably, and Big Dad put his hand to his face and shook his head.

What kind of crowd is this? Amanda thought.

Bunster ran in the cave first, violating the order to stay together. All the others followed, even the three ravens. Bill-Lee ran up to Big Dad to act as assistant search team leader. The cave got very dark and strange except for flashlight beams darting everywhere. "How much farther to the split?" asked Big Dad to Bill-Lee.

"About a mile," said Bill-Lee.

"A mile! You don't even know what a mile is; I remember you ran over to the park on Anderson Drive and were exhausted. You said it was a marathon! It was two-tenths of a mile!"

The group got to the low part of the cave and was called to attention by Big Dad. We have to crawl for a while. Bill-Lee says the low part is quite short, though. Let's go."

Everyone got on their hands and knees to start crawling.

"This is spooky," said Eddie's mother.

After a few minutes of groaning and shuffling in the dirt, they emerged from the low part of the cave.

"He hears trespassers, T; get in my coat, we get quiet now." Muzzie and T pushed back into their alcove. One beam of light landed on them briefly, but they were so quiet that the oncoming search team missed them entirely and went by.

"I didn't think I could crawl another second," said Mary Frances to H.S. as she brushed the dry dirt off her khaki pants and red socks.

"You did good, boss," said H.S., hoping a compliment would get him back in good standing.

"It'll take more than Lava soap to get this outfit clean!"

The group walked further, flashing their lights in every direction, looking for Eddie.

Amanda was listening and pondering. What was in H.S. Stevens' head when he looked at Cara and her? Suddenly, Big Dad's booming voice interrupted everything.

"OK, the cave splits here. We all go to the right; we will explore the left passage later, but remember, we have to stay together!"

The group continued trudging along.

"I hear something!" said Eddie's father.

9

THE BIG RESCUE

November, 2000

"**H**elp!Help!" could be heard faintly in the distance. The only problem was that it was coming from the other passage, not the direction they were heading.

"Dad, I think Bill-Lee went the other way on purpose!" shouted Amanda.

"I'm on it," said Big Dad as he walked off with Bunster. "Amanda, come with me. Everyone else, please stay here!"

"Oooh, I don't like what he's thinking," said Mary Frances. "Could be a prickly switch in Bill-Lee's future."

At the end of the other cave passage, Bill-Lee waited anxiously. He wanted everyone to see the wooden door at the end of the cave. All that was forgotten, though, when Big Dad and Amanda got to him.

"Restriction for a year or more, William Lee; here we are trying to find Eddie, and you can only think of yourself. You are tied to me like a chain for the rest of this day!" Big Dad grabbed Bill-Lee's hand and took off down the cave path. Amanda followed closely but then stopped in the dark.

"Rrrr."

What was that? she thought as Big Dad marched quickly away from her with Bill-Lee. Shining her flashlight in the direction of the sound, she saw the wooden door. Bunster crouched at the little moldy door, and he stared right at it. He was rigid like a statue. Bunster's low growl aimed at the door. What in the world? thought Amanda.

"Let's go, Amanda!" said Big Dad.

"Coming," said Amanda as she called Bunster, but in her mind she knew: I may have to come back here, and very soon. Bunster gave one warning bark and ran after Amanda.

Amanda, Bunster, Big Dad, and Bill-Lee, now known as the prisoner, rejoined the group. "OK, folks, now we can get somewhere," said Big Dad as he led the group up the left cave passage, still clutching Bill-Lee's hand.

"Dad, all the blood is out of my hand because you are holding it too tight. I think it's blue!"

"That's OK. After today, you will only need one hand and a stump!" growled Big Dad.

Amanda sidled up to Bill-Lee. "I think he's just kidding, but who knows," she whispered in his ear and flashed a grin toward Cara.

The group continued marching deeper into the right passage, when all of a sudden, the silence was shattered by, "caw, caw, caw." The three ravens took off and flew back toward the cave entrance. "I knew they were tired of this place," said Mary Frances. "No problem, they'll be outside when we get back." The big birds made it to a dead tree outside and two of them started cleaning themselves. Poe was pecking and not cleaning. Edgar and Allan looked, cawed loudly, and jumped on Poe. The black birds struggled over a small bag Poe had found on the cave floor. As they fought over the bag, three pork skins fell out. Each bird grabbed a treasure and went into nearby trees. The bag floated down on the path.

"Stinking birds…he hate dem birds," said Muzzie as he slowly released Toothless. "We's got to move and now." Stuffing his sleeping bag in the corner of the little alcove, Muzzie picked up his knapsack and tottered back out of his cave "bedroom" with T. Making a crucial mistake, Muzzie said, "We go to de lef passage, my friend." They picked up speed, hoping to find a new home away from people. "He sees a strange thing," he said to T. Muzzie and T stared at the half-opened moldy door. They crawled toward the door and pulled it open wider. Toothless barked loudly. "Shut yo trap!" Muzzie commanded. A roar started low and got louder in the area beyond the door. Not expecting anything but a bat, Muzzie whirled backward and fell against the cave wall. Never in his life had he heard a roar like that. He breathed deeply to calm himself.

"RRRRRRRRRR."

"What is that sound, T? He swear he see a stinkin' bear, a big un!" Muzzie quickly yanked off his knapsack and retrieved a red road flare. Quickly striking the end of the flare, it burst into brilliant flames. Muzzie held the flare and was in awe as he looked at a large man-made room filled with boxes. The large black bear was now cowering from the flames on the flare. Realizing he now had the upper hand, Muzzie grew bolder. "Git and git," Muzzie said as he maneuvered the bear toward the door. The bear started to charge, but as all wild things do, retreated out the door, away from the sparks and flames of the flare. "He said git and git." And the bear was out the door and down the cave passageway. "I wonder where he went," said Muzzie to T. "Oh well, home sweet home," said Muzzie as he shut the door and looked around the very comfortable new surroundings. There were shelves with boxes neatly arranged all around the earthen room. Only one box was not on a shelf. It was in the corner under a wide shelf. A cobweb-covered rocking horse was in another corner of the room. Muzzie stared at his new surroundings and took a deep breath. Yawning in the quietness, he realized how little sleep he had gotten the night before. Lying in the soft dry dirt and making a pillow with his jacket, he fell fast asleep with Toothless in his arms.

At the same time, in the right-side passageway, the eight-person, one-dog search team traveled along. "I'm getting hungry," said Bill-Lee.

"So, Pop-Tart six couldn't even last until ten o'clock. Only thinking of yourself, again. Suck it up, brother," said Amanda, "Eddie Creech hasn't had any breakfast today!"

"It's good, it's very good!" said Mary Frances to the group.

"What's good? What are you thinking?" asked Eddie's mom with tears in her eyes.

"My reading says Eddie is OK. We need to keep on a little further."

Eddie's mother and father stared at each other. Mrs. Creech was shaking in fear.

H.S. Stevens sidled up next to them. "I know what she just said sounds crazy, but she really can do magical things with her mind. I've been working with her for almost a year; it's amazing!"

At this statement, Eddie's mother just shook her head and turned away to wipe a tear.

After five more minutes of trudging through the cave, Big Dad said, "Everyone quiet, I hear something that sounds like growling."

They all kept walking quietly toward the growling sound. In just a second, they came to the hole in the floor of the cave and looked in. There, on the soft dirt at the bottom of the hole lay Eddie Creech snoring.

"His snoring always scared me too!" screamed Eddie's mom at the top of her lungs.

With a start, Eddie awoke and looked up. "Mom, Dad, everybody! I slept here last night by mistake!"

"Come here, baby," shouted his mom as she reached down the hole. "Oh, my arms are too short. I can't reach him!"

A thick rope sailed through the air and landed in the hole near Eddie. It had a Hester's Hardware Store tag and a price of $12.95 on it. "Did you buy that?" shouted Mary Frances.

"Yes, and I kept the receipt!" H.S. replied.

"Lord have mercy, help my boy out of the hole and forget about the rope!" screamed Eddie's dad.

"I'm almost to the top," shouted Eddie, and all of a sudden, six hands grabbed shirt, arms, and pants and hoisted a very dirty eight-year-old out of the hole.

"All's well that ends well," said H.S. as he observed the hugging and crying.

"Where's that receipt?" said Mary Frances. "We can get that rope back on the shelf; it's hardly soiled."

Just then the very frightened black bear raced up to the group. The beast had made a left turn at the large cave room, thinking he could find a place to sleep. Startled by all the noise, the bear stood up to his full five-foot stature and roared at the rescue party. His white teeth gleamed in the partial darkness of the cave. Six flashlights suddenly left Eddie in the dark and aimed at the panting beast. After a two-second silence, several people screamed.

Full of adrenaline and good feelings from finding her son, Eddie's mom screamed, "Nothing's gonna spoil my morning! Let's get him!"

The big bear was astonished as the entire group took off after him. He squealed like a little cub as the group pursued him through the cave. The bear pushed his fatted self through the low part and out into the morning sun. They chased him into a briar patch where he finally could be free. He did not stop running until he was deep into the woods.

"All right, team, good job," said Big Dad. "Now we need to notify the sheriff about our good news. He was waiting to hear from us and guess what—it's just ten thirty!"

"I know Sheriff Bernie Nyman and I'll call him right now," said Mary Frances as she pulled out her flip phone.

"Let's get this nasty tent cleaned up and folded," said Big Dad. "You girls get yours folded; it will be a long time before you use them again."

"We have got to get this rope wiped off and back on the shelf," shouted Mary Frances to H.S.

"I swear I've got the receipt, boss; it's in my pocket somewhere," said H.S. to a now smiling Mary Frances.

As the crowd broke up, Amanda and Cara took down the tent and stuffed it into the brown bag. Carrying the tent, Amanda threw her arm around Cara as they all walked down the trail. "Hey, girl, that cave was cool; it is full of secrets that need to be solved!"

10

NEW LIFE

November, 2000

SATURDAY MORNING AT HESTER'S HARDWARE, MARY Frances chuckled as she replaced the "rescue" rope on the shelf above the fishing equipment. She had just finished her ninth conversation about Eddie Creech's cave rescue. It was big news in Smith's Gap. People kept wanting to hear all the details. Midway through one of the "news conferences," Amanda walked in and joined in the rescue chatter. Soon everyone except Amanda left, and the store was quiet.

"A penny for your thoughts," said Amanda, staring at Mary Frances.

"Oh, I am ready to move away from the rescue phase to something new. I am feeling the need to help someone."

"Who?" asked Amanda.

"There was a man who came in here a few days ago. He got a little dog at the shelter."

"Oh yeah, Cara told me about a short man coming to the animal shelter. Isn't he an ex-prisoner?"

"Yes, and I realize that he now has real responsibilities, he has a dog, and he needs to learn to support himself. I have to step up and see what I can do."

Just then, the front door pushed open and, speak of the devil, there stood Muzzie Spicer with T's face sticking out of his coat. "Need worm pills and some pork skins."

"Coming right up! Let me introduce you to my friend Amanda," said Mary Frances.

Muzzie looked straight toward the floor and mumbled to Amanda, "Nice ta see ya."

"And I am glad to meet you," said Amanda as she extended her hand to Muzzie. Realizing that he was not going to shake hands, she withdrew it quickly with an embarrassed look.

Mary Frances hurried to the counter and dropped the items in a pile. Sitting on her stool behind the counter, she stared at Muzzie for a full ten seconds.

Muzzie looked down again in embarrassment.

"Hey, Muzzie, I got a brother in Hopewell, South Carolina, who may need some help. I've got some ideas for you. Let me make a phone call and see if you can work there. You know anything about fixing lawn mowers?"

"A little," he said with a smile.

"Well, let's see what we can do."

Within a week, Mr. Muzzie Spicer had a friend, a room, a boss, and a job, all thanks to Mary Frances Bradshaw. He was now working at Jenkins Small Engine Repair in Hopewell, South Carolina, over on Sanford Street. His boss was Newley Jenkins, who let him live in a small room at the back of the shop.

11

THE CEMETERY

November, 2000

BACK IN SMITH'S GAP, THE WILSON FAMILY WAS GETTING ready for a special field trip. Big Dad had planned the trip, remembering the words of the Raleigh therapist when she met with him privately before the move. He had told the therapist about his concern for Amanda's well-being and wondered about the effect of the move to the mountains.

"Your daughter has been through a lot and has made some progress," the therapist told him. "Moving is a big stressor. Be sure she knows she can talk to you about her feelings."

"There's another thing," said Big Dad. "The town we are moving to is very near the cemetery where my wife is buried; how do I deal with that with the children?"

"Bill-Lee should be fine with whatever happens, but I would wait a few months to make sure Amanda is settled before she goes to the cemetery."

"OK, kids, I just got some flowers. We are going to visit your mom's grave," announced Big Dad. "It's in a little cemetery near Heritage United Methodist Church just outside of town. I never thought I would be living so close to her resting place. We can walk there."

Amanda swallowed hard and took a deep breath. "It's kind of late in the day, Big Dad, can't we go tomorrow morning?" she asked.

Being sensitive to Amanda and remembering the therapist's advice, Big Dad relented, "I want these flowers to look good for her, but it can wait until tomorrow morning."

The next morning Big Dad reminded Bill-Lee and Amanda about the walk to the cemetery. The trio donned jackets and gloves and started the two-mile hike to the church and the cemetery.

"Why is she buried way up here when we lived a thousand miles away in Raleigh?" asked Bill-Lee as he walked fast to keep up with Big Dad.

"More like two hundred and sixty miles, my little friend. Anyway, your mom always loved the mountains and insisted that we both be buried here."

"Oooh, who wants to talk about stuff like that!" said Bill-Lee.

"I think it's time for you to stop talking about anything," said Amanda. "Big Dad, which path do we take?"

"We go to the right," said Big Dad. "One point six miles away." After a short walk along a forest trail, he shouted, "There it is," and the three looked out on a beautiful meadow of green grass and occasional purple violets next to a small wooden church.

A slow, cool wind went by Amanda's head, and she thought she heard something. I am getting freaked out, thought Amanda.

Amanda saw the gravestone and immediately grabbed her dad's hand. Her head drooped down, and she stopped. There at the top of the hill was a large marker with "WILSON" in big letters. Underneath it was written, "Julie Amanda Wilson, Born September 15, 1957, Died December 9, 1995, The Love of My Life." Amanda tasted salty tears streaming down her cheeks.

Again, she thought about her mom's last trip to the grocery store. What if she had just gone with her? She stood and looked and felt. Momentarily quiet. The same cool breeze drifted by. She bowed her head to say a prayer, "Oh, Lord, thank you for all my gifts and blessings. Please bless my mom who is with—"

"Look at the size of that stinking buzzard!" screamed Bill-Lee as he interrupted the prayer. "That's got to be a turkey buzzard; you know black buzzards are smaller and meaner!" The black raptor soared in a circle, then landed in a large nearby tree.

Amanda stared at it, and it stared back. Turning to Bill-Lee, she shouted, "Thanks for the bird lesson!" Everyone needs a loud little brother, she thought.

Big Dad knelt in front of the grave. He looked at the stone quietly for a good thirty seconds. Amanda watched him and grew sadder by the second. About twenty yards away, Bill-Lee found a stick and threw it to Bunster, who zipped over the grass to pick it up. "Did you see that?" he shouted as he pointed to the big yellow dog.

"Shush," commanded Amanda as she glared at her little brother.

Bill-Lee got very quiet as he watched his dad kneeling at the grave.

Wanting to appear strong and brave, Big Dad bellowed, "I think the flowers look great right here." Amanda noticed the yellows of the daffodils and the reds of the carnations in the arrangement. Little Bill-Lee got close to the arrangement and began to touch the leaves. He became trancelike as he felt the leaves between his thumb and index finger.

"Let me say a prayer," said Big Dad. "Oh, God, we come to this place on this special day to give thanks for all the good times we had with my beautiful bride, Julie. Please let her know that I am doing my best to raise our children as she would want me to. Help us to remember the good times and treasure them in our hearts. And, Lord, take good care of her. In Jesus' name, we pray. Amen."

"Let's race down the path," said Bill-Lee as he took off into the forest. Bunster joined him.

Amanda frowned as she watched her little brother and the big yellow dog.

"Don't fault him for this, Amanda," said Big Dad. "He only remembers his mom with pictures. When you are three, memories don't stick."

"My memories will stick," said Amanda, "like glue. I wish she could hug me one more time."

"God knows, I agree," said Big Dad. "There's so much I would like to talk to her about."

Just then, Amanda noticed her dad reaching for a handkerchief and quickly wiping his nose and then his eyes. Men cry? she asked herself.

In silence, father and daughter walked toward a sweaty Bill-Lee and a panting Bunster on the path.

As they walked on the trail back to home, Amanda lagged behind. Very quietly she heard a different sound. It was hard to make out, but it sounded like "May May." She pondered as she listened quietly. What was that? Amanda thought. It's probably just two limbs rubbing together. Wait, it sounds like a voice. "May May." OK, I'm crazy, Amanda thought. Her father and brother were almost out of sight. Just up the path, she noticed Bunster running toward her. "Hey, guy, thanks for keeping me company."

"May May." There it was again. Amanda noticed a path going off to the left. It was slightly overgrown but still discernible.

It seemed to be heading in the direction of the sound. She walked slowly, looking hard for poison ivy that could touch her legs. As she walked, she heard "May May." All right, this is spooky, Amanda thought. I have got to figure this out. She looked and saw Bunster like he had never looked before. He was staring and would not budge another inch. His fur was standing straight up on his back. Amanda stopped to comfort the scared canine and looked down the path. A huge, great horned owl sat in a tree about about twenty-five feet away. "You telling me you're scared of a bird!" Amanda said as she scratched Bunster's neck.

"May May." Bunster growled deeply. Amanda looked up, and the big owl was gone. I wonder if Mary Frances talks to owls, she thought. I will check that out.

Three days later, Amanda looked at Bill-Lee as he was coming in from school. His eyes were red and sopping wet. "What's wrong with you? You got pink eye or something?"

"Ha ha, no, my art teacher had us making Mother's Day gifts today."

"What! Mother's Day is in May. This is November. Doesn't she know how to read a calendar?"

"Yes, she does," answered Bill-Lee indignantly. "She says that mothers are so important we should honor them twice a year, not just once. All these guys in my class, including Eddie, are making presents for their mothers. You know, like Popsicle stick boxes and necklaces and stuff. Who do I give anything to? I got nothing, nothing!"

"Well, let's get creative here. What if you and I made something for Mary Frances? She doesn't have children, and we don't have a mother. It just might work."

"That crazy, frizzy-headed woman at the hardware store? I need to think about that," replied Bill-Lee.

Amanda spied a funny-looking Popsicle stick box on the side table next to Bill-Lee's bed. "Is that what you made? Why it's...it's..."

"Don't say it, I know it stinks. When you are the only one in the class making something for no one, it turns into a mess."

"Let's fix it," said Amanda. "We'll make the prettiest little box Mary Frances has ever seen. Mom would want you to." The two siblings diligently got to work on the box.

The next Tuesday was the new "Mother's Day," and Amanda and Bill-Lee marched down to the living room after school to see Big Dad. He was quite involved in reading an article in the paper about his beloved Atlanta Falcons trying to win a football game. "These Falcons, I just don't know if they can do it this year. What are you guys up to?"

"It's this, Big Dad," said Bill-Lee, and he put a beautifully decorated Popsicle box in his dad's lap.

"Wow," said Big Dad as he picked up the box and examined it. "What is this? And *why* is this?"

As Bill-Lee told his story, Big Dad's face softened and his eyes began to water. He thought about what it must have been like for an eight-year-old to see everyone in the classroom making a box for their mother except him.

"And so, Dad, I was going to put the crummy little box in the drawer until Amanda saw it. She had a pretty good idea."

"So what's the good idea?" asked Big Dad.

"Well, Amanda said we should spiff the box up some and give it to Mary Frances Bradshaw. You know, the crazy, I mean, the nice lady at the hardware store."

"That's an amazing idea! I am so proud of both of you! She has no children except those strange ravens; your mom would be very happy."

Amanda noticed her dad's eyes getting redder, so she quickly grabbed the box and ran to the kitchen counter to wrap it. "Time to get going, little brother. This should be fun, going to Mary Frances' house."

"You guys be safe and tell her I said, 'Happy extra Mother's Day.'" The door slammed, and Big Dad settled back into his newspaper-reading easy chair. He laid the paper aside and just sat with his eyes closed. "Amen," he said out loud as he smiled. "Julie, we have some good children," he said to himself.

Amanda and Bill-Lee walked quickly toward Mary Frances' house, which was about a mile away. "Hey, how do you even know where she lives?" asked Bill-Lee as he was breathlessly trying to keep up with Amanda.

"Cara and I were jogging one day and we passed by her house. It's pretty, but you know Mary Frances, it's kind of strange too."

"Eddie and I wondered about Cara and her fatness. She has been losing weight; I guess the jogging is helping."

Raising her eyebrows and stopping by the side of the road, Amanda stared at Bill-Lee and said, "Little brother, you got a lot to learn about girls. I hope I am the only person who has ever heard that statement! You may not live to your ninth birthday if any girl hears you talking about her fatness!"

"Don't worry so much about it. What Eddie and I talk about stays between Eddie and me."

"Well, you just violated that," said Amanda. "Hey, we are about to get to her house, just look at it."

Bill-Lee stood back to take it all in; it was a two-story house with dormer windows in the attic area. It had plants and vines everywhere, and there were pots with even more plants in them, although they were brown and withered from the recent frost.

Near the front door was a four-by-four post with a large shovel handle across it where the three ravens could perch.

"I see those big birds have been here a lot," said Bill-Lee as he pointed to several layers of bird droppings on the ground.

"Well, let's greet our honored hostess," said Amanda as she knocked on the door. Bill-Lee and Amanda stood and listened. Nothing. Amanda decided to knock again. Nothing. "I see her car around back, so I know she's here." Amanda knocked a third time. Nothing. The two siblings dejectedly started down the walk to leave.

"Go away!" they heard shouted from inside the house. "Private property!"

"Mary Frances! It's me, Amanda; we've got something for you."

Just then she heard a hasp lock rattle, and the front door flung open.

"Laws have mercy, girl, I didn't know it was you. I was getting 'stranger vibes,' but I guess that was from your little brother. You wouldn't believe the crazy people that come up to this door, selling books, encyclopedias, insurance, the Lord, magazines, everything. Well, come on in the house."

Amanda started into the house when she realized Bill-Lee had disappeared. "My little brother has a surprise for you—but he has vanished. Bill-Lee, where did you go?"

Everything was quiet, and then a small face appeared from around a mailbox down by the street. "What's your problem, Bill-Lee?" asked Amanda.

"She said to get off her property. Eddie told me the next thing that happens up here in the mountains is shootin', so I got scared."

"Come on in this house, boy, I didn't mean to scare you.

Besides, my gun isn't loaded today. But it is nice to know that an old lady like me can scare somebody."

Bill-Lee ducked his head slightly and walked from the neighbor's yard. He looked up at Mary Frances to shake her hand. Mary Frances smiled, put her arm around Bill-Lee, and ushered both of them into her house.

When they got into the kitchen, Bill-Lee's eyes grew wide. Up on a shelf, about five feet off the ground, was a row of twenty-five bottles and jars of various sizes. Some had plant stems, some had berries, some had dried lizard parts, and then there were three that had brown paper twisted around them.

"Whatcha looking at, Bill-Lee?" asked Mary Frances.

Bill-Lee pointed to the row of jars and bottles.

"Oh, that's my medicine chest, only it's not a chest of course. Let's see, there's preserved bee legs, some nice magnolia sap, dried spider egg sacs, and the green jar has emulsified crow feathers."

"Don't you have aspirin, Band-Aids, cotton balls, or anti-itch cream in your medicine chest, like normal people?" asked Bill-Lee.

Amanda punched him in the side.

"Well, my good friend, I guess you just answered your question. I am not normal. I quit trying to be normal about forty years ago when I was about the age of your beautiful big sister." Mary Frances turned and smiled at Amanda. "The big thing is to figure out who you are and be that person to the best of your ability."

"Peck, peck!" All heads turned toward a front window to see one of the ravens looking in on them.

"Laws, what does Edgar want?" Mary Frances grabbed her big glove, jumped up and ran to the front porch. In just an instant, she returned with the big bird on her wrist.

"Now what do you think he wants?" asked Bill-Lee.

"Well, these guys are very smart…and they are listeners. My guess is Edgar, here, agrees. Did you see him wink at me?" The raven continued to cock his head around, looking at the three humans. "Thanks for your contribution," Mary Frances said as she stroked his broad black back. "Now we must bid you goodbye. Can you hop over to the window and see yourself out?"

A flurry of large wings and a few pin feathers floating preceded Edgar, who flew over to a window with a shiny latch on it. The raven stopped at the window and looked back at Mary Frances.

"Go ahead and git. You see your buddies are waiting for you."

Very meticulously, Edgar pecked at the latch. In just an instant, they could see that he got the loose part of the latch in his beak and lifted it. The window inched open, and with six flaps, Edgar was sitting on the bird feeder.

Amanda and Bill-Lee looked and saw two other ravens sitting at a huge suet bird feeder in the yard.

"Now did you get all that?" asked Mary Frances. "He wants you to know that the big thing is to find your best self and be that best self. He knows who he is and he does it, day in and day out, rain or shine. OK, enough about life's lessons. What brings you two up to my crazy place on a Tuesday afternoon? Hey, what's that in the bag, Amanda?"

Almost forgetting what she was holding, Amanda looked at the bag and shoved it over to Bill-Lee.

"Drum roll!" Amanda said, and she began beating on the small coffee table in front of her. "Go ahead, little brother; it's your turn now."

"Well, in school, we were making things for our mothers and I…"

Mary Frances jumped up and grabbed Bill-Lee to hug

him. "Laws, boy, what are you trying to say? Did you make me something?"

Bill-Lee opened the bag and revealed a gift in red and white wrapping paper. He looked at it briefly and handed it to Mary Frances.

Mary Frances had already pulled a tissue out of her pocket when Bill-Lee handed her the gift. Very quietly she looked at it. A slight sniffing sound was evoked as she stared at the gift.

"Do you know how long it's been since I've gotten a gift?" Tears began to roll down her cheeks.

"Do you need me to open it for you?" asked Bill-Lee.

"No, no, sorry, I am kind of slow these days; I just don't know how to thank you."

"But you don't even know what it is," said Amanda as she stared at her emotional friend.

"OK, OK." And she tore open the wrapping paper.

"Would you look at this!" Mary Frances held up the little Popsicle stick box with beads and glitter glued to it.

"It has a lid, see," said Bill-Lee as he pointed to the top of the box.

"This is great!" said Mary Frances. "I've been looking for something to put my praying mantis egg sacs in. A Highland Peruvian priest came through town and taught me that you boil the egg sacs and rub them on arthritic knees."

Amanda stared quietly at Mary Frances in disbelief. A Peruvian priest? she thought. "We just wanted to remember you and what a friend you have been."

Blowing her nose into the tissue, Mary Frances looked at Amanda and Bill-Lee. "Come here, you two!" And she grabbed them and held them close for a few seconds.

All of the celebration and hubbub had covered up an arrival, however. A very dirty and old Mustang had pulled up in the woods behind the house.

"So, my crazy sister still lives here," said Lebie Jenkins quietly as he rolled the window down to take a closer look at Mary Frances' house. "Whew! I can feel a chill! Think I'll go south where I can stay warm for a few months. Maybe I'll come back up here. Who knows!" The Mustang slowly pulled away and was gone.

12

PORTER GRACE BAXTER

January, 2001

AFTER HIS QUICK NOVEMBER VISIT TO SMITH'S GAP, Lebie had just enough money for gas and some snacks to get from North Carolina south to Alabama. Seven hours on the road took him to the Johnson Motel just outside of Troy, Alabama. The small town of Troy and the warehouse at Smith Distributing Company would be his world for the foreseeable future. The manager at the warehouse liked Lebie's forklift skills and put him to work immediately.

A few months passed and the second semester had just begun at Jackson Middle School. Second semester meant January, and January in Smith's Gap meant cold and snow. There were four inches of crusty snow on the roads and the ground.

"Daniels Middle School in Raleigh would be locked up tight if there were four inches of snow," said Amanda to her friend Cara as they walked down the hallway. "I have seen empty toilet paper and milk shelves in the grocery store two days before the snow even starts falling."

"You flatlanders freak out with snow and ice; we mountain people just keep on truckin," replied Cara. "Some of the snow has melted off the roads, but hey, I was thinking. I haven't heard much about your brother, Bill-Lee, and his great friend, Eddie. I still think about that rescue we had a few months ago. That was the biggest thing to happen in Smith's Gap for years!" At the mention of Eddie, Amanda started sticking her finger in her mouth and making gagging noises.

"You know I make a lot of fun of Eddie, but he is my brother's only friend right now, and I've decided to keep quiet around Bill-Lee, who is a geek associating with another geek." They both snickered but then got very quiet.

"Hey, who's that girl at the water fountain?" asked Cara.

"Don't know," replied Amanda. "She must be new like me. Never seen so much makeup on an eighth grader."

They both got quiet and stared at a very elegant and overly made-up eighth-grade girl. She moved gracefully as she left the water fountain and started walking toward them.

"Look at the cover of this book," said Amanda, causing Cara to turn away from the new girl.

"Why did we do that?" asked Cara as the new student walked by the suddenly busy duo.

"I just wasn't ready for a meeting," replied Amanda.

They jumped into separate classrooms as the bell sounded. Amanda found her desk and was about to open her binder in English Language Arts class. The teacher, Mrs. Sanders, pointed silently to a message on the board stating that everyone was to do quiet reading and reflection for seven minutes. Amanda liked that class because she and Mrs. Sanders understood each other. Quiet reading and reflection appealed to Amanda, and she relished the thought of seven minutes where she could sit and think. She sat back in her desk in the silence. As she reflected, she took stock of where she was in life. Everything was OK up to this point. She was slowly getting over the darkness thing, and all the details of her life were working out: she occasionally saw H.S. Stevens at the hardware store, this morning she had fed Bunster as normal and petted him goodbye, she had kissed her dad at the carpool line, glared at Bill-Lee as normal, and she had found Cara at their usual meeting spot near the cafeteria. She sighed quietly and smiled. Life was really good now. All of a sudden she began to think about a song verse of one of her dad's favorite groups: Grateful Dead. She couldn't remember the exact words, but lead singer, Jerry Garcia, sang something about danger coming when life looks really easy and good.

Meanwhile, over at Hester's Hardware, Mary Frances was cleaning up the reduced-for-quick-sale table. She was humming and feeling very well also. One of the ravens, Edgar, was sitting on her shoulder. All of a sudden, a sharp pain hit her in the brain. "Oh," she said out loud. "Something is happening to my good friend Amanda. I have got to see about her today." Edgar squawked and flew away.

Back at school, the seven minutes of quiet reading was ending, and the "something" was about to happen. Mrs. Sanders announced, "Class, I am so happy to tell you that we have a new student today. All the way from Jackson, Mississippi, her name is Porter Grace Baxter. Isn't she pretty?"

Porter Grace wasted no time. She jumped out of her seat and moved in front of Mrs. Sanders. "I am so happy to be here and make new friends with all of you; I hope there is a student government here because I was vice-president of our student government at my former school."

Amanda felt sick and wished Cara was there for her. She looked over at Ashley, a girl she knew just slightly. Ashley put her finger in her mouth as if to vomit as she pointed to Porter Grace. They both giggled as they put their heads down on their desks.

Porter Grace continued the presentation of herself. "My mother is going to work as a civil engineer with the Roads and Bridges Division up in this area."

Amanda's mouth dropped open. *This little so-and-so's mother is going to be working near my dad! I wonder if she's as trampy as her daughter! Big Dad might need protection!*

Realizing that her class time was valuable and that Porter Grace was perfectly happy to talk the entire block, Mrs. Sanders interrupted, "Now, class, let's give our new friend, Porter Grace Baxter, a good old Snarlin' Possum welcome!"

The class erupted into a cacophony of snarls, growls, and hisses. This was the tradition at Jackson Middle School. Porter Grace's smile turned to a strange expression as she looked for her seat, glided into it, and crossed her legs in a ladylike fashion.

Back at the hardware store, Mary Frances was getting hit with a second wave of headache. "I have got to find my dried-mint bottle!" Mary Frances said to Edgar. "If things get worse, I may have to go for the emulsified beetle wings! A second something is happening to my friend at school!"

Mrs. Sanders' class was getting even more interesting back at Jackson Middle School. "Miss Baxter!" said a loud voice at the back of the room. "You just may be our next Snarlin' Possum queen!" All the students turned around to see that Principal Rifkin had come into the classroom. Standing next to him was a very pretty, but heavily made-up woman. "I'd like you to meet the other 'PGB,' Porter Grace's mother, Ms. Patricia Grey Baxter."

"Y'all can call me Patty Grey," said the woman as she lovingly looked at Mr. Rifkin.

Turning very red at the look she was giving him, Mr. Rifkin changed his tone and became very formal as he said, "Welcome, Porter Grace. Now, Mrs. Sanders, I think we should turn our attention to language arts." The two intruders vanished out of the classroom and into the hallway.

Amanda did not know what hit her. Who was this girl? Who was her bimbo mother? How would she fit into this school? She felt her pointer finger digging into her thumb, which was what she always did when she was nervous. The bell disrupted her thinking, and she found herself grabbing books and notebooks quickly so she could talk about this entire fiasco with Cara out in the hallway.

"Cara!" Amanda screamed as she saw her buddy walking toward her. "I don't know what just happened, but it may just turn our crazy world even more upside down."

"Tell it, girl!" exclaimed Cara.

"Don't have much time, but that new girl we saw earlier was in my English class. You know, she looks like a pageant girl, probably been in pageants since she was in diapers, I can tell."

"Whoa, whoa! Slow down. Did you actually talk to her before you put her on your hit list?"

"Well, I just know that H.S. would…"

"What did you say, Amanda? When in the world did you start to care about what hardware guy Stevens would say? I thought he only cut glass for you!"

"Bell's about to ring. See you."

"So long, Mrs. Stevens!" Cara shouted down the hall.

Amanda curtly turned and dashed into her next class. Thank goodness Cara is not in this class, Amanda thought. Maybe she'll forget about that crazy conversation. A more disturbing thought came to her. This Porter Grace person was already causing problems, and she had only been in the school for two hours!

About an hour later, Amanda and Cara were seated together at their regular spot in the cafeteria. Their conversation blended in well with the usual clamoring of trays and the squeals of sixth-grade students two tables over. "Sixth graders—I just cannot believe what they do over there!" said Amanda. "And to think my brother will be here in two years. Thank goodness, by that time I will be gone and in high school."

"Uh, can I sit here?" Amanda's and Cara's faces lost all their color as they looked to see Porter Grace Baxter holding a tray of food. Her freshly painted fingernails gripped the tray tightly.

"Oh, sure," said Cara, and both girls ducked their heads as if something really interesting was happening in their trays.

Cara's and Amanda's mouths dropped open, however, when they looked and saw Porter Grace move away and sit down at an empty table by herself.

Little did they know that Mr. Rifkin had been witnessing the entire event.

"What kind of a welcome is that?" he said. "And you, Miss Cara, are the assistant registrar at Jackson Middle School. I expect you to represent this school better than that!"

Cara jumped up and almost ran over to Porter Grace. They talked together for about thirty seconds, and then Porter Grace stood up and gathered her tray to move back to Cara and Amanda's table.

"Now that's better," said Mr. Rifkin. "We must remember that a Snarlin' Possum is also a friendly possum."

"Hey, Amanda, I want you to meet Porter Grace," stated Cara very formally as they both found their seats near Amanda.

"Oh, hello, nice to meet you," mumbled Amanda as she grabbed her roll and cut it in half.

"It's nice to meet both of you; I didn't know what to do when I first came to this table. All I saw were two death stares, so I left."

"Sometimes we can both be kind of reserved," said Amanda as she looked at Cara.

"Oh, it's OK to be shy. Shyness has never run in our family. I guess you remember meeting the other PGB this morning. You couldn't say that either of us is shy."

"I didn't say 'shy,'" Amanda retorted, "I said we were reserved."

"Whatever," said Porter Grace as she began nibbling her roll.

Amanda studied Porter Grace's fingernails and then looked at her own. Instead of seeing ten perfectly manicured and painted fingernails, she realized that only three of her fingernails were still nicely polished. The other seven had polish that was mostly worn off.

"Hey, who does your fingernails? They are beautiful," said Amanda, hoping to turn the conversation more positive.

"Why, thank you, there is a woman at Hannah's Nail Salon in Jackson that does them. My mother and I go there together; it's one of our 'together times.' I guess those days at Hannah's are over," said Porter Grace longingly.

"So, do you think you'll like it here?" asked Cara. "I have lived here all my life. It's a little town, but it's pretty nice."

"Well my mom says this place may just be a stopover. She wants a big administrative job in Raleigh at the state headquarters. Whoops, I think she told me not to repeat that. You guys can keep a secret, can't you?"

13

MEETINGS

Early March, 2001

SOME OF THE THINGS THAT MAKE LIFE EXCITING ARE meeting new people. So far in Smith's Gap, Amanda had met many new people. Of course, her latest meeting was a big one—the day she met Porter Grace Baxter. But she had met many other important people in her life in the last seven months. She had met her teachers at school. She had met Mary Frances Bradshaw, H.S. Stevens, Cara, and the other geek, Eddie Creech. Before Smith's Gap, in Raleigh, Amanda had her mom. Of course, Amanda didn't meet her mom. Her mom had just always been there. Until she wasn't. All of this would pale in comparison to the people she would meet in the next few months.

At dinner one Friday evening, Amanda talked to her dad about Luke's Pond. Big Dad interrupted loudly, "You know, Amanda, when we were searching for Eddie a few months ago, I was so preoccupied with his rescue, I didn't really notice a pond. Your mom and I came to Smith's Gap in the spring of 1986 when she was pregnant with you. We loved to hike on the trails in the woods, and on one of our hikes, we found a pond that was beautiful. I never knew the name of it. Your mom loved the whole area and enjoyed the solitude. I have been so busy settling into this new position; I would love to hike with you tomorrow. That may be the same pond; could you show it to me?"

The next morning after breakfast, the skies were dark, and it looked like rain or snow could start falling at any time.

"This looks like a better day to sit by the fire and watch basketball than to go into the woods," said Big Dad.

"But you know what the Danish people say," said Amanda. "There's no such thing as bad weather, just wrong clothes; let's get dressed and go."

"Where in the world have you heard Danish sayings?" asked Big Dad. "Oh well, let's get the 'right' clothes on and go."

With Bill-Lee and Bunster visiting Eddie's house, Big Dad and Amanda set out on their adventurous hike. After twenty minutes of hiking, they came to a small parking lot.

"Yes," said Big Dad, "this is where Julie and I parked the car nearly fifteen years ago and started our walk. She was about five months pregnant and was eager to exercise. She said it would make everything better, and she wouldn't be a fat woman!"

Amanda got quiet as she visualized her mom and dad walking in the same footsteps on the same path. Just then a sound echoed through the forest, "May May."

"What in the world was that?" asked Amanda as she looked at her dad.

"Oh, I think you hear an airplane or maybe a helicopter; the airport is just a few miles away."

"No, Dad, this was a voice, I think, and it said something like 'May May.'"

"You must be hearing things," said Big Dad as he walked a little faster.

Amanda and her dad walked in silence for several minutes.

Amanda soon became lost in thought about this strange place called Smith's Gap.

"May May!"

Amanda heard it again but did not respond. There it is, she thought. Why can I hear things and he can't? Either I am going crazy or it's some of that Smith's Gap magic stuff.

The two walked about a quarter of a mile farther and then, "There it is!" said Big Dad as the two approached Luke's Pond. "It's just as pretty as it was fifteen years ago. I almost feel like..." He stopped talking and just looked at the little body of water. He walked slowly and studied the path and the edges of the pond. Big Dad spoke slowly, "Your mom was tired, and we looked for a place for her to rest. We thought there should be a bench right along there," he said as he pointed to a level spot near the pond where about twenty large ferns waved in the breeze. "Since there wasn't a bench, we just sat on the bank and dangled our feet in the cool water. It was very refreshing. Her ankles were beginning to swell from carrying you, and the cool water made her feel much better."

"What do you mean, her ankles swelled because of me?"

"I guess I am being a little mean, no, many times pregnant women retain water in their bodies as their pregnancy progresses. Your mom's ankles would swell when she stood or walked for long periods."

Looking at her own ankles, Amanda decided to change the subject. "The pond must be pretty shallow, and the water is very clear. Back east, the ponds and streams were pretty dark; you could never see the bottom. I can see the bottom everywhere here. That looked like a small trout."

"I think I see little rose bushes growing on the other side. I bet it looks beautiful when the roses are in bloom...like heaven," said Big Dad.

"May May!"

Again Amanda got quiet and studied her father's face. Although he looked very sad, she could see no hint that he'd heard the call in the woods.

"Let's just sit here for a few minutes," said Big Dad as he put his arm around Amanda and ushered her to the bank. "This is so nice, but I must admit, even though I am tempted, it is just too blasted cold to put our feet in the water. That would really make it good..." his voice trailed off.

"There will be another time when it's warmer," said Amanda, suddenly feeling strangely like the adult.

"Wow, would you look at that!" said Big Dad. Fishing a small pair of binoculars out of his coat pocket, he turned the dial on the instrument. "It's a great horned owl! They seem so wise. Want to take a look?"

He handed the binoculars to Amanda, and after a few seconds, she found the big bird sitting near the middle of a large oak tree. She studied its face and then swallowed hard when she saw it wink at her. "It's...it's so majestic," she said as she handed the binoculars back to her dad.

"I've got to ask Mary Frances about that bird," said Amanda as she stood up from where the two were seated.

"Hey, we have a very large book on birds at the house," said Big Dad.

"Oh, I don't want to talk to Mary Frances about owls. I want to talk to her about *that* owl."

Big Dad removed his ball cap and scratched his head, "OK, May May, let's go back home. I am hungry for some lunch, and it's stinkin' cold out here."

"Why did you say that?"

"What, that I am hungry and want some lunch?"

"No, why did you call me 'May May'?"

"Oh, I don't know, I haven't thought about it in a long time. This place has just affected me, I guess. That's what your mom used to call you when you were very tiny. You were learning to talk; it was easy for you to say so we used it as your nickname for a while."

A lump formed in Amanda's throat and she looked back at the owl in the tree. It was gone.

After lunch and a warm shower at home, Amanda appeared at Hester's Hardware. Everything was quiet in the store, and Amanda was getting ready to yell for Mary Frances.

Suddenly a voice screamed out, "Laws, no! You can't mean it!" Peering into the car-wash section of the store, Amanda saw that Mary Frances was talking to nothing. As she crept closer, she heard a thick English accent, but she couldn't make out the words. Mary Frances continued, "Well, all I know is this, get back in there and build that web! There are too many skeets in here!"

"And what, my lady, is a 'skeet'?" asked the voice.

Amanda snuck up a little closer and could not believe her eyes. There on a shelf was a large, brown house spider. Mary Frances was talking to a house spider, and the darn thing had an English accent—very proper. Suddenly, Amanda sneezed, "Ahchoo!"

"What da?" said Mary Frances as she wheeled around. "Did you hear Victoria? I mean the spider is telling me that stuff? That has some deep meanings, Amanda." Neither of them noticed when the spider scampered underneath a shelf.

"I can't believe my eyes or ears, Mary Frances. That was a spider you were talking to. No, I did not hear what he said."

"She!" said Mary Frances very properly as she made a cup of coffee from the coffeemaker. "Most males don't make it past the spider wedding reception; many are eaten just like a piece of wedding cake! So, most of the adult spiders you see are females. It's getting darned cold in here! Where'd you go, H.S.?" Mary Frances looked toward the back of the store and then jammed some wood in the three-foot-tall potbelly stove a few feet from the counter. "He knows his job in the winter is to keep this place warmed up!" Flames started shooting from the opened door of the stove as she slammed it shut.

The bell hanging over the front door jangled and a man walked in. Amanda jumped out of the way as Mary Frances walked up to the man.

"Do you make keys, ma'am?" he asked Mary Frances.

"Yes, sir, and since my number one employee, H.S. Stevens, must be absent, I will be happy to help you."

While Mary Frances cut the key, Amanda wandered around the very interesting store. On the wall near the cash register, she saw a very old high school diploma. It was framed nicely but had a few stains on it. "The faculty of Smith's Gap High School is proud to present this diploma to Mary Frances Jenkins, June, 1968."

"So I see your last name used to be Jenkins," said Amanda.

"'Tis so. Hey, if that key doesn't work, come on back," Mary Frances said as the man paid two dollars, waved, and went out the door. She turned back to Amanda. "That's what you call a maiden name."

"That's what I figured, but…"

"What happened to my marriage to Mr. Bradshaw? Well, it's like this: Sometimes things are right, and sometimes they are wrong, and girly, Elvin Bradshaw was wrong, kinda like one of my brothers."

"Wait, wait, wait, I am hearing all kinds of stuff I didn't know anything about."

"Why don't you just sit yourself down, have some chocolate peanuts and listen to some great stories."

Amanda sat on an ancient wooden chair next to the bowl of chocolate-covered peanuts and prepared to listen. "I only got time for one story, but please tell me about this Elvin Bradshaw."

"Oh Elvin, where do I start with that crazy man? Oh well, we met in high school, tenth grade I think. He was a baseball player. He was tall and muscular. All I could think of when I looked at him was a hero like Mickey Mantle or Roger Maris."

"And who exactly are they?" asked Amanda.

"Stars and garters, girl, just about the best baseball players on this planet! They played for the greatest baseball team—the New York Yankees!"

"Well, I can see I hit a nerve there, Mary Frances. Can we get back to Elvin Bradshaw?"

"Do we have to? OK, after his high school glory days it was all downhill. Poor boy could not hold a job, but he had all the answers. 'Nobody's gonna tell me what to do,' he would always say, and then in two weeks he was fired. Lucky for me, I got to know old man Hester down here at the hardware store. I was able to keep the pitiful Bradshaw family going. After seven years of marriage, I threw in the towel and told him to get the heck out of the single-wide."

"You lived in a trailer?"

"It was called a single-wide mobile home, my dear, but yes, we did."

"But, Mary Frances, where did Elvin Bradshaw go?"

"Amanda, do you know the difference between ignorance and apathy?"

"What?" asked Amanda, quite puzzled.

"Let me tell you a quick story. One day a discipline-problem

110

fifth grader was half asleep in the back of the classroom during a vocabulary lesson. The teacher asked, 'Who knows the difference between ignorance and apathy?' Seeing the problem child half asleep on the back row, she decided to call on him. He disrespectfully answered, 'I don't know, and I don't care.' The teacher said, 'You are correct.' The boy was shocked, and the children clapped. Well, anyway, Amanda, that's a long way to answer your question. But here goes: I don't know where Elvin Bradshaw is, and I don't care where Elvin Bradshaw is."

"Well, I guess that settles that. Next time we'll cover your brother. Oh, wait; I need to tell you what happened at Luke's Pond this morning."

"Tell it, girl. Is the pond still frozen over?"

"Just a little, but today and over the last three months, I have seen this big bird. I think it's a great horned owl."

"Wow, Amanda, you saw her! I can't believe it!"

Mary Frances suddenly turned her back to Amanda and looked at the arm of her chair. "What? OK, OK, just a minute. Amanda, I need to ask you to excuse Victoria and me for a minute. Do you mind if she and I step to the rear of the store?"

"Sure," said Amanda as she frowned slightly and watched Mary Frances pick up the weekly newspaper with the spider on it and walk about twenty feet away down the long hall.

"Victoria, this better be good. I don't like keeping secrets from my buddy Amanda. What's up?"

"Well, milady, she is just not ready for all of this. My sense is that in a few months she will be a better partner in the enchantment area. We cannot talk willy-nilly about this important venue."

"She is making progress in the magic department. But I respect your thinking. I will wait a while. Now be off with you."

"Milady, that was rude. I wish to be returned to my web. I will be under the chair, listening."

Mary Frances smirked as she returned the spider to the chair. "Come on back over, Amanda," said Mary Frances. "Please don't mind Victoria; she just likes things to be 'proper.' Now the owl you saw is very important in the Luke's Pond neighborhood of animals. Did you talk to her?"

"No, but I kept hearing this sound: May May. My dad said that is the nickname they used for me when I was a toddler. Mary Frances, why is this happening? It's freaking me out!"

Mary Frances looked down at the floor and turned toward the chair. "In time," she said, "in time, I will tell you. You are not quite ready now."

Amanda frowned at Mary Frances. "I don't understand what you are saying, but promise me that you will help me interpret all this crazy stuff. It's giving me a headache right now."

"Sounds like a plan, my dear. We will walk this crooked path together."

14

TROUBLE

Saturday, May 5, 2001, and Monday, May 7, 2001

BACK IN HOPEWELL, MUZZIE SPICER WAS CELEBRATING his five-month anniversary on the job by enjoying a Saturday afternoon walk with his best friend, T. The little dog stopped abruptly and squatted near a bush. "He thinks that a good idea." And Muzzie and T went into the edge of the bushes near the road.

Meanwhile, the pride of Hopewell's police force, Officer Oscar Wilbert, was enjoying a pleasant afternoon in his cruiser as he motored slowly down the road. He was thrilled that he had gotten a promotion and was now permanently on the day shift, and he was looking forward to a quiet day of keeping the peace until he could watch his beloved South Carolina Gamecocks play baseball on TV at three o'clock. Just then, he spied a ragged-looking man relieving himself near a bush. Flipping on the blue light and hitting the siren for a second, Officer Wilbert pulled over to the man. "Get finished, buddy, and then come here!"

Muzzie looked at the officer and walked over to the curb.

"Look, this is a nice town, and we don't cater to people exposing themselves like you were doing! Find a bathroom next time."

"Yeah, boss man."

"Hey, buddy, where do you live? Our spring bluegrass festival is starting at six tonight and you look rather homeless."

"Suh, he, uh, I wok at Jenkins engine place," said Muzzie, pointing to the little business two blocks away.

"Oh, you are that new guy that Newley was talking about. What is your name?"

"Don't know about that," said Muzzie with his head down. Muzzie picked up T and headed in the opposite direction.

"Hey, friend, I am the police! I asked you what your name is!"

Muzzie ignored the command. He quickened his pace down the roadside.

Officer Wilbert frowned as he swung the car door open and jumped out. Running toward Muzzie, he shouted, "All right, that's enough! Get down on the ground! Hands behind your back! You are not showing respect to a law officer!"

With that shouting, Muzzie turned quickly and jogged into a nearby patch of woods. Officer Wilbert pulled his revolver out and shouted one more time. "I am an officer of the law, and I am ordering you to stop!" Being somewhat overweight, Officer Wilbert ran for about one hundred feet and stopped.

I almost swallowed my dad-blamed whistle, he thought as he leaned up against a tree, heaving for air. I got to start doing some exercises and cut back on the milkshakes...don't know where that wiry little stinker went, but guess what? I know where he lives and works. I'll drop by and visit with him and Newley soon. Right now, my shift is over. It's Gamecock baseball time!

Looking back over his shoulder, Muzzie carried T through several vacant lots to finally make it back to Jenkins Small Engine Repair. He was surprised to see an old and moldy 1986 Mustang parked at the gate. Just as he got to the gate, a familiar voice rang out.

"I see you finally got a friend; has he got any teeth?"

Muzzie turned and recognized Lebie Jenkins. Just as he spoke, the little Chihuahua in Muzzie's arms growled deeply. "It's OK, buddy," said Muzzie to T.

"Hey, calm down your German shepherd, Muzzie," said Lebie as he stared at the little dog. "If he goes after me, I'll be the last person he deals with. He will meet his maker."

"How you doing, Lebie?" asked Muzzie, wishing to change the subject.

"Not too good, buddy. What are you doing at my brother's place? You gettin' ready to break in? Maybe I just foiled a robbery."

"No, Lebie, he live and wok here…We do," Muzzie said as he looked down at T.

"All these years I have begged my older brother to put me up and give me a job, and he said no. This really gets me mad."

"Newley your brother?"

"Yes, brainchild, you know Lebie Jenkins and Newley Jenkins…same last name."

"You have a sister too; she sent me here," said Muzzie.

"Oh, you know crazy Mary Frances. You have made the rounds of my crowd! I won't use the word family; that usually means people love each other."

"You guys don't love?" asked Muzzie.

"No, it's closer to the other end of the spectrum."

"You saying hate?"

"That's a little strong. More like a good, sustained dislike," replied Lebie.

"Hey, where are you living, Muzzie? Can I bunk in with you tonight?"

"I guess," said Muzzie quietly. How Newley gonna feel about this on Monday? he thought.

The night and the next day passed without incident as Lebie slept most of the time. Lebie took the bed and made Muzzie sleep in his sleeping bag on the floor. The next morning Muzzie tinkered with a disabled lawn mower while Lebie slept. Lebie told him that he had been on the road for several days and was very tired. That was partly true. The real truth was that he had been on the run for several days. Trying to find work and start a new life had not worked out too well for Lebie Jenkins. His warehouse job in Troy, Alabama, went well for the first four months, but alcohol entered the picture and began to take more and more of his paychecks. That started the downfall. The evil drink coupled with a world-class know-it-all attitude turned out to be a nasty combination. Patterns of being one to two hours late for work followed by a heated argument with his boss ended the job before the fifth month. Lebie was so angry and desperate, he drove the four hundred miles from Athens to Hopewell in seven hours. He did make one criminal stop, to rob a convenience store in the boonies. Lebie felt like finding a job was getting more and more hopeless, and the fact that Muzzie was working for his brother really got his goat.

Monday morning came, and Muzzie got to work in the yard on a gas-powered leaf blower. As he was reaching for a wrench, he heard a car drive up. Almost instantly, Newley was standing in the repair yard.

"Morning, Muzzie, do you know anything about that old Mustang parked near the back gate?"

"Well...yes," said Muzzie quietly.

"What's wrong with you? Did something happen over the weekend?"

Just then, a police cruiser pulled up and parked in the lot outside the office. Officer Wilbert jumped out of the car, walked through the yard and pointed to Muzzie. At the very same moment, Newley spied a face he had hoped he would never see again as Lebie emerged from Muzzie's little room rubbing his eyes.

"Oh my gracious, a police officer in my parking lot and my long-lost brother popping up from nowhere; I've got to find out about all these revolting developments. OK, first things first, good morning, Officer Wilbert, how did the bluegrass festival go this weekend?" asked Newley.

"Morning, Newley, you know you can call me Oscar. After all, we've known each other over twenty-five years."

"Sounds good; how can I help you, Oscar?"

While the men talked, Muzzie and Lebie looked like two characters moving backward in a slow-motion movie. Lebie backed into the room, and Muzzie backed in the same direction.

"Hold on, pod'ner, stand still. We got some talking to do," shouted the officer to Muzzie.

"And who is that character that just disappeared into the background? Some suspicious-looking things are going on at Jenkins Small Engine. Come on, Newley, let's do some talking with these two gentlemen."

As the men approached Muzzie, T ran out of the little back room and started barking and growling. In the meantime, Lebie was pacing back and forth in the little room. What am I going to do? he thought. That little store I hit up Saturday morning for some food and gas couldn't have notified the police in another state this fast! Or could they? What a mess!

"Halt!" screamed Officer Wilbert to Muzzie as he saw him turning to walk away. When T saw the officer move toward Muzzie, he went after the police officer and sank both of his teeth in his ankle.

"Ow!" he said, and he kicked the little dog into a small set of briars.

When Muzzie saw T land in the thorny plants, he ran up to the police officer and smacked him in the face. Officer Wilbert fell back and drew his pistol.

"I have had enough of this! Stop! You are now under arrest for assaulting an officer."

Newley grabbed Muzzie. "You need to stop now, my friend. Just stop!"

"OK, everyone, calm down! Stand here, buddy, while I cuff you. It will be much easier if you cooperate," Officer Wilbert said, pointing to Muzzie.

"T! T!" shouted Muzzie at the little dog who was whimpering in the bushes.

"I will help your dog," said Newley. "We'll run him by the vet's office today. You go with the officer." Newley turned and mumbled to himself as he walked toward the office. "I have to call my sister about this guy. She seemed to think he was OK, but I have some bad feelings."

In all the confusion, Lebie had grabbed his hat, slipped out of Muzzie's room, gotten outside of the fence, and made it to the Mustang. He knelt beside the old car and as soon as the trio started moving toward the office, he opened the car door, turned on the ignition switch, and hit the road.

In the rearview mirror, Lebie spotted Officer Wilbert loading his friend Muzzie into the police car. OK, Lebie thought to himself, I am going to make my way up to visit dippy Mary Frances. All I know is Hopewell is too crazy. Maybe Mary Frances can get me a job and change my life.

Muzzie sat quietly in the back of the police car. Looking out of the smudged window, he thought, now he's done it, he done it again.

15

MORE MAGIC

Saturday, May 12, 2001

S EVERAL DAYS EARLIER, LEBIE JENKINS HAD MADE IT
from Hopewell to Asheville before the old Mustang blew a
tire and stopped. He decided to take advantage of the nice
weather and the laid-back nature of downtown Asheville to do
some panhandling. A crude sign that read "Wife in Hospital,
Please Help!" brought in some good money. He soon had
enough cash to get a room and buy a new tire for the old car.

Back in Smith's Gap, a warm front had brought good feelings to everyone. Amanda and Cara were enjoying the nice
Saturday afternoon by walking through the woods near Luke's
Pond. The air was cool but not cold, and the sound of birds was
all over the forest. Amanda marveled at the sight of the pond.
With the sun shining down, the glimmer looked like diamonds
floating on the surface.

"Remember last fall, I told you that these woods and the
Luke's Pond water have special powers?" Cara asked as she
looked across Luke's Pond. "Mary Frances used to come here
when she was a teenager and look at her now."

"She's a little crazy," said Amanda, smiling fondly.

"I would rather say...deeply intuitive," replied Cara. "All I know is they say wonderful things happen when you hang out here."

"OK, Cara, you just said that Mary Frances was deeply intuitive, right?"

"Yeah, so what?"

"I want to tell you something that happened a few weeks ago at this very spot."

"Girl, you are starting to scare me! Tell it!"

"OK, so my dad and I were walking along the bank, and he was very excited about remembering when he was right here at Luke's Pond with my mom back in 1986 before I was born."

"Yeah, so?"

"Be patient, Cara, this is big! As he was talking to me, I heard this sound—'May May'—coming out of the forest. My dad could not hear it!"

"Well, Amanda, as people get older, they start losing their hearing; maybe he has a wax buildup!"

Amanda's brow became deeply furrowed. "Or...Cara, maybe I am 'deeply intuitive'!"

Cara studied Amanda's face, then started looking at her hair.

"Cara, what is your deal? Why are you looking at my hair?"

"My friend, I figured if you were getting like Mary Frances, maybe your hair is getting like her frizz."

"Hey, this is serious. I took binoculars and looked in the direction of the 'May May' sound. There sat a great horned owl! Then the owl winked at me and vanished. Later, as we were leaving, my dad called me May May. I almost lost it. He said that he and my mom called me that when I was a baby."

"So they called you May May when you were a baby. That's pretty cute. I was always called Cara, as far as I know."

"But to think a big owl says, 'May May,' and then my dad talks about me being called May May, this is getting very weird."

"Pretty cool, girl, and *deeply* intuitive."

A week later, on Saturday, Amanda and Cara were again walking along the banks of Luke's Pond. "Why did you bring a gym bag for a walk in the woods?" asked Cara.

Suddenly, Amanda threw the gym bag down, ripped her shoes and jacket off, and dove into the pond, going down about six feet. As she approached the surface, she studied the shoreline. Instead of Cara standing there with her hands on her hips, she saw a man and a woman walking along holding hands. The woman was really fat—no, she was pregnant. That all disappeared when Amanda broke the surface, shivering and gasping for air. Amanda's hands hit the bank, and she pulled herself out onto a soft sandy area. The water was freezing!

"What da heck is going on?" asked Cara. "Girl, it's May! The ice on the pond just melted four or five weeks ago! Give this water some time to warm up. We've got time! The best time to swim is in July—late July—up here in the hills. You flatlanders don't know!"

"Cara, I must tell you this!"

"What? That you really are crazy and need to be sent somewhere?"

"Hey, girl, I'm not shivering because of the cold! You wouldn't believe it. I think—I think I just saw my mom and dad walking right where you are standing."

"Girl, you are crazy!" said Cara with her hands on her hips.

"Cara, get serious, but you've got to keep this between us. I'm going to see Mary Frances."

"Girl, put your hoodie jacket back on and go see that crazy woman. Don't forget we've got that current events report due Monday. Bye."

Amanda walked the two miles to the hardware store. What

did I see? she thought. My mom was so young and pretty! This place is full to the brim with secrets and magic! Just as she was leaving the woods, she saw a deep thicket of briars. That will have some great raspberries on it come July, she thought. Ten feet deep in the thicket, some eyes were watching Amanda. They were the large brown eyes of a black bear. *The* black bear. He stared at her as she walked.

In a second, Amanda heard leaves rustling in the thicket.

"What is it?" she said to no one.

Not yet, he thought, and he continued his quiet stare.

Amanda stood with her hands on her hips, looking at the thicket. Oh well, time's a-wastin' and I am freezing to death. I need to get going. Soon she made it to the freshly stained front steps of the hardware store and pushed open the door. The place was full of customers.

"Having a half-price sale today and tomorrow! Hey, H.S., those people look like they need help!"

"I need to talk with you, Mary Frances," said Amanda, "but I can wait. I'm going to the restroom to put dry clothes on."

"Suits me, little lady. Go get changed and then watch free enterprise at its best." Mary Frances turned to a woman looking at spray paints. "Now you can paint your grill or your car engine with these; they are high-temperature paints."

Amanda scooted toward the back of the store, holding her gym bag. After changing, she decided to warm herself at the potbelly stove in the center of the store. As she sat down in a rocking chair, she noticed a moderate-sized house spider climbing up the front leg of the chair.

"Milady, I have come to tell you something," said the spider.

Looking around and realizing no one was nearby, Amanda said weakly, "OK."

"He was watching you this morning; he wants to tell you something. You are just about ready."

Amanda looked around as two women burst out of the door and down the steps of the hardware store. "Tell me more. *Who* was watching me, and what does he want to tell me?"

"Your bear was watching you!" said the house spider. "He wants to tell you something, but it's not quite time."

Amanda stared at the little spider.

"That's all for now, toodle-oo!" said the house spider in a very British accent, as she jumped off the chair and vanished under a shelf.

Amanda took a deep breath. Just breathe, she thought.

The front door of the hardware store flew open again, and six people loudly walked out the door. Mary Frances held the door and yelled after them, "Now you folks come back soon, and let me know how that mixer works for you." She then turned to Amanda. "What's up with you today and why did you have to change clothes?"

"Mary Frances, I just did some swimming at Luke's Pond this morning. Cara said you might know some secrets about it. Is that true?"

As soon as Amanda finished speaking, she felt a tremendous push on her back. It was as if she flew to the back of the store. H.S. Stevens' eyes grew wide as he watched his boss and the girl vanish to the back of the store.

"Git, git, and git back here now," whispered Mary Frances.

Amanda swallowed hard as she was pushed down the hallway, past the bathroom, and into a small room she had never noticed before. Inside the room were three wooden chairs and a side table with a small 1950s table lamp on it. The room smelled very old and unused, but interesting. Mary Frances switched on the lamp and pushed Amanda into the closest chair.

"Now listen, girl, I have only told people a little about Smith's Gap being an enchanted place. Ever since those miners came here one hundred fifty years ago, there have been strange things popping up all over. In case you haven't realized, I am one of the conduits of the magic."

"OK, help me here, what does conduit mean? I think I remember it from science class last year."

"A conduit is like a wire or a cord with a plug. Just think of old frizzy-headed Mary Frances with a wire plugged into her head. The other end of the wire is in an outlet marked 'Smith's Gap Magic.'"

"Cool beans!" said Amanda. "Let's start spilling it to your 'adopted daughter.'"

"Not so fast, beans, there is a ton of ground rules that most eighth graders would have a hard time keeping secret. They all boil down to this: KEEP YOUR MOUTH SHUT about the magic!"

Amanda cowered back in the chair at this loud and harsh tone from her friend. All of a sudden, the sound of bells rang out at the front of the store.

"Who in the world is that?" shouted Mary Frances as she leaped up out of the chair to help a man and his son who needed a hacksaw blade.

Wow, she moves like a teenager. We could use her on the volleyball team, but I guess our high-level conference is over, thought Amanda. Realizing that the store was way too busy to do any more talking, she made her way to her gym bag by the stove and waved goodbye to Mary Frances.

"Do not forget what I said!" Mary Frances called out as she waved back.

"No problem," Amanda said, and she walked out the front door.

The next day, Eddie and Bill-Lee went exploring near Luke's Pond. They came upon a place completely covered by huge privet bushes. "This looks like a large fort," said Eddie. "Let's see what's inside." They got on their hands and knees and crawled under the bushes for about thirty feet. Soon they came to a clearing that was completely encircled by the bushes. Through the clearing ran a stream that widened into a deep pool. As they walked around the pool, they began to see pieces of plates and metal shovels.

"Bill-Lee, I think we are close to where the gold miners found the gold," said Eddie. "That pool looks very deep." They continued to walk around the secret camp when Eddie said, "Man, it's getting late; my mom's gonna kill me if I'm late for dinner again. Let's go. But first, Bill-Lee, we've got to promise that this is a secret place just for you and me. Don't tell your blabby sister about it!"

"I promise," said Bill-Lee. They crawled back out of the bushes and walked toward home.

As they neared the houses, Amanda and Cara saw them. "Hey, you dirty little skunks," said Cara, "where have you been? I hope you don't smell as bad as you look."

"You wouldn't believe what we found," said Bill-Lee. "It's like a magic fort, and it looks like where the gold miners found gold!"

"Really?" said Amanda. "I want to see it."

Just then Bill-Lee could feel some eyes staring through him. He looked over at Eddie.

"What a secret, *buddy!*" And Eddie walked home.

The end of school was coming up and performance on end-of-year tests consumed Amanda. Swimming in the cold Luke's Pond went down several notches on her to-do list. Finally, the tests were completed, and school was over. Warm weather returned to the beautiful mountains. "Hey, Cara, let's go back to

Luke's Pond. I want to swim again!" said Amanda in a phone call to her friend. Grabbing a towel, she met Cara standing on the edge of Luke's Pond in her bathing suit. "Time's a-wastin'," shouted Amanda as she leaped into the water. Although the air temperature was eighty-eight degrees, the water temperature at sixty-three degrees hit her and made her gasp. She came to the surface, took a quick breath and dove under the water again. As she looked toward the bank, she saw two pairs of ankles submerged in the water. One set of ankles was very familiar; it was her dad's, which she always considered large and muscular. The other set of ankles was smaller, more like her own, but they were different because they were swollen! Coming up for air, Amanda took another huge breath and went under the water. She steadied herself about six inches below the surface of the water, realizing now that this depth was the best vantage point to see the magic. On the shoreline were two adults. This time she could see her father. He had a lot more hair and looked like an overgrown college student. Quickly, Amanda broke the surface and gasped for air.

"Hey, why didn't you get in the water? It's pretty amazing!" shouted Amanda to Cara. "I saw my dad and pregnant mom again. I want to see if I can talk to my mother!"

Cara was very quiet and studied Amanda's face. "Girl, I believe you," said Cara. "I told you this place was magic. We probably should run this by Mary Frances. She can help refine your visits, maybe even get that conversation going. Who knows?"

"Great idea," said Amanda. "She will bring the magic quotient up considerably."

"Let's go visit the most interesting person in town," said Cara, and the two walked the two-mile trail as fast as possible toward downtown Smith's Gap.

"What can I do for these fine ladies?" asked Mary Frances as they entered Hester's Hardware. "Wait a minute; are you wet, Amanda?"

"Yes, ma'am, and you need to get wet also! Come and go with us to Luke's Pond!"

"Now, what do you think I am doing? Twiddling my thumbs here?" implored Mary Frances. "I have a business to run. I can't just go traipsin' off any old time."

Cara stepped forward. "This is important, Mary Frances, Amanda needs some magical assistance. It is four-twenty p.m. The store closes at five o'clock and surely 'guess who' can hold the fort down for forty minutes!"

"Now that's what I like: a strong, assertive woman. H.S.! Where are you?" In a flash, Mary Frances' handsome assistant burst from the backroom. Looking quite dashing with his green Hester's Hardware apron on, he looked over at Amanda.

"What happened to you? Get caught in a thunderstorm?"

Still in a serious mood and ready to take on the world, Amanda replied, "That would be a nun-ya, H.S., as in 'nun ya business.'"

H.S. ignored the assertive almost ninth grader and turned to Mary Frances. "I overheard the earlier conversation, and I can handle the store while you guys get wet or even wetter."

"Thank you, kind sir. Call me if you need me," said Mary Frances as she held up her flip phone.

"Let's go, ladies. I will drive 'cause I got to get my suit from home."

H.S. rolled his eyes at the mention of Mary Frances' bathing suit. Cara buried her face in her hands as she muffled a giggle.

"I saw that!" shouted Mary Frances to H.S. "Don't make me come around this counter!"

Soon they were all crammed into Mary Frances' 1972 cream-colored Volkswagen Beetle convertible. A quick park in her driveway and Mary Frances disappeared out of the car.

"I just have a question, Cara. Have you ever seen Mary Frances with a bathing suit on?"

"Oh my gosh, no, this will be something!" replied Cara.

Just then the front door slammed, and the two girls' eyes grew wide. Mary Frances had on a bright blue one-piece bathing suit with the letters "MF" on the front.

"Don't say a word, not one word," whispered Cara to Amanda. Amanda took a deep breath as she looked at the skinny fifty-one-year-old mountain woman in an old monogrammed bathing suit. Sensing Amanda's intrusive stare, Mary Frances tightened the cover-up around her shoulders.

"Don't say a word, not one word," repeated Mary Frances to the girls when she opened the car door. "I would say that is very good advice!"

In no time, the trio was parking near the trail that led to Luke's Pond.

As they reached the shoreline of the pond, Amanda quickly jumped in the cold water. Standing in a shallow section, she turned just in time to see Mary Frances don a bright yellow swim cap and a purple nose plug. Amanda started laughing and choked as she swallowed water.

"Girl, go ahead and laugh, but I was a two-time champion freestyle and backstroke swimmer. We didn't know about the breaststroke at my school or I would have won that too."

Amanda squeezed her fingers around her nostrils. "You sound like a different person with that nose plug on," she shouted to Mary Frances.

Cara emerged from her first dive in the water. "Hey, guys, I just saw something crazy—three old guys sitting around a little fire right near the edge of the lake."

"That was the miners," said Mary Frances. "I have seen them before when I have been swimming here; I call them Manny, Moe, and Jack. I have tried to get them to tell me about the box of gold, but I can't figure out how to communicate with them."

"That is a wonderful story, but we need to shelve it for right now because I want to see my mom," said Amanda loudly.

Amanda disappeared under the water and found her favorite spot six inches under the surface, near the area where her dad had said the bench should be. This time she saw a man and a pregnant woman walking hand in hand along the shoreline. Amanda pushed her hand above the surface of the water and moved it back and forth as if to wave. She was startled when the woman started pointing at her hand and screaming. Amanda could see her lips saying, "Someone is drowning."

What have I done? Amanda thought. She looked again and saw that the man had started to remove his shirt as if to jump in and save this supposedly drowning person. Quickly, Amanda broke the surface, and the image of the two was gone. of the two was gone. The ferns just waved in the breeze where there were none just seconds earlier.

"OK, guys, group meeting!" shouted Amanda to Mary Frances and Cara. As they huddled together on the shore, she recounted what had just happened.

"Laws, girl," shouted Mary Frances, "you didn't know that that was a cardinal sin! You don't just up and wave to people at Luke's Pond! This is not like the parking lot at the Walmart down in Asheville! This place is so full of magic, it'll make your head spin. Now look, the only proper way to communicate with those people on the shore is to write something down and show it to them."

"But I thought you just said you could not figure out a way to communicate with the three miners."

"That's right, Amanda," said Mary Frances as she removed her nose plug. "I slipped them a note on waterproof paper, but it didn't work."

"And why is that?" asked Cara.

"Well, let's see, it's 1870, only one in two kids even goes to school. Just the rich ones, mainly. Guess how rich gold prospectors are, and guess what, these guys probably never went to school; they are illiterate, and not one of them could read a word. I held up my waterproof note, and they just stared, and when one of them pulled a gun, I had to give up. I figured it was time to surface."

The three of them walked into the water again. "Well, we have certainly learned a lot today," said Cara as she swam up to Mary Frances and Amanda.

"Oh no, wait just a minute," said Mary Frances as she looked over at a log partially submerged in the water. Mary Frances drifted over toward the log about twenty feet from Amanda and Cara. "Yes, hello…Glad to see you again too…Oh, I've been fine…No, they're OK, and you are safe…You say what?… Hey, I am listening."

Amanda and Cara looked at each other and Cara started to make a circular crazy sign around her ears. Amanda smiled and then looked again at Mary Frances, who now was in a full-fledged conversation with the log.

"There's got to be something on that log," said Amanda, "and I bet you it has eight legs."

"Yes, ladies," said Mary Frances, "I am speaking to Dolo. She is a Dolomedes tenebrosus, which is the scientific name for a dock spider or fishing spider. Look at her, she is gorgeous!"

"Whatever you say," said Amanda as she drifted up and looked over Mary Frances' shoulder. "That thing is huge! I think I like your snake friends better."

"No, seriously, dock spiders do not bite humans. Dolo is getting ready to produce an egg sac; she will be very busy for the next few weeks. But she also has some very interesting information about the box, you know…the box of gold."

"Would you fine ladies close your mouths and listen! I can tell you are full of beans," said a very small, very English voice from the log.

Amanda, Cara, and Mary Frances stared in silence at the spider.

"I feel like I'm watching some old English movie," said Amanda in a whisper.

"Shh and shh," said the small voice. "Now look, the box was in the lake for a few years, but about eighty years ago, some forest people moved it to a cave room with a door. Can't talk anymore; I am cream-crackered and about to have a kip." With that, the large black spider found a hole in the log and disappeared.

"OK, girls," said Mary Frances, "you have heard the word, and now we just have to figure out where a cave room with a door is."

"Seriously?" shouted Cara, staring at the hole where the spider had gone. "I just have one question. How the heck does a very large black spider—yuck—know all this stuff?"

Mary Frances looked hard at the two middle school girls. "It's about time you two began to trust the magic; the animals around here know a lot of good stuff, and if you take the time to listen, they will tell you. I have learned that spiders, even large scary ones, want to tell what they know to help us. They live about a year or so, but they tell their offspring everything, so the story we just heard has been repeated through one hundred generations."

Amanda got very quiet. The image of a cave door came to her. She remembered the curve of the door and the darkness past it. Now there was a real reason to go back there. "But Mom comes first," she whispered as she looked at the waving ferns.

16

MEETING LEBIE

Thursday, May 31, 2001

L EBIE HAD WORN OUT HIS WELCOME IN ASHEVILLE. THE
police had warned him several times about the panhandling
ordinance, and he knew he was one step away from lock-up
if he continued holding his sign on the sidewalk. Time to hit
up my sis for some cash, he thought as he climbed into the
patched-up Mustang and drove out of Asheville toward Smith's
Gap.

Amanda woke up Thursday morning feeling better about
everything. During the morning, she was nicer to Bunster, her
dad, and even Bill-Lee. I am now a ninth-grader! she thought.
Instead of sadness, she smiled broadly when she looked at her
mom's picture on her bedside table. With this newfound joy, she
picked up the picture and moved it to her desk across the bedroom. "I still love you, Mom, and I always will. I'm strong enough
to do this now," she said as she looked at the picture in the new
spot. Grabbing the phone, she called Cara. "Hey, girl, it's me,
Amanda, and I have got a ton to tell you. Let's celebrate getting
out of school and becoming ninth graders!"

"Well OK," said Cara as she yawned, "how do we celebrate
in Smith's Gap?"

"I'll be over in ten minutes. Get dressed. Let's go see Mary Frances."

"Whoopee," said Cara half-heartedly.

In nine and a half minutes, Amanda was standing at Cara's door.

"What did you do, take a happy pill?" asked Cara, wondering why Amanda could not stop smiling.

"Let's say I am very motivated! How about we jog to Mary Frances,'" said Amanda. "It's mostly downhill." The two girls kept up a very good pace, covering the two miles in nineteen minutes.

"Wow, we may need to consider the track team next year in high school!" said an out-of-breath Cara.

After grabbing her knees and breathing deeply, Amanda stared at Mary Frances' house. "She's not here; let's go."

Amanda turned to see Cara taking off toward downtown Smith's Gap.

"Can't catch me!" shouted Cara as she sprinted off.

She has changed since I met her last summer, Amanda thought. She has lost weight and… "Hey, girl, wait up!"

In just a few minutes both girls were in sight of the hardware store, but Cara was still three lengths ahead. "We need to walk it in; we'll cramp up if we don't cool down. Now that we are almost track stars, we need to act like real athletes, not little girls running through a mountain town," said Amanda to a breathless Cara.

"Hey! Just remember our volleyball team came in second in the conference. It was really fun this year; you added a lot to the Snarlin' Possum team!"

"Thanks," said a sweaty Amanda as she put her arm around Cara.

"Uh, that's gross. You are wet and sweaty!" said Cara as she grabbed Amanda's hand and untangled herself from it.

"Hey, do possums sweat?" inquired Amanda.

Both girls giggled and walked up on the front porch of the hardware store still catching their breath. The only "managers" visible were the three ravens standing on the table near a food dish.

"Hey, guys," said Amanda to the three black "musketeers."

"Huh," said Allan.

"Did you hear that, Cara? This place is getter more and more interesting."

"Hear what?"

"That raven, Allan, he just spoke."

"No, he did not."

"Did too. He just said, 'Huh.'"

"OK, I'll take your word for it. Where in the world is Mary Frances?"

"Let's look in the back," said Amanda, and the two girls left the ravens and ventured down a hallway toward the back of the cavernous store.

H.S. Stevens, now an even more handsome tenthgrader, appeared from the stockroom and stood in their way. Amanda quickly gave him an approving once-over.

"You two go to the front of the store now!" commanded H.S.

"What's the deal? What's going on?" asked Cara.

"Mary Frances is back there with him, and you two need to stay away. They have been back there about thirty minutes, and I don't know what's going to happen next."

"Who is 'him'?" asked Amanda.

"Her brother Lebie; I don't know him very well, but he seems to be a nasty character."

"We are going back there," said Amanda.

"Hey, don't say I didn't warn you. Proceed at your own risk." With that, H.S. stepped aside and Amanda and Cara moved down the hall.

They crept slowly toward a door that had a sign painted "Employees Only." Amanda looked at Cara, pointed to the door, and said, "Shh." The ravens cackled as the voices grew louder.

"Oh no, no, no, little brother, sometimes I think you are the devil himself," said Mary Frances so loudly that it could be heard through the door.

Amanda and Cara shrank back in the hallway, but then inched closer. Both were trying to figure out what was going on.

"Sister, all I can say is I need help…big help," said a strange voice.

"How so?"

"Well you know, a lot of people have been getting me in trouble over the last few years…"

"Stop right there, little brother, let's take a little responsibility here. You have been getting yourself in trouble, and it's not just the last 'few' years; let's say twenty or twenty-five."

"Man, I did not come here to be condemned; there's plenty of that out there," the male voice said.

"What, what?" the girls heard Mary Frances say quietly. "Hey, we don't need to talk right now, go back to your web. There are still mosquitoes, flies and dad-blamed gnats out here."

Amanda squirmed a little closer and smiled to herself; she knew that Mary Frances was talking to a spider.

Cara stood back, confused by what she was hearing. In a moment, she sidled up next to Amanda, who had her ear to the door. "I'm going home, friend. I think this is none of our business. I'll catch up with you tomorrow."

Amanda nodded and was soon standing in the hallway by herself.

"Am I crazy? Are you having a fit or something? Are you talking to ghosts?" said the male voice louder. "Hey, I came here to get help. I did not come here to listen to a crazy person talk to ghosts!"

"Lebie, it's always been all about you, what you want, what you have done. I told you several years ago I had had enough, and that still stands."

"I'm desperate; I would not have come here if I was not desperate. I need money; I need food; I need work."

"I can tell you what you need…You need to turn yourself around and get out of this store and this town!" Mary Frances' voice rose several decibels. Amanda did not realize it, but the bench she was leaning on was about to break. As she pressed forward to listen harder, the front leg broke off. When the bench collapsed, Amanda went tumbling down on the floor.

Mary Frances ran toward the closed door and flung it open. "H.S., is that you?" she shouted as she looked toward the front of the store.

"No, it's me, Mary Frances," said Amanda in a quiet voice on the floor.

"Wow, that scared me to death!" shouted Lebie as he assumed a karate stance in front of Amanda. "Who the heck are you and where did you drop in from?"

With all the noise, Edgar, Allan, and Poe started screeching and cawing at the front of the store.

"And you stinking buzzards need to get quiet!" Lebie shouted to the ravens at the top of his lungs.

"All right, that's enough!" said Mary Frances. "It's time for you to take off, friend; you overstayed your welcome by about twenty minutes."

"I've only been here twenty minutes," said Lebie.

"That's what I mean. Now get outta here."

Lebie stared at Mary Frances for a full five seconds and then turned to leave.

"This ain't over," he muttered to himself. Then he opened the front door of the hardware store, walked out, and slammed it so hard that a seed display fell to the floor. Got to find me a room, he thought, got to do some thinking, and after all that, maybe some drinking.

"Sorry you had to see all that," said Mary Frances as she and H.S. knelt to pick up seed packets. "Now, Amanda, what did you want to see me about?"

"Uh, she's gone," said H.S.

Amanda's head was spinning from all the drama she had witnessed. She hurried down the sidewalk toward the edge of town where the road turned toward her house.

"What's your hurry there, little lady?" said a voice at the side of an abandoned auto shop.

Startled, Amanda quickly turned and saw Mary Frances' brother leaning against the wall with a just-lit cigarette hanging out of his mouth.

"Oh, hello, sir."

"I've just got one question," said Lebie. "How do you know my sister? You work there or something?"

Think, think, thought Amanda. "No...I don't work there. Mary Frances is just my friend. My mom was killed in a car wreck down east near Raleigh, and so Mary Frances is kind of like my adopted mother."

What is wrong with you? Why are you saying these things to this strange person? thought Amanda. Amanda didn't notice that her statement turned Lebie's face to a pale white and his expression changed from a wry smile to a frightened look.

"Well, bye," said Amanda as she quickly turned and left.

Lebie stood and stared at Amanda, "It's a small world. I got to find me a room." He took a long puff on the cigarette and trudged slowly down the alley toward the Mustang, shaking his head.

17

MUZZIE FREED

Friday, June 1, 2001

HOPEWELL POLICE CHIEF RYLAND STUBBS LOVED LAS Vegas, Nevada. He loved the glitz, the shows, the buffets, and the Strip. But most of all, he loved gambling. He got back to Hopewell on Thursday and spent just about all day talking to everyone in town about how he and his wife, Pinky, had just about paid for the trip with his blackjack winnings. "If I didn't like the retirement package, which I will get in five years, I would quit tomorrow and become a professional gambler. Just like Kenny Rogers says, sometimes you got to hold 'em, and sometimes you have to fold 'em."

The next morning, the chief walked into the small police station and watched as Officer Wilbert handed a tray of food to Muzzie Spicer. "Good lord, Wilbert," the chief shouted, "time has slipped up on me! This Spicer man needs to be released!"

"Whoa, Chief, Spicer is a menace to society!" retorted Officer Wilbert. "He assaulted me, an officer of the law! That is a felony! A violation of statute two-two-nine-dash-twenty-two-B."

"Whoa, whoa, big man," Chief Stubbs interrupted, "you know on your last evaluation I warned you about the badge-heavy tendency that you have. You kicked and injured his dog. If

140

this case went to trial, you would probably receive a reprimand from the judge, and we would be cited for unnecessary incarceration. Spicer has been in our jail for almost a month. He has been quiet and cooperative. He needs to go."

Officer Wilbert grumbled as he refilled his coffee cup.

"Wilbert, we should count ourselves lucky that a judge is not citing us for holding him so long. I believe justice has been done here. Overdone!"

The next morning Muzzie was a free man. As he stood in front of the Hopewell police station, blinking in the bright sunshine, Chief Stubbs shouted to him. "Go get your dog, Spicer! I just called Newley Jenkins and he's expecting you. Stay out of trouble!"

Muzzie trudged slowly down the road and turned the corner to the small engine shop. His steps quickened as he thought about seeing his beloved little Chihuahua, T. When he got to the shop office, Newley greeted him.

"Hey, boss man, he come back. Thanks for helping T."

Newley Jenkins was in the middle of a meeting with an auditor for his taxes and was not in a good mood. "Hey, Jenkins, glad you're out of jail. The bill for fixing up your dog was one hundred eighty dollars. I have a new repair guy, a young guy named Bryce, been here for about three weeks. He took the day off today. I like him, but you do a better job. It's good to have you back. Maybe I can have him stay on part-time and work with you."

All of a sudden a little dog scampered out of a back room and started licking Muzzie. "Thanks, he say thanks." Muzzie walked around the office and into the familiar surroundings of the repair area and his little bed. "Fresh water," said Muzzie as he poured water into a little pottery dish for T. The Chihuahua was thirsty and drank the bowl dry.

In another part of Hopewell a few days later, Porter Grace Baxter and her grandmother were shopping. They had been to five dress shops and Porter Grace's grandma, Memaw, started complaining. Unbeknownst to both of them, a tenth grader named Blitch Ann Taylor was jogging from her house outside of town into downtown Hopewell. She was the best runner on the high school track team, and she prided herself on running at least twenty-five miles a week. Her mother fussed at her about stressing her body, but Blitch Ann was determined that she would someday be an Olympian and gain the admiration of the world as she held up her gold medal during the playing of the national anthem in some faraway Olympic venue. "As long as it's a long way from Hopewell!" she often said defiantly.

Her favorite destination after her Saturday runs was the ice cream shop on the third street back from Main Street. The only bad part of going to get ice cream was that she had to cross in front of the small engine repair yard that was next door. It's not that she didn't like small engines, because she would often help her dad mow the grass at their house and the cemetery. The problem with the small engine yard was that it was, in Blitch Ann's opinion, a large junkyard where strange people would sometimes show up. Today looked like no exception. As she licked the two scoops of double fudge ice cream with purple sprinkles on them, her eyes met a shrimpy and creepy little man named Muzzie Spicer who was crouched next to a lawnmower. "Hey, you!" he said. "Got a minute?"

Oh Lord! she thought. What do I do now?

"He need help," said Muzzie as he pointed to a large self-propelled lawn mower on the ground. As he pointed, he moved closer to her and she shrunk back. Muzzie frowned at her. "Just forget it, he do it himself."

Blitch Ann watched as the man struggled to get the heavy mower up on the table. A loud thud signaled to her that he couldn't do it and she began to feel sorry for him.

"Hey, mister, I'm coming!"

"Thanks, grab there." Blitch Ann set her ice cream cone on a bench and cautiously moved toward the man and mower. In just a second the faded green machine sat on the table. "Hey, name is Muzzie Spicer, he an ex-con."

"Ex what? Hey, mister, glad to help, but I got to go." Blitch Ann turned quickly to leave but then felt his small dirty hand on her shoulder. Wheeling around, Blitch Ann shouted, "Buddy, you need to watch yourself!"

"Whoa, whoa, he saw a spider on your shoulder!"

Blitch Ann shrank back and felt her shoulder. This Muzzie-whatever man had gone from creepy to super creepy, and he had left a little greasy spot where the spider had been, if there actually was one. "Hey, no problem, friend, I am out of here." With that, she retrieved the ice-cream cone, stuffed the cone in her mouth, and began jogging up the street. After that crazy encounter, she knew she would have no problem running the last mile and a half home. Just as she hit her stride, however, a girl and an old woman stepped out in front of her. The three bodies collided amid shouts, yells, and finally groans.

"Ow, ow, I may have broken something," the old woman groaned.

"Just lie still, Memaw," said Porter Grace. "Hey, do you know first aid?" Porter Grace said as she looked at Blitch Ann.

"I'm sorry, but I gotta go." And Blitch Ann started running up the road to complete her training session.

"They call that hit and run!" yelled out Porter Grace. "We need your help. Haven't you heard 'love your neighbor as yourself'?"

A few more steps and Blitch Ann stopped. She thought about her Sunday school class and the commandments poster on the classroom wall. "Geez," she said and she turned back to the crumpled pair. "Let me help your friend up," said Blitch Ann to Porter Grace.

"Oh, she is my grandmother, Memaw, and my name is Porter Grace, from Smith's Gap in North Carolina."

"Well, I am sorry this happened," she said as she helped the old lady to her feet. "There's a bench right there. I think Memaw will be fine; after all, it was your fault. You guys stepped right out in front of me."

"Whoa, whoa, whoa, I believe this is a side*walk*, which means 'walk,' and you were running. That means you were speeding and almost committed a hit and run."

"Girls, girls, I think I will be alright," said Memaw, "but PG, can we just head back home so I can rest?"

Little did they know that nearby, Muzzie Spicer was listening and watching from a corner building. He has heard me some crazy names: Blitch Ann, Memaw, Porter Grace. Whatever happened to names like Linda, Sally, or Debbie? he thought.

Muzzie stepped away from his observation post and walked back to the engine repair table. He stopped short when he saw Newley Jenkins standing at the gate to the yard.

"I've done some thinking about this whole situation, Spicer; I don't need to put up with this—you can't even give me an honest day's work!" Newley spun around to go back to his office. "I need to think about your employment here!" he shouted over his shoulder.

In ten minutes, Newley came out to see Muzzie. He was holding an envelope. "Buddy, here's one hundred fifty dollars severance pay. Your employment here is over. You and the dog need to hit the road."

Muzzie gulped. "Severance pay, what? He don't get no second chance?"

"That was your second chance; I don't have time for all this. Get your things and your dog and get out of town. I saw you gawking at those young girls. We don't need your kind in Hopewell! Now go!"

"But!" pleaded Muzzie. "He didn't mean nothing!"

"Be out of here in thirty minutes!" said Newley.

Muzzie ducked his head and gathered his things in the small engine repair shop while Newley watched. "I am sorry it had to end this way. Here's a little bag to carry your things. Have a good life." Newley turned to walk toward the office.

"One question, boss man, where the bus station?" Muzzie and T got the directions and walked six blocks to the bus station, which in Hopewell, was also the front of a convenience store. A sign screwed to a post had a picture of a greyhound with "Bus" written underneath it. Remembering that he used to have a cousin in Richmond, Virginia, Muzzie bought a ticket and sat down on the bench, eating pork skins with T. The store clerk came out to smoke a cigarette and looked over at Muzzie.

"Hey, you know they don't allow dogs on the bus. Whatcha gonna do with that overgrown rat?"

Muzzie's temper flared, and he stood up. His fist clenched as he spoke. "You sorry..."

His tirade was interrupted as a shiny black and white Hopewell police car cruised up and stopped. Officer Wilbert, looking dapper in his starched uniform, lowered his window. "Any problems here, Mildred?" he asked.

"No, it's just a beautiful morning," said the clerk as she cut her eyes toward Muzzie.

Officer Wilbert pointed his finger at Muzzie, and the cruiser window went back up. Muzzie and the clerk stared at the Crown Victoria as it slowly pulled away.

"He's a piece of work," said Mildred.

"Yes, ma'am," said Muzzie as he gave T the last pork skin.

Muzzie settled into a chair in the waiting room and started to doze off. Just then the public address system blared, "Your attention, please; we have just gotten word that the bus to Richmond will be arriving here about four hours late. We should be boarding that bus about four-thirty p.m., five hours from now." Muzzie grabbed T and his bag and walked out of the waiting room to get some lunch.

"Now don't miss the bus, sir, and you still need to find someone to keep your dog. Remember, dogs are not allowed on the bus."

After getting some lunch and walking around Hopewell for a few hours, Muzzie went back to the bus station and found a seat. He had zipped T into the bag he was carrying. No one was going to separate Muzzie from his friend, T.

Thirty minutes later, a very sleek Greyhound bus pulled up in front of the convenience store. The sign on the front of the bus flashed "New York City." The driver looked at Muzzie and shouted, "All aboard and gimme your ticket. This is a late-night bus so get quiet and comfortable."

Muzzie grabbed his zipped-up bag and boarded the half-empty bus. "You're going to Richmond. That will be a six-and-a-half-hour trip. There is a bathroom on board but no smoking anywhere. Got that?"

"Sure do," said Muzzie as he found a seat and gingerly put the bag on the seat next to him. He patted the bag and unzipped it slightly. A little nose popped out. Muzzie jammed it back in. He leaned back in the seat and promptly went to sleep. He slept very well for about three hours until he was shaken awake by the driver.

"Hey, friend, we don't allow dogs on the bus! Now either the dog gets thrown off, or the two of you get thrown off! Which will it be?"

While Muzzie was asleep, T had made his way out of the bag and curled up in his lap. A passenger reported all this to the driver. Muzzie rubbed his eyes and looked at the driver. Several passengers who had also been asleep stared angrily at Muzzie. A man two rows back yelled out, "Throw him off! I've got to get to my daughter's wedding in Richmond! Let's get going!" In just five seconds, three more passengers started yelling as well.

"Where the heck are we?" asked Muzzie to the driver.

"We are in the North Carolina mountains. Let's see, we are near a little town called Smith's Gap."

"Oh Lordy! Oh Lordy!" shouted Muzzie.

"The Lord ain't gonna save you now!" shouted the man sitting two rows back.

The driver stood in the aisle with his hands on his hips. "There's a gas station about a half-mile away, and you can walk into town from there."

In five minutes the bus swished to a stop at a country store with two gas pumps. Muzzie got up to leave, and the entire bus started applauding. "Good riddance!" shouted a passenger.

"Sorry about that," said the driver to Muzzie, "but rules are rules. It would be like Noah's ark in here if we allowed animals. I once had a guy want to bring his python on the bus. Freaked me out! Anyway, have a happy life!"

Muzzie stumbled down the steps and turned to watch the bus roar away. It was about eightforty-five p.m. and the sun was setting. Putting a small leash on T, Muzzie looked down at him. "Well, T, he can get some pok skins." Muzzie grabbed the bag and the leash and walked across the small parking lot to the little store connected to the gas station. Not wanting any more trouble, Muzzie tied T to a bench in front of the store and went in to buy his favorite food.

"Hey, buddy, you are a lucky man. I am about to close this place up and go home. What you need?"

"He not a lucky man. Where is Smith's Gap?" he asked the clerk.

"By the road, three and a half miles."

"Too far. Shortcut?"

The clerk put the pork skins in a bag and stared at Muzzie. "Since I am a dog lover, I will tell you this: If you cut through old-man Homer Simpkins' farm, it will only be a two-mile walk through the woods."

"You the man!" said Muzzie excitedly. "Old man, he dangerous?"

"He can be, has a ten-gauge shotgun that he is not afraid to use. He is hard of hearing and spends most of his time in the house, so you can follow the path past his house and he probably won't even know you're there."

"He and T walk fast!"

"Hey, just don't tell him I sent you. This is where he buys gas and he'd be ticked off."

"He quiet," said Muzzie, and he walked out of the store into the twilight. T started wagging his tail and barking when Muzzie came out. "Hey, buddy, we got to be quiet soon." Muzzie and T walked across the road and up a hill about the length of two football fields. Muzzie saw a gravel driveway almost covered with grass, and an old mailbox with "Simpkins" painted on it. Dis is it, he thought as he picked up a now very tired Chihuahua. In about three minutes, Muzzie saw the lights of a small ramshackle house and realized he was approaching Homer's place. Since it was now ninethirty and very dark, Muzzie started looking for a place to sleep. Near the back of Simpkins' property sat a very dirty and elderly station wagon. That's probably Homer Simpkins' car, but I'll be in and out before he even gets up, Muzzie thought.

Little did he know that these sleeping arrangements were a serious mistake. Opening the car door quietly, Muzzie crawled into the back of the station wagon with T and the two of them fell fast asleep. Muzzie did not factor in two important things: First, Homer Simpkins was an early riser and liked to walk around his yard with a cup of coffee to "greet the morning." Second, T would give away their location by barking at Homer. When Homer heard a dog bark near the edge of the yard, he moved toward the house to get his weapon, the ten-gauge shotgun. He set the coffee cup down and walked toward where he thought he heard the sound of the dog. Homer could not figure out where the noise was coming from and was about to give up when he saw movement in his station wagon. Homer aimed the gun in the dawn light at the back of his car. "Get up, whoever you are!"

Muzzie Spicer raised up and then quickly ducked down in the car.

"Get out of here now!" Homer pulled the tailgate open and shouted at Muzzie. T rushed at Homer and began barking and trying to bite him. "You little…" There was a blast from the shotgun and the barking stopped.

"No! No!" screamed Muzzie. He started climbing out of the back of the car to look at T's motionless body.

"Get away from me now! You are trespassing!"

Deafened by his fury, Muzzie walked toward Homer with his fists clenched.

"Stop now, or you will be sorry!" A shotgun blast rang out, and Muzzie felt the burning of the shot pellets hitting his arm and chest. He stared at Homer and then began to run into the woods.

"Yeah, that's right. Run on out of here and don't come back!" Homer stood and watched as Muzzie ran toward the woods. He noticed that Muzzie started slowing down, so he yelled again. "Keep running, buddy, or you will get some more of this!"

Homer did not know why Muzzie was slowing down, but there were two reasons. One was that he wanted to see about his now deceased, only friend, T. The other reason, which he did not realize was that he was losing blood due to the shots in his chest and his arm. He looked back to see that Homer was walking toward his house. Muzzie stopped to rest and thought about what a mess this was. He heard something in the woods and turned quickly. Nothing. Anger and sadness mixed as he thought about his messed-up life. Feeling his blood-soaked shirt and the growing pain in his chest, Muzzie trudged back to the spot where his little friend lay dead. Looking quickly toward Homer's house, Muzzie pulled his shirt off and wrapped it around the little dog's body. As he held the body, he stood and almost fainted. A loud crunching sound caused Muzzie to stare down the path. He looked in the woods and saw nothing. He turned back toward the path but dropped T immediately when a five-foot-tall black bear stood in front of him.

"No, no, don't hurt me," he pleaded with the bear. The bear stared at Muzzie and was quiet. For about a minute, which seemed like an hour, they looked at each other.

"I know," said the bear quietly.

"You know what?" asked Muzzie, barely whispering.

The bear walked down the path, making no sound.

Muzzie stood still and watched. Something was so magical that Muzzie picked up T's body and started down the same path. In just a moment, Muzzie saw a pond and noticed the bear was lapping water. Muzzie realized how thirsty he was and went to the edge to drink also. The water was cool and refreshing, and Muzzie felt better as he sat on the pond bank.

Muzzie drew back as the bear walked toward him.

"You are hurt, and soon you will die," the bear said, sniffing the pool of blood next to Muzzie.

"You have a friend. We are looking for him. Soon he will die for his bad deeds," said the bear.

"My friend here is dead," said Muzzie as he looked down at T.

"No, the man-friend will die." The bear gave Muzzie one last look and moved toward the trees. Muzzie watched and wondered how something so big could be so quiet.

Man-friend, man-friend, what da heck does that mean? Muzzie thought. Could that be Lebie Jenkins? At least he will get what is coming to him. Muzzie lay back in the dirt near the pond for a few minutes and began to fall asleep. Blood continued to flow out of the wounds in his arm and chest. The loss of blood moved him from sleep into unconsciousness. In twenty minutes, unconsciousness moved to a deep coma, and finally, his breathing stopped.

All was quiet at the pond.

The bear, who had been watching from the deep forest, moved back into the light. He grabbed Muzzie's arm in his mouth and pulled his body into the deep water. Then he went back and picked up the little dog's body and placed him next to Muzzie. After floating for a time, both sank into the water. The bear splashed out of the water and disappeared into the woods.

All was quiet.

18

MOM, LET'S TALK

Saturday, June 2, 2001

THERE WAS ABOUT TO BE SOME DRAMA IN ANOTHER POND near Smith's Gap.

"Let's take a swim in Luke's Pond," said Amanda to Mary Frances.

"Sounds like a winner!" replied Mary Frances. "What about Cara?"

"Cara said she has to work at the animal shelter."

"Oh, I could have gotten Porter Grace to work for her," said Mary Frances. "She has been begging me for hours since the school year ended."

"I think work was just a convenient excuse," replied Amanda. "Cara told me all this Luke's Pond magic stuff is starting to creep her out."

As they approached the pond, Amanda put her towel down near the ferns and jumped into the cool water. Mary Frances decided it might be better to ease into the water. She had done some research and found a slate tablet with a stainless steel carabiner pencil that they could use to "talk" to Amanda's mother. Amanda took the tablet, turned away from Mary Frances and wrote, "THIS IS AMANDA, HELP ME! I CAN'T GET

OVER YOUR DEATH!" In all the busyness of getting into the water, Mary Frances did not read the words on the tablet.

"Now you get about six inches from the surface..." stated Amanda as she came up and wiped the water from her eyes.

"I know, I know," said Mary Frances as she gulped a huge breath of air and went under the water.

The first vision of the people on the shoreline was very fleeting because Amanda and Mary Frances were both gasping for breath from the walk and the entry into the cool water. The second vision was more detailed as they watched Amanda's mother and father walking hand in hand along the shoreline.

Coming up out of the water, Mary Frances looked sternly at Amanda. "OK, this is good; they are close to the shore. We can stay underwater, and you can lift the tablet above the water. Be careful not to lift your head or everything vanishes. Now let's get a good gulp and do it."

The two of them vanished below the surface again. Amanda and Mary Frances floated underwater near the shore and saw the two figures again. Knowing that they were only eight feet apart, Amanda lifted her hand with the board but mistakenly had it turned backward. The couple on the shore stopped walking and looked toward the upraised hand and the board.

"What is it?" said the woman.

Hearing her mother's voice for the first time in five years, Amanda sucked in a mouthful of water and gasped for breath. Instantly the vision of her parents was replaced by three ravens drinking water on the bank. Amanda threw herself on the bank, weeping and wheezing.

"Get a grip, girl, this is where my motto comes in," said Mary Frances.

"And what's that motto?" asked Amanda, still gasping.

"When the going gets tough, the tough chew spider eggs... it's worked for me all these many years. Hey, let me see what you wrote." As she read it, Mary Frances dropped her head. "We need to discuss what you want here; what do you want to hear from your mother?"

"Mary Frances, I want to talk about the anger I feel about her death being caused by some deranged drunken person and how I can get over my fear and bitterness."

"This is a real problem," said Mary Frances quietly, "because like everyone else, your mom does not know any of this. She cannot predict the future. What you are seeing is a pregnant woman in her late twenties who has no idea that she will be killed by a drunken person in eight or nine years. None of us knows what will happen tomorrow. Maybe I can help with your ideas and questions. Then you can enjoy seeing your mom."

Amanda got very quiet and stared at her friend. "OK, Mary Frances, I see your point. My purpose is not to make my mom miserable. But how can I move on? Cara has her mother. All the kids at school have their mothers. I want my mom. I want to talk to her."

"Amanda," said Mary Frances as she stared directly into her eyes, "how do you feel?"

"I hate the man that killed my mother. I hate how it changed my life. I hate how I have to be a mom to my little brother. I hate the weight on my dad's shoulders. I hate the fear I have of darkness. I hate the sadness. I want it to be over!"

Amanda sniffled and sobbed as she wrapped herself in the beach towel. Everything was quiet while Mary Frances put her arm around her.

"Thanks," said Mary Frances in Amanda's ear.

"What, what do you mean?" asked Amanda quietly.

"You have given me the great compliment of sharing your deep feelings. That's the best gift you could give me. Thank you!"

"Thank you for listening. It does feel better to get it out. But where do I go from here?"

Again Mary Frances stared into Amanda's face. "What would your mom want for you? Would she want you to be successful or would she want you to be bitter, scared, and angry your whole life?"

Amanda smiled as she looked over at the ravens who were pecking at a hole near the shore. "That's an easy one," she said. "My dad and mom always said they wanted us to be happy, productive, and responsible, so I know the answer."

"There you have it," said Mary Frances. "You know there is a lot of magic in this place, the birds, the bears, the spiders, the snakes, Luke's Pond. But the real magic for our lives comes when we figure things out so we can be happy. I have 'stuck' friends; you might say they're mired up in feelings and emotions that they hide from everyone. I know your mom would want all the best for you and that comes when you take the burdens away. Get rid of the fear and bitterness and flush it away, down the toilet."

Amanda looked at the words on the tablet and erased them. "You know, Mary Frances, thanks for listening and explaining. I see now that I don't really want to talk to my mom. I am happy that I heard her voice and saw her fat ankles, but to try to tell her these things would only trouble her. I now know what the answers are. I want that drunken person, uh, murderer, to be caught, and justice served."

"Absolutely," said Mary Frances as she slipped into the water. "Let's leave the tablet here on the shore and just enjoy seeing your mom one more time."

Amanda smiled and jumped in the pond. As she came

near the surface, she saw two figures walking on the shoreline. Amanda studied her mom's face, so young and beautiful. Her brown hair was long and shiny—almost radiant. She swallowed a mouthful of water, though, when another person walked up to her mom and dad. It was a woman with frizzy hair! Yes, Mary Frances Bradshaw was standing and talking to them on the shore!

Amanda burst out of the water and looked over at Mary Frances who was now standing on the shoreline drying off with a towel. "I just saw you with my mother and father! What is going on?"

"That's right, Amanda, I met them briefly when they were visiting in 1986. We spoke for a few moments. I am sure that your father doesn't remember the conversation because it was so brief. Your mother was very beautiful. You remind me of her."

Suddenly, Amanda jumped back in the water.

Mary Frances' mouth dropped open. What is she doing? she thought. "Amanda, get back here. Did you listen to a word I just said?"

There were no sounds except some gentle lapping of water on the bank caused by Amanda's sudden dive. Underwater, Amanda's mind raced. If I leap up, I will be covered with water, and for a split second, I can speak to Mom. I have to speak to my mom.

Amanda looked through the water and saw her mom walking alone on the shoreline. She could faintly see her dad walking away down a path into the woods. OK, I have a plan, Amanda thought. She found a shallow area about three and a half feet deep and stood up to get air. As she stood up, the images disappeared, and another image came into view: Mary Frances with her hands on her hips was staring at her.

"Laws have mercy! Young lady, what do you think you're doing? Did you not listen to a word of what I just said?"

Amanda stared at Mary Frances and smiled. Mary Frances started to feel a throbbing in her head. I am getting a reading, she thought as she spied a large tree log near the shore and sat down. She looked back at Amanda and noticed a change had come in her face. It was a little bit crazed but very determined. With a huge gulp of air, Amanda dove back under the water. All was quiet for eight seconds. Amanda could see her mom standing alone on the shoreline. Her dad had walked away from the pond into some trees. Like a jet, Amanda's body launched out of the water and she screamed, "Mom, it's Amanda, I'm fine! Fine!"

Just as quickly, her body vanished back into Luke's Pond. Mary Frances' head was now throbbing with readings. Spiders, praying mantises, owls all had seen what just happened. Amanda had disrupted the magic of Luke's Pond. Amanda Wilson, the little girl, had just taken it upon herself to redefine the magic and it worked! Mary Frances' head started spinning, and she realized she was on "readings overload." Amanda stood and turned just in time to see Mary Frances' eyes go up in her head. She fell off the log and fainted onto the ground.

Total quiet took over the pond and the forest. Amanda stood and caught her breath. She looked at the ferns waving along the shoreline. She saw the three ravens sitting on a branch overlooking the pond. She stared at the spot where she had just communicated with her mother. Her eyes moved over to a pair of mismatched hiking boots connected to the bony legs of Mary Frances lying just a few feet away. There was a sudden peace—a sudden strength. Amanda felt great strength because she knew what she had done.

I guess I better see about my buddy, Amanda thought as she stared over at the still-motionless body of Mary Frances. She hoisted herself out of the pond and knelt next to Mary Frances. "When life gets tough, it's time to chew spider eggs," she whispered into Mary Frances' ear.

There was no response. All was quiet, except for a little voice. Amanda squinted as she looked near Mary Frances' left ear.

"Get up, lady, get up!" a little voice said in a cockney accent.

"Oh, hello," said Amanda to a half-grown house spider. "What's her problem? Why won't she wake up?"

"Too many readings, milady, there has been a major Barney Rubble." The little spider pointed two of her eight legs at Amanda. "Caused by you, missy!"

Amanda looked puzzled in the quiet.

Soon she saw Mary Frances' eyes beginning to flutter. One eye popped open but then shut.

"Just wake up!" said the little spider in Mary Frances' ear.

All was quiet.

"Am I going to have to get him for you?" whispered the spider to Mary Frances.

Amanda was confused. Who was "him"? she thought.

Just then the hiking boots started shaking and jerking.

Mary Frances' eyes popped open, and she began to shout immediately. "Girl, I told you not to speak to your mother, and now you've done it! The magic at this pond has gone into a frenzy! You appeared before your mother and told her everything is going to be great. She has no idea who you are or what that means! All the connected animals and arthropods in this area are deeply confused. Some are in a stir, some are thinking about hibernation, some think it's mating season! They don't know what to do!" Mary Frances sat up against the log and hung her head.

"I feel great!" said Amanda loudly. "The magic in this place will calm down. My mom is fine. Here's the deal. I appeared to my mom for one point two seconds. I said to her, 'This is Amanda, and I am fine.' That's all I had time to say before I vanished back into the water. She will see it as a premonition. That's good, because now, whenever she questions the future, she will think of that vision. I know you told me not to do it. I had to. I just had to."

Mary Frances lifted her head and stared into Amanda's eyes. "Girl, don't know what I'm going to do with you. What about your father? What does he think now?"

"He had walked off in another direction to pick flowers. He didn't see me come out of the water. He told me about a strange thing that happened to my mom when she was pregnant, but he chalks it up to women's intuition, craziness or something."

Mary Frances breathed deeply and looked down at the moss on the bank. "Amanda, time will tell about the magic and the creatures."

"I know, and all that stuff about hibernation and mating season." Amanda completed the entire scenario. "All I know, Mary Frances, is that in my mom's final seconds of life, she will remember the vision that her daughter, Amanda, is going to be fine. I am happy about that. If it means a few sleepy bears or few hundred extra owls or spiders that's OK."

19

FEVER DREAMS

Sunday, June 3, 2001

AMANDA WAS STILL HIGH AS A KITE AFTER SEEING HER mother and doing the big scream from Luke's Pond. After church, she decided to drop by Mary Frances' to see about her readings and her general mental health. After knocking on the door and hearing some moaning, she went inside to find her friend lying in bed.

"Oh, ooh, I feel horrible, all that mess yesterday threw me for a loop. I think I've got a fever. Go get my thermometer."

After shuffling through a bathroom drawer, she found the instrument and stuck it in Mary Frances' mouth. "Get it under your tongue for a good reading," Amanda commanded.

"I know, I know," replied Mary Frances as she scowled at Amanda.

"Hmm, 102.6," said Amanda. "I have to call a doctor; isn't his name Doc Benjamin?"

"No doctor, especially not him! Doctors are quacks! Now get me three spider egg sacs out of the refrigerator, mix them with the emulsified crow feathers in the green jar, and boil for five minutes."

With a furrowed brow and trying to hold her breath to

block the smell, Amanda placed the ingredients in a saucepan. She looked over at the old-fashioned four-burner white stove and marveled at each burner covered with a decorative tin with red apples painted on them. She removed the largest tin cover and turned on the burner.

"OK, it's on the stove on high. I will sit with you."

In just three minutes, Mary Frances began snoring.

Hearing the concoction boiling, Amanda walked to the stove. What am I going to do with this junk? she thought as she moved the saucepan to a cool burner and turned the burner off. She stared at the gross brown substance.

Amanda turned as she heard a soft snoring sound coming from her frizzy-headed friend. She decided to enjoy the quiet moment by examining the bedroom of this very interesting and quite feisty lady. She saw stacks of books and some newspapers from South Carolina, North Carolina, and Georgia. In the corner of the room, she looked at an aquarium with a crocheted coverlet draped over it. What in the world is in that thing? she thought as she moved the coverlet back.

"Stop!" said a nearby voice.

For an instant, she thought the voice came out of the fish tank, but then she realized that Mary Frances had awakened.

"Here's your medicine," Amanda said to Mary Frances as she retrieved a tablespoon from the bedside table. "Open up!"

Mary Frances gobbled the brown goo in just six swallows. "I will be fine in the wink of a ferret's eye," she said, and she settled down against her pillow with her eyes shut.

Amanda felt a small pit in her stomach as she took the pot to the sink to rinse it out. I don't want this goo to harden. It will probably be like cement, she thought.

Soon Mary Frances was snoring again, and Amanda went

back to her detective work. She decided to look harder into the fish tank. Pulling back the coverlet, she estimated she was looking at a thirty-gallon aquarium. The glass enclosure was interesting because it was very neat inside. This wasn't some fish tank stored on the shelf; it served a present purpose. The question she asked herself was what purpose? In the tank was gray gravel, a small sunken dish with water, and a large, plastic mountain-looking thing with an entrance at either end. As she looked closer, she spotted a jittery white mouse huddled in one corner. On the top of the aquarium was a tight-fitting screen cover with a built-in door in the very center.

"I wonder what's in that mountain-looking thing," she said as she began to tug at the small door.

"What are you doing, little lady?" said a voice behind her.

Startled, Amanda turned and noticed Mary Frances sitting up in her bed. The color had returned to her face, and she looked amazingly healthy.

"Are you bothering Marvin?" she asked.

"Uh no, and who the heck is Marvin?"

Grabbing her bathrobe, Mary Frances moved over to the fish tank. "Come on out, you Southern gentleman," she whispered into the tank. Nothing. But in just a second, a black tongue began to flick at one end of the plastic mountain entrance.

"What is that?" asked Amanda.

"Marvin is a young corn snake who is not shy doing what corn snakes do best. He speaks in the nicest Southern way you have ever heard. I have been watching you, young lady, and it is time for you to enter the magical realm of Smith's Gap, North Carolina."

Amanda was startled. "What...what is going on?"

"See, in my view, you were brought here for a reason. You have a problem, and many residents of Smith's Gap have the answer.

Over the past few weeks, Marvin and I have been talking. He says he can help you. I don't know what he means. Let's sit back and listen."

Amanda slowly lowered herself into a chair in front of the aquarium.

"Yer sittin' too low, girl, put this pillow under you."

The pillow helped Amanda get eye to eye with the twenty-four-inch-long corn snake. She marveled at his tan body covered with burnt orange splotches. As she watched him, he turned toward the mouse and began to inch his way toward it. Without any fear, the little mouse just sat and began to wash its face and clean its body. Showing incredible speed, Marvin struck the mouse and wrapped his body around it. One squeal from the mouse and all was quiet.

"Corn snakes are constrictors; you may not want to watch this part."

Being an almost ninth-grade girl who wanted to conquer fear, Amanda stared even harder. She wished she had not. The cute little mouse struggled for fifteen seconds and then went limp. Marvin's jaws opened wide, and in about three minutes the mouse was history.

"You are a hungry little dickens," said Mary Frances. "I've got to get another three or four of those boogers for you."

They quietly watched as the "mouse" lump that was in his throat continued to move toward the center of his serpent body.

"Thanks, ma'am." A Southern voice emanated from the fish tank.

When Amanda heard this, she rocked back in her chair and fell backward.

"What tha!" shouted Mary Frances, and she grabbed the embarrassed young girl.

163

"Sorry about that," said Amanda, immediately staring into the fish tank.

"Don't be rude; say hello to this young lady!" Mary Frances commanded.

The young snake just sat for about thirty seconds.

"He's thinking...and digesting. Most animals are great thinkers—now possums, not so much," said Mary Frances. "We're waiting!" she yelled at Marvin.

"OK, OK...how ya doing, Amanda?" said Marvin with a beautiful Southern drawl.

"Uh, Mary Frances, what do I do?"

"Don't look at me, young lady, look at Marvin. He is expecting an answer."

Taking a deep breath, Amanda said, "I am very well, Marvin, and how about you?"

The young snake stretched himself as high as he could up the front glass of the aquarium. "Get me out of here!" he said a little louder.

"Laws, Marvin, we have covered that one hundred times before! When you are old enough and smart enough, you will have your freedom."

Looking at Amanda, Mary Frances continued, "That's the mantra for all confined beings, I guess. No one wants to feel trapped. Trouble is, his chances in these woods would be nil. Too many hawks, owls, and cars for an unschooled juvenile."

"Hey, hold your horses, I am seven months old and smart as a whip!" interrupted Marvin loudly. "And I am ready for a digestion nap, so can I tell this girl my revelation?" With that, he honed in on a fly that had landed on top of the screen mesh. In a flash, Marvin crashed his face into the top. The fly took off unscathed.

164

"Act like you didn't see that," said Mary Frances as Amanda tried not to stare into the aquarium. "Snakes are very proud creatures and don't like to make mistakes."

Amanda looked away quickly but then turned her eyes straight at Marvin. Staring at him through the glass, she said, "What's your revelation?"

Just as if on cue, Marvin turned his multi-colored body away from Amanda and disappeared into the plastic corner cave.

"Get your little rude self out of there!" shouted Amanda.

"Something you will learn about creatures…they take their time…they like to just be. Remember Allan, my raven. Dogs, cats, birds, insects, frogs, snakes, sometimes you will find them just sitting. Sometimes they are sleeping; sometimes they are just being. I think it is a renewal exercise. We humans need to do more of that."

"Hmmm," said Amanda as she thought about what a former minister said in Raleigh. "My friend Richard Wilmer told me that we humans are so busy because we are so empty."

"Great words," said Mary Frances.

Just then they both spied the flick of a black tongue coming out of the other end of the plastic cave. Slowly, Marvin moved completely out of the cave and curled up on the gravel in front of his two human friends. "Here's the darn revelation," he said. "It is with sadness that I tell you that I know who hurt your mom and caused her death."

Mary Frances gasped as she looked at Amanda. "I didn't know that was it," Mary Frances said quietly.

Amanda grabbed her mouth and ran out of the room. Cries and sounds of vomiting emanated from the bathroom.

Mary Frances stared at Marvin. "You could have been a little nicer."

"Diddly-squat, I'm a snake!"

"I know, you're a snake, give me a break," repeated Mary Frances, "I have heard that one hundred fifty times. Now be nicer."

Mary Frances got up and went to see Amanda. She found her seated on the edge of the bathtub crying. Putting her arm around her, she said, "I am so sorry. I didn't know that was his revelation. But we need to hear it. Right now, just be, Amanda, just be. You are a strong girl."

Amanda grabbed a tissue and blew her nose. "Honk."

"Wow, girl, that's a strong blow. Just take some time, and we will go back and visit Marvin...if you want."

"Yes," said Amanda, "just give me a minute."

Five minutes later, the duo went back into Marvin's room. Mary Frances gently took the lid off the aquarium and cradled the little snake in her arms. "What is that hanging out of your mouth?"

Amanda spied a brown cricket leg coming out of Marvin's mouth.

"Y'all interrupted my snack," said Marvin.

"All right, tell us what you know, serpent."

"I love it when you call me 'serpent,' it's so...manly."

"Marvin!"

"All right, all right, there is a man who has been through here lately that is connected to the accident that killed your mom."

"Do you know his name?" asked Amanda timidly.

Marvin curled around in Mary Frances' lap and then stared at Amanda. "His name is Muzzie Spicer, that small guy that doesn't speak very well. Heck, I speak better than he does and I'm a dad-blamed corn snake."

Marvin did not notice the sad look on Amanda's face, nor the surprised look on Mary Frances' face.

Marvin looked straight at Mary Frances. "Will you let me out of this fish tank now?"

"My stars and garters, Marvin, you must have the shortest memory in all of snakedom. No, no and double no!" Very carefully, Mary Frances lowered Marvin into the aquarium, and he slithered toward the plastic cave to sleep. Just before he entered the cave, he turned toward Amanda.

"Bless your heart, sweetie," he said…"Remember my friend, Mary Frances can get information from a ton of other sources out there." Marvin vanished into his cave.

"I guess I know what he means," said Amanda, looking at Mary Frances.

"Well, I can talk to all living things," said Mary Frances, "reliability and depth of knowledge vary greatly. In other words, just because I can talk to them doesn't mean they will talk back to me or talk back intelligently."

"What are your most reliable sources?"

"Most animals are reliable when they feel safe. They are very fearful of us, especially wild animals. Our size, our smell. It took Marvin about sixty days to open up to me. The ravens still don't want to talk. I have a few spiders and praying mantis sources, but they die every October at the frost. My overall goal is to see if I could talk to the master of the wild world up here."

"Who is the master of the wild world?" asked Amanda.

"It's different all over the world, but in these parts it's bears," said Mary Frances. "We need to think about bringing all sorts of creatures in to help figure this out."

Suddenly, the quiet was interrupted by Mary Frances' phone. "It's your dad; here you go."

"OK, I'm coming home now. Be there in fifteen minutes. Bye. He wants to take Bill-Lee and me to Asheville to shop for clothes. Mary Frances, I hope you start feeling better. I'm gonna take off now. I want to tell him what your snake said."

Grabbing the phone, Mary Frances looked at Amanda. "Any lead is worth pursuing. Can you wait about ninety seconds? I want to make one quick call."

Amanda listened as Mary Frances tapped on her phone. Soon a male voice answered.

"Hey, Newley, it's your sis…Oh, I'm fine…Say, whatever happened to that little short guy named Muzzie Spicer?…OK, I see, you say you think he has left town…No, nothing right now, just wanted to see how things were going. Gotta go. Bye."

Mary Frances closed the flip phone quietly as she lay back on her pillow. "Amanda, come give me a hug, girl, we got to see about some things to get this situation solved."

Later that evening, Amanda and Big Dad sat on the couch talking about the day.

"Yes sir," said Big Dad, "Muzzie Spicer, yes, we just might have our man. I'm calling the Raleigh police in the morning."

20

THE WISDOM OF RICKY ZINN

Sunday, June 3, 2001

THE BEAUTIFUL CAMPGROUNDS AROUND SMITH'S GAP had lured two familiar faces into the area. Mrs. Zinn decided that she and Ricky would spend ten days at Spooner's Campground, three miles out of town. To get ready for the adventure, they went into town to get some groceries and soak up some of the town's charm. They enjoyed the stores that lined Main Street and stared up at the mountain views that surrounded the town like walls around a fort. "This is why it is called Smith's Gap," said Mrs. Zinn to her son as she pushed the wheelchair along the sidewalk. "Travelers from the east could make an easy trip through the Appalachian Mountains at this point." Ricky's head bobbed around as he listened to his mother. "It's almost time for lunch, Ricky, let's find a place to eat on this pretty street." She looked and spied a restaurant two blocks away. It had a 1950's style rocket ship on its sign.

Two blocks away, a face from the past was walking toward them. Lebie Jenkins was heading back to his car after seeing Mary Frances. He had asked again if she would lend him money. "I am going out West to make a new life," he told her. "You know you want to help me get to California." As usual, the conversation did not go well. Lebie lost his temper and stormed out of the hardware store. Deep in thought, trying to figure out what to do, he was disturbed by the sound of a woman pushing a wheelchair toward him. The man in the wheelchair just bounced along with his head down as if he was asleep.

Why, that is Mrs. Zinn and Ricky! Lebie studied the two people. I know it's a long shot, he thought, but I'm desperate and maybe they can help me. Lebie ran and caught up with them as they were about to enter Scotty Rocket's restaurant.

"Oh my gracious!" said Mrs. Zinn. "I haven't seen you in a while, Jenkins. What's going on? How are you doing?"

"Hello, folks, it seems as though I have hit on some hard times. You know people don't want to give a guy out of jail a break…I cannot catch a break. Any chance you guys can help me out with some cash?"

Unbeknownst to Lebie and Mrs. Zinn, Ricky Zinn cocked his head to one side when he heard the familiar voice of Lebie Jenkins.

"Well there you are, little buddy!" said Lebie to Ricky.

Lebie moved his hand toward Ricky, intending to shake hands.

Quite uncharacteristically, Ricky pulled his hand away and proceeded to put both of his hands under his seat.

"The least you can do is give your old friend Lebie a handshake," said Mrs. Zinn.

Ricky just put his head down as if he was falling asleep. Lebie and Mrs. Zinn watched Ricky in the wheelchair.

"He gets very tired quickly these days and takes a lot of naps," she said with a sad look on her face.

Wanting to stay pleasant with an ex-prisoner, Mrs. Zinn quickly changed the subject and asked Lebie if he had seen Muzzie Spicer.

"Yeah, I was with him about a month ago. My last vision of Spicer was him getting hauled into jail for assaulting a police officer down in Hopewell. You know he gets in trouble a lot, always has."

Ricky again lifted his head to study Lebie.

Mrs. Zinn noticed the animation in her normally nonresponsive son. Something is going on in his head, she thought. "Lebie, I am sorry to say that I can't give you anything. I'm on a fixed income these days, and Ricky's doctor bills keep coming."

Realizing this was a lost cause, Lebie decided to conclude the meeting. "Hey folks gotta go. Ricky, give your old friend a good-bye handshake."

Their hands met, and Mrs. Zinn was surprised to see a slight smile come on Ricky's face. Quickly Ricky's eyebrows became furrowed.

"OK, that'll do, little buddy, you can let me go."

During the handshake, Ricky was taking matters into his own disabled hand.

"Hey, friend, I said let me go!"

Ricky squeezed hard and started pulling Lebie's hand toward the wheelchair.

"Hey, you crazy crip, let me go now!" Finally, Lebie yanked his hand loose. Losing his temper, Lebie pushed Ricky and the wheelchair away from him, shouting, "What in the world is wrong with you? You have always been about half crazy!"

Mrs. Zinn stepped forward and looked into Lebie Jenkins' angry face. "Hey, calm down, Jenkins, don't be pushing my son around like that! Haven't you hurt him enough?"

His anger boiling over, Lebie grabbed Ricky's knees and pushed him down a short hill on the sidewalk. Thinking and moving quickly, Mrs. Zinn lunged toward the wheelchair handles and grabbed them, but her hands slipped off the handles, and she fell on the sidewalk. The wheelchair began to pick up speed as it rolled faster down the hill.

"Oh no!" screamed Mrs. Zinn as the wheelchair rolled away. Just then, a young girl emerged from a dress shop and ran across the street to grab the handles of the wheelchair. She stopped the chair and promptly fastened the brakes, so the chair and Ricky were safe. Mrs. Zinn got up and ran as fast as a sixty-seven-year-old woman could and breathlessly got to the wheelchair.

"Thank you so much," she said to the girl. "What's your name?"

"Why, I am Porter Grace Baxter," she said, as she flipped her blond hair around.

Mrs. Zinn smiled at Porter Grace and then whirled around to see Lebie high-tailing it down the street toward his old Mustang. "I am calling the law, Jenkins. Ricky knows something!" Mrs. Zinn retrieved a flip phone from her purse and pushed 911.

Lebie did not notice, but Porter Grace stared at him with a determined look in her made-up eyes. If I slip down this sidewalk between the two buildings, Porter Grace thought, I should be able to cut him off. Nobody should be hitting or pushing a disabled man in a wheelchair! Running down the small alleyway toward the main street in Smith's Gap, she could hear the man's very heavy breathing around the corner. Soon she was next to him, running and yelling for him to stop. He only ran faster. She felt in her purse for some pepper spray in a pink case. Summoning newfound strength from her weapon and her anger, Porter Grace quickly caught up with him and jumped on his back. The two fell to the ground.

"Girl, I don't know who you are, but you're about to mess up. I'm gonna smack you so hard you won't remember yesterday."

Porter Grace stood back when she heard the utter meanness coming out of this man. "Hey, I don't know who you are either, but just get out of this town!"

Backing up a few feet from Porter Grace, Lebie shouted, "What are you, the sheriff or something? You need to mind your own business. Go back and re-blond your hair! I think I see dark roots!"

"Nobody talks bad about my hair!" said Porter Grace as her temper flared. She spied a smooth flat river rock and picked it up. With all her thirteen-and-a-half-year-old strength, she slung it toward the back of Lebie's head. The rock missed his head but hit him squarely in the center of his back.

"All right, that's it! You have really ticked me off! You're gonna get it now!" Lebie ran toward Porter Grace but did not realize that a reinforcement had just arrived.

The other PGB, Patty Grey Baxter, stepped out of a nearby store and shouted, "You better do what my baby girl says, or I will beat you up with my twenty-five-pound purse and stab you with my four-inch high heels! Now get out of here!"

That was all it took for Lebie. Two mad blond-haired women were too much to handle. I'm out of this crazy place; I need to go to another state and quick, he thought as he spotted the old Mustang still parked on a side street. When the cloud of the Mustang's blue smoke cleared, Smith's Gap suddenly had one less resident.

21

THE CAVE AGAIN

Sunday-Monday, June 3-4, 2001

TWO MILES ON THE ROAD, LEBIE'S OLD CAR DIED. WHITE smoke billowed from the chugging engine, and the temperature gauge registered "hot." Lebie saw a state park parking lot and pulled into a space near the entrance. Raising the hood, he figured the thermostat had broken. He also realized he had forgotten for the last three months to check the oil level, and he had been riding on mountain roads with very little oil in the car. The engine seemed to melt before his eyes. He kicked the rear wheel, and a rusty wheel cover fell off and rolled into the curb. Lebie laid his head down on the trunk of the car and breathed deeply. He was at the end of his rope. Looking for a solution, Lebie pulled two tall-boy beer cans out from under the seat, drank them quickly, eased the driver's seat back, and fell fast asleep.

The next morning at six a.m. sharp, a loud knock on the car window woke Lebie. As he rubbed the grime off the window, he noticed an almost thirty-year-old state trooper staring at him. "There's no overnight parking here, sir!" said the young trooper authoritatively. "There are some campgrounds down the road, but you can't stay here!"

"Yeah, yeah, yeah, I hear you, buddy, but my car is dead. I have a sister in town that can help me; that's where I'm going now."

"About twelve hours from now, your vehicle will be towed and stored," said the young trooper very properly. "That's statute number..."

"OK, friend, I hear you! I got twelve hours!" Lebie got out of the car, slammed the door, and started the two-mile journey back into Smith's Gap.

The officer grimaced at the tired-looking man and turned to write down the Mustang license number.

Knowing that it was too early for the hardware store to be open, Lebie walked straight to Mary Frances' house and banged on her front door; Mary Frances scowled when she saw him. "Brother, I am about to call the sheriff. Laws, man, I want you to leave here now!" Her voice became even louder as she studied her bedraggled brother.

"Just hear me out. I need quick food and a place to stay for one night, so I can get myself together."

"I told you a few weeks back; I can't help you, Lebie, and now I am calling the law!"

"Ok, here's the deal. Give me some food and direct me to a place to stay. I'll have to walk since my car just died."

"Stay here, stay right here," said Mary Frances as she vanished into her kitchen. "Here's a chicken leg and a thigh, and some cole slaw," said Mary Frances as she handed him a paper plate covered in aluminum foil. "Consider this a take-out meal. Now git."

"What about a place to stay?"

"About the only places that come to mind are the caves in the park; it's not gonna be here!"

Lebie cradled the paper plate of food and walked down Mary Frances' front walk. Suddenly, a sleeping bag sailed past his head and dropped in the weeds. "Take this bag and go find a cave. There's a bottle of water and a flashlight in the bag. Merry Christmas, happy birthday or whatever, and tell the bats in the cave, I said hello! Have a happy life."

With a scowl, Lebie walked down the road into the forest. As he got near the woods, he saw blue lights flashing in the distance. The overzealous young trooper had called in reinforcements and a tow truck. Law enforcement surrounded Lebie's old car. "Good-bye, old pony, old bedroom," Lebie said as he watched the tow truck lift the car. He slunk back in the woods and walked down the path. Soon he found a log that was just perfect for sitting. "Looks like time for a chicken meal!" He made short work of the coleslaw and meat on the plate. I did not sleep worth a ding-dong in that car, Lebie thought. It's time for a nap, and I am ready. Throwing the paper plate in the bushes, Lebie located the bottled water and the flashlight. Shining the flashlight into the cave, he noticed that it flickered slightly. "This'll do, this will have to do," he muttered. After crawling through the low part, he stood up in a large area, which had a small alcove to one side where Muzzie had slept a few months before. Stowing the sleeping bag in the alcove, he said to himself, "Let me see if there are better accommodations in this 'hotel.'" Coming to the fork in the cave passageway, he made a left turn. Soon his flashlight illuminated a wooden door at the end of the passageway. "Holy moly," he said, amazed that a wooden door would be this deep in a cave. The flashlight flickered on and off as he crept forward. It was quiet, oh so quiet. A low growl beyond the door broke the hush. The flashlight died, leaving Lebie and the growler in total blackness. Feeling around in his pocket, Lebie realized that he had left his handgun with the sleeping bag. "Think, think," he said to himself. He wanted to get beyond the door, but he was sure that the growl was something big and nasty. Lebie pushed the flashlight button on once more. It came on brightly. As two huge eyes reflected the light, he noticed shelves and boxes in the room. One more growl and Lebie became a leaping gazelle, running out the door and back to the alcove. Fishing around for his gun, he sat on the sleeping bag, panting heavily. He listened hard for the bear. Nothing. Exhaustion took the place of fear and soon Lebie was zipped into the sleeping bag, snoring.

That afternoon, Bill-Lee and Eddie were busy with an adventure of their own. They told their folks they were going to the movie theater. As they got out of sight of the house, Bill-Lee turned to the left toward the woods.

"Hey, buddy," said Eddie, "downtown and *Teenage Mutant Ninja Turtles* are that way. What's up?"

"There's just something I have got to check out," said Bill-Lee. "You know we were studying the directions of east, west, south, and north in school last week. I've been thinking about the direction of the left fork of the cave. It goes directly east according to my compass. My house is also directly east. Could this mean that the left fork passage of the cave goes under my house? We need to check it out way more than we need to see *Teenage Mutant Ninja Turtles* right now."

"But I like *Teenage Mutant Ninja Turtles* and I've got ten dollars saved for the admission and some good buttered popcorn," retorted Eddie.

"Then go on, but I'm exploring; I've got to figure this out."

Eddie watched as Bill-Lee walked down the path and knelt near a tree. He soon realized that Bill-Lee was untying Bunster from a large oak tree.

"OK, I'm going with you. How did you convince your dad that you could take Bunster?"

"I snuck him out; we may need him for protection."

"This is the first time I've been in the cave since you know when," said Eddie in almost a whisper. "I sure don't like to think of that time."

"What a weenie!" said Bill-Lee.

"Hey Bill-Lee, you were in that nice warm sleeping bag all night, and I was lying on cold dirt listening to my stomach growl while you ate all the Pop-Tarts."

"You like dirt! I've seen you eat it!" shouted Bill-Lee to Eddie. Eddie started to reply but got quiet as they both approached the entrance to the cave. Since it was two in the afternoon, the cave opening looked much less scary to both of them. Both the bear and Lebie were asleep in their respective "bedrooms" as the boys entered the cave. The loud voices of Bill-Lee and Eddie awakened Lebie. He watched quietly as the trio walked by his alcove. Bunster stopped and sniffed toward Lebie as the boys walked by. Like a large centipede, Lebie pushed a few feet deeper into the alcove until his head hit something and he stopped. Must be the wall, he thought. Bunster again growled quietly as he looked into the small opening. The boys had already walked about fifty feet ahead when Bill-Lee whistled for Bunster to come. One more slight growl and Bunster took off toward the boys.

I can breathe, thought Lebie, but those boys are headed for trouble. Oh well, big deal, he thought as he lay down, zipped into his sleeping bag. I got enough troubles of my own. Turning in curiosity, he shined the flashlight on the thing that had hit his head. "It's a box," he said out loud. Closer examination brightened his grimy face into a wide smile. "I think that's gold! I could be rich; this is mine, all mine!"

Back up the passageway, the boys were making progress. "See, Eddie, I have always thought that our house had a basement," said Bill-Lee. "Today is a big day; I will prove my theory right."

"There's the door," said Eddie, but before he could say anything else, Bunster barked and growled and ran past them into the opening.

About two hundred yards away, a tiny seed of guilt blossomed in a normally uncaring soul. Lebie decided he needed to check on the boys. If that big bear gets a hold of them, they are mincemeat, he thought. Lebie pulled out his small handgun and resolutely walked down the narrow cave path toward the boys and the bear. What are you doing? he thought. Lebie looked down at his dirty pants and shoes. After what I just found, maybe it's time to do something right. My whole life has been filled with wrongs. Holding the gun, he proceeded up the left passage. His pace quickened when he heard the barking and growling of the dog. Then he heard a sound that chilled him to the core. "Was that a dog screaming?"

Bill-Lee and Eddie were frozen with fear as they looked into the cave room beyond the old wooden door. What they both saw would be seared into their minds for eternity. Bunster had jumped to attack the bear, but eighty pounds and four hundred pounds don't mix very well. The bear swatted Bunster, the big dog screamed and then fell into a whimpering heap in some boxes at the back of the basement.

Growling deeply, the angry bear turned to the boys. Bill-Lee and Eddie turned to run but were shocked when a dark form ran by them screaming and yelling at the top of his lungs. Lebie ran toward the bear with his gun drawn. Loud blasts came from the gun, and the bear roared in pain. The boys ran down the passage, away from the cave room. Bill-Lee turned and saw a motionless Eddie staring at the fight.

"Come on, let's go," shouted Bill-Lee to Eddie, who was frozen in place. Bill-Lee, knowing he had abandoned his friend in the cave before, turned and went back to stand next to him. What they saw was incredible. Lebie Jenkins had loaded all six bullets in his handgun, but only two had been shot. The bear rose up and swatted Lebie. Lebie was knocked into the back corner of the basement. Lebie pushed himself under a shelf and grabbed his gun with his bloody hand. Two more shots rang out. The bear growled furiously and slumped down dead. Silence. Not really, though. The boys heard the very quiet whimpering of Bunster and the hard breathing of Lebie. "It sounds like they are both alive," said Bill-Lee, "but what do we do now?"

As Bill-Lee suspected, one floor above this mayhem sat Big Dad in the den of their house. He had been disturbed while going over some work papers, just above the fray. With wide eyes, Big Dad put his ear to the floor and listened to gunfire, dog barking, and bear growling. Putting two and two together, Big Dad pulled at the wall-to-wall carpet and spotted a discolored three-by-three square of wood flooring. After working with a crowbar to remove the flooring, he slowly lowered himself into the cave room. The two stunned boys looked at Bill-Lee's father descending from the ceiling. "We have got to get this man and Bunster out of here and to doctors," he shouted to the boys after taking a second to assess the mess. Quickly, he called for help, and in less than ten minutes, the rescue squad had reached Lebie.

"I think he will be OK, but I'm not so sure about the dog," said the attendant. The EMTs carted Lebie into the ambulance. As they walked away, one yelled back, "Mr. Wilson, we are taking him to the Asheville hospital."

"Thanks," said Big Dad.

All the while, Lebie moaned and cried out.

Big Dad stepped up on some wooden boxes and hoisted Eddie up through the opening into the den of the house.

"Wow!" said Eddie as he stood up and then looked down the hole at Bill-Lee and Big Dad. Soon Bill-Lee and Big Dad had pulled through the opening and were standing next to him.

"Eddie, I have called your mom to come and pick you up. Bill-Lee, come with me. We will take the wheelbarrow to the cave entrance to get Bunster. We have to get him to Melvin Nichols' place." Dr. Nichols was the veterinarian in Weaverville, about fifteen miles away. Bunster growled and moaned quietly as he was loaded onto a blanket, pulled slowly through the cave and loaded onto a wheelbarrow.

Bill-Lee watched his father as he worked to get Bunster out of the cave, into the wheelbarrow, down the path, and to the SUV. He had seen his father mad, but never this mad. Bill-Lee actually wished his sister was there with him. "Where's Amanda?" asked Bill-Lee.

"She's fine," grumbled Big Dad. "We'll call her soon."

As they drove out of the driveway, Bill-Lee peeked over the seat into the back. He listened as his big friend breathed heavily in the back of the SUV.

"Bunster is unconscious and may have several broken bones," said Big Dad as he glanced at Bill-Lee. "We will talk about your problems when we get home, but right now I have got a world of stuff to look into."

"How did you know where we were and how did that hole get in the floor?" asked Bill-Lee.

"We will talk when we get home. I have always learned that you should not discuss things when you are beyond capacity."

"What does that mean?" asked Bill-Lee.

"It means don't talk things out when you are just this close to losing your temper." As he pulled up to a stoplight, Big Dad held his pointer finger and his thumb up to Bill-Lee. Studying his father's fingers, Bill-Lee noticed that they were almost touching.

"I am this close to the end of my rope!"

Bill-Lee quietly thought about that statement and decided the best thing he could do would be just to sit. The father and son rode the next twelve miles of mountain roads in complete silence.

"There's the animal hospital," said Big Dad as they pulled into the parking lot.

"Stay in the car while I see if Dr. Nichols can help me bring Bunster into his office. While his dad was gone, Bill-Lee climbed over the seat and peered down at Bunster. There's so much blood; he thought as he put his hand on Bunster's head to pet him. To Bill-Lee's surprise, Bunster let out a low growl. Quickly, the back of the SUV popped open, and Bill-Lee stared at Dr. Nichols, his dad, and a boy who was about fifteen. The three of them gently picked up Bunster and his bloody blanket to carry him in for the examination. "Bill-Lee, sit in the waiting room; I'll be in there soon."

"But I want to stay with Bunster!" said Bill-Lee.

"Do as I say, and do it now!" commanded Big Dad.

Bill-Lee ducked his head and walked straight into the waiting room. Inside the old knotty-pine-paneled room, there were three people and three animals. First was a very overweight black cat and a very skinny owner, sitting at the far end of the room was an elderly black and brown dachshund that barked constantly, and in another corner was a four-month-old golden retriever puppy. Bill-Lee went into the room and slumped into a chair as far away from people and animals as he could get.

"You bringing your dog in for some shots?" asked the young woman with the puppy.

"Uh, not sure, don't want to talk about it," mumbled Bill-Lee as he looked at the floor.

The door to the examining room opened quickly. Big Dad pointed at Bill-Lee and motioned for him to come into the room.

"I thought about just letting you sit and not be involved," said his father, "but you are old enough to see and deal with this."

Bill-Lee noticed his dad's eyes were red and as he stood, he looked slumped over like he had been defeated. The next thing he noticed was the smell of the small room; a strong odor of disinfectant wafted around them. In the center was a mass of fur and blood that used to be Bill-Lee's best friend, Bunster.

"Is he…?"

"Bunster is still alive," said Big Dad, "but he was injured so severely that he will have to be put down."

"Put down, put down, what does that mean?" Bill-Lee started to cry as he thought about what it probably meant.

"Son, it means he will be put to sleep. He cannot recover from this. We either do this, or he lies in pain for several hours and will die naturally."

"But I know Dr. Nichols can make him well! That's what animal doctors do! We have to try!" Bill-Lee went to the corner of the small room and slumped down, whimpering.

"I probably made a mistake here, Doc. Sorry about this, but you know I am the only parent, and he had to come with me."

Dr. Nichols reached out one hand to Bill-Lee and the other to Big Dad. "Let's say a short prayer. Father in heaven, we all know that dogs go to heaven; please be with Bunster so that he can go and wait for his family in heaven…and Lord, reach out your hand and take care of this wonderful dog. Amen."

Bill-Lee turned slightly from the corner as the prayer ended and stared up at the two men and Bunster. "Do you want to give your friend one last pat on the head?" asked Big Dad.

Bill-Lee slowly got up and walked over to the examination table. He spied Bunster's ear that was near the edge. He picked up the ear and whispered very quietly, "I love you."

A disturbance broke the moment of tranquility in the waiting room. "There's a girl out here that's very loud and she says she is related to everyone back here. Can I bring her in?" said the attendant from the front desk.

"That's my daughter, Amanda," said Big Dad.

"Yes," said Dr. Nichols, and with a rush, in walked Amanda.

"What da?" And she ran to Bunster but reeled back when she looked at him.

"Amanda, Bunster was trying to defend Bill-Lee and Eddie from the bear. He is severely injured and…"

"Why didn't you come get me? You knew I was at Cara's house."

"No time, there was a man involved also, and he should be at the hospital in Asheville by now. We need to focus on Bunster, who is in great pain."

"They are going to put him to sleep," said Bill-Lee to his sister.

"Why, why?"

At this point, Dr. Nichols breathed deeply and spoke, "Amanda, many of Bunster's organs are damaged, his back is broken, and his lungs are filling with fluid. He is a strong dog who could lie here for several hours, but he is in great pain. If he lies here and dies later, he will be suffering."

Amanda stared at the doctor as tears ran down her cheeks.

"Now this first shot will relax him." Dr. Nichols gently

placed a needle in Bunster's hip and pushed the milky fluid into his body.

Bunster's eyes fluttered open for a few seconds as he looked at his friends. Then they closed.

Big Dad, Bill-Lee, and Amanda all stared as he gently took another syringe from the tray.

"This one will stop his heart."

Everything was quiet in the examination room as he pushed the second needle into the big dog.

Very meticulously, Dr. Nichols put the ends of his stethoscope into his ears and placed the chest piece on Bunster, moving the fur so he could get close to the skin. Everyone watched the eyes of Dr. Nichols. Closing them slightly, he turned away from Bunster and faced the trio.

"He's gone on now."

Big Dad grabbed his children and hugged them. All was quiet except for sniffling and moaning.

"Will you want the body so you can bury him?"

"Of course," said Amanda, not waiting for her father to answer.

"She's right; we will bury Bunster at our home. Can we come by tomorrow to pick up his body?"

"Just let us know when you are coming."

"Thanks for your help, Dr. Nichols."

With that, Amanda and Big Dad touched Bunster's fur and walked toward the door. Bill-Lee, however, hung back and was holding Bunster's front paw.

"He gave his life for me and Eddie, he protected us, he saved our lives." Then Bill-Lee climbed up on a stool and hugged Bunster's body.

"That's gross," said Amanda quietly to her dad.

185

"Let him be; just let him be."

Amanda and her dad stood in the parking lot outside the veterinarian's office. The afternoon was warm and springlike. "Just wondering," said Big Dad, "how did you know where we were?"

"I was at Cara's, and Mary Frances came by and said that something told her you were here. That's all I know."

"That lady is something. You know, as an engineer, I live in a world of numbers and facts, she seems to live and thrive in a world of intuition, magical intuition; it's amazing." Big Dad shook his head and started staring at the veterinarian's door. "Where is that boy?"

"Over here," said Bill-Lee as he wandered over from a wooded area. "I just didn't want to walk through the waiting room with all those happy people and dogs, so Dr. Nichols showed me a back exit."

"Now we need to find out about the man in the hospital. They took him to the Asheville hospital." said Big Dad.

The Wilson family loaded into the SUV and headed toward Asheville. "I can't believe it," said Amanda sniffling quietly. "I was just playing with Bunster this morning...now he's gone."

22

LEBIE IN THE HOSPITAL

Tuesday-Wednesday, June 5-6, 2001

BIG DAD'S CELL PHONE RANG AS THEY DROVE TOWARD Asheville. "Yes, Mrs. Creech, how is Eddie doing? Uh-huh...Uh-huh...So you think we should get the police involved? And why is that?...Well, go ahead, it's probably not a bad idea...I know, Bill-Lee doesn't know where he came from either... Yeah, he is at the Asheville hospital; we are going to see him now. We'll talk later. Goodbye."

As Big Dad hung up the phone, he looked at Amanda and Bill-Lee. "This has been a crazy day, but we need to visit this man in the hospital. Bunster certainly did all he could to stop the bear, but this man shot and killed him. He really could have saved your life and Eddie's."

The three rode quietly to the hospital. There wasn't much talking because everyone was exhausted. Fighting back sleep, Bill-Lee spoke, "I don't know where he came from. We were standing there, the bear attacked, and he just popped out of nowhere."

"Sounds like a guardian angel," said Amanda.

"Here's the hospital," said Big Dad as he wheeled the SUV into a large parking lot. "Do we even know his name? This is going to be interesting."

187

Amanda and Bill-Lee followed Big Dad across the parking lot and into the front of the gleaming white hospital. As they approached the front desk, a woman greeted them with a smile. Big Dad took charge. "There was a man brought here by ambulance about two hours ago, from up near Smith's Gap. Can we visit him? Is he OK?"

The woman's smile faded. "You two look like you have been through it," she said.

"You mean, you 'three,'" said Bill-Lee as he put his dirty fingers on the counter.

"Oh excuse me, you three," said the woman, slightly perturbed. "Let me make a call. You guys take a seat, looks like you could use a rest."

Big Dad, Amanda, and Bill-Lee all turned to sit and wait. After thirty minutes, Bill-Lee fell asleep, and Amanda was getting very fidgety. Big Dad slowly walked back to the desk. "Could I leave my phone number if there is no visiting allowed today?"

"Hmm," said the woman at the counter, "let me try making one more call." Amanda appeared next to her father, and both stared at the woman as she dialed the phone.

"Yes, the man that was brought in about two hours ago... Oh, his name is Mr. Jenkins? What's his condition? Is he able to see visitors?"

Amanda's hand went to her mouth as she heard the name "Jenkins."

"He is in ICU. He has regained consciousness, but there is a limit of two visitors at a time. Here are two name tags."

"Uh, Dad, you and Bill-Lee go ahead," said Amanda as she punched Bill-Lee to wake him up.

"Are you sure? All right, well just stay here, your brother and I will be back in ten minutes or less. I don't even know the guy."

Amanda sat down and grabbed a magazine while Big Dad and Bill-Lee walked toward the elevator.

"What floor will you be on just so I'll know," shouted out Amanda.

"Uh, floor six," replied Big Dad as the elevator made a dinging sound and the doors opened.

Amanda scanned the room. She looked at the slightly bored woman at the counter, the two older people holding handkerchiefs to their noses as they whispered to each other, the old man four chairs down who was now snoring, the restrooms, and finally a magical sign over a door that said "stairs." Amanda stood up and walked straight to the women's bathroom and then at the last minute turned and vanished into the stairwell. I am on a mission, she thought. This name "Jenkins" needs complete investigation. While Amanda was climbing the six flights of stairs to get to the ICU, Bill-Lee and Big Dad were now standing at the bedside of Lebie Jenkins.

"Hello, sir," said Big Dad, "we just wanted to thank you for jumping in to fight the bear. You may have saved this guy's life." Big Dad put his arm around Bill-Lee, who was standing back near the door staring at the wires, tubes, and beeping screens that surrounded Lebie Jenkins.

"Yes," said Bill-Lee in a loud whisper, "my dog and you helped us to escape."

Lebie was staring at the ceiling but turned his head toward Bill-Lee when he heard his voice.

"I, I jus' thought it was the right thing to do. I was glad to do it, guys, but I got to get some sleep. This has been some day, and my body has got a lot of mending to do."

Meanwhile, in the stairwell, Amanda stopped to catch her breath when she saw the sign that read "Floor Six." She peered through the wired glass of the door and noticed two large doors with the letters "ICU" over them. As she stared out of the window in the door, the two doors swung open and a gurney with a patient and two nurses flew through the doors. That's it, she said to herself, I can stand just outside the doors and when they swing open I can sneak in. Amanda crept outside the door and stood to look up and down the hallway. Just then the doors opened and Amanda walked with great deliberation straight toward them.

"Hey, you!" said a voice down the hall. Amanda shrunk back but then realized that a security guard was shouting out to a nurse that had just passed him. Relieved, Amanda burst through the now small opening of the double doors and stood still to get her bearings. There were about ten alcoves with curtains in front of each of them. At this point, she saw no nurses or doctors that would mess up her spy plan. Someone sneezed behind the curtain of the fourth opening, and she knew immediately that Bill-Lee and Big Dad were there. Quietly she crept over to the curtain and pulled it open slightly. Bill-Lee's head was right in the way, but then he moved to the left, and she caught a full view of the patient. That's the guy! she thought almost out loud. That is Mary Frances' brother Lebie Jenkins, and he is a super-creepy dude. Just then, a hand came down on her shoulder, and she turned to see a young woman in a striped uniform staring at her.

"Can I help you?" asked the young woman.

"Uh, I was just leaving," said Amanda, and she burst back through the double doors and into the stairwell. She made it down the six flights of stairs and was just seated when the elevator dinged. Big Dad and Bill-Lee exited the elevator and walked toward Amanda. "The man said he wants to see you," said Big Dad.

"I am really tired, Dad," said Amanda, "and he probably needs rest."

Slightly perturbed and puzzled, but too tired to argue, Big Dad looked at Amanda and Bill-Lee and said, "You are probably right. All of us have had a major day, not that good, but very eventful."

The ride back to Smith's Gap from Asheville was quiet. Bill-Lee went back to sleep, and Amanda just stared out the window. As they approached Smith's Gap, Amanda asked, "Did you find out his name, Dad?"

"A kind of unusual name: Lebie Jenkins."

"That means I will have to make a special visit tomorrow," said Amanda.

"What for?"

"I met a man about a week ago at Mary Frances Bradshaw's store; his name was Lebie Jenkins. He is her brother; she needs to know about all this."

As they pulled into the driveway, Big Dad's cell phone started ringing. "Quick business call. Amanda, can you help your brother into the house and make him take a bath? I have to get this call."

"Sure, Dad," she said as she tugged at Bill-Lee's shirt.

Big Dad shot a thumbs-up and ran up the steps into the house.

"Wha, wha," said Bill-Lee as he almost fell out of the car.

"Wake up and walk, little brother, I can't carry you!"

Bill-Lee stumbled and fell on the ground.

"Oh my gosh, they are gonna get me for brother abuse!" Amanda whispered in her brother's ear. "We wish you a merry Christmas; we wish you a merry Christmas…"

"Be quiet!" Bill-Lee shouted. Rubbing his eyes, he walked quickly toward the house. When he got to the steps, he felt Amanda's hand holding up his arm.

"Let me go!" he shouted again.

"OK, OK! Go get in the bathtub and clean yourself up!"

The next day, Amanda walked quickly through the woods, through the edge of Smith's Gap, and up the hill to Mary Frances' house.

"Hey, girl!" said Mary Frances from her front porch swing.

"Hello, have you been in the garden?" asked Amanda, spying the dirt on Mary Frances' long pants and seeing a purple Minnesota Vikings sweatband on her head. Mary Frances was a sight as always.

"What's going on with you? Whatever happened about the premonition from yesterday?" asked Mary Frances as she hugged Amanda.

"A boatload is going on with me. Can I sit next to you on the swing?"

"Anytime, Amanda, anytime." She slid over on the green-painted swing and patted a spot for Amanda to sit.

Amanda almost breathlessly recounted the story to her friend. Because she went through the story so fast, she never revealed the name of Lebie Jenkins, only referring to him as "this man in the cave."

"What a crazy thing, and I am so sorry about Bunster. He was a great dog and a great friend to you." Mary Frances said this as she was looking out over the woods. When her eyes returned to Amanda, she realized that Amanda was weeping quietly as her head was buried in her hands.

"He was a friend, a real friend. He was with me when Mom was killed, and now he gave his life for Bill-Lee and Eddie."

"Do you know about the Rainbow Bridge?" asked Mary Frances.

"No," said Amanda quietly.

"When dogs die, they go to this large field. It's a beautiful field where they run and play with other dogs."

"So it's like dog-heaven?"

"No, because at the far end of the field, there is a beautiful bridge, but it's roped off, so no dog can go there."

"What's the purpose of the bridge? I'm confused."

Mary Frances put her arm around Amanda and took a deep breath. "One exciting day Bunster will get to cross the bridge. He will look up from playing in the beautiful field; he will see his master coming toward him. Because you see, his master has died and is going to heaven. He runs to his master and the two of them cross over the Rainbow Bridge together into heaven. I believe that is what will happen."

Again Amanda buried her head in her hands, and Mary Frances hugged her tighter.

"This may be too early to say, Amanda, but there are about three young pups down at the shelter that would love to live in the Wilson household."

Amanda lifted her head and smiled. The two just sat for a moment.

"What about the man with the gun? He is also a hero, and I would like to shake his hand for saving my two buddies, Bill-Lee and Eddie."

"Well, Mary Frances, that is the other reason I wanted to come and talk with you. He is in the hospital in Asheville, and we went to visit him. The docs think he will be OK."

"That's great, did you get his name? I have lived here almost all my life; maybe I know him or his family."

Amanda swallowed hard. "I know that you know this man because the doctors said his name was Lebie Jenkins."

Mary Frances drew in a monstrous breath, her eyes were

as big as silver dollars, and the color all came out of her sweaty cheeks and forehead. She grabbed her Minnesota Vikings sweatband and flung it to the other side of the front porch. Two of the ravens that had been asleep on the porch railing awoke with loud cawing and crowing. "My stars and garters!" she shouted. "Not in a million years would I have thought that name would come up! I want to say that this is a crazy, unpredictable world. My brother Lebie Jenkins has never done anything heroic or even noteworthy. I am speechless!"

"Well, not really!" Amanda replied with a smile. "You have been going on now for three straight minutes."

"Let me get a glass of water, girl. You want some?"

"Sure." And then Amanda found herself alone on the swing. It was so nice, she thought, to have someone to talk to about all this. Mary Frances was a great substitute mother and friend.

Bang! The screen door flew open and out came Mary Frances with two glasses of water and some Thin Mint Girl Scout Cookies.

"Don't eat these sugary things except on a special occasion. I guess I will be taking a trip to Asheville to visit my new and improved brother, Lebie Jenkins."

"I want to go with you," said Amanda.

23

THE TRIP TO ASHEVILLE

Wednesday, June 6, 2001

THE AFTERNOON WAS WARM AND BLUSTERY. "MIGHT GET a thunderstorm during our trip," said Mary Frances as she drove toward Amanda's house.

"Yep," replied Amanda as she jumped out of the car to tell her dad about the second visit to Asheville. Big Dad was still in a low mood after the crazy Tuesday but he conceded that she could go and see Lebie. "We will be burying Bunster in the back yard after supper tonight, so don't make any plans, Amanda," he said quietly. Amanda gave him a quick hug and ran toward Mary Frances and the Volkswagen in the driveway.

Mary Frances and Amanda rode in silence for the first fifteen minutes of the trip.

"A penny for your thoughts," said Mary Frances, wanting to lighten up the somber mood.

"I'll give you a dollar's worth," replied Amanda. "Someone told me that every minute is precious and we should enjoy each one. I think about all the times that Bunster would come up to me to get a pat on the head. I would ignore him and do something else. Now," she sniffled slightly, "now I can never be with him again."

"Talk it out, girl, talk it out, get it out, don't leave those sad thoughts inside. And thanks for sharing them with me. As you have sad times, always remember to find a friend to talk it out. That way you can heal inside. Maybe you should get a picture of Bunster and put it in your room, next to your mom's picture."

"That's a great idea, and thanks for letting me talk. Hey, I want to tell my dad and Bill-Lee about Rainbow Bridge after our burial ceremony after supper. I know they will love it. Now tell me what you are thinking about your brother, Lebie."

"Oh, that's a big one," said Mary Frances as she took a turn toward Asheville Hospital. "I have always thought about redemption, you know, being forgiven for all the bad things you have done. My brother may have just found redemption for the horrible life he has led."

The Volkswagen puttered into the parking deck outside the hospital. Mary Frances grabbed the parking ticket as she approached the gate, and she quickly found a space in the third row. Pulling up the emergency brake between the seats, she looked over at Amanda. "Hey, girl, thanks for coming with me. I have lived alone for a long time and can do a ton of things by myself, but it's good to have a friend sometimes."

Amanda smiled, jumped out of the car, and slammed the door. "Let's go find him," she said.

Entering the hospital, Amanda quickly realized that the same woman was at the counter. She smiled at both of them and then quickly stared at Amanda. "Haven't I seen you before, only more tired and with a grimy little boy?"

"Yes, ma'am, I was here last night with my father and my grimy little brother."

"Too bad only two can go into ICU. I watched you sitting by yourself as your dad and brother went up to see Mr. Jenkins."

Amanda's eyes dropped as she realized her sneaky journey to the sixth floor had gone unnoticed.

The woman handed two name tags to Mary Frances. "Hopefully, your little brother has had a bath by now."

"Oh, yes, we scrubbed him clean last night, but he hates baths. One time he went eight straight days without a bath."

"Well, you tell your brother, by the way, what's his name?"

"Bill-Lee."

"Well, you tell Bill-Lee I can't wait to see him again after his bath!"

"That's enough about your little brother," said Mary Frances. "Now let's go see my little brother." She grabbed Amanda's hand, winked at the counter lady and moved quickly toward the elevators.

"Floor six," said Amanda as the elevator doors silently shut. "When the doors open, take a right into a short hall and then go into ICU."

"I thought the counter lady said you didn't come up here yesterday. How do you know all this stuff about the ICU?"

Amanda smiled a sad smile. "She urged me to find a way to see him."

"Who urged you?"

"I think it was my mom; I knew I just had to get up to see him."

"Girl, you are becoming a conduit! It has its advantages and disadvantages, but I am glad we can work together. Magic is a fascinating thing!"

"It's right in here; he is in the fourth bed behind these curtains."

Mary Frances moved toward a nurse, flashed her name tag, and said, "I am here to see my brother Lebie Jenkins. How is he doing?"

"If you had asked me six hours ago, I would have said 'pretty good,' but lately his vital signs have been deteriorating. We have a constant watch on him. I'm sorry."

Mary Frances pulled the curtains apart, and she and Amanda looked at Lebie. He had two tubes going into his mouth and several tubes connected to his wrist. His skin was colorless, and his breathing labored.

"Lebie, it's your sister. Wake up!"

There was no movement from the bed.

"Let's just sit here with him for a minute and let me close my eyes," said Mary Frances.

"Are you saying a prayer?" asked Amanda.

"Not exactly; I am getting a reading."

Amanda stared at Mary Frances but said nothing. Three minutes passed with just the electronic sound of the heart monitor beeping. Finally, Mary Frances opened her eyes and looked at Lebie. "You don't think you can, but you can. You can live; you can live!" Mary Frances stared at her brother for a full ten seconds, then wheeled around and looked at her friend. "Amanda, let's go downstairs and get a Coke." Mary Frances quickly flashed through the curtains and dashed out of the ICU doors to the elevators.

"Wow, getting a reading must make you thirsty!" Amanda took one look at Lebie's motionless body and followed her friend to the elevator.

As they watched the elevator doors close to take them to the snack bar, Mary Frances again closed her eyes and got quiet. The elevator dinged at floor five, and six people trundled into the small space. A ten-year-old boy watched Mary Frances standing in the corner with her eyes closed. He grabbed his mother's arm. "What's the matter with her?" he asked.

"Sh, sh, she just may be very sad," replied his mother in a whisper.

"No, actually she is getting a second reading," said Amanda to the group.

The elevator dinged again, and the group of six crowded to the door to leave. A few of the group turned to catch a glimpse of Amanda and the strange woman in the corner with her eyes closed.

"What's a 'reading'?" said the little boy to his mother.

"Didn't I tell you sh, sh!" And the mother grabbed his hand and pulled him out of the door.

Amanda looked at Mary Frances. "Uh, we are on the first floor. Do you want to go to the snack bar?"

"Yes, but I need a chair. Get me to a chair with my eyes shut; if I open them, the reading may be lost."

Amanda grimaced, shook her head, and reached for Mary Frances' hand. "This way," she said as she spotted two chairs in the waiting area. Mary Frances stumbled as she moved to the chair in the waiting area. She settled into the chair and Amanda stared up at a wall-mounted TV.

Then she heard it: "In other news, an old case is being re-opened; more details after this message." Amanda looked around the room during the news show commercial. Her eyes settled on the lady at the front counter. The lady motioned to Amanda. Amanda looked at Mary Frances and then walked over.

"What's up with her?" asked the woman.

"It's a long story," replied Amanda as she looked back at Mary Frances.

"Well, I've got some time," said the woman as she looked deeply into Amanda's face.

"Sorry, but she seems to be rousing, maybe later." And

Amanda returned to sit next to Mary Frances. Mary Frances' eyelashes began to flutter. Suddenly both eyes popped open.

"OK, you really embarrassed me this time!" said Amanda to her friend. "I am having to deal with the looks of all these people and…"

Just then a female reporter came on the TV screen and resumed the previous story. "It appears that there is a break in a cold case in the death of a woman five years ago in Raleigh. On a tip, Raleigh detectives are planning to travel to the small town of Hopewell, South Carolina, to talk to police about a man that had been held in the local jail. We will bring more details as they are available."

"Ow, ow." Mary Frances held her head in her hands. "OK, this headache will go away soon. Let's go get that Coke, and I'll tell you what is going on in my head."

Turning from the TV, Amanda dutifully followed Mary Frances into the snack bar.

The snack bar was crowded with people chatting and eating. No one seemed to notice the interesting duo that entered the area. Mary Frances had one hand on her head and the other on her chest. Amanda stared at her and whispered, "Can you please sit over there, and put both your hands on the table. I am really self-conscious walking around with you holding your head and your chest. You look like you should be one of the patients!"

"Oh, sorry, didn't realize…Something is coming to me; let me just sit here."

"I know, Mary Frances, something is coming to you, your eyelids are starting to flutter again!"

"Just get me a Coke, girl!"

Amanda dutifully walked over to the drink chest and selected a Diet Coke and a full strength Coke. I need all the sugar

I can get right now, she said to herself. After she paid for the drinks, Amanda turned and found that Mary Frances had left. No one was at the table. Sighing loudly, Amanda walked to the table and sat down. It was good to rest in a secluded place, but what in the world was she learning today? She thought through the events. It was a giant blur. Just then she heard a call near the other side of the room. Through some tropical plants, she could see Mary Frances staring at her and motioning for her to come.

"I just had to get to myself," said Mary Frances as she sipped on the soft drink. "Things are coming to me. I'm ready to tell you what they are saying."

"Spill it," said Amanda.

Frowning slightly, Mary Frances took a deep breath. "OK, first, I am getting that Lebie is going to get better. Second, you can't always trust a juvenile snake. I am getting that Marvin is wrong about Muzzie Spicer."

The clock in the waiting room showed six fifteen and Amanda suddenly realized the quiet demand her father had made. She was going to miss the "funeral" if they did not leave immediately. "Mary Frances, can we talk about this on the way home or maybe tomorrow, I must get home now!"

"No problem, my head is feeling better, my brother is not going to die, and maybe some things in this crazy world are getting worked out. Hey, Amanda, thanks for letting me talk this out and thanks for hanging with me."

"Glad to do it," said Amanda as she stood and guzzled the last of her drink. "Let's hit the road."

"Yeah, let's hope for a good trip home. We've been here quite a while."

Upstairs on the sixth floor, there was another activity going on. Lebie had heard his older sister's plea that he could live. He began to feel better, and his mind started working. "Hey, nurse, got any grub around here?"

A young man in crisp white garb pulled the curtain open quickly. "Mr. Jenkins, nice to see you feeling better. I will be glad to bring you dinner. Tell me your order."

"Fried chicken, collards, mashed tators, and does that TV work?"

"Sir, you need to refer to the menu, but we are thrilled that you are doing better. Let's see, OK, here's the nightly news, is that OK?"

"I appreciate it, and whatever you can bring for dinner is fine; I am really hungry!"

"Be right back, sir."

Lebie settled back and grabbed the TV remote. He turned the volume up just in time to see a young reporter standing in front of the sheriff's office in Hopewell, South Carolina.

"As we reported earlier, there is a break in the five-year-old case where a woman in Raleigh was killed by a hit and run driver. It seems that information had implicated a man named Muzzie Spicer, so Raleigh detectives have made it to Hopewell to talk to police officials there. Unnamed sources have told TV25 News that Spicer is not the hit and run driver. A man with the name of Jenkins has come up as a possible suspect. It is believed that several witnesses have confirmed that this man named Jenkins may have been driving the car. This is Katharine Davis with TV25 News."

Lebie Jenkins quickly hit the mute button on the remote and sat very still.

"Here you go, Mr. Jenkins, I think we have a smorgasbord of delightful food here."

Lebie looked at a tray with a piece of fried chicken, a piece of meatloaf, a roll and some french fries. "Looks great, thanks."

As he gobbled the food, Lebie realized that hospital check out time may be coming soon.

24

CAMP TOOLS

Saturday, June 9, 2001

MARY FRANCES WALKED OUT ON HER FRONT PORCH TO enjoy the beautiful spring mountain morning. "Guys, I think I can make it today," she said to the trio of ravens as they all sat on the railing of the front porch. Five days had passed, and Mary Frances was recovering from a cough and cold she was sure was caused by a combination of stressing about her brother Lebie and a customer who'd insisted on sneezing down every aisle of the hardware store. The ravens each sat on the porch railing and stared at their friend. "I know why you're staring… you can't fool me…it's almost feeding time…don't look at me like you love me…I know I'm just a great big food vending machine to the three of you." Mary Frances vanished into the house and appeared again in her back yard. She picked up a very old skillet and hit it three times with a broken stick. "Come on, you three," she said as she poured a mixture of fruit, nuts, snails, eggs, and grubs. In just four seconds, there was a flurry of activity at each of the three spots in the yard. "Hey, you two stop fighting and go to your correct spot!" Mary Frances moved quickly to Edgar and Allan, who were fighting over one pile of food. "Well, you guys have certainly given me some humor and energy this morning.

I think I'll do fine at the hardware store today." With that, she went into the house to call H.S. Stevens. "Yeah, I'm feeling better today. Nothing like spider egg sacs and emulsified crow feathers to get you back in shape! Go ahead and open up. I'll be down there around nine; see you then."

When Mary Frances got to the hardware store, there sat Amanda on the bench near the front door. "Well, good morning, young lady! How are you this fine June day?"

"Pretty good," said Amanda. "Are you feeling better?"

"Straight up like an oak tree!" replied Mary Frances.

"OK if I hang out here for a while? Bill-Lee and my dad have gone fishing near Canton."

"That will be great; maybe I can give you some pointers on business management."

Amanda spied H.S. Stevens stocking some shelves with nails and other fasteners. She saw him roll his eyes at Mary Frances' pronouncement.

The trio was interrupted by the clamor of a lady pushing a young man in a wheelchair through the front door. "Good morning!" said Mary Frances. "What can we do for you fine folks today?"

"Hi, I'm Nora Zinn, and this is my son, Ricky. We are camping outside of town and need some tools for our camper. A pair of pliers, a hammer, and an adjustable wrench is what we need."

"Hey, it's nice to meet you folks. I'm Mary Frances Bradshaw, this is H.S. Stevens, and over there is my sweet friend, Amanda Wilson. Hey, Old Jeff Spooner has got one of the best campgrounds around, and I know the views are incredible," said Mary Frances.

"How do you know so much about the campground?" asked Mrs. Zinn.

"Well, I'm fifty-one years old, and I've been in Smith's Gap fifty-one years. I even remember when old Spooner got kicked out of school for smoking in the sixth grade. But enough of that. H.S., take them down to aisle six so they can browse through the tools."

In just a minute, H.S. brought some shiny tools to the counter. "Thank you, sir!" said Mary Frances. "That will be $19.22 with tax, Mrs. Zinn. By the way, where are you from?"

"These tools look like just what we need. Oh, I am from South Carolina, just retired about a month ago. My son enjoys nature, and I wanted to take in the sights and smells of spring-time in the mountains."

Mary Frances walked over to Ricky who was sitting slumped in the wheelchair. "Hello, Ricky, how are you?" She squatted next to him and looked in his eyes. They were blank, and a small amount of drool was coming out of his mouth. Mrs. Zinn quickly retrieved a tissue and wiped his mouth.

"Ricky, can you smile at Mrs. Bradshaw?" The disabled man raised his head slightly and then dropped it again. "He was in a bad accident when he was about twelve; this has affected his nervous system and his speech. I can assure you he is as smart as a tack and is listening to everything we are saying," she added. "Ricky, dear, can you give a thumbs-up to how beautiful the campground is?" They all watched as Ricky made a fist with his right hand. In just a second, his thumb came up and jerked from side to side.

"Yay, and good for you!" said Mary Frances as she patted Ricky on the back.

A slight smile appeared on Ricky's face.

"Hey, guys, do you know anything about leveling a camper? I have tried, but it still seems to be leaning. I am not very mechanical."

"Sure," replied Mary Frances, "Hey, H.S., can you do it? I'll pay overtime!"

"No, ma'am, kinda busy. I have a date."

Mary Frances and Amanda frowned at H.S.

"I can drop by after dinner tonight," said Mary Frances as she frowned at H.S. "I would love to see how you get Ricky and the wheelchair into the camper."

"Great," said Mrs. Zinn, "could you come about seven?"

"Sure. How about you, Amanda?"

"I think I probably could…I'll need to check with my dad."

"Sounds great," said Mrs. Zinn, "see you both tonight. Campsite number sixteen."

At about six thirty that evening, Mary Frances was getting into her Volkswagen.

"Hey, wait up!" shouted Amanda.

"Oh, I'm so happy you can come; it's nice to show hospitality to our visitors," said Mary Frances. The two jumped in the Volkswagen, which now had the top down. "I'll turn some heat on so we can be warm. It's turning into a cool evening."

Amanda pulled her sweater up around her neck. "Uh, Mary Frances, who is H.S. going out with?" she asked.

"I think it's Porter Grace," replied Mary Frances.

Suddenly Amanda did not feel the need for her sweater up around her neck as her face and neck turned red. That little biddy! she thought.

"So you know Porter Grace?"

"Yes, she's new to our school, but I've met her a couple of times."

"Uh-huh," said Mary Frances as she entered the campground. I wonder about Porter Grace, thought Mary Frances. "This looks like the campsite, yes, number sixteen, I'll just swing in behind her truck."

Mrs. Zinn ran up to the car, greeting Mary Frances and Amanda warmly. "So glad you could come. Ricky and I just had dinner, and I have a fire going. These mountain evenings are a lot cooler than our South Carolina nights. Let me show you the stabilizers."

While the camper was being leveled by Mary Frances, Amanda walked into the campsite and saw the back of Ricky Zinn in the wheelchair faced toward the fire. "Good evening, Ricky," she said, "it's nice to see you again." She found a seat in an old camp chair. Ricky was slumped down in a camp chair with drool dripping from his mouth.

Amanda's mouth watered as her eyes drifted to a large dish of sliced strawberries, some sponge cake, and a soup bowl full of whipped cream.

"It would be great," announced Mrs. Zinn, "if you and Amanda could join Ricky and me for some strawberry shortcake."

"How did you know that was my favorite dessert! I know we are in. Can I help with anything?" asked Mary Frances as she motioned to Amanda to get out of her seat and help.

"Sure," said Mrs. Zinn, "I will have to help Ricky eat, if you two could serve yourselves."

Mrs. Zinn seated herself next to Ricky and slowly lifted a fork to his mouth. He opened his mouth and hungrily swallowed the berries and cake.

"You said you just retired from a job in South Carolina. What type of work were you doing down there?" asked Mary Frances.

"I was superintendent of a small prison farm near Greensburg."

"Well, this is a small world. My brother was in prison down there. Did you know someone named Lebie Jenkins?"

The quietness of the campsite was violently interrupted by a gasping and gurgling from Ricky Zinn. When he heard the name Lebie Jenkins, he started choking. For the first time, Amanda saw his eyes. They were wide and wild as he tried to catch his breath. Mrs. Zinn jumped up and put her arms around her son. "Now, now, Ricky, it's alright; let's try and finish your dessert."

Amanda and Mary Frances were shocked and watching. They were both impressed that Mrs. Zinn was so quick to jump to Ricky's aid. As soon as he began breathing normally, she turned his wheelchair so it faced away from the group. Behind his back, she pulled out a notepad, jotted a few words on it, and handed it to Mary Frances. Amanda looked at the note as Mary Frances went for her reading glasses. It said:

Let's change the subject until I can get him quiet and in bed.

Mrs. Zinn produced a washcloth and wiped off Ricky's face and his shirt, which had strawberries and cream all over it. In about two minutes, Mrs. Zinn turned his wheelchair around, and he was back with the group.

"But, wha—?" asked a wide-eyed Amanda. Mary Frances elbowed her in the side.

"You two keep your seats," said Mrs. Zinn as darkness descended on the campground. "Enjoy the fire; there's some more wood over near the lantern. Ricky has had a big day, and I need to get him ready for bed."

"Good night, Ricky," said Amanda quietly.

Ricky's head moved slightly toward Amanda's voice, but he continued looking downward.

"You folks need any help?" asked Mary Frances as she watched them approach the lift near the camper door.

"No, we are experts at this, been doing it for a while."

Mary Frances and Amanda watched as Mrs. Zinn pushed

the wheelchair onto a metal sheet. One push of a red button and the camper lift took the two of them up to the door where they vanished into the camper.

With her eyes on the crackling fire, Amanda spoke to Mary Frances. "What was that all about?"

"Well, I guess we'll find out shortly. Ricky seems to have some crazy reaction about the mentioning of my brother's name. That's understandable because, until one week ago, Lebie has never done what's right. He does what he wants, and it's usually wrong. I do seem to remember some trouble Lebie got into before he was expelled from school. I was busy with my life and was trying not to keep up with what Lebie was doing. Maybe I should have. My folks were overwhelmed. Can you get one more piece of wood for the fire? I am getting the feeling that we are going to hear some interesting stories."

"Sure," said Amanda as she jumped up and walked to the small pile of firewood.

"You people need to be very careful about what's going to happen next. Could be in for some Barney Rubble. Need to be sure you're getting brass tacks," said a very small, very English voice from the top of the woodpile.

Startled, Amanda stared at the wood in the darkness. Shining a flashlight, she saw a small jumping spider staring right at her. "Mary Frances, come quick, one of your friends wants to see you."

Grabbing her sweater and pulling her arms through, Mary Frances walked over to the woodpile. "Hello there, my friend, can you repeat that?"

"I said… you people need to be very careful about what's going to happen next. That's what I said, and that's what I meant, now if you will excuse me! Ta-ta." Then the little jumping spider did just that. She jumped off the woodpile into the leaves and vanished.

Mary Frances stared at the leaves. "Where is that little dickens?" she asked as she rummaged through the leaves. Finally, she stopped and turned toward Amanda who had gone back to the campfire. "I am getting a reading, and my head is hurting."

Amanda watched Mary Frances stroking her forehead in front of the dying fire.

"Did you two have trouble picking out some wood?" asked Mrs. Zinn as she rejoined the group.

"Naw," said Mary Frances, "I just got a little sinus headache, so we sat down for a few moments."

Mrs. Zinn grabbed two small logs and carefully crisscrossed them on top of the fire. In thirty seconds, flames engulfed the logs.

"Well, Mrs. Zinn, how is Ricky?" asked Mary Frances.

"Please call me Nora," said Mrs. Zinn. "Ricky is better. He generally sleeps very soundly all through the night."

"Tell me, Nora, about your relationship with my brother Lebie. You probably don't know that he is in the Asheville hospital recovering from a fight with a bear."

"My goodness, we just saw him downtown about a week ago. Will he be OK?"

"Lebie is pretty tough, and I think he will be fine. Tell me more about Ricky's story. This has piqued my curiosity and my head."

Amanda snuggled down in her jacket and stared at the fire. She was somewhat uneasy about Lebie Jenkins because of all that had gone on in the last few days. He gave her the creeps, but she had great faith in her buddy Mary Frances to work things out.

"I have known Lebie since he moved in with his aunt and uncle in Hopewell when he was a ninth grader in 1977. I guess you remember the details about that."

"Wow, that brings old cobwebs out of the closet! Yes, that was a rough time in our family, the school, and Smith's Gap. Nobody could handle Lebie. He was obstinate, violent, and disrespectful. Always getting into fights at school and in town."

Mrs. Zinn continued. "Our paths crossed again when he entered the prison farm where I was superintendent. I always wondered if he had a handicapping condition, like bipolar disorder or autism?"

"No, none of those. We always called his condition 'MAH.'"

"MAH? I have never heard of that condition," said Mrs. Zinn.

"Well around here, MAH stands for something that Lebie exemplified: Mean As Hell."

"I must admit, Lebie was always up to something, a sneaky devil, he was way meaner than his prison buddy, Muzzie Spicer," said Mrs. Zinn as she held back a slight snicker.

"Oh my goodness!" shouted Amanda from deep in her chair near the campfire. "You also know Muzzie Spicer! Mary Frances, isn't he the little man that Marvin was talking about? Didn't you help him get a dog and a job?"

"Correct, Amanda! And my brother Newley tells me that Muzzie was put in jail for assaulting a police officer."

For just a few seconds, the three sat in silence, staring at the burning fire. "I was looking forward to a pleasant campfire dinner, not this!" said Mrs. Zinn.

"Mary Frances, you know what Marvin said. Could it be that Muzzie is worse? I mean, meaner than Lebie?" asked Amanda.

Another set of ears heard Amanda's question. Ricky had not gone to sleep, and with the windows open he was listening and getting very agitated. All of a sudden "Bang, Bang!" came from the camper. Three startled faces turned and saw something none of them would ever forget. They saw the distorted face of Ricky Zinn through the screen in the camper window. "Lebie, Lebie!" screamed Ricky.

Mouths dropped open as Mrs. Zinn ran to the camper window. "What in the world, darling! What are you saying?"

"No, no! Lebie! Lebie is bad! Lebie is bad!" Ricky's voice grew softer and softer as his strength was sapped from the outburst. The screaming had worn him out. They all watched as Ricky's face vanished from the camper window.

Mary Frances and Amanda sat down and eyed each other. "I don't know what to say, Amanda, this is all so crazy. How are you doing through all of this?"

"I guess we should leave soon," whispered Amanda.

Mary Frances realized there was no color in her face. "Are you OK?"

"Not really, I'll probably have nightmares for the next week. I don't know what to think right now."

I kind of hate to leave Mrs. Zinn in this predicament. Both you and Ricky are so shaken up."

"Let's just be," said Amanda, staring into the campfire.

The two of them sat in front of the fire. Suddenly, there was a sound in the deep darkness of the forest. Both Mary Frances and Amanda sat motionlessly. The sound grew louder and louder as if it was approaching them from the edge of the forest.

"May May! May May!"

"I have to see what that is," said Amanda quietly to Mary Frances. "Will you come with me?"

Mary Frances glanced at the camper. "Sure, I will. What do you think it is?"

"According to my dad, my mother called me Amanda May

when I was very little, and sometimes she shortened it to May May. I have heard this sound several times over the last few months. Let's walk on the trail and see what it is."

Armed with a flashlight, the two walked in silence into the dark. Suddenly the sound of a large bird flapping its wings made them stop.

"That bird scared me to death," said Mary Frances. "Let's turn around since Mrs. Zinn does not have a clue where we went. I hate to worry her anymore."

"OK," said Amanda, and they both spun around and turned back. In the darkness, they saw a large form cross the trail in front of them. "OK," said Amanda, "this is scary, sorry I suggested it."

Walking very fast to get back to the campsite, they froze. "Stop. May May, I need to tell you, I need to tell you," said a deep voice. Rustling in the leaves they saw the large form coming toward them. "Do not be afraid; I'm here to help." The black form came out of the woods and sat on the trail, blocking their way to the campsite. A large male black bear.

Amanda looked down at her legs, which were shaking and beginning to buckle. She smelled the great black being.

Then he spoke. "The magic of the pond has been stirred. The woman on the shore wants you to know the truth. Ricky is right; Lebie Jenkins is…"

Suddenly a large stick sailed through the air. The bear growled as the stick struck its back. He vanished into the thicket as Nora Zinn came screaming down the path.

"I didn't want you two to be injured by a wild thing like my son was. I hate wild things. They should all die."

25

THE HISTORY OF RICKY ZINN

Saturday Evening, June 9, 2001

STILL CATCHING THEIR BREATH, AMANDA, MARY Frances, and Nora Zinn limped into the campsite and settled into chairs.

"What is that smell?" asked Mrs. Zinn as she approached them.

"Believe it or not," said Mary Frances, "the bear we just encountered is a male. It's June, and that means mating season for bears. Males put out a musky smell during mating season."

"OK, I guess I should expect bears in this area, even though I don't like them. What should I do?" asked Mrs. Zinn, slightly anxious and shivery.

"Make sure you keep food locked up and throw trash away in the locked bins. I wouldn't worry too much about the bear we saw. That guy left in a hurry," said Mary Frances with a grin. "Maybe he had a date."

Amanda giggled at Mary Frances' sense of humor.

"Would anyone like some coffee?" asked Mrs. Zinn, wishing to change the subject.

She poured two cups of coffee and was slowly stirring in the cream.

"Sure," answered Mary Frances.

"Do you have any Diet Coke?" asked Amanda.

"Just a moment, sweetheart. And, Amanda, I am sorry you have to endure all this."

Mary Frances shook her head, thinking about screaming Ricky and the huge bear. "I know this is very personal," she said, "about Ricky and his condition. But since it involves my brother Lebie, I feel I must ask you about the history of Ricky, Muzzie, and Lebie. Would you mind if we talked about them?"

Just then the dark campsite was illuminated by headlights as a car slowly glided down the camp road.

"That's my dad," said Amanda as she got up to walk toward the car.

"Good evening, folks!" said Big Dad as he exited the car and approached the campsite. "Bill-Lee is spending the night with Eddie, so I thought I would come and see how my beautiful daughter is doing and maybe give her a ride home."

After making introductions, Mrs. Zinn took a deep breath and stared at the group assembled around the fire.

"Mr. Wilson, it's nice to meet you, and I am glad you are here," she said. "Through my experience as a resident of Hopewell, South Carolina, and as a prison superintendent, I have gotten to know a lot about Lebie Jenkins and Muzzie Spicer. Lebie and Muzzie also were friends with my son, Ricky. I was just about to talk about my experiences with them."

"Of course," said Big Dad, "I am sorry for barging in uninvited. Do you mind if I pull up a chair and listen?"

"No problem," said Mrs. Zinn, "I just don't have any more chairs."

Big Dad turned toward his car and popped the tailgate. "Just like a good Boy Scout," he said, pulling out a folding chair. "By the way, where is your son, Ricky? Amanda told me he was with you."

"He is very tired and has gone to bed," replied Mrs. Zinn.

She took a long sip of coffee, took a deep breath, and stared at Big Dad, Amanda, and Mary Frances. "I hope you all will please call me Nora. I think that by talking about Ricky, Lebie, and Muzzie, it will help me vent my feelings and listen to your opinions."

"Not only that," said Big Dad, "but my family is dealing with a great loss that happened about five years ago. It is possible that this guy Muzzie Spicer is involved. There is a rumor that he may be the person who took my wife away from me. The Raleigh police are looking for him. He was in jail in South Carolina." As Big Dad spoke, he looked over at Amanda who had slumped down in the camp chair. "I mean she was taken away...from us," he said softly. His eyes turned from Amanda, and he faced the group. "There was a great evil that happened in the past; it looks like justice will finally be done."

For a moment all was quiet at the campsite, darkness encircled the group who sat mesmerized by the crackling fire. Big Dad got close enough to put his arm around Amanda.

"Mr. Wilson, it's amazing how we four are all interconnected with this. I truly cannot know the sorrow in your heart," said Mary Frances, almost in a whisper.

"Go ahead, please tell us the story," said Amanda as she stared at Mrs. Zinn.

"OK, here goes," said Mrs. Zinn, clearing her throat.

Everyone listened with rapt attention as Mrs. Zinn told the story of Ricky's past. She mentioned her struggles as a single parent, the wasps, the meanness of her mother, Ricky's meeting with Lebie, and the attack that Lebie and Ricky initiated on Zulu

Zinn's home. Her voice lowered as she spoke about the death of her mother. She ended the twenty-minute monologue with a description of the injuries to Ricky. "He was injured so severely," she said, "that he lost his ability to walk and speak."

"But we just heard him speak about an hour ago," said Amanda.

"That's what makes this night so special…and scary," said Mrs. Zinn. "Tonight is the first night I have heard his voice in over twenty years."

Everyone in the group stared at Mrs. Zinn.

"What exactly did Ricky say?" asked Big Dad.

Mary Frances stood up and walked over to Big Dad. "Mr. Wilson, he said, 'Lebie is bad!' several times."

"Hmmm," said Big Dad rubbing his chin thoughtfully. "We need to make another phone call to Raleigh tomorrow."

26

ADVENTURES IN HOPEWELL

Sunday-Monday, June 10-11, 2001

RALEIGH POLICE CHIEF CLINTON JEFFRIES NORMALLY did not like to work on Sundays, but something was happening. Detective Avie Swindell had urgently requested that they meet. "OK, Swindell, this is a five-year-old cold case, tell me what you've got."

"This is what we know so far…" said Detective Avie Swindell. "OK, for a start, we had a number of people, the frizzy-haired-hardware-store woman, a fourteen-year-old-girl, and the tall guy all say they were sure that this Muzzie Spicer guy is the one who killed the Wilson woman in Raleigh five years ago."

"And how do they know this?" asked the chief.

"Well, sir, that's the problem, no eyewitnesses. But then we have another suspect; his name is Lebie Jenkins. He and Spicer served short sentences down at the prison farm near Greensburg, South Carolina."

"Whatcha got on Jenkins, Avie?"

"Jenkins has a long rap sheet, but here's where this thing gets creepy—there's this invalid named Ricky Zinn. He has not spoken or moved for several years."

"What's wrong with this Zinn guy, you know, that he can't speak or move?"

The detective rambled through a history of Lebie, Ricky, his grandmother, Zulu, and the Doberman pinscher.

"That's a great story, Avie, but what do you say we do now?" asked the chief.

"I would suggest that we question seven people: Bill Wilson, Lebie Jenkins, Muzzie Spicer, Nora Zinn, Ricky Zinn, Amanda Wilson, and the frizzy-haired woman."

"All right, Avie, let's get professional here; let's give the frizzy-haired lady a name."

"The frizz...oh yes, it's Mary Frances Bradshaw."

"OK, so tell me about this conversation between Mrs. Zinn and Mary Frances Bradshaw."

"Mrs. Zinn told Bradshaw about her stint as a prison superintendent in Greensburg, South Carolina..."

"What, Avie, you're telling me is that this Mrs. Zinn was also at the little prison farm down there?"

"Yes, sir, small world isn't it? And it gets smaller; turns out this Mary Frances Bradshaw's maiden name is Jenkins. She is Lebie Jenkins' sister. But here is the best part: During the last twenty years or so, Ricky Zinn sits and stares or sleeps in his wheelchair. This all changed when he started to hear about the prison and the names of Muzzie Spicer and Lebie Jenkins. He lifted his head and stared right into the eyes of the frizzy-haired lady."

"Wow, I am glad we got the tape recorder going on this. I'm getting lost in the weeds."

"OK, so here's Mary Frances Bradshaw talking with Mrs. Zinn, and they start talking about Mary Frances' favorite person in the world."

"And who is that, Detective Swindell?"

"That is the fourteen-year-old girl I mentioned at the start of the deposition. Her name is Amanda Wilson."

"*Wilson?*" asked the chief haltingly. "How does Bradshaw know Amanda Wilson?"

"Yeah, boss, the Wilson family moved to the mountains about a year ago. Amanda Wilson and Mary Frances Bradshaw became friends. You know the tall man I mentioned a few minutes ago?"

"It seems like hours now, Swindell, but yes, I remember."

"The tall man is William Randolph Wilson, the husband of the deceased Julie Wilson and the father of Amanda Wilson. I didn't want to mention all the names up front because that may cloud your thinking."

"Nothing clouds my thinking, Detective, my mind is a steel trap...proceed."

"Well, back to the time Mrs. Zinn was with Mary Frances, Ricky uncharacteristically started moaning and shouting. He knows something; he may be our best witness!"

Detective Swindell went on to tell about Nora and Ricky Zinn and how they got to see Lebie Jenkins and Muzzie Spicer at the prison farm.

"Well, Detective, what are we waiting for? Let's talk to these seven people you have mentioned. We should start with Spicer and then see the other six."

"Sounds great, Chief, but there's a problem, we can't find Spicer or Jenkins. They have vanished into thin air."

"Swindell, it says on this sheet that Spicer was in jail recently in Hopewell, South Carolina."

"Yes, sir."

"Spicer is a suspect, and I want to know everything about

him. Call the sheriff down there and let's do some talking. We may need to take a little road trip to Hope Mills."

"It's Hopewell, sir. Hope Mills is in our state."

"Hope this, hope that I just hope we can get some information and move this case along."

"Boss, I'm ahead of you. I already called them, and they are ready for us. They said to come on whenever we want to."

"Good job, Swindell. It's all coming back now, I remember I had just been appointed chief of police when the Wilson woman was killed five years ago. I'll never forget that little girl screaming in the dark when I talked to Mr. Wilson. I want justice done here."

Early the next morning, Swindell and Jeffries left for the four-hour trip westward through Charlotte and Gastonia. Around eleven o'clock, they arrived in the village of Hopewell, South Carolina. Carolina. As they parallel parked in front of the station, Chief Jeffries remarked, "Wow, I feel like Andy, Barnie, and Gomer will come running out at us anytime!"

It was a cool but very clear morning, and Officer Oscar Wilbert had just poured his second cup of coffee from the coffee maker located near the men's room. Suddenly the front door burst open and in walked two neatly dressed uniformed police officers. "Hello, gentlemen, I am Lieutenant Oscar Wilbert, and I want to be the first to welcome you to Hopewell, South Carolina. We need you guys to sign in right there."

The two men shook his hand and turned to a spiral notebook to write their names, positions, and purpose of visit. The chief spoke first. "It's nice to be here, Officer Wilbert. Can we interview the witnesses now?"

"Didn't know exactly when you would be here. If you guys want to get a cup of coffee and have a seat in the conference room. We have Newley Jenkins and a minor, Blitch Ann Taylor. They should be here shortly. In the meantime, I can tell you my experiences with being brutally assaulted by Spicer."

"What?" asked Chief Jeffries. "You were assaulted?"

For the next hour and twenty-seven minutes, the two police officers sat and took notes as they listened to Newley Jenkins, Blitch Ann Taylor and Oscar Wilbert. More than a few times, they raised their eyebrows at what they were hearing. One of the big takeaways was a belief that Officer Oscar Wilbert was incompetent. As they were leaving, they stopped off by the bus station to find out more information from Mildred, the store clerk.

"Kind of a nice little guy, certainly loved that dog," she said. Mildred then gave them the cell phone number for the bus driver.

They called the driver and left a message. "Looks like our next field trip will be to this little place called Smith's Gap, in western North Carolina. Let's plan to go there on Wednesday."

As they drove back to Raleigh, the cell phone rang. Chief Jeffries grabbed it and said, "Hello, yes, this is Clinton Jeffries, thanks for calling back...What! You threw him off the bus! Where?"

In just a few seconds, there was even more reason to go to Smith's Gap.

27

LEBIE'S ESCAPE

Sunday, June 10, 2001

S UNDAY AFTERNOON BIG DAD, MARY FRANCES, AND Amanda sat huddled at the Wilson home. The topic of discussion was their call to the Raleigh police about Lebie. "I just don't think a man that saved two boys' lives would do something like this," said Amanda emphatically.

"Amanda, we are not convicting him, we are asking that they talk to him," retorted Big Dad.

Mary Frances just sat quietly with her hands on either temple.

"What do you think, Mary Frances?" asked Big Dad.

"Go for it, make the call," was the reply.

"No, no, and double no!" screamed a voice coming down the steps. Bill-Lee stood in front of the trio with his arms crossed. "He saved my life; I wouldn't be here if he hadn't come. He got hurt to save me!"

Big Dad stared at his son. "As I said earlier, this phone call to the police does not convict Lebie Jenkins. It just makes it easier for them to do their job. A great wrong was done, and we need to make sure there is justice." Big Dad opened the flip phone and dialed the number.

Earlier that day, Lebie Jenkins was lying in his hospital bed staring at the ceiling. After a week in the hospital, he had made a lot of progress toward better health. His ribs were healing, and the pain had subsided. The scratches and claw marks on his face, arms, and legs responded well to the bandages and antibiotic creams that the nurses had fussed over for the last six days. Lebie knew he had to get enough rest to rejuvenate himself so he could escape from the hospital. The heat was on. On his bedside television, he had heard that the police were looking for a suspect named Muzzie Spicer. He grimaced as he remembered the meeting with the Zinns and how Mrs. Zinn was dialing 911 as he left them. He was sure Spicer would squeal if the cops found him. Taking a deep breath, Lebie looked at his arms. Even though he was moved from ICU three days ago, he still had two needles in each arm delivering antibiotics and saline solution. He slowly started working the IVs on his right arm out. That wasn't so bad, he thought, and he lay back on the pillow to gather strength for freeing the other arm.

"Uh no, no, no, and triple no!" The voice and body of a very large nurse came bursting through the curtains. "What is going on here? Are we going to have to put a watch on you? Mr. Jenkins, I am Nurse Erin, and I am telling you to leave these IVs alone! Don't you want to get better?"

"Just needed to get to the bathroom!" said Lebie just as loudly.

Leaning over into his face, Nurse Erin spoke loudly again. "You have a catheter, sir, just let 'er rip!"

Knowing he was beaten, Lebie leaned back on the pillows.

"That's more like it, sir. We want you to get well. Just lie back and watch some TV." Nurse Erin grabbed the remote and pressed power. Lebie could see a reporter standing in front of the city hall in Raleigh, North Carolina. He grabbed the remote and pushed the power button. The screen went blank.

"Need to sleep," he said to Nurse Erin and he closed his eyes.

"I am keeping my eagle eye on you!" said Nurse Erin, pointing her finger at Lebie.

There was no response. Lebie just kept his eyes shut and did some planning. Escape, box of gold, success, happiness. My whole life is gonna change; everything will be different. Coming back to the present, he thought, I need a diversion. What could that be? His eyes fixated on a fire alarm pull that was on the wall directly outside his door. He smiled and shut his eyes.

With his entire life planned out, Lebie was snoring.

Thirty minutes later, a metal cart clattered into his room. "Got just what you want, a brat, some sauerkraut, and a roll. What a banquet!"

Lebie rubbed his eyes and looked at the tray.

"Here you go.Now when I get back, this tray better be empty." Nurse Erin grabbed the TV remote and clicked it on. "Mr. Jenkins, you need some entertainment, so here you go," and she pushed the tray of food with the remote onto a tray table that swung over his stomach and chest. "Ring me if you need something. I'll come back and check on you."

Lebie turned the volume down on the TV and began eating his lunch. With half a brat in his mouth, he saw another reporter in Raleigh.

"Raleigh police are telling us that they are ramping up efforts to solve the five-year-old hit-and-run case that occurred in Raleigh, North Carolina. There is speculation that a task force is being formed to bring more answers."

He quickly clicked the TV off and looked at the clock. It was now one thirty in the afternoon and Lebie knew it had to happen. Pulling the curtain back from his bed, he could see the fire alarm pull. Next to that was a janitor's closet. The IVs in each arm came out easily, and after almost biting his thumb off to offset the catheter pain, that plastic tube lay on the floor, quickly forming a urine puddle from the bag slung under the hospital bed. Lebie knew he was now free. He grabbed his clothes out of the nearby cabinet, walked weakly toward the hallway and pulled the fire alarm. People began to scream, and loudspeakers started wailing as Lebie vanished into a janitor's closet. He stuffed the hospital gown toward the back of the janitor's closet, pulled on his grimy clothes, and pulled the door open slightly.

"Lebie Jenkins! Lebie Jenkins! I know you're up here! I know who you are! I will find you! You best believe that!" Lebie watched Nurse Erin storm down the hallway still shouting and dialing a cell phone. He quickly moved into a stairwell door and limped down the steps. He smiled as he realized how much the rest and medical care had helped him, and in just twelve minutes he had left the hospital grounds and was standing on a small rural road with his thumb out. Something told him to go back to Smith's Gap. That could be a bad idea, but he also knew the woods and the caves in the area very well.

Soon a late model car screeched to a halt, and Lebie jumped into the front seat. Realizing his name may be his biggest enemy, Lebie took quick action to become another person. "Hey there," he said, "I am Johnnie Jones, and I appreciate you stopping. I'm trying to get to Smith's Gap." The man in the driver's seat did not speak. He glared at Lebie and pushed the accelerator. After ten minutes of riding in silence, he looked at Lebie.

"You smell like a hospital, buddy. You sure you got discharged on time?"

"Oh, yes, sir, I was completely cured, and I am ready to take on the world."

"Hmm," said the man as he gave Lebie a once-over. "I'm not going as far as Smith's Gap. Gonna drop you off in about a mile, I'm heading up toward Virginia."

"That's just fine," said Lebie. "You have helped."

The door opened, and Lebie found himself standing on a very lonely stretch of the rural road three and a half miles outside of Smith's Gap. I am pretty sure that the next driveway goes to old Homer Simpkins' house, he thought. Don't know if he still lives there but he and I always got along pretty well. Lebie was glad to get off the road and headed slowly up the driveway. The pains in his side and legs were getting more intense. Lebie was pretty sure they were just strained muscles, so he kept limping along, and in just a few minutes, he saw the house. This place has gotten nasty, thought Lebie. I don't know if the old man is still living or not.

"Don't want you here; don't want you here!"

"Who is that?" shouted Lebie, shaking in his boots.

"You don't deserve to live after the life you have lived. Get out of here, now!"

Lebie squinted through the bushes and trees and saw nothing. Then he looked down and saw a king snake coiled up in front of him. Picking up a stick, he started to back away.

"Either you leave, or I tell the leader, and he will take care of you."

Lebie realized that the snake was talking to him. "Look, little buddy, you are not poisonous, and I don't know who this 'leader' is…so scoot."

The snake stared at Lebie. Its tongue flicked in and out. "Suit yourself, sir; the leader will not be happy that are here. You don't deserve to live…"

"I know, I know. Friend, I am going to see Mr. Simpkins, and you can tell your leader I am ready whenever he is."

Realizing that the stick made a pretty good walking cane, Lebie limped over to the door of Homer Simpkin's house and knocked. Nothing. Lebie took a deep breath and pounded on the door. Leaning against a column that was peeling paint, Lebie wheezed from the physical stress of walking up hills and beating on the door. He heard a slight noise coming from an open window about twelve feet away. Out of the window slowly emerged the blue steel of a double-barrel shotgun.

"Get off my front porch now. This is private property, and you are about to meet your maker!"

"Homer, is that you? This is your old friend Lebie Jenkins!"

"Can't hear nothing, buddy!" A loud blast from the shotgun and for a moment the world stopped.

Lebie ducked quickly, fell back, and landed in a bush off the porch. Crawling away through the weeds and sticks, he finally made it out to a wooded area. Looking back toward the house, he saw the shotgun disappear from the window. Soon the front door opened and an ancient bent-over man holding the shotgun emerged.

Lebie's eyes grew wide as he looked toward the house. The old man stood for a moment before going back into the house. In two minutes, he emerged again, sat in a rusty lawn chair on the porch, put the shotgun on his lap and popped open a beer. Seeing this made him realize how thirsty he was from his eventful day. Looking ahead down the path, Lebie spotted an opening, which revealed a small pond. Water! I must have water! Leaning against trees and his makeshift cane, Lebie made it to the water and drank from the mostly clear pond. Minnows and small bream scattered as he ducked his head into the watery paradise.

"Enjoy your last sip!"

Lebie wheeled around, trying to get up to defend himself when he saw a dark shadow near the tree line. "Who is it? Just let me rest and I will get out of here!"

"Too late, sinner, you have violated so many rules; it's over."

Lebie sniffed the air. I swear it smells like a big bear is near here, he thought. As Lebie studied the tree line, the dark shadow moved and then stood in the sunlight.

"Get out of here!" Lebie waved his stick at the bear, hoping it would run away. The bear walked toward Lebie, staring at him constantly. Knowing he was quite weak, Lebie covered his face and lay motionless as he had been taught by his big sister Mary Frances when they were small children. Mary Frances, I wonder what she is doing now. Slowly the bear watched and just as slowly, Lebie could feel a weakness coming over him.

The bear sat twelve feet away.

Lebie's thoughts now were of total loneliness and bewilderment.

"Now you know how Amanda's mother felt the night you killed her," said the bear slowly. "You are accountable for what you have done, and you will soon be breathing your last breath just as she did. It's all in the plan for people that are liars and murderers. You have been living a lie for five years and never wanted to own up to it. Even when you met Amanda, you couldn't do it."

"But I saved her brother's life! Isn't that worth something?"

"Not enough," said the bear, "not enough." The bear sat quietly watching Lebie, who was now halfway in the water.

The bear did not know that something was watching him from a short distance away. Two objects hit the bear and cut a gash in his head. The bear roared as he turned to see Homer

Simpkins getting ready to throw his third full beer can at the bear. Remembering the gunfire from Homer's house, the bear took off quickly into a briar thicket.

Homer ran out of the forest and grabbed Lebie. With great effort, he pulled Lebie completely out of the water and onto the dry sandy shore.

Lebie squinted to see an old man with a Budweiser shirt on standing over him.

"I wasted two full cans of beer on your rescue. Now put your arm around my shoulder and let me get you in the house. I don't like you much, but I can't stand a goldarn bear messing around my property!"

The two limped back to a golf cart partially hidden in the woods. "OK, you sit there and let me see if I can find my two cans of beer, never knew they would be such good weapons. The black bears around here don't want a lot of trouble, but they will get into everything!"

Homer found the two full cans floating in the edge of the pond and retrieved them. He slid into the golf cart seat next to Lebie.

"This weren't no normal bear, sir, this one could talk!" said Lebie to Homer.

Homer started the golf cart and took off down the path.

"Didn't you hear me? Are you deaf or something, that bear could talk!"

"Two things, buddy. First, you show me some respect right now! Second, you are delusional; bears don't talk, and to tell you the truth, it would be great if you made like a bear and didn't talk either!"

The loud duo pulled in front of Homer's house. "Put your arm around my shoulder. I'm taking you to the extra room.

There's an old bed out there. Tell you the truth; I haven't even looked into that room in years. My son lived out there, and after he got killed, I just shut the door."

"How did he die?" asked Lebie.

"How do you think? A goldarn bear got him."

Lebie stayed with Homer for three days to recover from the exhaustion. As they talked and drank beer together, Homer remembered some of the funny things that Lebie did as a child. He started to take a liking to the injured man. Lebie had other ideas, however. He still believed he had the answer to all his problems: the box of gold. It still lay undisturbed in the cave.

At the end of the three days, Lebie gave Homer a handshake of thanks and took off toward Smith's Gap and the box of gold. Homer gave him directions through the woods. "This shortcut will save you some walking," Homer said as he slapped Lebie on the back.

Lebie started walking through the woods and then turned back and stood in front of Homer Simpkins. "Hey, Mr. Simpkins, I want to thank you for your help. I do have a big favor to ask."

"What's that, Lebie?"

"I know Smith's Gap is a small town, but you can't tell anyone you saw me, especially my sister. She and I are not on good terms, so she doesn't need to know anything about this."

"Hey, no problem, I have enjoyed the company, my lips are sealed. Have a good trip; wherever you're going."

28

THE REVELATION

Wednesday-Thursday, June 13-14, 2001

LEBIE LEFT HOMER SIMPKINS' HOUSE AT MIDDAY thinking he was on top of the world. He walked through the quiet woods unaware that Smith's Gap had become a hotbed of police work. The Raleigh police officers thought they were within a fingernail of arresting Muzzie Spicer for the death of Julie Wilson, but he could not be found. There were still questions about Lebie Jenkins, who was also missing. The police had searched the room in Asheville that Lebie had rented, the cave room where he shot the bear, the hardware store, and the cave passages. In a stroke of good luck for Lebie, they missed seeing the alcove with the box of gold. Mary Frances, Amanda and Big Dad had all been interviewed. The Zinns were asked to extend their camp stay for two days so they could have a discussion with the police.

During that conference, Mrs. Zinn pulled a scrap of paper out of her purse. "I almost forgot," she said. "Ricky scrawled something here." She handed the paper to the chief.

"It says 'bear pond.' What in the world does that mean?" Chief Jeffries looked at Officer Swindell, shook his head and handed the paper to him. "Don't see how this means anything, but let's keep it," he said. "Swindell, we need to put out an APB on this Jenkins guy. He could be anywhere." The two officers concluded the interview, stood up and headed out the door.

After the police conversation, Mrs. Zinn and Ricky went to the hardware store where they found Mary Frances and Amanda deep in conversation. "A bear pond! I guess that's a clue, but what does it mean?" said Mary Frances as she looked at Amanda.

"I am clueless!" said Amanda. "I thought ponds were full of water—not bears!"

"This statement has got me confused," said Mary Frances. "I am trying to get some readings, but nothing is coming up."

H.S. Stevens stepped up to the counter from the back storeroom. "Old-man Simpkins has a minnow pond on his farm, and he always tells me about the bears that go into the water. It seems they like to eat the minnows. He said he is about to lose all the minnows, doesn't know how to run them off. He told me he is worried about the bears breaking into his house. He is thinking about draining the pond because he doesn't need minnows anymore."

"Let's go!" said Mary Frances. "H.S., this is family business. I got to take care of it; mind the store please."

"No problem, boss, do what you got to do." The young man pulled a cheese stick out of his pocket and began to peel the plastic off of it.

"Hey, is that provolone or cheddar?" asked Amanda.

"Girl, stop thinking about food. We got to rev the VW up and take off. Old-man Simpkins is about twenty minutes away on these curvy mountain roads. And H.S., it's not break time just because I am leaving. That whole paint section better be straightened up by the time I get back."

"State law, boss, I get two 15-minute breaks per day."

Mary Frances started toward H.S., but Amanda pulled her back. "Let's figure this out, Mary Frances. It'll be dark in a few hours."

Mary Frances glared at her employee who was neatly finishing up the cheese stick.

"That was good!" he said as he tossed the plastic wrap toward the shiny metal trash can. The wrapper bounced off the can, fell on the floor and rolled near the edge of the counter.

"Come on, H.S., work with me here," said Mary Frances as she pointed her finger at him.

"I got it, boss, drive safely."

Amanda pulled Mary Frances out the back door of the store toward the elderly Volkswagen.

"Hey, thanks for doing this, Mary Frances."

"Girl, I am doing it just as much for me. He is my brother, you know."

The two rode in silence as the cream-colored Volkswagen lurched around the mountain curves. Amanda found a strap near the seat and hung on. Mary Frances looked at her and smiled, then pushed down the accelerator. The trip was over as the little car went up a gravel driveway with a very crooked mailbox at the end of it. "Simpkins" was hand-painted in green on the rusted mailbox.

"Yeah, Homer Simpkins was the mayor of Smith's Gap about thirty years ago. After his wife died, though, he could not stop drinking, so nobody much sees him anymore. This should be interesting."

Amanda looked at an old farmhouse that had seen better days. Ivy grew up the sides of the house and covered some of the windows. There were bushes in the front of the house, which she could tell were once beautiful, but they were now out of control and blocked the windows. Unmowed grass and weeds grew up in the front yard.

"We should have brought the tick spray. Watch where you step. Let's go see the man."

Two raps on the front door brought a shout from around the backyard.

"What do you want?"

"Hey, Mr. Simpkins, it's Mary Frances Bradshaw, we came out here to see you!"

The two walked through the weeds to the backyard where they saw an eighty-year-old man in overalls sitting under a beautiful spreading oak tree in a rusty lawn chair. In the shade, they could see a red cooler next to him, and on the cooler sat one can of Budweiser beer. Six empty cans were placed neatly in a row underneath his chair.

"Well laws, laws!" said the man. "I ain't seen Mary Frances Bradshaw since I don't know when. What brings you out to my resort?" He looked around at his unmowed yard, his ramshackle house, and two buildings on the property, both of which had caved-in roofs.

"Mr. Simpkins, we heard that you had a little problem with your minnow pond, that bears are around your pond all the time and that you are considering draining it."

"Hmmm," said Mr. Simpkins, "I love living in a small town where everybody knows everything, or at least they think they do. I see bears up here all the time. I saw one bear a few days ago. A great big one. He looked different from all the other bears I have ever seen. It's almost like you could talk to him. He looked me straight in the eyes. Not mean-like; he just looked at me like he was interested in having a conversation."

"Well, what did you do? Talk to him?" asked Amanda.

"Heck no, I threw a beer can at him. I am not up here in the wilderness wanting to make friends with great big smelly wild things! Now if he had had a hat on with the name Smokey on it, I may have treated him differently, but whatever." Homer sat back and took a sip out of his beer can. The discussion about bears seemed to drain his energy. He rubbed his face like he was waking up in the morning. "You guys have come at a great time. I've got Jamie Baker's excavating company coming tomorrow to drain the pond. I don't need it anymore, and maybe I can plant a garden up there. Jamie and his crowd are coming at eight thirty tomorrow morning. Y'all come on out, and we can watch them drain the pond."

Already reading his mind and knowing that this was his seventh beer, Mary Frances hastened to move the conversation along. "Do you have another chair or two? I need to tell you some things, and I am getting tired of standing here like I am appearing before the mayor."

Homer laughed out loud. "Mary Frances, you are something. Feisty as ever. Kind of like your brother, I guess." Knowing he had made a promise just a few hours earlier and realizing he had consumed a lot of beer, Homer Simpkins took a deep breath.

"You talking Lebie or Newley?" asked Mary Frances with a quizzical look on her face.

"Oh, Newley, of course. I don't remember seeing Lebie around much. I just remember Newley when he was a boy and seeing you today reminded me of him," replied Homer quickly.

Changing the subject and the interrogation, Homer got back to the chairs. "Hey, I don't have any out here. Y'all come on in the house, and we can sit and talk." As they walked through the tall grass to the house, Mr. Simpkins stopped and stared at Amanda. "Mary Frances, by the way, who is this pretty little thing you got with you?"

"Oh, sorry, Amanda, I've been rude. Mr. Simpkins, this is my good friend Amanda Wilson; we both have a real interest in what I am about to tell you."

Homer Simpkins pulled open a screen door that had several big slits in the screen, "Yep, darn bear did that several years ago. I got a good shot at him, but he took off, so I think I missed him."

The trio stepped into the house that led to the small kitchen where Amanda noticed every inch of counter was covered with pots, pans and kitchenware of all types. Homer pointed into the next room.

"OK, guys, this is my living room, so find a chair and let's do some talking."

Amanda stood back as she surveyed the room. The word "hoarder" popped into her head as she looked around. There were newspapers all over the floor, at least three inches deep over most of the floor. She saw an old rug and a type of wood flooring under the edges of the newspaper piles. She had never seen floors like those in a living room. "What sort of material is your floor?" Amanda asked.

"I built this house myself, and I was about to put wall-to-wall carpet down when my wife died fifteen years ago. I just haven't felt like doing anything with this house. What you see is called subfloor. I also do a lot of recycling. I save all paper so that it can be used again. Don't want any more trees cut down than we have to. Don't you agree, young lady?"

Amanda shook her head and continued looking around the house. Next to the living room was a small dining room covered with cardboard. The cardboard pile was about two feet high. At the edge of the dining room were several blankets and a pillow.

"Is that where you sleep?" asked Amanda. "Don't you have a bedroom?"

"Got two bedrooms right down this hall. Just don't use them except to store my recycling material. OK, that's enough of a tour. You ladies have a seat and let's talk about what's on your mind."

Amanda and Mary Frances moved some newspapers and some beer cans off the sofa and sat together as Homer Simpkins fell back in his recliner. "Mr. Simpkins, about five years ago in Raleigh, Amanda's mother was killed in an auto accident. A drunk driver ran a red light and hit her."

"Wow, I'm sorry to hear that," said Homer as he looked at his beer. "This stuff can do a lot of damage."

"The driver left the scene of the accident and was never identified," said Mary Frances.

"So who was the driver and how does this involve me?"

"My younger brother, Lebie, is a suspect, and he may be in this area."

"Your brother Lebie! He was one of the wildest kids in Smith's Gap. Didn't your family ship him off somewhere when he was a teenager?"

"I know he's my brother, Mr. Simpkins, but I think he is touched in the head somehow. He is very smart, but there's something wrong with him. He never learned right from wrong, so he chooses the wrong things constantly."

Homer got quiet as he thought about Lebie's visit just a few days before. Was he keeping a secret that would hurt this pretty teenaged girl? A promise is a promise, he thought. After all, he is only a suspect; no one is sure that Lebie committed a crime.

The conversation was quickly degenerating as Amanda and Mary Frances could tell that beer number eight was starting to slur Homer Simpkins' speech. "Mr. Simpkins, we have to go now, but we'll be back tomorrow morning." Amanda and Mary Frances exited quickly after they extended their hands for a cordial handshake.

"That was a real experience," said Amanda as they approached the Volkswagen.

"Girl, sorry you had to hear a man who could hardly pronounce his words. On the bright side, I am getting some readings that tomorrow will be quite interesting. Are you up for coming out here?"

"I wouldn't miss it," said Amanda. "I have been wondering about the truth for five and a half years. Maybe we can find it out. Can you pick me up at eight o'clock?"

That evening Mary Frances called and said that she had heard from Homer Simpkins. The excavator, Jamie Baker, was not coming to his house until one thirty, so they changed their plans accordingly. On their way that afternoon, they had stopped to get a gift for their host. A dozen sugar doughnuts were presented to Mr. Simpkins, who hungrily ate one and a half before taking a breath. "These sugar doughnuts are just what you need sometimes," he said as white powder stuck to the four-day-growth around his mouth.

"Let me get you a napkin," said Amanda as she walked toward the kitchen.

"Ain't got any napkins; I don't like to use up paper on unnecessary things."

Mary Frances and Amanda frowned as a yellowed handkerchief popped out of Homer Simpkins' back pocket. Just then a knock on the door startled the trio. "That must be Jamie Baker; I'll get the door." Homer Simpkins peeked out the side window next to the door. "Git where I can see you! OK, I see you." Homer pulled the door open, hobbled over to his recliner and fell into the big chair. "Step on in, Jamie. You need to see Mary Frances Bradshaw and meet her friend Amanda."

"Hey, folks, haven't got much time for yik-yak. Homer, I will be up at the pond tearing down that dam. Y'all come up if you want, but stay out of the way. It's pretty interesting what you find in a pond when you drain it. Especially this one, since it's over one hundred years old. Correct, Homer?"

"My granddaddy built it in 1896." Mr. Simpkins began to gather up some beer to put in a small cooler. "Let's go watch this, ladies; it should be fun."

The minnow pond was about a quarter mile walk through the woods. Mary Frances, Amanda, and Homer Simpkins got in a golf cart and followed a dump truck and backhoe up to the site. As they rode, Amanda was amazed at how much duct tape held the seat cover together. I guess if you have to reupholster something, duct tape will work fine, she thought.

Once they got to the pond, Mary Frances started looking along the shoreline.

"Ain't gonna see any tracks, if that's what you're looking for," said Mr. Simpkins. "We have had several good rains in the last few days."

"I do see a few bear tracks," said Mary Frances.

"Of course, but I got this beer can ready if the real thing appears. Come to think of it; I did have a commotion up here about a week ago. I had to shoot at some man that came by wanting something."

"What was his name? What did he look like?" asked Mary Frances.

"Do I look like the FBI? I'm just an old man trying to protect myself. I just shot, and he left. I didn't hear anymore, so I just continued going about my business."

"What business is that, Homer?"

"Well, at that time of the day, my business was taking a mid-morning nap, so I climbed back into my bed and went to sleep."

The conversation was soon interrupted by the loud diesel sound of a large backhoe that was digging at the soil on the dam.

"They will drain it slowly, so the folks down the way don't get flooded," said Homer Simpkins. "Hey, ladies, I just thought of something. I do have some lawn chairs in one of my buildings. I'll be right back."

Mary Frances looked at Amanda as things got very quiet. All they could hear was a group of crows cawing and the occasional voices of Jamie Baker and his men standing on the dam, planning its destruction.

"Girl, we have come a long way this last year. I had no idea that so many things would be resolved in the twelve months that I have known you. You came into my life, Muzzie Spicer came into my life, and my brother Lebie. You know, things work out for good, they do."

Amanda stared out at the pond. "I feel like something else is going to happen, but I don't know what it is. Thanks, Mary Frances, for helping me work through all this stuff. The magic around here is incredible."

"Got 'em!" shouted Homer Simpkins as he rumbled back up the path on his golf cart. Amanda was amazed to see three substantial wooden folding chairs. Homer produced a cloth towel and began wiping a chair off. Mary Frances grabbed the towel and wiped another one of the chairs off.

"You sit while we clean this last one," she said as she unfolded the chair near the shoreline. Soon they were all seated in the quiet of the woods.

"Need to look at my old pond one last time," said Homer. "I have been swimming in it and fishing in it for many years. Now maybe it will be a great garden for some good corn, squash, and maters."

The three just sat until some birds began screeching loudly. "Oh no!" said Mary Frances. "My boys have found me. I was getting some thoughts that they were on their way." Just then, the three ravens, Edgar, Allan, and Poe, landed on the shoreline near the chairs and began drinking water furiously.

"Where the heck did these buzzards come from?" asked Homer.

"They are not buzzards, they are purebred ravens, I will have you know," said Mary Frances indignantly.

"OK, fine, just make sure they don't fly over and poop on me!" said Homer. "Hey, it looks like they are about to start tearing it up."

Just then Jamie Baker came by, walking fast toward the house. "Just need to get a tool from my truck," he said.

"Hey, take my golf cart; you'll save your time and my money," shouted Homer.

Jamie jumped in the golf cart, waved and vanished down the path. Again it grew very quiet. Edgar, Allan, and Poe walked along the edge of the water, occasionally drinking and picking up stones. Just then Poe's head snapped into the water, and he came up with a small minnow, causing Mary Frances to laugh.

Amanda looked behind them in the woods and stared into the dark trees and thicket.

"Whatchalookin' at?" asked Homer.

"Thought I saw a dark shadow in the trees," said Amanda.

"Wouldn't be a bit surprised. I have got my beer can ready if it is a bear, but as soon as the backhoe starts up, that should not be a problem."

"Not unless there is an urgency," stated Mary Frances emphatically. "I think I am getting a reading right now. There may be an urgency."

"Mary Frances, I don't know what you are talking about," said Homer. "I am gettin' a reading that you might be crazy!"

"OK, Homer, here's the deal. You two did not see the king snake on the way up. The king snake winked at me as we rode by. Now my ravens are here. I am quite sure that is *the bear* behind us in the woods. Something is happening. I think we are in for some excitement."

"It will be exciting," said Homer, "when I hit that stinkin' bear in the head with this beer can." Homer looked down at his crunched-up beer can.

Just then the backhoe started up and began to gouge at the earth in the twelve-foot-high dam. It made several cuts and placed the soil gently in the bed of the dump truck. After the dump truck was filled and unloaded twice, the water line was only two feet from the top of the soil.

"This next shovelful should start the draining," said Homer as he leaned forward in the lawn chair.

The backhoe hit the now soft soil very hard, and the water began spilling through the hole. Backing up slightly, the backhoe again dug deeper into the dam. Reddish water was now pouring out of the pond and heading downstream. The backhoe reversed and moved to the more stable pond shoreline, where the driver stopped the motor. Jamie Baker began walking over to see Homer.

"We'll give this about twenty minutes and then finish the job. In forty minutes you will have a big wet field for your new garden."

"Would you look at that!" shouted Homer as he stood up. "My granddaddy never did tell us where he put that Model A Ford. I think I see the top of it!" In the corner of the pond, a very red, flat surface started to appear. It was the top of an antique car being reborn on this day.

243

"Is that the 'reading' you were getting, Mary Frances?" asked Homer as he looked excitedly at the shell of the car.

"I don't think so, but that is neat. You can drive it this year in the Smith's Gap Christmas Parade!"

"Yeah, shoot me thirty thousand dollars and I can. No, it will be a great yard ornament! I'll drag it down the path and enjoy it. Might paint it red or purple or something."

The water was now down to the cut in the dam, and it stopped draining. The Model A was halfway covered, and it was obvious there would be no Christmas parades in its future. Large rust holes appeared throughout the body, and the headlights, tires, taillights, and rumble seat were completely rusted away.

As everything got quiet, Amanda again turned and looked at the forest behind them. Nothing. The ravens began walking out in the wet soil that was now uncovered for the first time in a century.

Jamie Baker shouted from the shoreline near the dam. "OK, folks, last cut; this one will drain the pond completely."

The backhoe roared to life and began moving toward the opening in the dam. Mary Frances looked down and started whispering to something in the chair. Amanda knew what was happening. She inched closer to Mary Frances and heard a very slight English accent coming from the side of Mary Frances' chair.

This is what Amanda heard: "Just a few moments, my dears, and he will come; he wants to be sure you find everything you need."

Amanda's eyes shot back to the backhoe on the dam. The cut was now down below the waterline by about five feet. Two more shovelfuls and water would be pouring through the cut and emptying the pond. There it was! The backhoe had completed its job of tearing into the dam. Muddy water was now pouring through the cut and draining the pond.

"Your pond will be just mud in about five minutes," shouted Jamie Baker. The ravens starting cawing loudly as they jabbed at wiggling minnows trapped in the shallow water.

"Hey, you guys want some tartar sauce with your fish dinner?" asked Homer. All three ravens turned and stared at Homer.

"They don't like disrespect; that sounded condescending and sarcastic, plus they have very sensitive little raven stomachs," scolded Mary Frances.

"All right, this is getting crazy. Aren't there any normal dumb animals around here?" asked Homer.

Amanda giggled when Mary Frances whispered, "Just one," and pointed to Homer behind his back.

The group stood and watched the pond turn from a body of water to a future vegetable garden. Amanda buried her head in her hands. A rumpled, muddy shirt and pants had come into view. The sight of a body was different from the old tree stumps, cinder blocks and the old Model A Ford.

Mary Frances and Amanda walked into the mud. Amanda examined Mary Frances' face and noticed a very strange look. Homer Simpkins stayed in his chair with his hand over his mouth, completely astonished. He watched as they stood looking at the body that was face down in the mud.

Deciding to play dumb, actually because he was dumbfounded by the sight of the body, he slushed up beside Mary Frances. "Sorry for your loss, Mary Frances," he said. "But if you don't mind, I'm gonna turn him over. Haven't seen old Lebie's face in a long time." Homer took a large stick he had brought from the shore and pushed it up under the body. The body slowly flopped over on its back and then slopped into the mud. The mottled face stared at the sky.

Mary Frances and Amanda gasped when they looked at the face. "THAT'S MUZZIE SPICER!" screamed Mary Frances. "Where in the world is my brother Lebie?" Amanda and Mary Frances looked in disbelief and then grabbed each other and hugged.

"What do we do now?" asked Amanda.

"I would say we need to call the sheriff," said Homer. "Got to give this poor dude a decent burial, whoever he is."

"That's the thing, we also need to call the Raleigh guys," said Mary Frances. "We know this man; he was a friend of my brother Lebie."

Amanda looked closer at Muzzie's body. "What is that next to him in the mud?" she asked.

"Hey, Jamie, you got a cell phone?" shouted Homer. "Can you call Sheriff Nyman and tell him what we found? We are going to have to get the law involved in this."

Amanda knelt near Muzzie's body. "It's a little dog's body. It's T."

"Yeah," said Mary Frances, "named him T. Stood for Toothless. This whole scene is blowing my mind. I knew I was getting some crazy readings from everywhere. Now the bear in the woods is completely gone. I do not understand this at all, Amanda."

"Well, all I know is I got to pay my man, Jamie Baker," stated Homer emphatically. "You ladies have certainly brought a lot of excitement to me and my old worn-out homestead. You are gonna have to hang around for the sheriff. You are now witnesses to finding this Monty guy."

"His name is Muzzie, Homer. Laws, laws, give some respect to the dead!"

"You are just like you used to be, Mary Frances, you won't

back down on anything. Just like you ran that Bradshaw guy away back when."

"Back when, what, Homer, stars and garters! That Elvin Bradshaw needed to be run off, and you know it!"

Homer laughed. "Just like I said, a lady with some spunk. OK, let's change gears. I see some blue lights near my house. Gotta get me a beer and be ready to be interviewed."

Sheriff Bernie Nyman stepped out of his sheriff's car and walked up to Homer's house. Directly behind him came a shiny black Raleigh chief car. The golf cart loaded with Amanda, Mary Frances, and Homer rumbled up in a cloud of dust to the sheriff's car.

"This shouldn't take long," said the sheriff. "Just need your statements and to let the coroner do his thing."

"Slow down, big guy," said Chief Clinton Jeffries, "we need to do a thorough examination."

A third car brought a cloud of dust up the gravel driveway.

"Hey, Clarence, you don't have to drive so fast up my road. You gonna get these fine ladies all dusty!"

Clarence C. Clever had been the coroner in Wickens County, North Carolina, for twenty-eight and a half years. He had seen plenty of gruesome sights in those years. From people hanging themselves to shootings to beatings to car wrecks. "Where's the body?" Clever asked.

"Up there at the old pond," replied Homer as they looked at the Raleigh officers standing in the mud over the body. You two get in; this golf cart will hold all of us."

"You go ahead," said Clarence Clever, "I'll walk with the sheriff. He can fill me in while we walk."

"Suit yourself," replied Homer as he motioned for Mary Frances and Amanda to get in the golf cart.

The examination and questioning took about ten minutes. "I've got to notify next of kin," said Coroner Clever.

"Don't have any idea, but I know a woman who may know. I will have a Mrs. Zinn call you," said Mary Frances quietly.

In half an hour, Amanda and Mary Frances headed back to Smith's Gap.

"What in the world happened there?" asked Amanda as Mary Frances shifted the VW into third gear.

"I have got to get in a quiet place and listen," replied Mary Frances. "I'll drop you at your house; it's been a big day. Come see me tomorrow around ten o'clock at the store. We'll talk some more."

Amanda didn't realize how tired and hungry she was as she exited the VW at her house. Big Dad and Bill-Lee stood at the door as she walked up the yard. Climbing the steps, she asked if dinner was ready.

"Got you some fried chicken and mashed potatoes!" said Big Dad. "Tell me about your afternoon. I saw several cars roaring out of town as I was heading home from work."

Amanda rushed into the bathroom to wash her hands and get ready for dinner. After the blessing, the family wolfed down the chicken, salad, and potatoes.

As they were eating, Amanda looked at her dad and brother seriously. "I have two things to say. First, the whole world is looking for Lebie Jenkins. Second, there is a law called 'Stand Your Ground' that may save Homer Simpkins from jail time. The officers said that Muzzie died from a combination of drowning and being shot with a shotgun—maybe Homer Simpkins' shotgun. I could not believe the bodies were Muzzie Spicer and his dog."

"Wait a minute," said Bill-Lee, "I thought the guy in the

pond was the guy that saved our lives. I thought he was the guy that got hurt by the bear and got out of the hospital! What's going on here?"

"That's exactly what we thought, too. We were completely dumbfounded. I am going to see Mary Frances tomorrow morning. The police are on this, and so is she. She is doing a lot of thinking and getting some ideas."

Big Dad and Bill-Lee just shook their heads. How did Muzzie make it up to this area? wondered Big Dad. And...where the heck is Lebie Jenkins?

29

TRUE JUSTICE

Wednesday-Friday, June 13-15, 2001

EBIE JENKINS LEFT HOMER SIMPKINS' HOUSE AND started the two-mile journey through the woods to the cave. He was feeling great. He was almost completely recovered and was formulating a plan that was going to change his life. Get in the cave, get the gold, cash it in, and start a new life somewhere.

OK, there it is, Lebie thought as he recognized the trail that led to the cave. A large king snake slithered across the trail. "Git, git, and git!" shouted Lebie as he kicked at the retreating serpent. The snake was not retreating, but was hurrying to report what he had seen.

Little did Lebie know that half a football field away, a strange sight was occurring. The king snake was approaching a bear that was eating raspberries voraciously. As the king snake was making the journey, he noticed several spiders of all types— house spiders, dock spiders, garden spiders—going in the opposite direction. They barely looked at each other, but the king snake knew they had been on an earlier part of the same mission. The snake climbed up on a log near the bear and shouted in his best Southern voice. "Hey, big guy, got some news."

The big bear ignored the snake and kept gorging himself on

raspberries. Finally, the snake became impatient and with a skill-ful tail, flicked a small stone at the bear's back.

"Ow!" said the bear as he wheeled around to face the king snake. "I heard you and your crazy Southern accent. I just want to eat as many of these berries as I can before the other bears find them. They're really good!"

"Hey, friend, we got to get moving," said the snake. "The tim-ber rattler will meet us at the cave entrance. The rattler is loaded with venom and feels if he can get a good shot, we can take this evil guy down easily."

"I will be there for backup. It's so hot out here, there are not many humans around, so our plan should work," said the bear.

Homer had given Lebie a flashlight, food, and five beers for his journey. He stopped near Luke's Pond to eat before getting to the cave. As he chowed down on a dried-up ham sandwich, he said to himself, "You'll be eating steak and caviar in a few days." A cold wind interrupted his daydreaming. He looked around suspiciously.

Back on the forest trail, Lebie was planning as he walked. Gonna get the Mustang fixed up. No, heck no, gonna get a new car! Buy me a double-wide trailer...No, heck no, get a house! Wow, this will be great! he thought.

To celebrate, he popped open a beer and entered the cave. He did not notice the six-foot-long timber rattler coiled in the briars near the cave entrance. Slowly he crawled through the low section of the cave, got to the large part, and looked over at the alcove where he was staying when Bill-Lee, Eddie, and Bunster went by several weeks earlier. What a mess that was! he thought. Maybe I should have let the little boys get killed. I've been through it since that little battle!

Just for old times' sake, Lebie took the left passage and

approached the wooden door near the end of the cave. He was dismayed when he looked inside. Over the last few days, Big Dad had built steps from the den into what was now the basement. Can't stay here too long, he thought. I am actually in someone's basement!

Walking back toward the alcove, Lebie popped open his second can of beer. A big smile came on his face when he looked and saw the edge of a box. The box that would change his life!

Lebie pulled the top off the box and smiled as he looked inside. There were eight large rocks and several small ones, all with flecks of gold. He breathed deeply as he picked each one up and studied it.

The entrance to the cave was busy with activity. Several spiders had begun making webs that were intended to cover the opening. The timber rattler was weaving his way back and forth as if he was rehearsing. "Don't start your rattlin' until he has gotten through the webs!" said a voice in the bushes. "You will slow him down, and if I am needed, I will stop him."

"Yes, suh!" said the rattler in his best Southern drawl. "Now everyone get quiet and let's just wait."

About fifteen minutes went by, and the spiders moved the edges of their intricate web. They had now built a substantial structure, and they were sure it would slow and distract their prey.

Finally, scraping noises interrupted the work, and all the animals looked at each other. This is what they had waited for. Their job was justice in the magical realm of Smith's Gap and more importantly, Luke's Pond. About fifty feet above the cave entrance sat three very quiet ravens. Edgar, Allan, and Poe had been sent by Mary Frances to oversee the operation. Since they did not engage in conversation, Mary Frances could not find out directly from them what was happening. She did, however, get readings from them. In other words, she could read their little minds.

Lebie Jenkins finally dragged the box to the cave opening. Catching his breath, he pulled it into the light of the entrance. Sticky spider webs covered him from head to toe.

"What da?" Lebie shouted as he dropped the box and began struggling with the endless webs that were on his face, body, and hands. He finally got through the webs and started to pull the box. His eyes widened when he heard the loud rattle of a very heavy six-foot-long snake. Lebie started to reach for a knife when the snake struck his ankle and sank its teeth deep into the skin.

In the bushes, the large bear studied the fray. Lebie screamed at the bite and stomped down on the snake. When Lebie stomped down, however, he lost his balance and fell on the path. The snake recovered and quickly bit Lebie in the neck below his ear. At this point, Lebie changed quickly. The venom raced into his bloodstream through his leg and his neck. Lebie crawled about ten feet along the path and slumped down. All was quiet.

The bear stepped out of the bushes onto the path. "Everyone OK?"

"Kind sir, we are fine, and we hope you have a bloody good day!" said the three spiders.

"I ain't feeling that great. He stomped me hard, but I'll recover," said the big snake.

"Good job, guys, I'll take over from here." With that, the big bear grabbed a now unconscious and dying Lebie Jenkins by the back of the shirt and dragged him into the cave. "We wait. It's not time, yet," he said as he looked at the near-dead Lebie Jenkins.

The next day, the Wilsons and Mary Frances were notified that Muzzie's body was being released from the coroner's office.

"He is ready for burial," said Clarence Clever to Mary Frances as they stood in the morgue. "Since we can locate no family, I guess you guys can handle his final arrangements."

"You mean 'their' final arrangements," said Mary Frances as she looked at T's little body. "We can handle it, sir."

That afternoon, the Wilson family, Mrs. Zinn, Ricky, and Mary Frances were all busy getting ready for an event. "I need to call Cara and let her know what is going on," said Amanda as she was looking in her closet for a dress.

"I think Porter Grace and her mother will be coming," said Big Dad. "You know her grandmother is from Hopewell and knew where Muzzie worked."

"I hope she doesn't come," Amanda said. "Porter Grace has never met Muzzie and she is such a drama queen she will expect applause when she gets there and will probably want to speak."

"Amanda, I am afraid I need to tell you two things. First, I have already told Porter Grace's mother, Patty Grey, about this while we were at work; second, this funeral is not private. Anyone can come if they want to."

Amanda frowned at her father and grabbed his cell phone. "Hey, Cara, I need to tell you that tomorrow at two p.m. at Heritage United Methodist Church there will be a short grave-side service and I would love it if you could come. You and Mary Frances have been like family the last year, and you know how I get when I go to that cemetery where my mom is buried... Yeah, we are having a short ceremony to bury that little man that adopted the sad little Chihuahua...Yeah, you remember he named the little dog T... That's him, the guy that liked pork skins and called them 'pok chops.' Anyway, he has no family, and we thought he should have the dignity of a small funeral. Can you come?...Great." Amanda hung up the phone and went into the living room where Bill-Lee, Big Dad, Mrs. Zinn, and Ricky were sitting watching television. Ricky was not watching; he sat drooling with his head down.

The next day at the cemetery, Mary Frances smiled as she sat on the front row in a dress. There were three rows of chairs, five chairs in a row. On the front row also were Big Dad, Bill-Lee, and Amanda. On the next row were Cara, Porter Grace Baxter, Patty Grey Baxter, Eddie, and his mother. There was a third row with three empty chairs, a wheelchair space for Ricky Zinn and a chair for his mother. Mrs. Zinn smiled because she could see that Ricky was quite attentive during the seating. He was dressed in a black suit with very shiny dress shoes.

Amanda punched her brother as they looked back at Ricky. "He looks so good! And look at those shoes, they are so shiny! They look brand-new!"

"They look brand-new because they never touch the ground to get dirty!" Bill-Lee looked at his slightly scuffed-up Sunday shoes and glanced back at Ricky, whose head was now facing downward.

Amanda looked at the small box on the table in front of the chairs. Bill-Lee jabbed Amanda in the side. "Stop it, you little twerp!" Amanda said out loud. Big Dad frowned as he looked down the row.

"Shh," said Big Dad.

Bill-Lee whispered in Amanda's ear. "Why is the box so small?"

"Because Muzzie was cremated."

"Cream what?" asked Bill-Lee.

Porter Grace heard the comment and started giggling.

"I will tell you all about this later; you will see there is a small box for Muzzie and an even smaller one for T."

Pastor Steve stood up at a small podium. "Friends, we are gathered before the Lord to honor Muzzie Spicer and his good friend T. Let us have a moment of silence." Everyone bowed their heads.

The church was about a mile down the path from the cave. The black bear realized that it was now time. He dragged Lebie's cold body along the path toward the gathering.

At the funeral, Pastor Steve was finishing the reading of the twenty-third Psalm. "Surely goodness and mercy shall follow me and the days of my life, and I will dwell in the house of the Lord forever. Amen.

I want to thank everyone for coming. The ceremony is now over."

Everyone stood up and began to murmur, hug and shake hands. Eddie grabbed Bill-Lee, and they chased each other around the tombstones. Eddie landed a picture-perfect tackle on Bill-Lee, and they both rolled into a large headstone. Eddie's mother grabbed Eddie, stared at the grass stains on his dress pants, and trotted him toward the car. The Baxters were already leaving in their shiny black Lexus. Pastor Steve walked over to talk to Big Dad. Mrs. Zinn was whispering to Ricky as she pushed the wheelchair toward the car. Amanda looked back at the chairs and noticed Mary Frances was still seated.

"What are you doing?" asked Amanda.

"Sh."

Amanda sat next to her and studied her face. A slight headache started to hit Amanda as she stared at Mary Frances.

"Amanda, we need to stay here for eight to ten more minutes. Go tell your father."

Amanda rushed over to tell Big Dad.

"Amanda, it's a workday and I have to go. What is this about?"

The two of them walked over to Mary Frances who was still sitting quietly with her head down.

"What's going on?" asked Big Dad.

"He is here."

Big Dad and Amanda quizzically stared at Mary Frances. No one noticed the three ravens who had just landed quietly in the top of a tall tree. A large owl watched quietly from a magnolia tree.

Mary Frances looked up at the ravens; then she glanced over at the magnolia. "OK, it's time. Everything is now coming together. Mr. Wilson, please call Sheriff Nyman and the Raleigh boys. We are going to need them."

Big Dad started to question the command, but Amanda put her hand on his arm. She looked so solemn and determined that Big Dad reached for his cell phone. Normally, he would ask more questions, but Amanda's face was so serious and Mary Frances' voice was so stern he felt like a little boy being directed by his teachers.

Suddenly there was a scraping and sliding sound and a large black being emerged from the path. Amanda whirled around when she heard the words "May May" coming from the forest near a magnolia tree. She could see nothing in the tree.

Still holding his cell phone, Big Dad shouted, "I'm going to get my gun. Why is that huge bear coming out of the woods toward us?"

"Just call the sheriff. We are perfectly safe," scolded Mary Frances.

Mrs. Zinn shouted from the edge of the cemetery as she looked at the bear. "I have got to get Ricky out of here!"

Mary Frances stared at Mrs. Zinn and held her hand up like a stop sign. "Sit," she commanded.

Mrs. Zinn ignored Mary Frances and kept walking. "I have got to get my son to a safe place!"

Mary Frances grabbed a folding chair and walked briskly over to Mrs. Zinn. "Everyone is safe; I said sit!"

Mrs. Zinn frowned and sat on the folding chair next to Ricky.

They all looked back at the bear and noticed it was dragging an object.

"That bear is pulling a body!" said Big Dad.

All eyes were on the bear as he stopped and dropped the body on the ground within twenty-five feet of the group.

"It is done," the bear said, and he turned to go toward the cars and the church. Mrs. Zinn noticed that he was walking straight toward Ricky who was now slumped in his wheelchair.

"Oh no, don't hurt him! I knew I should have left this crazy place; now it's too late!" Mrs. Zinn screamed as she watched the bear approach her son.

Mary Frances grabbed Mrs. Zinn's jacket. "It's OK," she said.

"Why, you, let me go! You people will not take my beautiful son's life!"

Mary Frances did not let go of Mrs. Zinn's jacket, and they both stared at the bear. The big animal walked up to Ricky and looked at him for a full ten seconds. He then turned toward the church, went into a set of thick woods and was gone. There was no sound, just Mrs. Zinn's heavy breathing.

Big Dad walked over to the body. The others followed quietly.

"You are a crazy person, and I will be looking into legal action! We could have all been killed!" exclaimed Mrs. Zinn, shouting within one inch of Mary Frances' face.

As Amanda predicted, Mary Frances did not back down. "Bring it, sister!" The two ladies stared at each other.

"Law enforcement will be here in five minutes," Big Dad announced, hoping to cut some of the tension.

Mary Frances walked over to the body. It had turned an ashen white. "It is Lebie; he has finally gotten his due." Mary Frances pulled out a very frazzled tissue and wiped her eyes as she studied the body of her brother. "Something else is about to happen," she whispered as she put her arm around Amanda.

"Mama! Mama!" The group looked toward the sound, and all mouths dropped open. Ricky Zinn was standing next to his wheelchair and slowly walking toward his mother. Mrs. Zinn screamed out and ran toward her son. Her new son. "I am healed, I am healed; the bear took the evil away and I am healed!" Ricky shouted. He stumbled slightly but did not want to stop walking or talking. After over twenty years confined in a wheelchair, he did not want to stop. "Mama, the bear told me that I am healed; the magic has worked!"

Mrs. Zinn could not stop hugging her son. Then she looked at Mary Frances.

"Hey, no problem; magic is not always clean and neat!" Mary Frances walked over and hugged Mrs. Zinn and Ricky.

"What kind of a strange funeral is this?" shouted Sheriff Nyman as he and Chief Jeffries and Detective Swindell got out of their cars and surveyed the scene. Everyone crowded around the confused lawmen and started talking.

"Hey, y'all, one at a time!" The sheriff walked over to the body, felt for a pulse and proceeded to call the coroner. "All right, we'll do this quick. Everyone have a seat. We will call you up and get your statement." Sheriff Nyman looked over at Ricky Zinn, who continued to walk around the cemetery. His new black shoes were beginning to get scuffed up. "Hey, boy, I said take a seat."

"Get off your high horse, Bernie!" said Mary Frances. "You wouldn't believe what has just happened to him!"

Acting like he didn't hear her, Sheriff Nyman motioned for Big Dad to come and give his statement. All the others soon followed. Another car drove up. Coroner Clarence Clever jumped out of the car.

"Laws, laws, every time here lately that I investigate a dead body, there stands Mary Frances Bradshaw and that young girl!" said Clever as he got his briefcase out of the back seat. An ambulance with two attendants roared up and parked behind Clever's car.

"Good to see you again," said Mary Frances. "This is my brother Lebie."

"You mean 'was,'" said Coroner Clever.

"I guess so," said Mary Frances. "I have got to call my other brother, Newley, and let him know about this, but first we need to go to the cave. I am getting a reading, and there appears to be one more good that is about to happen today."

"My gracious! I'm just going to call in to take the whole day off!" said Big Dad, holding his cell phone up to his ear.

Being dismissed by Sheriff Nyman and Coroner Clever, Mary Frances watched as her brother's body was loaded into the ambulance. She immediately walked over to Mrs. Zinn and Ricky. "I know you have both been through a lot, but there is one more short excursion we need to make."

"We are tired, but we can do it," said Mrs. Zinn as she happily put her arm around Ricky.

After Big Dad made sure Sheriff Nyman and Coroner Clever had everything they needed, he walked over to the beginning of the trail where Mary Frances had assembled the group. She led them to the mouth of the cave. As they approached the cave, only Mary Frances noticed a very tired timber rattlesnake in the bushes near the cave entrance. "Just as I thought," said Mary Frances as she pulled a leaf back to show the group the snake. "This is a large poisonous snake, probably six feet. He is very tired now; it will take him two to three weeks to get enough venom to kill his prey. I have a feeling that this is how Lebie died. Generally, if you get bitten, you can get to a hospital to get the antivenom."

"The what?" asked Bill-Lee as he stared at the lethargic snake.

Mary Frances continued. "Antivenom helps you live through a snake bite. Lebie had no way to get to a hospital. The wildlife crowd made sure of that. They wanted to rid the world of Lebie and his bad ways."

"I think I see something at the edge of the entrance," said Amanda as she walked toward the box.

Bill-Lee ran ahead and opened the box. "Just a bunch of rocks," he said as he ran back out of the cave.

Big Dad Wilson walked over to the box and quietly looked inside. "Bill-Lee, you told us about this several months ago. This is the box that is in The Legend of the Box that you had heard about. Bill-Lee, if I am not mistaken, this is GOLD!"

Mary Frances called Big Dad, Amanda, Mrs. Zinn, and Ricky over.

"I'm coming. It will take me a minute," said Mrs. Zinn, who was now on her eighth tissue because her happy sobbing would not stop. "I have my son back; I never thought this would happen. There is truly good and evil in the world, and the evil of my mother and Lebie Jenkins has been erased. My son, Ricky, can live! He can live!" With that last statement, Mrs. Zinn grabbed her ninth tissue and hugged Ricky.

Mary Frances looked deeply into the eyes of Big Dad, Amanda, Mrs. Zinn and Ricky,all who had huddled around her. "There is magic here, and it has worked for the good. Mrs. Zinn, the gold in that box is to go to you and Ricky so that he can be completely rehabilitated and lead a successful life. Evil has robbed him of twenty years, and he deserves the best from now on. Amanda, please remember what I have said about living life…"

"I know…I need to be responsible, productive, and happy. I will, Mary Frances, I know I will. Mary Frances is right," continued Amanda. "For me, this started with evil done to my mother; making things right is what she would have wanted. I feel her with me. Giving everything to Ricky is the answer. Justice is now done!"

ABOUT THE AUTHOR

 Dr. Gary Ridout is a long-time resident of North Carolina and has always had a fascination with animals of all types and a love for people. He spent over forty-five years in public education. During his time as an elementary and middle-school principal, he would have discussions with children about their fears and their triumphs. In getting to know the children, he found that many of them would brighten up when they discussed their pets and other animals. Dr. Ridout and his wife are the parents of three grown children and four grandchildren who regularly enjoy his creative stories about animals.

Made in the USA
Columbia, SC
16 May 2020

97530875R00162

REBELS
OF THE LAMP

REBELS OF THE LAMP

OF THE

MICHAEL M.B. GALVIN
& PETER SPEAKMAN

𝒟ɪsɴᴇʏ · HYPERION
LOS ANGELES   NEW YORK

Printed in the United States of America
First Edition, May 2015
1 3 5 7 9 10 8 6 4 2
G475-5664-5-15046

Library of Congress Cataloging-in-Publication Data

Galvin, Michael M.B., author.
   Rebels of the lamp/Michael M.B. Galvin, Peter Speakman.—First edition.
     pages cm.—(The Jinn Wars)
   Summary: "Parker Quarry is only twelve years old, and he's about to enter a war that has been brewing for centuries. When his mother sends him to New Hampshire to stay with his cousin Theo, Parker expects to be bored out of his mind. But then he stumbles across an ancient container—with a real genie inside—and life for Parker gets way more exciting. But there are those who seek to unleash the devastating power of the genies onto the world, and he may be humanity's only hope at surviving."—Provided by publisher.
   ISBN 978-1-4231-7957-3
[1. Genies—Fiction. 2. Magic—Fiction. 3. War—Fiction.] I. Speakman, Peter, author. II. Title.
   PZ7.1.G35Re 2015
   [Fic]—dc23   2014029969

Visit www.DisneyBooks.com

THIS LABEL APPLIES TO TEXT STOCK

ACKNOWLEDGMENTS

Thanks to Eddie Gamarra, Eric Robinson, Jeremy Bell, and Peter McHugh of the Gotham Group, Valerie Phillips and Trevor Astbury at Paradigm, Jim Garavente, Russell Hollander, Faye Atchison, all the friends and family members that put up with us while we're writing, and everybody at Disney • Hyperion, especially our patient and tireless editors Kevin Lewis and Ricardo Mejías.

For Laura, Devon, and Zachary: the best adventurers for the biggest adventures.
—P.S.

For Chelsea, of course.
—M.M.B.G.

PROLOGUE

PARKER QUARRY HAD NEVER DRIVEN a car a hundred and fifty miles an hour before.

Actually, if you want to get all technical about it, Parker had never driven a car at all before. Not even once. Not even in a parking lot. They don't let you drive cars when you're twelve years old. He had checked.

He grinned. This was, without a doubt, by almost anybody's definition, cool.

"Dog!"

Parker heard Reese scream out, but he had already seen the dog in the middle of the road. He had spotted him almost a mile away. What was it, exactly? A Boston terrier? Some kind of a retriever? A labradoodle? It was hard to say. All of Parker's senses seemed sharper, but he wasn't really a dog person.

"Parker!"

"I heard you, Reese. Sheesh," Parker said.

It would have been impossible for him not to hear her. Reese was wedged into the backseat of the red Porsche 911 Turbo S, and her head was only three inches from Parker's ear. It was a backseat designed more for small children or groceries than actual people. Reese wouldn't have been comfortable back there even if she was alone, and she wasn't. Parker's cousin, Theo, was crammed back there, too, one hand gripping the side of the car so hard his knuckles were turning white, and one hand held up to his mouth in case he got any sicker than he already was.

The backseat was not suitable for two junior-high kids. It would be perfect for, say, a Boston terrier, or some kind of a retriever, or a labradoodle.

Like the one that the car was hurtling toward.

"Parker!"

Parker thought that Reese might actually have a heart attack. With all the skill of an F1 driver, he downshifted the Porsche and turned the wheel, missing the mystery mutt by a good foot and a half. The dog was safe to resume his life of barking happily at skateboarders and urinating on things that needed to be urinated on.

The Porsche growled as Parker stabbed the gas again and continued his automotive assault on the winding, tree-lined back roads of Cahill, New Hampshire.

"I think I'm gonna throw up," said Theo.

"Deep breaths, buddy," Parker said. "In through your nose and out through your mouth."

The man in the passenger seat sighed and crossed his arms against his broad chest. He feared that he would never get used to twelve-year-olds or cars. He was tall, with sharp features, and eyes that never seemed to decide what color they wanted to be. He was dressed in black robes. He might have been twenty or he might have been fifty. It was hard to say.

"Um, Parker?"

"Yes, Theo?"

Theo was too ill to get the words out, so he just pointed. A police car was turning onto the road behind them.

"Oh. Well, maybe they're not after us," Parker said.

The cop turned on his flashing lights and sirens and stomped on the gas, his rear tires erupting in smoke as he joined the chase.

"Huh. Well, that's not a problem."

Parker shifted again, and the sports car lurched forward as if someone had attached rockets to the back bumper.

"Five hundred and sixty horsepower," Parker bragged as the police car faded from his rearview mirror. "I don't think they're going to catch us."

"They don't have to catch us," said Reese. "They have radios."

She pointed. Three more police cars were parked sideways, blocking the road about a mile ahead. The cops were standing behind their cars, guns drawn. The officer in charge held up a bullhorn.

"This is the Cahill police. Stop your vehicle."

Reese turned pale. "I think he wants us to stop."

Parker just smiled.

"I mean it, Parker. I can't get in trouble with the police. My mom's expecting me to apply to Harvard in four years. My safety school is Stanford!"

"There's no way out," said the cop. "Stop the car. Now."

Parker frowned. On the one hand, it was a beautiful day and he was really enjoying the drive. On the other hand, policemen with badges and shotguns seemed to really, sincerely want him to stop the car.

It was a no-brainer.

"Guys," Parker said, "You might want to hang on to something."

Theo groaned. "I knew this was a bad idea. I just knew it."

Parker mashed the gas pedal. The Porsche accelerated like it was dropped out of a plane. It was headed straight at the roadblock.

"Are you ready, Fon-Rahm?" Parker asked.

The man in the passenger seat nodded.

"Then do your thing, please."

Wisps of smoke came from the man's eyes.

"I just knew it," said Theo.

The cops saw the car speeding toward them. The officer with the bullhorn shook his head. "I don't think that guy's going to stop," he said.

He was right, too. The Porsche was going to smash into the police cars. At a hundred and fifty miles an hour.

"Um, I'll be over there," said one of the officers, pointing toward the side of the road.

"Wait! Stay here!" said the top cop, but it was too late. Every one of his officers had abandoned the roadblock.

The officer in charge thought for a moment. Then he dropped the bullhorn and ran off the road to be with his buddies. His wife was making tacos for dinner, and he liked tacos, and he wouldn't be able to eat them if his teeth were scattered all over the highway.

The Porsche charged at the cop cars. This was going to be messy.

"Now!" said Parker.

Fon-Rahm lifted his left hand and waved it through the air, bored. Smoke rose from the ground, and bits of wood, sheets of metal, and street signs leaped up from the sides of the road and magically shaped themselves into a makeshift ramp.

The cops stared with dropped jaws as the Porsche hit the ramp and sailed over the police cars. It landed with a thud and a storm of sparks past the roadblock, and it didn't pause for a second before speeding off.

Reese scrunched up her face. "Well, at least we're not getting arrested," she said.

"Please, Parker, please stop the car," said Theo.

"I will in just a few minutes." Parker looked the man in black over. "I know we're the only ones who can see you, but those robes really give me the willies. How about changing into something a little more contemporary?"

A light mist filled the car. When it cleared, Fon-Rahm's robes were gone, replaced with a sleek black suit.

"Is this more to your liking?" he asked.

"Very sharp. The color fits your personality."

"You try my patience, boy. I am Fon-Rahm of the Jinn, not a dress-up toy."

Parker shook his head and clucked. "Fon-Rahm, I'm surprised at you. Have you not been wearing your seat belt this whole time? Put in on, please. Safety first."

Fon-Rahm put his seat belt on and continued sulking.

"And cheer up, Rommy, old pal. This is what us humans call fun."

Parker stepped on the accelerator and grinned. You know what was cool? Having your own personal genie.

That was cool.

1

TWO WEEKS EARLIER

THE GODS STARED DOWN FROM THE ceiling.

Mercury blasted through space, wings flapping at his ankles. Venus lounged on a cloud, her long, black hair flowing behind her. Jupiter held lightning in his hands as if to warn humans not to get too close. Atlas held up the world, weary but unbroken. Imagine propping up the entire planet on your shoulders for all eternity. It was a thankless job, but somebody had to do it.

Mr. Ardigo knew the feeling.

"All right, all right, settle down, please. Please. Please."

He had volunteered—no, he had *begged* to bring his class to the Griffith Observatory. The place was, as the kids would say, sick.

It was equipped with massive telescopes and a planetarium, and it was set smack-dab on the edge of a cliff overlooking the entire city. The view was amazing. From the right angle you could even see the Hollywood sign. "It'll be educational!" he had said. "It'll broaden their horizons! It'll show them the grandeur of space and how small we are compared to the rest of the universe!"

If it showed them anything, though, it was that one teacher (okay, two, if you count Mrs. Haverkamp, but she was useless. A nice woman, sure, and great with computers, but when faced with screaming kids she was as handy as a Nerf hammer) could in no way hope to successfully wrangle forty seventh graders through a Los Angeles landmark. There were just too many of them. Mr. Ardigo was simply outmanned.

The kids were all standing around a circular hole in the floor of the marble rotunda, watching a pendulum swing from the center of the mural of the gods overhead. That was fine, he thought. The pendulum's swing was proof that the Earth was rotating, and that was a science lesson in itself. He wanted the kids to learn.

What he didn't want them to do was act like what they were: twelve-year-olds on a field trip. The boys shoved each other into walls while the girls kept up a regimen of near constant shrieking. What was there to scream about? The pendulum was neat, in a nerdy way, but really? The second these kids stepped out of school, they lost their minds. He thought they might burn off some of that extra energy on the bus ride over, but their supply seemed limitless.

Mr. Ardigo had a headache already. He checked his watch. They had been at the observatory less than fifteen minutes.

"The planetarium show starts in twenty-two minutes," he said over the roar. "And then everyone will get a chance to look through the telescope."

He checked his guidebook. "Apparently, we'll be looking at a very rare planetary alignment. The last time it happened was over three thousand years ago. Kendra!"

Kendra stopped leaning so far over the railing that she would absolutely fall in and looked at him blankly. A small, small victory. She did not stop shrieking, though. They never do, thought Mr. Ardigo.

"There's a lot to see in here, and I want to get to it all, but you're all going to have to cooperate, okay? Guys?"

Mr. Ardigo noticed that he was tapping his foot, and made a conscious effort to stop. He was always drumming his fingers or clicking a pen. Stuff like that drove his wife nuts. She was right. He was too nervous. He had to learn to relax. He also had to make more money. Mrs. Ardigo's dream was that her husband would ditch teaching altogether and open up a Quiznos.

He would never do it. He loved teaching. Well, not on this particular *day*, but in general, he loved teaching.

"Okay, let's go, let's go."

His class broke away from the pendulum in one noisy lump and rushed past him on their way into the exhibits.

"Stick together, please, and keep your hands to yourself," Mr. Ardigo said. "We're going to be quiet and we're going to be respectful. That goes double for you, Parker."

The teacher froze. He scanned the line of kids once, and then again. No Parker.

"Parker? Has anybody seen Parker?"

Nobody had. Mr. Ardigo let out a sigh and stared at the ceiling. Atlas, he thought. Atlas had it easy.

Parker twisted the puzzle again. It was a series of four interlocking metal squares, and the idea was to make them all line up. It should be easy, he thought, except for some reason, it was ridiculously hard. He would get two in the right place, and then one would be way out of whack, and then he would fix that one, and ruin all the work he had done before. The thing was impossible. Maybe if he could take the price tag off.

"I can never figure those things out," said a woman behind him.

She was about sixty years old, and she was wearing a blue shirt with a collar and a Griffith Observatory name tag that read JUNE.

Parker smiled sweetly at her. He was just an innocent kid browsing the racks of a gift store. There's nothing less suspicious than that.

"Me neither," he said, putting the puzzle back on the shelf with the astronaut ice cream and the Lunar Lander play set. "But, you see, it's not for me. I'm looking for a present. For my mother."

"Aren't you sweet! Is it her birthday?"

"No, she's . . ." His eyes found the floor. "She's in the hospital."

"Oh, I'm so sorry," said June. She was, too.

"Yeah, she's pretty sick. I thought maybe, since I was here, I could get her something to cheer her up. I got her some flowers and stuff but it's still pretty depressing in her room."

"Well, how about a stuffed animal? People love these!"

She held up a stuffed monkey wearing a NASA space suit.

"That's great! Really great! But I was thinking maybe something like that?"

Parker pointed to a crystal sculpture of a shooting star lodged at the top of the highest shelf in the store.

"Oh!" she said. "That is pretty."

June bit her bottom lip. She was a small woman, smaller than Parker, even, and he was twelve. If she was going to get that sculpture, it was going to take some effort.

"Let me just get that for you."

June stood on her toes and reached as high as she could.

As soon as her back was turned, Parker expertly grabbed the metal puzzle and slipped it into the pocket of his jacket.

June's fingers touched the sculpture. For a second it looked like it might fall, but June caught it and showed it triumphantly to Parker. "Ha! Got it!"

Parker looked at the light sparkling off the crystal.

"Is it okay if I come back for it later?" asked Parker. "That way I won't have to carry it around with me the rest of the day. I might break it. I'm pretty klutzy."

"Oh, you are not. I'll bet you're a natural athlete."

"Could you set it aside for me? Please?"

"Of course. You come back for it whenever you would like."

Parker thanked her and walked out the glass doors. It was that easy, he thought. If only he could get up the guts to grab some stuff out of a real store. Then maybe he wouldn't be the only kid he knew without a decent skateboard. Or a flat-screen TV. Or an iPhone.

He smiled a sly smile. Then he looked in the window of the

gift shop and saw June struggling to put the crystal star back on the shelf.

Parker sighed.

He walked back into the gift shop and steadied June while she put the thing back. Then she thanked him, and he sneaked the metal puzzle out of his pocket and back on the shelf. He never would have solved it, anyway.

Parker left the gift shop. He had better get back. Mr. Ardigo might have noticed he had left the group, and the last thing Parker needed, really, was to get in trouble again. His mom would kill him. Before he could take two steps, though, Parker was confronted by two of his classmates.

"Hey, Parker, what are you doing in the gift shop? You know you can't afford anything in there."

Great, Parker thought. Jason Sussman and his buddy Adam. They were two kids with more money than brains, and they were not fans of Parker. Both Jason and Adam were bigger than he was. In fact, almost every guy in his class was bigger than Parker. His mother told him he was going to hit a growth spurt soon, but Parker would believe it when he saw it.

"Jason. Adam. What's up?"

"Adam and I were just admiring your shoes," said Jason. "Hey, where do you think I could get a pair like that?"

Parker gritted his teeth. He was wearing sneakers from Payless. The worst thing that could happen to a kid was to get caught wearing sneakers from Payless.

"My uncle brought them back from England, so you probably can't get them. Sorry."

"He bring you that shirt, too?" asked Jason. "It looks like something you would get at Kmart."

Caught again. Parker hated going to school with rich kids.

"Ouch!" he said. "You got me. Well, see you later."

Parker turned to go. He would walk away. He would stay out of trouble.

Jason stepped in front of him. "Come on, Parker. What's your hurry? Let's hang out for a minute."

"You know, Jason, I would like to, really, but I think I had better be getting back. If Mr. Ardigo finds out I'm gone, I'll be in detention for the rest of my life."

"Yeah, well, it's just that Adam and I have a question for you." Jason stepped right up to Parker. "What's it like being poor?"

Parker bit his lip. He would stay cool. "You know what they say, Jason. Money can't buy you love."

"Yeah, but it can buy a lot of other things."

Parker couldn't help himself. "Obviously, not a decent haircut," he said. "It looks like you got yours in a helicopter in the middle of a tornado."

Adam guffawed, but the smirk on Jason's face disappeared. Parker knew he had made a tactical error. Rich kids can dish it out, but they can't take it.

"Kidding!" he said. "I'm just kidding around."

"Oh, we know," Jason said. "You're a funny guy."

"Great! So we're cool?"

Jason shook his head. While Adam stood watch, Jason shoved Parker against a wall.

"I hate funny guys," said Jason.

Parker stepped back, but there was nowhere to go. He was boxed in.

"Come on, guys," he said. "This is stupid. Let's just go find the class."

"Wow. Now you're saying I'm stupid? You just don't know when to shut up, do you?"

Jason raised his fist and laughed when Parker flinched.

"See that, Adam? He's just a talker. Parker's jealous. He knows that we have futures. We'll go to college, and then we'll get killer jobs and make lots of money, and he'll be watching from the sidelines. See, Parker here doesn't have a future. He's trash and he'll always be trash. He'll probably end up in jail."

Jason leaned right into Parker's face.

"Just like his father."

And that's when Parker snapped. The fingers on his right hand closed into a fist and he punched Jason in the face as hard as he could.

Jason fell to the ground, and for a moment, everything was calm. Jason clutched his nose, Adam stared in disbelief, and Parker stood, his hands still clenched, shocked at his own outburst.

Then Jason pulled his bloody hand away from his messed-up nose and broke the tension.

"Oh, Parker," he said. "You are so dead."

Parker looked at Jason. Then he looked at Adam. Then, for a split second, he looked at June, who was watching horrified from the gift shop. Then Parker made maybe his best decision of the day.

He decided to run.

VESIROTH'S JOURNAL, CIRCA 1200 B.C.

The war came to us.

I had heard of the battles, of course, when I went into town to barter for goods, and I saw the soldiers when I sold my crops in the city. No one could tell me what the war was about, though rumors abounded. Some said it was a dispute about land. Others thought it was a battle to control the river that sustains us all. Perhaps it was not about anything so practical. Perhaps someone's great-great-grandfather had insulted someone else's great-great-grandfather hundreds of years ago and everyone was still upset. Such things are what make wars.

I was a farmer, not important enough to be kept informed, too busy to find out for myself. The fighting meant nothing to me. It did not affect the seasons or the way the sun hit the

soil or the way the sands shifted in the north.
I was concerned only with my crops and with my
wife and with my daughters. I had no time for
politics. There was always work to do.

The day that changed my life forever
progressed like any other. I was in the fields,
the hot sun on my back. My youngest sat near
me in the dirt. She was playing with a toy
stallion I had carved from a spare piece of
wood. I remember how she looked up at me and
how she smiled. She was beautiful and young and
perfect, and I adored her. When I winked at her,
she giggled.

I cherished those moments, and I knew that
when the workday was over and our simple meal
was eaten, my family and I would gather by the
fire. My hands would be sore and my back would
ache, but my daughters would make up stories to
entertain me, and we would all laugh. We would
sing songs and play silly games. I would send
the children to bed, and my wife and I would
share a quiet moment, knowing we were blessed.
My life was hard, but I would not have traded
places with the sultan. I was happy.

My daughter went back to her toy, and I
returned to my work. That is when I saw the
soldiers riding toward the house.

I was confused. I was no one. Their war had
nothing to do with me.

My daughter abandoned her toy and hurried to

meet them, her black hair flowing behind her as she ran. She loved horses, and she had hoped that the men galloping to us in a storm of dust were part of a circus. She thought the best of people, always. Children do.

I knew better. They carried torches and swords. These men were part of no circus. I dropped my scythe and I ran.

I grabbed my daughter in my arms and I put her inside our little house. I knew my wife would be grinding meal by the fire. I knew my oldest child would be tending the animals nearby.

I gathered them together and told them to stay inside. I took my copper ax, the finest tool I owned, and I went out to meet the soldiers.

Surely, they would listen to reason. Surely, they would see that we were no threat, that we were a humble family with no ties to power, no stake in their fight.

The men stopped their horses in front of me. I raised my hand in greeting.

I was rewarded with a club to the side of my head.

I fell to the dirt.

I tried to get up, but my legs would not stay beneath me. I saw these men dismount from their horses and kick in the door to my house. I stumbled toward them, but I could do nothing as they raised their torches.

The soldiers laughed as they set fire to my

home, laughed when my daughters and my wife cried out from inside, laughed when I tried to stop them.

I was weak. They batted me away like a toy. I fell again, and one of the men grabbed me by the hair. He held my arms behind my back and forced my face down into the fire. I could hear my own skin as it sizzled like cooked meat.

Thankfully, I blacked out. I would not have to hear my family's cries as they died.

Hours later, as I faded in and out of consciousness, I felt myself being dragged from the smoldering ruins. It was an old man. I tried to tell him to leave me where I was. Everything I had was gone. I had no reason to keep on living.

Before the words could come, the blackness took me again. That is how I came to travel with Farrad, alive but with all meaning for my life stripped away.

2

PARKER RAN DOWN A SET OF STAIRS
and straight into the observatory's crowded main exhibit floor.
He pushed his way through a group of Cub Scouts looking at a
video slide show of the stars, and by a family with six (six!) kids
in matching T-shirts who were testing out a set of scales that
showed you how much you would weigh on Mars.

He ran behind a statue of Einstein sitting on a bench, and then
up another flight of stairs, using kids and guides as shields, but
he couldn't shake Jason and Adam. They were right behind him.

"You're dead, Parker!"

I know, thought Parker. I know.

He poured it on and got ahead of the kids chasing him. The
next level of the building was a long hallway full of exhibits
stretching in both directions. Parker ducked out of sight behind a

massive globe of the moon. He stayed perfectly still while Adam and Jason rounded the corner and ran the other way.

A little kid with a toy rocket stared at Parker, and Parker grinned back, relieved. He was in the clear.

When he stood up, though, his jacket caught on the metal stand that was holding the globe up. Parker's grin vanished as the globe came spinning down and landed with a thud at the rocket kid's feet. Then it started to slowly *roll.*

Someone yelled, "Hey!"

Great, thought Parker. A security guard. Where was he when I was being threatened by my buddies Jason and Adam?

The guard ran to Parker, clutching his belt with his left hand so his radio and flashlight didn't bang into his legs.

"Don't move! Stay right there!"

Good advice, thought Parker. But not great advice. He ran again.

"Hey!" said the guard. Parker looked over his shoulder and saw that the huge globe was gathering speed and scattering people left and right as it cut a swath through the museum. The Cub Scouts scrambled for cover, tangling up the guard, who watched helplessly as the globe smashed into Einstein's bench and knocked the statue over.

Mr. Ardigo's not going to be happy about that, thought Parker. He ducked under a brass railing and burst through some closed doors into the planetarium, where the show he was supposed to be watching was just getting started. A machine rose up in the middle of the room and projected lights and colors onto the domed ceiling to make you feel like you were looking at space.

The show's narrator explained how far away the stars were and talked about how the different constellations got their names, and pointed out the Milky Way and the Crab Nebula. The seats were laid back so you didn't have to crane your neck to look up.

Parker didn't have time to enjoy the show. He ran straight to the exit on the other side of the room, the security guard on his tail.

"Parker!" said Mr. Ardigo from one of the seats. "That had better not be you!"

"It's not!" Parker said as he got through the exit door, just steps ahead of the guard, who had renewed the hunt with a very red face and a burst of not-so-good-natured intensity.

Parker ducked behind a wall, and the guard ran right past, barking into his radio.

Parker put his hands on his knees, out of breath from all that running. An old man stared at him.

"The scope of the universe," Parker panted. "It takes my breath away."

Parker had escaped. He had no idea what to do next, but the important thing was that, for the moment at least, he was safe.

"Hey, buddy," said a voice behind him.

Parker turned. It was Jason and Adam.

"We've been looking all over for you."

Parker ran once more, this time heading for open space. He slammed the handle on some glass doors and found himself outside.

The exterior of the observatory was even more impressive than the inside. There were walkways on every floor, with coin-operated telescopes mounted to the railings so you could look at Los Angeles. Girls posed while their boyfriends took their pictures in front of the city.

It really was some view. From here, LA didn't look half bad.

Parker stopped. The sweaty security guard was coming the other way.

He was in it now. If he went left, Adam and Jason would get him. If he went right, he'd run straight into the security guard. He was toast.

Parker didn't know the place's layout, but he knew that the levels were all connected by stairways. Piece of cake. He would jump the wall, land on the stairs, and run down to the bottom level. Easy. Elegant, even. Parker put his hand on the railing and vaulted over.

Except the stairs were on the other side of the building, and Parker had just launched himself over the edge of a cliff. The only thing there was a hundred-foot drop and some very unfriendly looking rocks.

Holy crap, thought Parker. Jason was right. I really am dead.

I have been with Farrad for weeks now.

He is an enigma to me. He dresses in tattered robes and worn sandals. He has no friends and mentions no family. Even his age is a mystery to me.

We never stay in one place for more than a few days. He trades household objects out of his battered wagon, earning just enough silver to keep us in food and his old horse in oats. I do not know where he comes from or where he is heading. He seldom speaks, and when he does he says no more than a few words at a time.

He has taken great care to nurse me back to health. He fed me broth until I was strong enough to take solid food. He covered my damaged face with bandages. He gave me clothes and a place to lay my head. At night we sit by the fire in silence. Farrad stares into the flames and thinks his thoughts. He has asked me no questions about myself, although he must know what happened to me. If he takes any

satisfaction at having saved my life, he does
not show it. His kindness to me feels less like a
good deed and more like atonement for past sins.

I can think of nothing but my family and how I
failed them.

One day, while Farrad was away trading,
the grief I felt over the death of my wife and
daughters finally overwhelmed me. I felt I could
not bear another night of loneliness, another
night of black dreams that ended in me sweating
through my bandages and screaming myself
awake. I had nothing to live for, and my despair
was so great that I sought to do myself harm.

I searched for something, anything I could
use to take my own life. Perhaps Farrad had
foreseen my joyless mood, for the wagon was
devoid of weapons of any kind, and even the sham
ointments foisted off on gullible peasants as
a cure-all for anything from coughing fits to
baldness were gone.

In my desperation, I tore the wagon apart.
Just when my mood was at its bleakest, my hands
felt a weak spot in the wood of Farrad's driver's
bench. I pried it open and found hidden within
an ancient book, so old that at first I dared
not open it lest the pages crumble into dust.
I found my courage, though, and I opened the
volume to read.

What I found astounded me. The book is an

ancient compendium of arcane magick, written
by hand and bound in some kind of hardened
leather. It describes something called
the Nexus, which is a force of magick that
surrounds everyone and everything. With the
right spells, potions, amulets, and talismans,
the book claims that it is possible to tap into
the Nexus and amass great power.

The book is the first thing, the only thing,
to hold my interest since the destruction of my
family. I became obsessed. I read it through
that night and put it back in its hiding place
before Farrad returned. Now, whenever he is
gone, I go back to the pages. They pull at me,
call to me even. They quiet the screams of my
wife and daughters when they threaten to smother
me. The secrets of the universe are contained
within them.

I am especially beguiled by the book's
concluding page. There is written a fragment
of an incantation that promises ultimate power.
The spell is incomplete, but it intrigues me and
haunts my sleep.

Perhaps in the Nexus I may find the peace that
eludes me.

3

APPARENTLY, MERCURY AND THE REST
of the observatory gods were feeling...benevolent.

Mr. Ardigo, out looking for his favorite student and for once
in his life at the exact right place at the exact right time, grabbed
Parker's arm and stopped him from getting all the way over the
railing and splatting to a messy death on the rocks below.

He stopped Parker in midair and dragged him back over the
wall. Mr. Ardigo didn't let go until they were both lying in a
heap next to the wall.

"Thanks," said Parker, his eyes wide with amazement. "For a
minute there I was in serious trouble."

Oh, thought Mr. Ardigo, you have no idea what serious trouble is.

* * *

"Suspended. Well, that's just great, Parker. That's just about perfect."

Parker stared out the window of the ten-year-old Saturn sedan as his mother drove. The car was once tan, but most of the paint on the roof and the hood had blistered off in the California sun. The back door on the driver's side was red, replaced after an accident years ago, but never repainted. His mother had assumed she would scrape together the cash to do it someday, but someday never came.

"You talk back. Your grades are terrible, you lost all your friends, and now you're getting into fights. Awesome. You're future's looking brighter every day."

"I don't know why I'm the one that's in trouble!" he said. "Those guys were beating on this little kid and I told them to stop and they turned on me! I should be getting some kind of a reward!"

"Don't. Don't even . . . Just don't."

Parker shut his mouth. His mom was wearing her Denny's uniform, and she smelled like French toast and pancake syrup. That meant that the school called her at work, and *that* meant that she had to get someone to cover the rest of her shift, and *that* meant that her boss, Antonio, was not happy, and that was bad news for everyone involved.

"When I think about what a pain it was to move just so you could be in a better school district . . ." She trailed off. A lot of people told Parker that he looked like his mom. They both had dark brown hair and hazel eyes. Nobody ever told Parker he looked like his dad.

"You know you broke that kid's nose, right? We'll be lucky if his parents don't sue. His dad's a lawyer. Or a tax guy. Something like that. That's just what we need."

She stopped the car at a red light. Parker looked up at a palm tree. In the movies, they seemed so glamorous, but they were everywhere in LA. This one was outside a liquor store with a broken sign.

Parker's mother sighed. Her sarcastic tone was gone when she spoke again.

"I'm trying, Parker. I'm trying so hard, but I'm doing it all alone, and you're not helping me. It's just..." She looked out her window. "It's just not working."

The light turned and the car drove on, the two of them sitting in silence.

"I talked to your principal, and I talked to your school counselor, and they suggested that maybe it might be a good idea if you spent some time someplace where you could stay out of trouble. Someplace with a yard and some fresh air where you could take a break and maybe make a fresh start. We thought that maybe if you stayed with your cousin for a while in New Hampshire..."

Parker was stunned. He had expected the usual riot act, the yelling, the empty threats. He hadn't expected this.

"You're sending me *away*?"

"No! No!" said his mom. "Just for a little while."

Parker couldn't believe it.

"It's hard for you here. I'm working all these double shifts, and you're alone half the time. It's not good for you. And you need some positive male influence in your life."

Parker let that one sit there. He knew she was talking about his dad, and he knew that she was right. Parker's father was nobody's role model.

"Let's just try it. Let's both agree that it's an experiment and that we'll both try to look at it like it's a positive thing. It'll be an adventure."

Parker sulked. "Yeah, New Hampshire is known for adventure."

"It won't be for forever. Just until things improve a little bit."

"So this is a done deal, then? I don't even get a say in it at all? I thought this was a democracy."

"Don't be so dramatic, Parker. You're not going to a mental institution. You're going to New England."

"Same difference."

Parker's mom's voice turned cold again. "This is happening, buddy, so you might as well get used to the idea. I've already talked to your aunt Martha and uncle Kelsey. You're going this weekend."

"This weekend? I can't go this weekend! I have things to do here!"

"Really? Like what, exactly?"

Parker opened his mouth, but nothing came out. He didn't have anything planned. Not a single thing.

"Really, Parker, what have you got to lose? What's here that you'll even miss? Maybe you'll like it out there. You certainly don't seem to like it here."

She had a point.

"And it's not like I'm abandoning you. You're going now, and then I'm coming out in three weeks for Thanksgiving."

Parker shook his head. He knew his mother. That was never going to happen.

"I am!" she said. "We'll spend Thanksgiving together!"

"Sure, unless you have to pick up an extra shift or you can't afford the ticket."

"I'll work it out."

"Or you decide to go see dad instead."

Parker practically spit the words out. His mother opened her mouth to say something cutting right back to him, but she took a breath instead. She let herself calm down before she spoke.

"Sooner or later, you're going to have to forgive him," she said.

Parker stared ahead.

"I'm not excusing what he did. It was stupid and it was selfish, and he's paying the price for it. We're *all* paying the price for it. You know, it hurts his feelings that you won't go and see him."

"He's a crook."

Parker's mother glared at him.

"He's the man I married. And when this is all over we're going to be a family again, even if it kills me."

They drove in silence for a moment. The button for the passenger-side window was broken. There was a Chiquita Banana sticker Parker had stuck on the dashboard in sixth grade.

"New Hampshire will be good for you, honey. It'll be good for you to have people around that are going to be there for you. It'll be good for you to have people you can count on."

"You can't count on anybody," Parker said. "They'll always let you down."

His mother drove on. Parker knew that she was hurt, but at that moment, he didn't care.

Tonight, Farrad came back from trading earlier
than I expected him.

  He found me reading the book by the light of
an oil lamp. I was so engrossed in its secrets
that I did not hear him until he was already
upon me. He jerked the book from my hands and
began to scream, furious at my transgression
and betrayal. I had never seen Farrad display
any emotion at all, and to see him so angry was
a surprise to me. At first, he railed against
me, but soon his rant took on a different cast.
He began to warn me against using magick. He
said that any attempts to connect with the Nexus
would only lead to my ruin.

  I listened to his outburst with a chastised
heart. The book was his, and I had no right to
take it. He had saved my life, after all. I was
in his debt.

  But emotions I had never before felt flooded
over me, and my guilt became bitter resentment.
Who was this pathetic peddler to tell me what to

do? Why should I follow his example, when he was so clearly a worm of a man? He had nothing. A wooden wagon rotting from the wheels up. A load of worthless trinkets. A bucket of meal. A horse close to death. If he were to simply skim the surface of what the book promised, he could be swimming in gold.

I knew then that Farrad was a fool. I remembered the pages of the book and I raised my hands. I summoned up but a paltry sliver of the Nexus's power and cast my first spell. A ball of green light appeared in my hands, and Farrad was blown out of the wagon. He landed heavily in the dirt.

The book was mine. I climbed down from the wagon and leaned over Farrad. For a brief moment, his eyes flashed with anger, and he raised his hands as if to cast a spell of his own. I backed away, suddenly afraid. I sensed a great power unleashed in Farrad, as if I had roused a sleeping beast into action.

Then, as suddenly as it appeared, the fury in Farrad was subdued. He seemed tired and resigned and older than I had ever imagined. I approached him warily, and I pried the book from his hands. He stared ahead, powerless to stop me.

I felt the sting of my own betrayal as I mounted his ancient horse and rode off into the night, but the promise of the book urged me on. I had a new reason to live. I would find the men who had slaughtered my family, and I would use the spells at my disposal to make them pay.

4

PARKER STEPPED INTO HIS NEW
bedroom and dropped his bag on the floor.

"This is Martha's crafts room," said his uncle Kelsey.

Parker could tell. There was a sewing machine shoved against
the wall, and the quilt on the twin bed was handmade. The wall-
paper had pictures of flowers and vines, and it was torn at the
corners where the walls met the ceiling.

"I asked her to clean it out, but I think she just shoved most
of her stuff into the closet. Not a lot of space here. Still, it should
be big enough for you. Good thing you travel light."

Uncle Kelsey put Parker's duffel bag on the bed.

It was a farmhouse, deep in rural New Hampshire. The land
had once been a working apple orchard. There were still some
trees, and a battered old barn with a cider press, and a tractor with

a seized piston. The Merritts' house needed paint and new windows. The pipes groaned when anyone ran the water. It was old, but it was solid and it was big. It was a world away from Parker's two-bedroom apartment in Los Angeles.

"Theo! Your cousin's here!"

Uncle Kelsey ran a hand through his thick hair. He was a big man with an outdoorsy look about him. He had a goatee and work boots. His stomach hung over his jeans. He looked like a guy who knew how to get broken things to work again.

He crossed his arms on his chest.

"I know this is a big change for you, Parker. It's a big change for us, too. But there's no reason this shouldn't work." He paused for a moment. "I know it's been tough on you, with what happened with your dad and everything. I want you to know that you can come to me or your aunt, either one of us, if you have any problems."

Sure, thought Parker. There was about as much chance of that happening as there was for Parker's shoes to spontaneously transform into singing frogs.

He put his hand on Parker's shoulder.

"We want you to think of this as your home."

Parker didn't react. Uncle Kelsey removed his hand. When he turned around, Parker's cousin Theo was in the doorway.

"Hey, Theo," Uncle Kelsey said. "Great. You can help your new housemate get settled in."

Uncle Kelsey walked out and down the stairs in search of his wife, leaving Theo and Parker.

"Hi, Theo," said Parker.

Theo wore an MP3 player strapped to his arm, and gym shorts

and a Robert Frost Junior High T-shirt soaked with sweat. He had braces and a crew cut. He took the buds out of his ears.

"This is crazy," Parker said. "I mean, one minute I'm whooping it up in LA, and the next thing you know I'm in the sticks. It's like living in the eighteen hundreds, am I right?"

Theo just stood there.

Parker took a breath and, for just a second, let his defenses down.

"I'm glad to see you, Theo. Really. You're, like, the only person I know in this entire state."

Theo shook his head. "The bus comes at seven fifteen," he said. "I get the first shower."

"Wow. Okay. You're going to show me around and everything, right? At school and stuff?"

Theo just put his earbuds back in and walked off.

"Theo?"

Theo was gone.

Parker looked at the nightstand by the bed. His aunt Martha had placed a framed photo there of Parker with his mom and dad. He remembered the day it was taken. They were on a trip to the Grand Canyon. His dad had bought Parker a cowboy hat and a badge that said US MARSHALL. They were all smiling. Happier times.

All at once, the fact that he was separated from both his parents finally sank in, and a single sob erupted from Parker's lips. He clamped his hand over his mouth and stood absolutely still. He closed his eyes. He took a deep breath.

When he had everything back under control, Parker opened his eyes, turned the picture facedown on the table, and started to unpack.

After weeks of searching, I found the soldiers who destroyed my life.

They were in a tavern, drinking and laughing and telling one another lies about great battles they had won. They paid no attention to me as I made my way to their table. Why would they? I was just a peasant dressed in rags and bandages. I was harmless.

Then one of the men jeered at me, and another threw a piece of wet food at my head. I was beneath them. I did not deserve to be in their presence.

I closed my eyes. This was the moment I had been waiting for.

I spread my arms to my sides, and I felt the power surge through me. I had chosen a spell carefully and had practiced it day and night since I had abandoned Farrad. I would not trip over the strange words. I would not hesitate. I would not fail.

I took a deep breath and began. As I said the

words, my bandages fell away and the burns that disfigured half of my face were revealed.

Did the soldiers recognize me? Did they look on me and feel regret for what they had done to me and to my family?

The air turned cold, and smoke rose around me. The sounds of drinking and conversation gave way to panic as fear took hold. One of the soldiers, realizing too late that his fate was sealed, sprang at me with a knife. Before he reached me, my spell was done. As I finished the incantation, I closed my eyes tightly and brought my hands together in one mighty clap.

There was a roar, and then silence.

When I opened my eyes, I saw that everyone in the room was dead.

For a moment, my heart sank. I had tried to move beyond my anger, to let things lie. I had tried to think of my family and what they would have thought of my dark pursuits. I had tried to put their deaths behind me. But always the Nexus called to me. Always I had found myself turning the pages of the book, studying its arcane secrets.

And now, though my family was avenged, I saw that I had only brought more sorrow into the world. Did these men not have families? What of the innocents caught in my own war of vengeance? What would my daughters think of me now, surrounded by the corpses of my victims?

I saw then that these soldiers were but a symptom of a larger disease. The enemy was war itself, and I knew that I would not rest until I had ended the very idea of war.

My future is sealed. In order to forever end war, I must assume dominion over all men. I must rule the world.

5

REESE WATCHED THE NEW KID TWO tables over.

He was small and scrawny, even for a seventh-grade boy, but, man, was he confident. One day of school and he was already surrounded by admirers.

"Oh, sure, we had a box at Staples Center, so I got to know some of the Clippers a little bit. Blake Griffin, Chris Paul. One time I got to sit on the bench for a game. They play so much, though, and sometimes I just wanted to hit the bars on Sunset with my friends. A lot of them are in bands."

Reese knew that everything that came out of the new kid's mouth was a crock, but the kids at his table hung on his every word. Sheep, she thought. They'll believe anything.

"How did you get into *bars*?" Jenna Conroy asked, her mouth hanging open. That girl would believe anything.

Parker shrugged. "I know people."

Parker looked at Reese, but she immediately buried her head back into her art history book. She was an eighth grader, and she didn't want him to get the mistaken idea that she was interested in anything he had to say.

She turned the pages of her book slowly. She wished that Robert Frost Junior High actually taught art history, but no dice. The high school didn't, either. She wouldn't be able to take it until college. Until then, she would have to be content sitting through classes taught by teachers who didn't want to be there, and filled with dopes, airheads, soon-to-be burnouts, and class clowns.

Reese's mom had gotten her the art book, along with the poetry and the Russian novels. She had also enrolled Reese in a pile of classes outside of school. There were the viola lessons, of course, and the piano, and the French, and the extra math (Reese was already far, far ahead of her high school-age tutor, a kid with bad skin and rimless glasses, who spent more time texting his girlfriend than formulating quadratic equations), and the swimming (Robert Frost didn't have a pool, but they did have a new scoreboard for the football team), and the ballet (this one Reese actually sort of liked, although she would never, ever admit it to anyone), among others.

Reese's mom was hell-bent on getting Reese into a good college on the first try, and in her opinion, it was never too early to start pushing. Overachievement was not enough. Reese had to be stellar in everything, all the time.

After years and years of constant pressure, Reese was just now starting to push back. She still got the grades, sure, and she still went to the classes (sculpting! There was a sculpting class for a while there!), only now she did it with magenta streaks in her short black hair, and enough rings for any six emo kids. She wore sweaters with long, long sleeves, and she mumbled whenever her parents spoke to her.

All of this was designed to get a rise out of her mom. It failed utterly. If Reese's mom noticed any of it, she kept it to herself as she taxied Reese all over Cahill for extracurriculars. Reese was starting to wonder if she was going to have to actually start listening to goth or death metal, which would be a real sacrifice. In her heart of hearts, Reese remained a Taylor Swift fan.

"Did you ever meet any movie stars?" another one of Parker's new pals asked.

"Meet them? Are you kidding? When I was a kid, Selena Gomez was my babysitter."

Reese watched Parker's table out of the corner of her eye. Theo Merritt rolled his eyes and shook his head. Reese was pretty sure that somebody had said the two boys were cousins.

"Yeah, it's a shame I had to leave Hollywood, but I crossed some pretty intense guys, and the police thought it would be in my own best interest if I got out of town for a little while."

"Wait. Wait."

Jenna again. This girl was more gullible than a four-year-old whose uncle kept pulling quarters out of his ear.

"You're hiding out here? From a *gang*?"

"Gang is an overused term. Let's just call them a well-organized group of guys with similar taste in clothes. They thought I should join, but I had other ideas."

Reese saw the jocks before Parker did. They were eighth graders that had been her classmates since kindergarten. She wasn't sure why guys became tools when they got together in a group and put on uniforms, but in her experience, that seemed to be what happened. She would look it up. Somebody must have done a study on it.

"Wow," one of the eighth graders said. "Look at this, guys. We have a real action hero here."

Parker grimaced before he turned to face the jocks. There were guys like this at every school. Somebody had to run the places. Otherwise, kids might actually enjoy themselves.

"Me? Nah," Parker said. "I'm new here. I'm just, you know, trying to fit in."

The lead jock picked a Tater Tot off Parker's plate. Parker liked Tater Tots. Everybody likes Tater Tots. "Well, you're doing a bang-up job at it so far."

"We got off on the wrong foot. I'm Parker."

"Why, hello, Parker. My name's Evan . . ."

Of course it is, thought Parker. Of course your name is Evan.

". . . and I'll be teaching you a lesson in how to respect your elders."

The jocks with Evan grinned. Reese saw Parker look to his cousin for help.

"You guys don't scare Parker," Theo said with a grin. "He's from the city. He's faced down guys with guns. To him, you're just a bunch of pansies. That's what he was saying before you got here, at least."

Parker turned red and started to stammer.

Cold, Reese thought, as the jocks escorted Parker up from his seat and quietly out of the cafeteria. Reese ate her lunch alone, and she finished the chapter in her book alone, and she checked the time on her phone. She still had five minutes before the bell. She picked up her book bag (black, of course, and covered with pins that infuriatingly did not annoy her mother) and walked out the back door to the alley behind the school.

She stopped at the Dumpster. Reese put both book-bag straps on her shoulders and pushed the lid open. There was Parker, covered in the remnants of today's lunch. And yesterday's lunch. And the day before's lunch.

"Thank you," said Parker.

"No problem. You know, you really should stay away from those guys."

"Yeah, thanks. I'll keep that in mind."

Parker slipped on some pretty rancid old tomato sauce on the bottom of the Dumpster but righted himself before he fell over.

"I'm Reese."

"Parker."

He held out his hand, but Reese just eyed him warily.

"Do I smell that bad?" he asked.

"No. I'm just not sure if I should be friends with you or not."

"Why not?"

"You don't seem like you're going to survive the week."

Reese hoisted her bag and walked away. She hated to admit it, but her mother was right about one thing: boys were nothing but trouble.

The tastiest books are always the hardest to
come by.

The really good ones are banned, and all
are rare. What sellers I can find are slippery
men who live in the shadows and are not to be
trusted. I could slash their throats, I suppose,
but why bother? They would just be replaced.
There is an endless supply of scum in the
world, and I can't help but admire the survival
instincts of the common rat.

I have rented a charmingly decrepit room in
the city, and I toil alone until my eyes hurt
from reading by the dim light of candles. I
dress in rags, and when I go outside I cover
my face with a filthy bandage so as not to show
my scars. People avoid me. They assume I am a
beggar, or worse.

They are right. I am worse.

My landlord pounds on my door and threatens
to throw me out into the street. It might amuse
me to summon a demon to drag him away, but there

would be a mess, and the smell would linger for days. I take the prudent course and instead conjure a handful of silver coins. I pay him his rent and slam the door in his face. He walks away in a huff, with no idea how close to oblivion he has just come. There is a certain pleasure in living in ignorance.

In my centuries of study, I have learned many things. I have discovered magick that makes me powerful, and amulets that can be used as fierce weapons. I had practiced the arcane arts for only thirty years before I discovered the spell that would allow me to live forever. I am told that this knowledge is in the hands of only a select few sorcerers. I do not associate with my peers, although I know I walk among them. I feel no need to socialize with a group of magickal malcontents, all trying to outdo one another with tricks and amazements.

The key to immortality is mine, and yet I find it a trifling thing. War still rages around me. What good is eternal life if I cannot enforce my will on the world? Is a life never ending a gift or a curse?

I search always for the missing pieces that would complete the incantation at the back of Farrad's book. This is the ultimate weapon. This is the key that will make me the world's master.

The spell's creators are shrouded in mystery.

They are men discussed in hushed voices, wizards whose past deeds are known now only as myths and legends. According to the tales, they were the Elders, the first sorcerers who ever bridged the gap between our world and the Nexus. They pooled their wisdom and between them created the most powerful spell yet in existence. Why did they never cast their masterpiece? No one knows. There are theories that the Elders were afraid of the power that would be unleashed, and others that suggested a traitor among them turned the Elders against one another. Whatever the true history of the Elders, their most powerful magick is to this day unused.

Was Farrad one of the Elders? I fear I will never know. I have searched for him, but even with my resources I can find no trace. It is as if the man has vanished from the face of the earth.

No complete copy of the spell remains, but bits and pieces float through the world of the arcane and the occult. Through the years I have collected all but one piece of the lost spell. The last, missing fragment torments me. I know it is out there somewhere. It waits silently for me and me alone to find it.

I suppose there is no need to rush.

6

CAHILL UNIVERSITY WAS A SMALL
school set on top of a large hill. The grounds were well-tended
and the brick buildings were old. Classes were done for the day,
but a few students sat on the grass and the low, stone walls reading, talking, and enjoying the fall weather that they knew would
turn nasty in just a few weeks. A kid with dreadlocks played
an acoustic guitar under a tree. The guy in the CU sweatshirt
discussing politics with the pretty girl handing out flyers for an
upcoming rally assumed that his jokes about Congress distin-
guished him as the kind of witty, sophisticated, well-read college
man that babes found irresistible. In fact, the girl had little to no
interest in him. She was obsessed with a guy in her intro business class who got drunk at parties and then burped the entire
Pledge of Allegiance.

Uncle Kelsey parked the old truck in the university parking lot and got out along with Parker and Theo.

"I won't be long, guys," Uncle Kelsey said. "I just have to move some stuff in Hilliard Hall and stop by the administrative offices. They always have something for me to do over there. There's a snack bar where you can do your homework. They make pretty good chocolate-chip scones. Theo can show you."

He locked the truck.

"I'll meet you guys back here at seven. Try not to get in any trouble."

He winked at Parker, and Theo rolled his eyes.

Uncle Kelsey went left. Theo hoisted his book bag and went right.

"Do you want to wait for me, please?" said Parker, running to catch up with his cousin.

Both kids were glad to get out of the truck. It didn't have a backseat, so Parker and Theo and their book bags were crunched together with Uncle Kelsey in the front, and since Theo was barely talking to his cousin, the trip was awkward.

Parker caught Theo and they walked in silence. A Corvette drove by and Parker thought that he might as well try again.

He said, "Those are nice. A friend of mine in LA has one. We like to buzz up and down Hollywood Boulevard looking at girls. They have tons of power, but I like something a little more exotic, myself. I got to drive my buddy's Ferrari once...."

"Will you please shut up?"

Parker stopped walking. Theo continued for a few steps before stopping and turning to face him.

"I was doing all right, you know," Theo said. "Straight B's.

I made the baseball team. I'm not a starter, fine, but I'm on the team, and I'm *this* close to being able to hit the catcher from all the way out in left field, and people at school are actually starting to notice that I'm alive, but just when I finally, finally get something going for myself, you show up with all of your BS about Hollywood..."

"It's not BS!" said Parker.

"...and you ruin everything!"

Parker had never seen Theo so angry. He was turning red.

"Why couldn't you just stay in California?"

"I wanted to! You think I wanted to come live in Hick Town? I didn't have a choice!"

"Oh, that's right. A gang was out to get you."

Parker closed his mouth. He knew that the gang thing was far-fetched. What could he do? At the time, he was on a roll.

"You cause problems, Parker. Everywhere you go."

"That's ridiculous."

"Yeah? Do you remember the last time we were together?"

Parker did. Theo and his family had come to California to go to Disneyland when the kids were ten. They were all having a great time until Parker disappeared. Everyone was frantic looking for him, and his mom pulled in park security to join in the search. They eventually found him. He had sneaked into a cotton candy stand and had eaten so much of the stuff that he was rolling around in the bushes, clutching his stomach. They had to call it a day. Theo never even got to ride Space Mountain.

"Come on. That was years ago!" said Parker.

"And what about when we were nine and you pushed me off the roof?"

"I didn't push you! You jumped!"

"I jumped because you said if I didn't jump you would tell everyone I still wet the bed!"

"Okay, that was mean, and I never would have actually done that. Plus, it really wasn't that high."

"You always have to be in the spotlight. It always has to be The Parker Quarry Show."

"It's not my fault I'm charismatic!"

"Well, all I know is that my parents and I are happy living out here in the boondocks, and we don't need you screwing things up for us the way you screwed up your family."

That stung, worse than Parker ever would have thought. It brought up a lot of feelings that he simply didn't want to deal with. It hurt. Parker stared at his cousin for a moment. Then he turned and made a beeline for the nearest building.

"The snack bar is this way," Theo said.

As Parker walked, he took a key ring from his pocket and jingled it at Theo. "There must be something fun to do around here. It's a college."

Theo was stunned. "You stole my dad's keys?"

"I *borrowed* your dad's keys. I just want to do a little exploring."

"You can't do that! We're supposed to go get scones!"

Even Theo knew that was lame. He thought for a second and blurted out the nuclear bomb of threats.

"I'll tell my dad!"

Parker turned, ready to call his cousin's bluff. "Come on, Theo," he said with a grin. "No one likes a snitch."

Parker walked away. After a moment of indecision, Theo rushed to join him.

Against all logic and contrary to my better
judgment I have taken on an apprentice. Perhaps
I am growing feebleminded in my advanced age. I
am over three hundred years old, now. I think.

She calls herself Tarinn. She is a young girl,
an orphan. She considers herself a sorceress.
What she is is a pest.

She was sitting outside of my door. I assumed
she was begging for food or money. She was not.
She told me she was looking for the mighty
wizard that people in the city spoke of in
whispers. She wanted to learn. She offered
me her services as a cook and an assistant. I
pushed her aside gently, considering I could
easily have turned her into, say, a centipede,
and continued on my way.

She was there the next day. And the next. And
the next.

Last week I needed a fresh eagle's heart for a
particularly delightful potion. I was in a rush.
I had much to do. I always have much to do.

I stepped outside and Tarinn was, as always, there. Underfoot. In my way.

In my anger, I raised my hand to strike her, but when she gazed up at me, I paused. Everywhere I go, people turn their eyes from my ruined face. As if by instinct they seem to know I am a man best avoided. They fear and hate me. But this street urchin was not frightened! Her eyes were bright, and for a moment my mind was clouded by thoughts of my own daughters, dead now for centuries. I had assumed that I had banished all memories of my life as a farmer and a father, but now they came flooding back. After all this time, any feelings besides anger and ambition felt alien to me. Have I been so corrupted by the Nexus that I am no longer capable of feeling compassion?

I reached my hand down to her, and in an act of kindness of which I would not have believed myself capable, I pulled her from the gutter.

I made her an offer. Lodging and food, for her help with my experiments and study. She jumped at the chance and actually attempted to embrace me. I pushed her away, my mind clear once more. Tarinn is not my daughter. She is simply a tool in service to my goals. I will send her to do my chores, so I can more fully devote my mind to unlocking the treasures the Nexus still keeps at bay.

She thinks she will learn my secrets. She is mistaken. I will teach her worthless tricks and keep my true plans hidden. When she is no longer of use, I will destroy her or turn her back to the streets from which she came.

Maybe she will end up a centipede, after all.

7

PARKER PICKED A BUILDING AT
random and strolled in like he owned the place. Years of experience had taught him that was the key to getting into places he
didn't belong: act like you were supposed to be there.

Theo followed him. "Parker! Cut it out! We're going to get
in trouble!"

"We're not going to get in trouble."

It was an anthropology building, or maybe archeology. Parker
knew there was a difference between the two things, but he didn't
know what that difference was.

All he knew was that if he was looking for something interesting, and he was, he had come to the right place. The hallway
was lined with exhibits of old pottery and tools. Parker knew the
good stuff was around somewhere.

He stopped outside an office door and got out his keys.

As he worked, Theo started to sweat. "Stop it."

"I just want to take a peek inside."

"I'm serious, Parker. My dad could lose his job."

Parker found the right key. He slid it into the lock and put his hand on his cousin's shoulder.

"We won't get caught. It'll be okay, I swear. You're allowed to have a little fun. Theo, if you're this wound up at twelve, you'll be dead of a heart attack before you hit twenty. You have to learn how to enjoy life."

Theo thought this over. Finally, he nodded. He didn't really need his cousin's approval, but he didn't want Parker to think he was a wuss, either. The door opened and the kids stepped into the office.

"See, this," said Parker, "*this* is what I'm talking about."

Professor Ellison's office was a wonderland of fantastic stuff. The shelves lining the walls were overloaded with skulls, dusty weapons, and weird relics. The professor's desk was buried under teetering piles of unread mail and unopened boxes. No one had sat there for weeks.

Parker went right to the good stuff.

"Egypt, South America, Africa...There's stuff here from everywhere," he said, checking out a tiki idol almost as tall as he was.

Theo stayed by the door.

"Okay, Parker, you've had a look around. Can we please leave now, please?"

"Come on, buddy, hoist up your skirt and live a little. Where's your sense of adventure?"

Theo walked tentatively into the room. With the utmost respect for someone else's personal property, he looked over some ancient scrolls and a mad tangle of necklaces that seemed to be made out of gold and teeth. He shuddered at a dead monkey floating eerily in a jar of yellow formaldehyde.

"Creepy," he said.

Parker hefted a brass dagger and gasped when he saw a row of what could only be genuine shrunken heads. He got face-to-face with one. It was the size of a baseball. Its skin was jet-black, and its eyes and mouth were sewn shut.

"Too cool," he said. "Do you think anyone would notice if something went missing?"

"Yes!" Theo said, flicking the tag on a stuffed monkey. "It's all cataloged! Don't take anything!"

"I won't," Parker said.

Theo glared at him.

"I won't! I swear. Sheesh."

Parker put the dagger down and wandered over to a series of newspaper articles and Web site printouts taped to a wall. Some were torn and yellowed with age. Some were brand-new. He read the headlines aloud.

"'Disturbance in South Korea.' 'Strange Sighting in Istanbul.' 'Government Attributes Odd Reports in Tennessee to Methane Gas Leak.'"

Theo wasn't listening. He had found a door to another room and was checking to see if it was locked. It wasn't.

Parker squinted at an article featuring a grainy photo. It was a picture of a man holding some kind of a large metal cylinder. The photo had been crossed out with a red marker.

"'Tanzanian Miners Make Unusual Discovery.'"

Parker reached for the clipping. Just before his fingers touched it, he stopped. There were voices coming from outside the office door.

Tarinn has been with me for fifteen years now.
The time slips away like rain sloshing down a
gutter.

She has grown to be a capable and determined
woman, and she has surprised me by earning
my grudging respect. She is not my equal,
naturally, but she studies for long hours and
she has learned much. Perhaps someday she will
be something more than worthless.

For the first time in hundreds of years, I
have a source of true companionship. Against
my will, I find myself somehow drawn into
discussions with her of the nature of the
Nexus, and we argue over our differing views
of the power the Nexus affords. Tarinn grows
increasingly convinced that overexposure to
the Nexus erodes the soul, and that magick used
in anger will lead to one's own destruction.
What does she know about anger? She is naïve.
Perhaps when she has lived as long as I have,
her thinking will be more clear.

Always I search for the conclusion to Farrad's spell. Always it eludes me. This failure is beginning to affect my usually pleasant disposition.

8

PARKER AND THEO BOTH FROZE.
Then, with the reflexes of twelve-year-old boys caught someplace they shouldn't be, they both scrambled into the office's
back room.

The room was for storage, and it was a mess of boxes and racks.
They didn't have time to close the door, so Parker and Theo flat-
tened themselves against the wall. A black dread grew in the pit
of Parker's stomach. Less then a week in New Hampshire and he
was already in deep, deep trouble.

The door to the office opened, and Parker and Theo could
hear a woman escort a man in.

"Where did you say you found it?" the woman asked.

"One of the guys on my crew dug it up," said the man.

Parker and Theo heard the thump of something heavy being placed on the desk.

"At first we thought it might be an unexploded bomb from over at the shipyard, but one of my guys was in the army and he said that wasn't it. Myself, I think it's probably an Indian thing, right? Some kind of sacred idol or something? I don't know. Anyway, I asked around, and people told me this kind of thing is right up Ellison's alley."

Parker scrunched up his face. His curiosity was killing him. Theo frantically shook his head no, but Parker couldn't resist peeking out the door. He had to see the thing they were talking about.

He couldn't see the woman, but he saw the man's back. He was wearing filthy jeans and a paint-splattered shirt, and he was unwrapping a dirty towel from the thing on the desk. When the man shifted, Parker could see that it was some kind of a container, a metal cylinder about two feet long, covered with weird engravings half-buried under the patina that came from being buried underground for a long, long time. The ends of the object were capped.

Parker couldn't tell if it was just his imagination, but the thing seemed to be faintly glowing.

"It's an interesting piece, that's for sure," the woman said.

"I was wondering . . . I mean, you think maybe it's made out of gold or something? Do you think it's worth any money?" asked the man.

"It's not gold," the woman concluded. "Gold wouldn't tarnish like this. I couldn't tell you if it's worth anything."

The man turned around, and Parker ducked his head back just in time.

"The thing is..." the man said. "The thing is, that thing's weird. I mean, it acts strange. We had a devil of a time prying it out of the ground. The pick Tommy was using flew out of his hands when he hit at it, and none of us could really get a grip on the thing. It's like it's made out of magnets or something. I put it in the back of my truck, and my dog just sat there growling at it. It's just... weird."

"Well, like I said, the professor's away at a dig until Wednesday. If you like, you could just leave it here."

"That's fine by me. I'll be happy to get rid of it, to tell you the truth, even if it *is* worth a few bucks. Whatever that thing is, it gives me the creeps."

The woman led the man out and shut the door, leaving Parker and Theo alone in the office. Home free.

But one of the straps on Theo's book bag was caught on something. He gave it a mighty tug and pulled an entire rack of iron spears over. They clanged when they hit the floor, making slightly less noise than a plane crash might.

Parker and Theo braced for the worst, but they were okay. The assistant and the man had gone.

Parker smirked at Theo, who shrugged back. Parker went back to the other room as Theo started to pick up the spears.

Parker saw the metal canister on Professor Ellison's desk. He walked over and put his hand near the object before pulling it away. He couldn't stop staring at it.

In the back room, Theo struggled with the spears. He would

get them all upright, only to see one tip over into the next, causing all the spears to go down again. He was contemplating the idea of just leaving the stupid things on the floor when he noticed something strange about the wall behind the rack.

It was shimmering.

Not a whole lot, but walls don't usually do that at all, so even a little bit of shimmering is bizarre.

Theo reached out his hand, mesmerized. When his fingers touched the wall, Theo was blown backward as if he had touched an electric fence. He hit the floor on his back, the papers from his book bag flying around him.

Theo just stayed there for a moment, catching his breath. Then he got to his feet and crammed his homework back into his bag, never taking his eyes off that glistening wall.

He ran to the other room, where he found Parker zipping up his own book bag.

Theo grabbed his cousin's arm.

"We have to get out of here. Now."

"Right behind you," said Parker.

Parker turned off the office lights before he closed the door. The towel was still on Professor Ellison's desk.

The weird container it had once covered was gone.

The spell is mine!

In the commission of her daily chores,
Tarinn stumbled upon a tattered book that had
fallen into the hands of a novice wizard. The
intellectual titan had attempted to cast the
spell fragment but managed only to annihilate
himself in a burst of fire.

Tarinn handed me the book, triumphant. She
knows that I search for something, but in
our years together I have managed to keep my
true aims hidden. She thinks bringing me this
book will endear her to me. In fact, it only
underscores the fact that I no longer need
her.

I hold the book in my hands and I run my
fingers over its charred pages. I can feel the
strength that courses within. Soon, the world
will be mine.

I should have known that I could not keep my plans from Tarinn forever. I admit now I underestimated her hunger for knowledge. She grows more powerful every day, and I begin to suspect that someday her connection to the Nexus will rival my own.

She watched me for days as I pieced together the spell fragments, experimenting with different orders. Finally, she made her own calculations and realized what the spell was.

She was horrified. She tried to reason with me. Me, the great Vesiroth! She attempted to convince me that I am making a mistake and will grow to regret the path I have chosen, as if I had not spent centuries formulating my plans for a world at peace, with me as its sovereign. Tarinn could never understand the wisdom of my true goal. She once viewed the Nexus as an aid to mankind, but now sees it as a threat. She is convinced that no one can control magick this strong.

She is a fool. I have put all weakness behind me.

When she saw I had no intention of backing away from a lifetime of work, she snatched the pages from my table and ran to the fire. All reason fled from me. Furious, I cast a spell of binding that swept Tarinn up and violently pinned her high against a wall. My rage knew no bounds. The papers fell to the floor as I raised my hands again, intent on reducing my apprentice to ash. As the temperature in the room rose, Tarinn's eyes grew wide with horror.

In all the time Tarinn was with me, she had never shown fear in my presence. Tarinn alone seemed to see past the thing I have become and glimpse the man I once was. Now, she was like all the rest, cowering in the company of a thing driven past reason by dark magick.

What had I become? Was I truly now a monster, bringing nothing but sorrow to anyone who would dare approach me? I lowered my hands, and Tarinn fell to the stone floor with a thud. I gathered my papers while she crawled to the door. When I turned back, she was gone, and with her the last vestiges of anything within me that could be considered human.

I have no further need of her. I can run my own errands and cook my own food. Let her go back to her children's tricks and illusions. Simpletons like her should leave the real magick to men of vision.

I am Vesiroth. I stand alone.

9

PARKER DRANK A COKE AND PONDERED his next move.

He had been futzing with his stolen container for hours in his room, with his door shut and his blinds closed, in what might be considered to be a waste of a perfectly good Saturday. He looked at the mess he had made so far. A hammer, a rusty saw, and a monkey wrench were laid out next to him on the bed. He had tried banging on the canister, and sawing at it, and prying at the caps. Nothing worked. As far as he could tell, he hadn't even put a scratch on the thing. It just would. Not. Open.

He put the can of soda back on the table and hoisted the metal cylinder. Heavy, he thought. Well made. The endcaps turned, but no matter how much he tried, they didn't unscrew. The etched markings on the canister's sides were deeply grooved, and if you squinted at them, they glowed slightly green. What could make it do that? Emeralds, maybe? Whatever was inside there was something special, he just knew it.

He wiped his hands on his jeans and picked up a flat-head screwdriver. After a moment's consideration, he jammed the screwdriver's tip into the slight gap where one of the thing's end-caps met its body. He pried at it with all his might, but nothing happened. Well, if there was one thing that Parker had learned in almost a full half a year of junior high school, it was that sometimes what was called for was sheer brute force. He set the canister on the floor, inserted the screwdriver, and stepped on it, applying every ounce of his one hundred and eleven pounds. Parker thought that the cap actually gave a little, so he stepped down harder. Suddenly, an arc of blue electricity came off the thing. The lightning made a sound like a bug zapper as it traced the walls, floor, and ceiling of the room. When it touched the overhead light, the bulb inside exploded, plunging the room into darkness.

Parker took the screwdriver out and the lightning subsided. He was, frankly, more than a little freaked out. He could smell the burning ozone in the air.

He reached out to touch the canister again and there was a knock on his door.

"Parker? You in there?"

Theo. Why not? thought Parker. The guy did live here.

"Hang on! I'm..."

"You're what?"

Parker couldn't think of anything he might be doing that wouldn't make Theo suspicious, so he gathered up the canister and the tools, wrapped them in his blanket, and threw them on the bed. "Nothing. Come on in."

Theo opened the door to find Parker standing by the bed.

"What are you doing in here in the dark?"

"Just, you know. Thinking."

"Thinking? Thinking about what?"

"Just thinking."

Theo jammed his hands into his pockets and stepped carefully into the room. He spent a few moments looking around. There wasn't much to see.

"I got the keys back to my dad. He didn't even know they were gone."

"That's good," said Parker.

"Yeah," said Theo. "Yeah."

He walked over to the bed. Parker cast a worried eye down to his blanket, but Theo didn't sit. He turned to Parker.

"Look," he said. "I'm sorry about what I said yesterday and just, you know, about how I've been treating you in general since you got here. I know that what happened in your family wasn't your fault. It must be tough to move three thousand miles away from all your friends and your mom and everything that you know."

Parker was more than a little surprised.

"It is," he said. He meant it.

Theo ran a hand through his own hair.

"So, anyway, me and a couple of guys I know are going over to this go-kart track in Tramerville, and, you know, if you want, you can come along. If you want."

"Yeah! Great! Absolutely!" said Parker. "Just let me get changed."

Theo stared at his cousin.

"You don't have to wear a tux. It's a go-kart track. In *Tramerville*."

"Well, yeah, but still. There might be girls there."

Theo rolled his eyes.

"Fine. Whatever. I'll wait."

Before Parker could stop him, Theo threw himself down on the bed. He hit his elbow on something hard and grimaced. Theo's face fell.

"Parker," he said. "What's under here?"

I performed the ritual alone, near my new
lodgings deep in the empty desert. No one was
there to witness the greatest act of the world's
most powerful sorcerer. I need no audience. I
crave no glory.

I dug the pit and lined it with rare jade
as the book demands. I set the burning sulfur
in bowls of obsidian facing the north, south,
east, and west. I garbed myself in robes covered
in runes that were ancient even before this
continent had a name.

I fasted for nine days and nine nights,
sitting motionless by the pit's edge. When my
mind wandered, I dug a golden spike into my leg
to regain focus.

At midnight on the ninth day, I stood. My body
was weak with hunger, but my will was girded
with iron. There was no turning back. My time
was at hand. I would succeed where every other
man who had ever lived had failed.

I chanted the age-old spell. My eyes filled

with smoke as the words took effect. The ground beneath me shifted, but I was not deterred. When the moon reached its highest point in the night sky, I said the last words and I plunged the sword into the pit.

The earth responded with a roar and I was thrown through the air. I heard the low, moaning sound of pain, and I staggered back to the pit.

Through the gloom of smoke and the stench of hellfire, I saw him in his first moments of forming. He was shaped as I am, and he had the features of my face. He was clothed in robes as black as the blackest reaches of the night sky.

He rose before me, floating above the ground in a cloud of mist. He was a creature of untold power. I admit that even I was awed by the sight of him, and even I was visited by doubt. Was he a thing that could not be controlled? Had I created a beast that would destroy me? Was Tarinn right all along?

Then my creation bowed his head and in his first words called me "Master," and I knew that I would have my way. I named the genie Fon-Rahm.

The world is mine.

B66015
His power is immense.

He has the gift of flight, and he has dominion

over lightning and smoke. He can cause men
to overlook him as if he is not there. He can
conjure objects at will. Men are like insects to
him. He is a marvel of magick.

I have spent weeks inside with Fon-Rahm,
teaching him the ways of man. He learned
quickly, drinking information and knowledge
like a child drinks his mother's milk.

In many ways he is a child. My only child.

I find myself weakened after creating
Fon-Rahm. I assumed it was temporary, but my
condition persists. I will study my texts until
I find the cause.

It is a small concern. Soon I will bring my
genie out to the city, and all will know the
glory of my creation.

I really cannot wait.

B66027
He will not obey!

I called him into being from nothingness.
Without me, he was just an idea, an
impossibility, a dream that could not be
real. I am his creator, the most powerful
man to ever walk beneath the sun.

And he will not obey!

When I felt that the time for books and
schooling was over, I took Fon-Rahm into the
city. He looked with wonder at the buildings

that towered overhead. The achievements of man were fascinating to him, proof that mankind is a race of artists.

I know better. I know that mankind is a race of killers.

I waited, and I watched him explore. I knew that soon we would come across some tempting target.

And soon we did.

The soldiers were blocking the street. In their arrogance they assumed that there were none more important than those in their own ranks. Everyone else in the city was there simply to be bullied and spit upon. These were men just like the men who killed my family.

My time had come.

I smiled at my creation. Fon-Rahm had been called forth from the void to be my sword. With his might I would be ruler of all men. War would be a thing of the past.

I issued my command. Fon-Rahm was to wipe the soldiers from the face of the earth.

And he would not obey.

I spoke again, with more force. He was to kill these men, with no mercy. Their deaths would be an example to all armies of my awesome might. To defy me would bring about their destruction.

He would not obey.

Fon-Rahm spoke. He told me that he would not

kill a human being, any human being. He would not submit mankind to my rule. He said that man must be free to make his own decisions, for good or ill. A world ruled by a wizard was a prison.

I was enraged. I spit at him to do what I commanded. I was his master! He was nothing, a clump of sand in a hole I dug in the desert. He would bend to my will!

But he would not obey.

I heard laughter. The soldiers had heard my pleas, and they saw me, an old man with half a face, begging an empty space in the air to do his bidding.

Humiliated, I returned to my books with greater intensity than ever before. What had gone wrong? Why was my creation weak?

I found my answer. The spell demanded that I create Fon-Rahm using a shard of my own life force. A portion of the power that gives me life and energy was taken from me and went into the genie. It gave him life, and it gave him power that was no longer mine. That life force was charged with my thoughts and emotions at the exact moment it was transferred to my creation. In my excitement and naïveté, I had called on the most pure and incorruptible parts of myself, the memories of my wife and children, parts years dormant but not yet extinguished. I know now that Fon-Rahm represents me at my most merciful. Goodness and mercy were built into him, and they would always come before any commands to subjugate man.

I had failed. On every level, my creation was inadequate.

A rare misstep. I wash my hands of this pathetic creature. If this genie will not obey me, I will create another who will.

10

AS PARKER FAILED TO FIND AN explanation about the stolen container that would satisfy his cousin, a black Cadillac Escalade stopped at an intersection outside of Cahill. Another car pulled up behind it. The light changed, but the Escalade didn't move. The car behind honked, waited, and then pulled around the big Caddy and drove off.

The driver of the Escalade rolled down his window. He was a tall man with blond hair and deep, cold blue eyes. His jaw was clenched. He stared intensely out at the landscape as two passengers in the truck's backseat argued. Like him, they wore black suits with no ties. One was from Spain and the other from Thailand, but they spoke in a shared language any linguist would tell you had been dead for generations.

As their argument grew more heated, the driver raised his hand. His passengers instantly shut up.

The driver reached down and pulled a coat aside to uncover a tablet on the passenger seat. It was about the size of a laptop computer, and it seemed to be made of the same metal and to be from the same era as Parker's canister.

The driver closed his eyes and placed his hand over the tablet. Slowly, the metal plates on its surface began to rearrange themselves. When they stopped moving, the plates had formed an arrow that pointed to the right.

The driver covered the tablet and rolled up his window. The Escalade drove through the red light and made a right turn.

I returned to my pit and I chanted again.

I had learned my lesson well. This time I summoned the darkest and most cruel parts of my nature. I would not repeat the mistake I made with Fon-Rahm. This creature was to be cold-blooded and without mercy. He would follow my instructions completely, without pity for the deluded humans I was born to rule. He would respect the power of fear.

My new creation was born in a ball of fire, and as he rose to meet me, flames engulfed him. His robes were red. I was surprised to find that he, like Fon-Rahm, resembled me, but where Fon-Rahm adopted a look of deep contemplation, my new son wore a sneer.

He was perfect.

I called him Xaru. He and I will reign over this world. Men will cower in fear before us.

B66051

Xaru has proven to be every bit the student that Fon-Rahm was.

I am fascinated in the differences between my two creations. Fon-Rahm is always willing to give man the benefit of the doubt. He takes for granted the fact that man is, at his heart, good. Xaru scoffs at the idea. To him, man is an animal to be tamed.

Unlike his older brother, Xaru is not content to sit inside. While Fon-Rahm pouts in his corner, watching us like a chaperone, Xaru paces. He is restless. Energy radiates off him, and he seems eager to follow my every command.

He, like Fon-Rahm, calls me Master, but in Xaru I sense defiance and anger. I see him often watching the fire, delighting in the way it consumes everything it touches. I have told him to wait, that soon his power would be unleashed, but I feel his patience is coming to an end.

Xaru craves violence. He is far more my son than Fon-Rahm.

We are going to have lots and lots of fun together.

11

THEO STORMED OUT OF THE HOUSE.
Parker followed him, the canister cradled in his arms like a baby.
A heavy, weird, metal baby.

"I had to take it! It was like it was calling to me! It was like I was supposed to take it!" Parker said.

"You mean you were supposed to *steal* it?"

"Who said I stole it?"

"It's not yours, is it?"

"It was buried in the ground! It's not anybody's!"

"We have to take it back," Theo said. "Today."

"Just let me have a little time with it."

"Today."

"Let me get it open, at least. I won't keep it, I promise. This is something special. It's important. I just have to find out. If I give this thing up without ever knowing what's inside of it, I'll never think of anything else for the rest of my life."

Parker planted himself in front of his cousin.

"Let me keep it for the rest of the weekend," he said. "No one will even know it's gone until Monday. Come on. Please."

Theo shook his head. It was just like Parker, he thought, to put him in this position. Parker was the one causing all the trouble, and now he was making Theo feel guilty about doing the right thing.

Parker said, "We'll take it back on Monday before school. First thing."

Theo sighed. "First thing on Monday. You swear it?"

"Absolutely. You have my word."

Theo threw up his hands. "I guess that's okay," he said.

Parker smiled. He had always been able to talk his way out of stuff like this. It was a gift. Poor Theo never stood a chance.

Theo looked at the canister.

"Can I see it?"

Parker handed it over and Theo hefted it.

"There's a crowbar in the barn," he said. "Under the screw jars."

"Great!" said Parker. As he ran to the barn, Theo walked to the side of the house for his mountain bike. He cradled the canister in one arm and pushed off.

Parker saw his cousin stand on the pedals.

"Hey! Theo!"

Theo started down the long dirt driveway. Parker chased after him.

"You said I had until Monday!"

"Yeah," said Theo, building up speed. "I say a lot of things I don't mean."

Parker chased Theo down the driveway, past the mailbox, and onto the street. He got about fifty yards before Theo faded off into the distance, leaving Parker panting by the side of the road. The six-year-old girl who lived next door to the Merritts gawked at him from the seat of her pink-and-purple Disney bike. It had training wheels, laser streamers, and a white basket with pictures of princesses on the front.

Parker waved to her.

After months of silence, Tarinn came to me. She had heard of a demonic sorcerer that had gone mad in the desert, and wanted to assure herself it was not her old benefactor, Vesiroth. So nice to have company! I offered coffee and pastries, which she rudely refused, and with great pride I presented Tarinn with Xaru and his sulking elder brother, Fon-Rahm. I was sure that when she saw the majesty of my creations she would finally understand my work. Instead, she was horrified.

She felt her fears confirmed: I had gotten too close to the Nexus, and the exposure had driven me insane. She said she could see the change in me from just weeks before. This is, of course, ridiculous. Would a madman have accomplished such miracles? I have never felt more in control of my mind.

Tarinn was also different. Her brush with death had changed her. Her smile was gone, replaced with a look of grim purpose. She

shunned my genies and issued me a warning.
A warning! From a second-rate conjuror not fit
to change my sheets! She told me that if I did
not contain my genies, she would. As if she had
that kind of power! I am the great Vesiroth, who
cannot die. I was destined to crush this world
under the heel of my shoes.

I dismissed Tarinn, and she left me with one
glance behind her. Was it pity in her eyes, or
hatred? No matter. I need counsel from no peer.
With Xaru at my side I will be unstoppable.

When Tarinn was gone, I felt a weakness
well up inside of me. I collapsed to my knees,
and Xaru had to help me back to my room. The
transfer of power that had brought forth
Fon-Rahm and his brother has left me fragile
and in a pitifully debilitated state. The power
that is rightfully mine will remain in my
creations until they are destroyed, and they
will never be destroyed. They sap my potency
with their very existence.

No matter. There are only two. I have strength
enough to do what needs to be done.

12

THEO GRIPPED THE CANISTER UNDER his arm. It was awkward to carry, but doable, and he might as well get used to it. He was planning on going out for football the next year.

He did a double take when he heard Parker behind him.

"Come on, Theo! Wait!"

He turned, incredulous, to see Parker on Suzie McLanahan's bike, pedaling furiously.

Theo groaned. "Give it up, Parker. I've been running wind sprints all fall. I'm a trained athlete."

"Yeah, trained to sit on the *bench*."

Theo turned off the pavement and onto a dirt bike trail, picking up his pace and leaving Parker and his tiny, tiny bike in the dust.

Okay, that was a tactical mistake, thought Parker as he followed his cousin off road. Shouldn't have mentioned the bench.

As Parker pumped the bike's pedals, the black Escalade passed him going the other way, the two men in back still arguing in their dead language. The driver heard a scraping sound and uncovered the metal tablet in the seat next to him. The plates on the tablet's surface rearranged themselves again, this time pointing directly at Parker and Theo.

The driver slammed on the brakes. His unbelted passengers hit the backs of the front seats as he executed a perfect bootleg turn in the middle of the road. He turned onto the bike trail, lined the Caddy up with the kids, and stepped on the gas.

Parker was already winded. Too much TV and not enough physical exertion, he thought. He shouldn't have quit soccer. When he was nine.

As he huffed and puffed, Parker heard the black Cadillac pull up alongside him. Weird, Parker thought. The Escalade was bouncing over brush and rocks on a trail meant for bikes, not cars.

And it was getting awfully close.

The Escalade swerved slightly in at Parker, almost hitting him.

Parker slammed his fist into the side of the truck.

"Back off!" he screamed. "Share the road!"

The driver of the truck rolled down his window. He smiled apologetically at Parker, and then he stuck a machine gun out the window. As the driver aimed the gun directly at Parker's head, Parker began to wonder if there was anyone in the world who wasn't really, really mad at him.

I have created a monster.

As with Pon-Rahm, I took Xaru to the city. We soon came across a group of soldiers marching through the streets. I commanded Xaru to kill them. I held my breath, fearing that Xaru would be subject to the same weak-kneed pangs of conscience that afflict Pon-Rahm. I am pleased to note that my concerns were unfounded.

With one concentrated blast of fire, Xaru annihilated the soldiers where they stood. The very ground underneath their bodies was melted into glass from the heat.

As the ash that was once the soldiers floated into the desert sky, I turned my face toward my son, Xaru. He was smiling, content, and finally free to express his only purpose for being.

It was as I had hoped. Xaru has proven more than eager to kill. What I did not expect was that his zest for bloodshed would be more overwhelming than my own.

With no soldiers left to slaughter and my curiosity settled, I was ready to go home. I strode down the street, gratified to see the eyes of merchants cowering in their stores, terrified by the carnage following me.

But Xaru was not finished.

He turned his power on the witnesses. There was nowhere for them to run, and they died in shock. Then Xaru burned the buildings that lined the street. Fascinated, I allowed him to cut down the running peasants like the scum they were.

But then I saw three figures cowering by a pile of rubble. It was a mother, trying in vain to protect her two young girls from the destruction that rained down upon them. The woman turned her face to me, and a cold chill ran down the length of my spine when I recognized her. It was my own wife, somehow back from the grave with our daughters, and returned to me.

I shouted at Xaru to stop before my family was once again ripped from me in a wave of flame. My wife and daughters must be spared!

The look on Xaru's face was one of pure resentment. He obeyed my command, but it was clear he would as soon vaporize me for my insolence.

I turned back to the carnage, my eyes searching madly for my family, but they were gone. I ran up and down the ruins of the street, but I could find no trace that they were ever there. Did I really see them, or was this a cruel hallucination to mark my descent into madness? Was Tarinn right after all? Was I mad?

Xaru cast his eyes away from me. I must remember not to turn my back on Xaru. He is ruthless, single-minded, and filled with the lust for blood. He is just as I made him.

B67020
I can no longer restrain Xaru.

My will is weakened by his very existence, and I fear he has learned that my hold on him is uncertain. I made him too well.

He takes a perverse delight in killing, and it is clear that the city will become a slaughterhouse if he is not contained. My life's work is to be undone! Men were born to bow to me, not the genie Xaru!

If Xaru is destroyed, the life force I have placed within him will return to me and I will grow strong again. As much as I hated to lose such an exquisite creature of destruction, I felt it prudent to make the preparations that would cast him back into nothingness. I cast the spell, but it failed to strike even a minor blow. I am too weak. Xaru knows he has the upper hand, and he will soon come to the well-reasoned

conclusion that he does not need me at all.
Clever genie!

Tarinn was right. I have unleashed magick
beyond my control.

Fon-Rahm has vowed to do battle, but he and
Xaru are too evenly matched. Neither genie could
destroy the other.

I saw Xaru reading my ancient books. What
could he want with the knowledge within? I saw
the spell he wished to cast and I burst into
laughter. Xaru is indeed my son and heir. He had
been hard at work mastering the spell I used to
create him and his cursed brother, Fon-Rahm.

Xaru wishes to create genies of his own.

13

THE ESCALADE HIT A RUT AND bounced high on its twenty-two-inch chrome wheels.

The bike trail was rough going, but the Cadillac could take it with no problem. It had four-wheel drive and a beefed-up suspension, along with the V-8 engine, a huge navigation screen, and wood trim in burled walnut and olive ash. The men in suits had stolen a very nice car.

A car, however, even a car as dope as this car, could not be expected to glide smoothly over the rugged terrain next to this particular Cahill, New Hampshire, bike trail, and this car didn't. The bouncing threw off the driver's aim, and his shots thudded into the dirt harmlessly instead of blowing holes straight through Parker Quarry.

Nadir, the driver of the Slade, swore. Not out loud, of course.

He had taken a vow of silence when he had taken control of the Path, and he was not going to break it over some undersize American teenager in a Dodgers T-shirt. He swore to *himself*. He had expected the lamp to at least be stationary, buried still, or perhaps on the shelf of a museum too stupid to realize what they had, but now here he was chasing two children down a trail made for dirt bikes, not three-ton luxury trucks. This was getting annoying. Nadir was not a man who welcomed annoyances.

He shut out the yapping of the Path members in the backseat and swapped out a clip for his submachine gun. The gun had once belonged to a police officer in Illinois. The police there had executed a raid on Nadir and his men, thinking that they were part of a terrorist group. The police were right, sort of. Nadir was a terrorist, all right, but not like any terrorist the cops had ever seen. After the raid was over and all of the police officers were dead, Nadir took the gun. He liked guns and he hadn't been able to bring any of his favorites with him, airport security being so tight these days. He and his men had to dispatch the policemen with swords and knives, just like in the old days.

Parker rode faster than he ever had before in his life. He could hear the Caddy roaring ever closer when he caught up with his cousin.

Theo was stunned to see him. He figured he had left Parker in the dust when he turned off the main road.

Theo said, "What are you—"

He didn't get any further than that, because Parker rammed his bike into him, crashing both of them into the wide drainage ditch that ran next to the bike trail. They tumbled down the side of the ditch, smashing their shins and elbows on rocks and hard ground as they fell, tangled up in their bikes. When they landed, thought Theo, *if* they ever landed, he was going to kill Parker.

They landed, finally, knotted together in a cloud of dry dirt. The canister from Cahill University slid to a stop a few feet away.

Theo gasped. He was already furious at Parker, and that was before the jerk ran him off the road. He could hardly believe his cousin was that intent on keeping the stupid canister.

"You could have killed me!" Theo said. "You could have broken both my legs!" He wasn't in any actual pain, but that didn't mean he was okay. He was certainly scraped and definitely bruised.

And the worst part was, Parker wasn't even looking at him. He was staring at the top of the ditch, some six feet up.

When Theo asked, "What is wrong with you, Parker?" Parker had the gall to actually hold up his finger in a "please be quiet I'm on the phone" sort of way.

"They're coming back," he said.

Theo looked up, incredulous. "Who? What's going on?"

"I have no idea," said Parker.

On the bike trail, Nadir calmly stopped the truck. He and the other men got out. There was no hurry. The children were trapped, unarmed, and they had the lamp with them. There was no one else for miles. They could take their time to claim their prize.

The three men took their police-issue guns and walked over to the side of the trail. They peered down through the dust into the ditch.

Parker and Theo gawked backed at them.

Nadir smiled and raised his gun.

"I can't believe it," Theo said to Parker. "You weren't making it up. You really do have a gang after you."

Parker just gaped. Think of something, he thought. You're good at this. Talk your way out of whatever this was.

"Uh, look, guys," he said as the three men inched their way carefully down the side of the ditch. They clearly didn't want to mess up their suits. "I, um, think maybe you've made a mistake, here? I think maybe you're looking for somebody else and not us?"

He looked to Theo, who nodded.

"Just a misunderstanding of some kind, is what I'm saying. It could happen to anybody. But whoever the guys are you're looking for, I can assure you, it's not us. We're in the *seventh grade*."

Parker really thought that last bit would sell them. Nobody would kill a seventh grader with a machine gun. That would be excessive.

The men, now at the bottom of the ditch, looked at one another. One of them turned to another and said something in a language that neither Parker nor Theo had ever heard. The other guy laughed. Parker smiled. Maybe he had gotten through to them. Maybe they realized they had cornered the wrong guys. Laughter is the universal language.

"Great! So . . . great! Then we can go?" he said with all the hope of a girl being asked to the prom.

The men stopped laughing. Nadir shook his head as he aimed his gun at Parker and Theo.

"Parker!" said Theo.

Parker and Theo scrambled backward, but there was no place to go. They were going to be killed and left there, literally dead at the bottom of a ditch.

Parker, desperate, grabbed the metal canister. It was the only thing within reach that could possibly pass as a weapon, and even then, it was still just a metal canister.

"Get behind me! This will block the bullets!"

"I don't think it will!" said Theo.

The kids shut their eyes as Parker held out the canister.

The lamp, Nadir thought. Finally. It would be his. He aimed at Parker's head.

Later, Parker would wonder why he twisted the canister, and, more important, how he managed to turn the caps on the thing in the exact right way, in the exact right sequence, and then he would come to the conclusion that the thing (or really, what was *inside* the thing) had wanted him to open it and had somehow given him the combination. That almost made sense, when he thought about it later.

There in the ditch, though, he wasn't thinking about anything other than how great it would be if he and his cousin weren't going to die. He was hoping, really, deeply hoping that someone, or something, would save them. You might even say he was *wishing* it.

Chaos reigns in the city as the war between my
genies rages on.

Xaru has created an army of his own, ten
brother genies that obey him and him alone. Each
of his genies is, as he is, a clone of me, but
the farther they get from the Nexus, the more
twisted they become. They are copies of copies,
with each flaw magnified. One genie, I know,
has four arms, and two are horrible twins,
conjoined at the head. One is made entirely of
swarming insects. I hear talk of the others,
but alas, due to my constrained circumstances,
I have not been myself witness to them. There is
a rumor, spoken in hushed voices, that there is
one more genie, a genie that Xaru creates as I
write this. The last of his brothers will be an
abomination, a monster so grotesque as to turn
all those who see him immediately into glass.
Impressive! If this is true, he will be the
greatest power to walk the Earth.

How proud I am of my son Xaru! If not for
my condition, I would be standing beside him,
laughing as my fellow men are cut down by
fire and magick. Xaru is right! There is no
reasoning with humanity! They must be put down,
one by one, until their wills are broken and
they beg for mercy.

Fon-Rahm, the fool, stands with the humans.
He is brave but deluded. He cannot win against
Xaru's beautiful genie army. I can hear them as
they battle in the skies above the city, and I
can feel the ground shake as they trade mighty
blows. Buildings fall. Fires burn. Humanity
is doomed, no matter how valiantly my first son
strives to fend off the inevitable. Men will be
slaves, perfectly docile pets for their genie
masters.

Some even know that this is for the best. In
the West, a cult has sprung up based only on
spoken stories of Xaru and his brothers, a group
of fanatic men who worship the genies as gods.
I applaud their enlightenment. They may be the
only wise men left.

The specter of my dead family haunts me. They
follow me everywhere now, always in the shadows,
never saying a word but simply staring at me
with pleading eyes. They are in my chambers
even now. I try to talk to them, begging them

to forgive me for not saving their lives, but my voice goes right through them, as if I were the one that did not really exist. The sight of them tortures me, but my time grows short, and I suppose I will not have to bear it for much longer.

Word has reached me here that Tarinn has struck a deal with the sultan. He knows that his claims to power fade like smoke from a dying fire, and he is desperate to keep his hold on the city. Tarinn believes that she can trap the genies in metal boxes. She has no chance for success. Her sorcery is strong, but she is no match for my magnificent creations. Let her try and be destroyed with the others for her impudence.

Would that I could be there to see her extermination at the hands of Xaru and his genie army. But I remain rooted here.

Each genie that Xaru creates further takes a piece of my own life force. I, Vesiroth, immortal wizard of untold knowledge and might, am reduced to a state of living death. I move as slowly as the oldest man. Each gesture takes hours instead of seconds. It has taken me days to write this, my final entry before I am frozen like a stone statue for eternity.

My only wish now is to see the triumph of horror over mankind, but it will have to go on

without me. When Xaru completes his last genie,
all my life force will be gone from me. I will
be frozen, a living statue, able to think but
not to act. Soon, I fear I will no longer be able
to mov

*[TRANSLATOR'S NOTE: The author's handwriting here trails
off in an indecipherable scrawl.]*

14

THERE WAS A CLAP OF THUNDER. BOTH
Parker and Theo agreed on this, later on. They didn't mistake it
for gunfire, either, because it didn't sound like gunfire. It sounded
like what it might sound like if a bolt of lightning had struck
about, say, two feet in front of them.

They didn't see what happened, because both of them had their
eyes squeezed shut in the completely unfounded belief that what
they couldn't see couldn't hurt them, but they could still hear,
and what they heard were gunshots. Lots of gunshots.

Parker, pleasantly surprised to find himself intact and unshot,
opened his eyes first. It didn't help. The ditch was filled with
a deep fog so thick that Parker couldn't see anything at all. He
walked a step and tripped over the now-open canister. It was

empty. He looked up to see Theo inches from his face. Theo looked as confused as Parker felt.

They heard the men yelling in their strange language, and then more gunfire lit up the fog. One of the men screamed, and Parker and Theo ducked as the man was thrown over their heads. There was a loud crash, and then another loud crash, and then Parker and Theo mashed their hands against their ears as the air was filled with the excruciating sound of tearing metal.

Then there was silence. Parker and Theo rose slowly, waving their hands in a vain attempt to clear away the fog. They stepped over the remains of their bikes and climbed carefully out of the drainage ditch.

The air reeked of electricity. The smell reminded Parker of an old electric train his dad had set up to run around the Christmas tree when he was a kid. His mom eventually made him take it down, because she was afraid it was going to start a fire. It was dangerous.

Through the rising mist, Parker could just make out the three men in suits as they ran away as fast as they could.

Parker stared, his mouth open. Theo tapped him on his shoulder, and Parker looked where Theo was pointing. One half of the black Escalade was in the middle of the trail, and the other half was lodged in the top of a maple tree. The Cadillac had been torn in two.

"Um, Parker?" Theo said.

"Yeah?"

"What just happened?"

"What just happened. Well, there's got to be some kind of a

rational explanation, right? I mean, maybe there was some kind of an electrical storm that..."

Parker trailed off. He could feel, behind him, some kind of a presence.

He looked at Theo, and Theo looked at him, and they both turned slowly to see what was behind them.

There, in the thinning fog, was a motionless figure dressed in billowing black robes. Smoke drifted out of his eyes, and lightning crackled down his outstretched arms and off his fingers.

Theo nudged Parker and pointed. The figure was standing, if *standing* is the right word, two feet off the ground.

"Uh," said Parker. He couldn't think of anything to add, so he repeated himself. "Uh."

After what Parker assumed was two or three weeks, the figure finally moved. Parker and Theo gasped as he landed gracefully in front of them. The figure crossed his arms and took a step toward Parker.

At least we won't be shot, Parker thought. We'll be fried by a weirdo with lightning coming out of his fingers. That's something.

But instead of vaporizing Parker, the genie Fon-Rahm knelt on one knee. He gritted his teeth and spoke his first words in three thousand years.

"You have freed me from my prison," he said in a voice gravelly from disuse. "I am bound to you. I am in your debt."

Theo gaped at Parker, and Parker said the first thing that came into his mind.

"Uh," he said.

"Oh, man," said Theo.

Theo pointed once again. Reese was in the middle of the bike trail, wearing a sky-blue helmet and sitting on an electric-assist bike her dad had gotten her for Christmas. This was the first time she had ever taken the trail, which promised to be a shortcut from her class at the community college (Latin! Useful!) to her house.

With all of that extra schooling, it was no surprise that Reese could find the word that Parker was groping for.

"Wow," she said.

15

PARKER, THEO, AND REESE SAT ON THE
edge of Reese's bed and stared at the figure seated uncomfortably
in the purple beanbag chair.

The room was predominantly pink. This was not something
Reese could blame on her mother. Reese chose the color for the
walls, and she chose the dresser, and the bookcase, and even the
purple beanbag chair. In her defense, she was ten at the time. If
she had a chance to remake the room, Reese would throw out the
academic ribbons and trophies and paint the whole thing black.
That would show her mom. Of course, it would be an awful place
to sleep or read or talk on the phone. (Not that she talked on the
phone much. Who would she talk to?) But all that would really
be beside the point.

Reese supposed it didn't really matter. No one was ever in her room, anyway.

Until now.

"So you were trapped in that thing for how long?" she asked.

The genie shifted and pulled his robes away from his legs.

"Three thousand years. Give or take."

"And you don't want a sandwich or something?"

Parker looked at her like she had three heads.

"Really? We find an actual, swear-to-God genie, and all you can think to ask him is what he wants for lunch?"

"He's a fictional creature of Arabic folklore. What am I supposed to ask him?"

"Uh, where did he come from? Who were those guys that were trying to kill us? Why is he here?"

"These things would be beyond a child's comprehension," said Fon-Rahm.

"Who are you calling a child?" said Parker.

"This is so weird," said Theo.

They had debated what to do with the genie when they were still on the road. Theo wanted to call the police, but Parker wasn't super interested in explaining how he wound up with the canister in the first place. Besides, this was too good to turn over to somebody else. Even Theo had to see that. Reese suggested that they take him to her house. It was closest, and her parents were at work. They could hide out until they decided what to do. Parker readily agreed. Sooner or later, someone was bound to notice half a luxury SUV jammed into the upper branches of a tree and, quite frankly, he didn't want to be around to explain what happened.

The genie did not object when Parker told him the plan. Parker, Theo, and Reese got on their bikes and told Fon-Rahm to follow them, and he did. Parker looked back as they were riding and saw Fon-Rahm, his robes billowing in the breeze, as the genie glided over the trail. Parker had expected the genie to be looking straight ahead, but he was surprised to see that Fon-Rahm was actually staring directly at him. It made Parker uneasy.

They made it to the house with no problem. Now they were inside, away from prying eyes, and no one had the slightest idea what to say.

"You're a genie," said Reese.

"I am of the Jinn, yes."

"And we freed you."

Fon-Rahm raised a finger and pointed at Parker. "*He* freed me."

Parker perked up.

"Right!" he said. "I freed him! So he's mine!"

He turned to Fon-Rahm. "So how does this work? I get three wishes, right?"

Fon-Rahm sighed. He hated to say what he was about to say, but he had no choice.

"No," he said. "There is no such limit. I must do your bidding forever."

"I wish I could fly!" said Parker.

"I cannot make you fly."

"I wish I was bulletproof?"

Fon-Rahm closed his eyes.

"The scope of my power is boundless, but my ability to use it is not. Since you are my"—Fon-Rahm took a deep breath and practically spat the word out—"*master*, I cannot harm you, and I will not allow harm to come to you. I am compelled to obey you, but there are limits. I cannot change you physically. I cannot turn back time. If you see something you would possess, I can make it yours for a time. I can bestow knowledge in an instant, but it will fade in weeks or days. I cannot make another love you. I cannot change the human heart."

"Could you take out a few jocks for me?" asked Parker.

"Parker!" Reese said, appalled.

"I don't mean he necessarily has to *kill* them."

"I cannot harm an innocent on your whim."

"Can't or won't?"

"I will not harm an innocent on your whim. I will follow your commands, but I will not use my power for destruction and ruin."

Parker thought for a moment.

"Lame," he said.

"This is . . . This is . . ." Theo stammered for something to say. "It's unreal. Parker, do you realize what he's saying to you? You can have whatever you want. You can do whatever you want."

"That's true," said Parker. "I can."

There was a knock on the door. Parker, Reese, and Theo froze.

"Marisa? Are you home?"

Reese gasped.

"It's my mom."

"I thought you said she was at work!" said Parker.

"She came home! She does that after she's done working!"

Reese popped up and ran to block the door, but it was too late. Her mother pushed the door open.

Reese gasped. "Mom! I can explain!"

Reese's mother stood in the doorway and took in the scene. Reese knew she was done for. There were two strange boys on her bed and one exceedingly strange man sunk into a beanbag chair made to fit a ten-year-old girl. And, on top of everything else, Reese was supposed to be studying.

Grounded? No, not grounded. There wasn't a word for what was going to happen to Reese. Buried, maybe.

"Reese," said her mother, staring at Theo and Parker. "Who are these boys?"

Reese was surprised that her mother wasn't more upset.

"Uh..." she said.

"Um, I'm Parker? Parker Quarry? And this is my cousin Theo?"

"And why are you here?"

Theo raised his hand. Parker glared at him and he put it down.

"School project?" Theo said.

"Oh," said Reese's mom. "Oh. That's all right, I suppose."

She looked at her daughter, who was practically hyperventilating.

"It's fine, Marisa. You can have friends up here. I just want to know about it."

"Yeah. Okay."

Reese's mother looked back at Parker and Theo. "Do you want some carrots or iced tea?"

"No, thank you, Mrs...." Parker started.

"Lorden," said Reese.

"Mrs. Lorden. Thanks, though."

"All right. If you want anything, let me know." She turned to her daughter. "Don't forget. Viola lesson at six o'clock. Keep the door open, please."

And just like that, she was gone. She hadn't seen Fon-Rahm at all.

Reese quietly closed the door behind her.

Theo pointed to Fon-Rahm.

"You're invisible!" he said.

"I'm not invisible. If needed, I can ... encourage people to overlook me for short periods of time. It saps my strength, but it can be done."

"So ... you're invisible," said Theo.

"No," said Parker, fascinated. "People just can't see him."

He flopped backward on the bed, knocking a pink pillow onto the floor.

"Okay," he said. "Okay. So, first, I think we can all agree that this is something we need to keep to ourselves, right? I mean, this is *major*. This is the biggest thing since ... This is the biggest thing that has ever happened to anybody, probably. We can do whatever we want! We can be rich! We can rule the school!"

"I don't want to rule the school," said Reese.

"We can be rich!" said Parker.

"Stop," said Fon-Rahm.

The kids looked at him. Even squashed into a beanbag chair, Fon-Rahm was a commanding figure. His eyes gave off a faint blue light. He was stern and he was scary.

"I am Fon-Rahm, the first of the Jinn. When I was created, the mountains quaked and the skies turned black. I possess the might of ages. My power is a nation without borders. My eyes bring fear, and my hands, bolts of lightning. I could be the savior of the world or I could be its destroyer. I am not a plaything and I am not to be taken lightly. I will not be used for fun and trifling novelties."

Theo and Reese were suitably cowed.

Parker, however, sat up. He nodded thoughtfully at the genie and then broke into a grin.

"So," he said. "Have you ever heard of a Porsche 911?"

16

PARKER SKIDDED THE RED PORSCHE to a halt. Theo was thrown once more across the tiny backseat and into the window.

"Ouch," said Theo.

Fon-Rahm sat stoically in the passenger seat, staring straight ahead. His new suit fit him perfectly, unwrinkled even after Parker's insanity behind the wheel.

"You can relax now, guys," Parker said. "We're home."

Well, not exactly home. They were in some bushes in the middle of a field almost a mile behind the Merritts' house. Reese was already gone, dropped off near enough to her house so that she could get home on foot, but far enough so that no one she knew would see her get out of a hundred-and-fifty-thousand-dollar sports car being driven by a seventh grader.

She wasn't happy about it. It was going to be a long walk.

Parker and Fon-Rahm climbed out of the car, and Theo clawed his way out of the back. Theo was thrilled to be stationary. Until very, very recently, Theo never got carsick. Now he could barely look at the Porsche without getting dizzy. One more thing to thank his cousin for.

"Look at that!" Parker pointed at the 911. "Not a scratch on it!"

That wasn't even remotely true. The car was a mess. It was dirty and scratched, and one headlight had exploded when they landed their big jump over the cop prowlers. The jump had also seriously damaged the suspension, so the Porsche sat a little lower than it was supposed to. These little modifications made the car look like it was exhausted. If it were human, it might have sighed.

It didn't really matter. The Porsche was already disappearing, fading out of their existence and back to the Nexus. They could already see through the bumpers. In a few hours the whole car would be gone, leaving nothing behind besides tire tracks, confused policemen, and the smell of burned rubber.

"It's a shame we can't keep it," Parker said.

"No, it's not," said Theo. "You drive like a lunatic."

"I drive like a NASCAR driver." Parker turned to Fon-Rahm. "How long is that going to last, anyway? My new abilities, I mean."

"Days. Perhaps a week," said Fon-Rahm.

"When it fades away, I suppose there's nothing to stop me from wishing for it again."

Fon-Rahm gritted his teeth. "I suppose not."

"And I can always get another car. A Lambo next time, I think.

Or that Mercedes with the gull-wing doors. Of course, there's no backseat in either of those things. . . ."

"Good," said Theo.

Parker grinned. He had woken up with, let's face it, not a whole lot going for him. Now, here it was, less than ten hours later, and everything had changed. Everything he ever wanted was his for the asking or, more accurately, the wishing. From now on, things were going to go his way. He was exhilarated.

He was also wiped out.

"Let's go home," he said.

"Yeah, about that." Theo gestured to Fon-Rahm. "What are we supposed to do with him?"

"Way ahead of you, buddy. I got it all figured out."

Moments later, Parker, Theo, and Fon-Rahm were standing in the Merritts' old barn. At one time it had housed an imposing wooden cider press, and the sweet smell of apples still hung in the air. Now the barn was a catchall toolshed for Theo's dad. It was filled with long-handled rakes and pitchforks. There was a stocked workbench holding just about any kind of a tool you could possibly need, along with a half-finished remote-control plane that Theo's dad had tried and failed to get his son interested in. There was also a forty-year-old tractor that ran most of the time and a box of Christmas decorations that hadn't been touched in a decade.

Parker showed Fon-Rahm to an empty space in the corner.

"I guess you can sleep over here."

The genie stared through him. "I need no sleep," he said.

"Okay," said Parker. "Well, if you get hungry, I could leave you some . . ."

"I need no food."

"Water? Oxygen?"

"I am not alive in the way that you are alive. I am a creature of magic. You are merely flesh and bone."

"Yeah, well, I'm the boss of you."

"I'm going in," said Theo, looking warily at Fon-Rahm. "Are you sure he's going to be all right out here?"

"He'll be fine," said Parker. "He's a creature of magic."

Theo closed the barn door on his way out.

Parker yawned. "Okay, Fon-Rahm, get some rest. I have a lot planned for you and me."

"You try my patience, child. I am Fon-Rahm of the Jinn, not a toy."

"Whatever you say, Rommy old pal."

Parker put his hand on the barn door, but he stopped himself from opening it. He paused for a moment before turning back to the genie.

"What was it like? When you were in the lamp?" he asked.

Fon-Rahm contemplated this.

"It was like a dream," he said. "I could feel the centuries as they passed, but time itself was meaningless to me. It was, perhaps, like it was for you, before you were born."

The genie looked deep in thought.

"Now I find myself far from home, and in a world I do not fully understand. It is . . ." He searched for the word. "Difficult."

Parker knew the feeling. He was far from home himself, and often felt like he would never truly fit in.

He shook it off. He had an image to maintain.

"See you in the morning," he said. "Try not to destroy the world."

"You don't have much faith in me."

"That's true, but I wouldn't take it personally. I don't have much faith in anybody."

"Relying on others is not a sign of weakness. It is a sign of strength."

Parker shrugged.

"Huh. Well, great. I'll try to keep that in mind."

Fon-Rahm stood in his corner, his arms folded against his chest, as Parker walked outside and closed the barn door.

As he made his way to the house, Parker was struck with a sudden dull ache behind his eyes. He stopped and closed his eyes tight. The pain didn't go away. A headache, thought Parker; uncomfortable but nothing to worry about. If it got any worse he could always have Fon-Rahm conjure up some Advil.

He walked into the house through the kitchen door. Something was bubbling on the stove, and the whole house smelled like mashed potatoes. Parker pulled the lid off a pot to see what was inside, and he saw his aunt Martha sitting alone at the set table in the next room. She was Parker's mother's younger sister, but Parker thought she looked older. Her back was to him and she was talking on an old cordless phone.

"Why not?" she said. "When?"

She pulled absently at one of her apron strings.

"Well, get somebody else to do the double shift! He's expecting you to be here. I mean, it's Thanksgiving. . . ."

She turned her head to see Parker in the doorway.

"Oh! Parker!" She was suddenly all smiles. "Your mother's on the phone. Would you like to talk to her?"

Parker turned on his heels and walked away. He wasn't interested in hearing any more of his mother's excuses.

"Parker?"

Parker walked up the stairs to wait for dinner. His head was killing him.

17

THE ICE STRETCHED FOR MILES IN every direction, and a freezing wind cut through the barren plain. There were no trees or mountains or houses. The night held nothing but snow and the promise of a cold, cold death. It was forty degrees below zero.

The ice crunched under Nadir's boots as he stepped onto the tundra. He had been in the country for less than an hour. It had taken four flights to get to Greenland and, as he had slit the throats of the two Path members who were with him in New Hampshire, he had made the trip alone. The men proved worthless in the fight with Fon-Rahm. Worse, if they had survived they would have told their brothers in the Path about the fiasco, and Nadir could not let that happen. It would undermine his authority. It would show weakness.

He was angry with himself for losing Fon-Rahm. If he could have taken possession of the lamp, unopened, things would have gone much easier. Now the first of the Jinn was free and would have to be dealt with accordingly.

Nadir was not worried. Fon-Rahm was bound to a child. It would be no great challenge to defeat him.

Especially since the discovery here.

In the near distance, six men stood in a circle. They were bundled up in boots and thick gloves and coats with fur hoods. They carried picks and shovels, and one had a chain saw. As Nadir approached them, he could see their breath in the air and he could hear their teeth chatter.

The men stepped aside so Nadir could see what they had found.

It was a block of ice the size of a refrigerator, cut from the ground nearby. Inside, Nadir could make out some dark object.

Nadir pulled the guiding tablet from a bag on his shoulder. The metal plates on its face slowly worked themselves into a new pattern. The arrow pointed directly at the frozen object. Nadir put the tablet away and nodded. He stepped back as one of the men started the chain saw and cut into the block of ice.

When the lamp was free, two of the men placed it on a low stone altar set up on the ice. Nadir ran his hands over the metal cylinder. At last, his destiny was to be fulfilled.

Nadir raised his hand slowly and pointed to one of the men. The man nodded solemnly and stepped forward. He stripped off his winter clothes and donned a purple robe covered in ancient runes. Shivering, he knelt before the altar. He offered up a silent prayer and placed his trembling hands on the lamp. He twisted the ends first one way, and then another, until there was an audible pop and the hiss of escaping gas.

The man's face flooded with fear. The lamp opened with a roar and a storm of orange flame. Instantly, the sky was ablaze. The men turned away, their eyes burning. Some fell as the ground melted beneath their feet. Only Nadir kept his gaze fixed on the hurricane of fire in their midst.

The fire died down. Again the air was calm. When the smoke lifted, the genie Xaru hovered above the altar. His features were sharper than Fon-Rahm's, and where Fon-Rahm's robes were black, Xaru wore a brilliant crimson. He was like a more feral version of his older brother. At the sight of him, the men of the Path threw themselves to the ground in worship.

The man kneeling at the altar looked to the reborn genie, terrified. Xaru peered down at him, suppressing a sneer.

"You have freed me from my prison," he said. "You have my eternal gratitude."

The man simply whimpered.

Xaru looked to Nadir, power recognizing power.

"Of course, I am now bound by magic to do this man's bidding, and I am prevented from causing him any harm. While he lives, I am nothing but a slave."

Nadir nodded to one of his confederates, and the Path member presented him with a wooden box, lacquered black, its corners blunt from centuries of use, an image of a grinning skull carved into its lid. Nadir set the box on the ground, removed the rusting metal pin that held the lid closed, and reached inside.

He pulled out a small glass vial stopped with an age-old cork. The liquid inside was thick and oozy and as dark as tar.

As Xaru looked on, curious, Nadir removed the cork and let a single black droplet fall to the ice.

After a moment, the drop began to move.

The trembling man at the altar bowed his head. His whispered prayers grew louder as the black droplet creeped toward him. By the time it disappeared under his robe, his eyes were wide with terror. Soon, his legs were coated with the vile stuff. He swatted at himself, half mad with panic, as it engulfed his chest and arms, and his last scream was smothered when the black tar covered his face and his head.

Then, somehow, the goo began to contract. The kneeling man, now a writhing shadow, grew smaller and smaller. Finally, he was still, and all that was left was a single droplet staining the ice black.

Nadir put the opening of the vial on the ground, and with his finger drew an ancient symbol in the ice. At his command, the droplet rolled back into the glass tube. He replaced the cork and put the vial back into its box.

Xaru smiled, now truly free.

"That's so much better," he said to Nadir. "I can hardly wait to get started."

18

WHEN HE OPENED THE BARN DOOR the next morning, Parker found Fon-Rahm standing in his corner, arms folded against his chest, exactly as Parker left him. The genie had literally not moved a muscle.

"Good morning, sunshine. I would ask you how you slept, but you don't sleep. I didn't have a great night, myself. My head was killing me. I feel better now, though, thanks for asking."

Fon-Rahm stared straight ahead.

"Okay, then," said Parker. "Here's what's going to happen today. Theo and I promised my aunt Martha that we would run to the store with her to pick up some perennials, whatever they are, and after that, you and I are going to get up to some serious wish-granting. I have been toying with the idea of a helicopter."

Fon-Rahm seemed distracted. He didn't even appear to be listening.

"You with me, buddy?"

Fon-Rahm said, "Something has happened."

"Wow. Here's a command for you: be less cryptic. *What* has happened?"

"I do not know. Something has changed. The balance in the Nexus has shifted."

"Okay, I'll bite. What's a Nexus?"

"It is the force of magic that surrounds Earth. I sense dark waves on the horizon."

"Oh. Well, in that case..." said Parker. "No, I still don't care. I'll see you in about a half an hour."

Parker left the barn. His headache returned the second he shut the door behind him.

"Come on, Parker," said Theo. He was waiting with his mother in the driveway in front of a ratty Subaru station wagon.

"I'm coming, I'm coming."

With each step Parker took toward them, however, his headache got worse. By the time he reached the car, he was pressing his palms into his eye sockets to try to relieve the pressure.

"Parker?" asked his aunt Martha. "Is something wrong?"

"No, I just...I'll be okay. My head hurts."

"It's probably allergies. People who aren't used to the country get them."

Theo got in the car. Parker opened the door to the backseat and grimaced when he climbed in. His aunt looked him over.

"Maybe you should go inside and lie down for a while."

"But..."

"Go, Parker. Theo? Why don't you stay with your cousin? There's some allergy medicine in the bathroom."

Theo grumbled and got out of the car with Parker. As soon as Aunt Martha drove off, Parker collapsed onto the driveway.

"Jeez, Parker, are you okay?"

"The barn," Parker said.

Theo helped Parker to his feet. As they neared the barn, Parker's headache vanished. They swung open the barn door to find Fon-Rahm rising from the ground, recovering from a headache of his own.

The genie looked at Parker.

"You, as well?" he asked.

A half an hour later, Parker, Theo, Reese, and Fon-Rahm were standing under the uprights in the visitors end zone of the Robert Frost Junior High School football field. It was set behind the school, hemmed in on one side by hills. It was also deserted on a Sunday morning, which made it perfect for an experiment like this one.

"I don't know, guys," Reese said, scrolling through a Web site on her phone. "I can't find anything anywhere about genies and their masters being attached by the head."

Parker and Theo stared blankly at her. Boys, thought Reese. Really.

"You two didn't even consider Wikipedia?"

"I do not know what knowledge this Wikipedia contains, but the spell that binds me to Parker has clearly also created some kind of a tether between us." Fon-Rahm turned to Parker. "My suggestion is that you walk down this shorn meadow...."

"It's a football field," said Theo.

"This football field, then, until the pain forces you to stop. That way at least we will know how far apart we are permitted to go."

"That's not a bad idea, Rommy," Parker said. "But, of course, losers walk."

Parker pointed to the other end zone. Fon-Rahm rose off the turf and began to float slowly down the field. Reese counted off the yards as he went.

"Ten. Twenty."

"My head already hurts," said Parker.

"Thirty. Maybe he should slow down a little."

Parker rubbed his temples.

"Wow. Yeah, it's getting much worse."

"Should we stop?" asked Theo.

Parker said, "Uh-uh. We have to know."

The pain was obviously getting very bad for Parker. He clenched his eyes shut and began to sweat.

"Forty. Fifty."

"Okay. That's enough," Theo said.

"Sixty."

Reese was starting to sound as nervous as Theo.

Parker fell to his knees. In the distance, Fon-Rahm tripped out of the sky and landed on the grass. The genie struggled to his feet and continued on foot, slowly and in great pain.

"Seventy."

"That's it," said Theo. "Call him back!"

Parker gritted his teeth.

"Just a little bit farther..."

"Seventy-five."

Reese sounded more than a little panicked. Fon-Rahm began to weave. He was continuing on willpower alone.

Parker dropped to all fours. Theo ran to his cousin. By the time he got to him, blood was running from Parker's nose and ears.

"Fon-Rahm!" Theo screamed. "Come back!"

He yelled to Reese.

"Make him come back!"

The genie was no longer moving. He was collapsed eighty yards down the field.

"Reese! Help me with him!"

Reese ran over. She and Theo each grabbed one of Parker's arms. They dragged him as quickly as they could down the field toward Fon-Rahm. As they got closer to the genie, the pain in Parker's head began to go away. They reached Fon-Rahm and they all fell in a heap, spent.

Reese studied the genie's face.

"Fascinating," she said. "What do you think would happen if you got farther apart than that?"

Fon-Rahm and Theo just stared at her.

Parker said, "Let's hope we never have to find out."

19

THE PUCK SLAMMED INTO THE GLASS right in front of Parker's face. Theo and Reese both flinched, but Parker kept right on smiling. Fon-Rahm looked like he would rather be back in his lamp.

"And this is what, exactly?" the genie asked, gesturing to the ice stretched out in front of them. "Another football field?"

"Close! Good, Rommy!" Parker said, nodding his head approvingly. "Actually, what this is is a hockey rink. People put metal blades on their shoes, like so." He held up his new ice skates. "So they can go really fast, and then they use sticks to push a hard piece of plastic into a net." He gestured at the goal.

"Ah. It is a waste of time."

"Nailed it in one," said Reese.

Parker shrugged. "Maybe. What I just said is literally one hundred percent of everything I know about hockey."

The rink was vast, with high ceilings and mainly empty bleachers lining the sides. The floors off the ice were concrete and covered with black rubber mats. The plexiglass topping the barrier that surrounded the rink was cloudy and scratched. It was a classic rink, open since the fifties, and it had been home to countless hockey games, birthday parties, skating lessons, and first dates. There was a snack bar that sold Snickers bars and popcorn, and a pro shop where you could buy gear and get your skates sharpened.

It was so cold inside the building that the kids could see their breath. Fon-Rahm, of course, didn't breathe.

"Then why are we here?" he asked.

Theo said, "Because those jerks are here."

He pointed at the guys finishing up their hockey practice on the ice as they gathered in the center of the rink and took off their helmets. They were the jocks that had tormented Parker on his first day of school. The goalie took off his mask and shook the sweat out of his hair. Then he turned to the bleachers and nodded at a group of bundled-up eighth-grade girls watching from the bleachers. Caitlyn Masters, the redhead Evan had been after all year, turned and whispered something into the ear of a friend. Evan smiled to himself. Caitlyn was having a party later that night and, if he played his cards right, he just might be able to get her alone for a couple of minutes.

"Why, hello, Evan," Parker said.

Theo shook his head. "Let's grab a seat," he told Reese. "This is gonna be good."

The Robert Frost Junior High hockey coach was a patient guy. He liked kids, mostly, and he *really* liked hockey. He had, in fact, briefly played minor league hockey for the rough-and-tumble Syracuse Crunch, but he spent a lot of time on the bench, and he hung up his skates when he realized that if he couldn't start for the Crunch he was probably never going to play left wing for the Canucks. He brooded about it for a few months, but then he met Debbie and bought the place in New Hampshire, and he never looked back. He kept in shape by running laps at the school, he built a deck for the house all by himself, and things had worked out pretty well at the tire shop. Plus, he got to spend his free time teaching kids the game he loved. Not so bad at all. Coach Decker was that rare guy who was completely content with his life. Let the other idiots break their necks trying to get rich and run the rat race. He thought he had it all, and on occasion, he *acted* like he thought he had it all.

He blew his whistle and skated out to his boys. "All right, you doorknobs, let's wrap it up," he said.

Parker finished lacing up his skates and turned to the genie. "Okay. Wait till I give you the signal."

"What is the signal?" Fon-Rahm asked, genuinely confused.

"Um, I'll go like this." Parker shot imaginary guns with both sets of fingers.

"Ah. And where shall I be?"

"Close! The whole effect will be ruined if my head explodes."

"I concede the point."

Parker put on heavy gloves and hobbled to an opening in the wall. He had been on skates once before, with his father, but he was just a little kid then. The only thing he remembered about that whole day was the cup of hot cocoa his dad had bought him after. That was right before his dad took "the job" that turned into "the trial" that turned into "the jail."

Now he placed his left foot gingerly on the ice. It immediately got away from him, and he had to wave his arms in the air to keep from going straight down.

"Poor Parker," said Reese, settling into her seat.

"Yeah," said Theo. "He's not the most coordinated guy in the world."

Parker balanced himself on the wall. "Here we go," he said, and he pushed off.

"Oh, come on. What the"—Coach Decker glared at him, so Evan changed his sentence midstream—"*heck* is this jerk doing?"

The other guys snickered.

"Hi!" said Parker, slipping on the ice. "Whoops! Sorry!"

"Can I help you?" asked the coach.

"I'm Parker Quarry? I'm here to try out for the team!"

"Are you kidding me?" said Evan.

"All right, guys, just . . . I'll handle this." Coach Decker turned to Parker. "Tryouts were last week. We're already practicing."

"Yeah, but I'm new! I just found out about it."

"I would love to let you try out, really, but it just wouldn't be fair to the other . . ."

"Let him try out!" said Evan.

Coach Decker sighed. "Evan, come on."

"No, he's right! We should give him a shot. You don't know. He might be the next Sid Crosby!"

"More like the next..." Evan's friend searched his brain for a good person to compare Parker to, but he had nothing. "The next *loser*."

"Yeah, um, it's Parker, right?" said the coach. "I don't mean to be harsh, but have you ever played before?"

"Nope. But I was watching you guys, and I have to say, it doesn't look all that tough."

A wise guy. Coach Decker knew the type, and he knew how to deal with it.

"All right. You want to try out, let's do it."

"Great!"

Caitlyn Masters and the other girls in the bleachers laughed as Parker lurched on the ice. He managed to stay upright, but just barely.

The coach touched Evan on his shoulder. "Get in the goal." Evan put his mask on and skated gleefully to his spot. "Parker, I'll tell you what we're going to do." He put his hand on Parker's back, causing another near wipeout, and dropped a puck in front of Parker's feet. "Evan's going to stand in front of the goal, and all you have to do is give this puck a whack with your..." He saw that Parker didn't have a stick. "Coleman! Give Parker your stick."

Coleman handed it over. "Ah, man, it's brand-new. I got it for confirmation."

Parker took the stick and used it as a prop to keep himself standing.

"Hit the puck into the net," said the coach. "That's it. You make three goals, you're on the team. Do you think you can do that?"

"I'll do my best, Coach!"

"All right. Good luck!"

Parker grinned and held out his hands out awkwardly, trying to signal Fon-Rahm, but was stymied by his bulky gloves.

The coach said, "Um, what are you doing?"

Parker scanned the arena in search of Fon-Rahm. "I'm, uh, shooting you with imaginary guns."

"Why?"

"It's, um, it's a signal to…for…" Parker broke into a cold sweat. The girls in the stands laughed and pointed as he craned his neck looking for his genie. Without Fon-Rahm, Parker was just a moron in for the humiliation of his life. He would never live it down. Where could the genie have gone? Finally, Parker leaned his head back and spotted Fon-Rahm twenty feet in the air directly above him. Parker waved to the genie madly. This caused him to lose his balance for good, and he went down hard on the ice.

"Ouch!" said Theo.

"That's going to leave a bruise," said Reese.

The girls roared, and Evan grinned behind his mask. This was almost too good.

Parker struggled back to his feet, peeled off his gloves, and gave Fon-Rahm the signal just as his legs went out from under him and he felt himself going into what would be an incredibly uncomfortable split.

This time there was no missing it. The genie nodded almost imperceptibly, and Parker's legs stopped moving out. He straightened himself up and slowly put his gloves back on. He grabbed the stick, held it out to gauge its balance, and slapped it down on the ice.

"Okay," he said. "Let's go!"

With that, Parker swung the stick back and drilled a shot bullet-straight at Evan. It came in so fast that Evan, scared, dove out of the way. The puck caught the center of the net and dropped to the ice.

The arena was silent. Then a lone voice came from Caitlyn Masters.

"Holy crap!"

Evan pushed himself to his feet. He grabbed the puck from the net and slapped it back to Parker. "I thought you never played before!"

"Yeah!" said Parker. "But I think I'm getting the hang of it!"

Theo looked over at Reese. She was watching Parker, rapt. "I can really skate, you know," he said, turning red the second the words left his mouth. "I mean, without using magic."

Reese smiled at him. "I'll bet," she said.

Coach Decker motioned to three of his players. "Get in there and play some D." They skated out, ready for Parker's next attempt. Parker looked them over and began to skate in slow, lazy, clockwise circles. Then, when he was good and ready, he broke fast to his right, his skates spitting frost as he deked past one defender after another, finally speeding past the goal and slipping the puck in, untouched, past Evan's reaching pads.

The girls started to cheer, and Parker raised his hands in triumph as he took a graceful victory lap on one leg.

Theo couldn't help but smile at the kid's bravado. Theo himself would never be able to muster that kind of guts.

"All right. Everybody on the ice," said the coach. "Everybody. Whitten, Spinelli, everybody!"

The entire team took to the ice. Parker raised his eyes to Fon-Rahm and broke into a huge smile. So. Much. Fun.

When Coach Decker blew his whistle, guys came in from all sides. With the genie hovering unseen ten feet overhead, Parker glided elegantly down the ice, faking one way and then going another, flipping the puck with amazing dexterity as he literally skated circles around his defenders. He saw two Robert Frost Fightin' Poets coming at him from opposite directions, and put on the brakes so quickly that they ran into each other. He stopped and actually gave the puck away to one of the eighth graders, only to steal it back and leave the kid flat on his butt on the ice. He destroyed an entire team, little by little making his way to the goal. When he got there, he raised his stick for a slap shot. Evan buried his head in his hands, waiting terrified for the shot to blow past him. Instead, Parker tapped the puck with the utmost gentleness, and it slid delicately into the goal.

The jocks deflated. They were beaten—worse, they were *dismantled*—by a seventh grader. From *California*.

Parker skated balletically to the wall. Before he climbed off the ice, Coach Decker grabbed him.

"Where are you going? You made the shots. You're on the team! Parker, I'm telling you, I have been around hockey my entire life, and I have never seen anyone play like you. You're going to be the greatest of all time. Better than Robitaille! Better than Guy Lafleur or Bobby Orr or Espo! Better than *Gretzky*! Evan, get this kid a jersey!"

Evan hung his head and skated for the bench. He wouldn't be going to Caitlyn Masters's party tonight. He might not even be going to school tomorrow.

"No thanks, Coach," said Parker as he joined his giggling friends outside the rink.

"What? Why not?"

Parker shrugged. "I think I might take up basketball."

Theo and Reese laughed out loud as Parker unlaced his skates, but Coach Decker was crestfallen. His life was changed forever. He was no longer content, and he never would be. He had lost the greatest hockey player in history.

20

THE NEXT FEW DAYS WERE THE BEST of Parker's life.

He still had to go to school, sure, and with Fon-Rahm hanging around mopey, unseen, and always within ten or twenty yards, that was a bit of a drag. Still, the genie came in handy. He produced correct test answers with only a whispered wish from Parker's lips. He gave Parker the ability to dunk a basketball in gym, stunning the teacher into a stupored silence. He guided Parker's brush in art class, producing a perfect likeness of the hottest girl in school. For the first time in years, Parker really enjoyed the process of learning.

The best stuff, though, happened after school was done for the day. Parker, Theo, and Reese had a blast coming up with new and increasingly more ridiculous uses for Fon-Rahm's power. They stocked up on all the trendy gadgets they could stuff into their closets without getting caught. They jumped off a bridge a hundred feet over the Merrimack River, using only Fon-Rahm's magic as bungee cords. Parker laughed as his beloved Dodgers crushed the Boston Red Sox 31–0 at Fenway, hitting home run after home run directly into his and Theo's gloves in the stands. They tore through the woods, playing paintball on souped-up Segways. Parker learned Spanish, Italian, Greek, and even won an argument with Reese in Latin. When Theo wished for an entire outfit of Ed Hardy clothes, Reese and Parker laughed so hard they thought they might pass out. They had a never-ending supply of milk shakes and Doritos and tacos without getting sick. The only things holding them back were the parents, aunts, and teachers, who would suspect something was seriously wrong if they didn't keep everything hush-hush, and the constant scowl on Fon-Rahm's face that reminded them that the genie was not sharing in their fun. At all.

Parker, Theo, and Fon-Rahm walked into Theo's house. They had spent the afternoon watching Theo use his new instant guitar-shredding talent to shut up the guy in the guitar store before dropping Reese off and heading home.

"Maybe we should leave him in the barn," Theo said, nodding at the genie.

Parker poured himself a glass of water.

"I'd just as soon keep him close. You never know when we might need him for something."

Theo's dad called to them from the next room. "Theo, Parker, come in here for a minute."

Parker and Theo exchanged looks before walking into the living room. Fon-Rahm stayed by the door.

Uncle Kelsey was sitting in a battered but insanely comfortable old easy chair.

"We have a visitor," he said. "Theo, you remember Professor Ellison."

Professor Ellison sat with her back to Parker and Theo on the couch. She turned to the kids.

"Hello, Theo," she said. "Who's your friend?"

Busted, thought Parker. Busted hard. Busted bad. Busted in new ways he had never even been busted before. Busted, busted, busted.

Uncle Kelsey said, "That's Parker, my wife's sister's boy. He's staying with us for a while."

Professor Ellison smiled. If Parker had expected a rumpled old academic, he couldn't have been more wrong. She was an elegant older woman, maybe sixty years old, with long limbs and expensive clothes. Her eyes were a cold gray that matched her perfectly styled hair. She owned the room. The couch was old and covered with a poorly made quilt, but it might as well have been a chaise longue at a five-star hotel's pool.

"It's nice to have family," she said.

"The professor and I were just talking about security at the university. She was telling me that some things have turned up missing from her office."

"Really?" Parker said. "That's weird."

"What did you say was taken, Professor?"

"I don't know about *taken*," she said. "Let's just say it was misplaced. It's nothing to get too worked up about, anyway. Just a worthless artifact someone dug up a few miles from here."

She stared at the boys.

"A metal canister, about yay big. I don't suppose you lovely boys have seen it floating around, have you?"

Busted busted busted busted busted

Theo stammered. "Us? No. Nope."

"It was a long shot, I admit, but you never know. Sometimes missing objects turn up in the strangest places."

Parker felt himself turning red. When the professor suddenly stood, both he and his cousin jumped.

Professor Ellison shook hands with Uncle Kelsey.

"Thank you, Mr. Merritt. We'll discuss the new locks and so forth at your convenience."

"Whenever you're free."

"Such a charming man." She turned to Theo and Parker. "Theo. It was nice to meet you, Parker."

Parker didn't even realize he was holding his breath until Professor Ellison walked to the door and he let it out.

"Oh, Theo," she said, turning back around. "I almost forgot. You might need this."

The professor reached into the Louis Vuitton bag she carried with her everywhere and handed Theo a piece of paper. It was one of his old science homework assignments. His name was right on top. It must have fallen out of his bag when everything went flying in the professor's office. He got a C on it.

Professor Ellison stared at him. "Study hard, Theo. The world needs more great thinkers."

As she walked past Fon-Rahm on her way out the door, Professor Ellison froze. Impossibly, she knew that something was there. She whirled on Parker and Theo, furious.

"You let him *out*?" she screamed. "Are you insane?"

Parker and Theo turned white.

Uncle Kelsey was confused.

"Um, what?"

Professor Ellison took a deep breath and got herself together.

"Sorry. I thought the . . . cat had escaped."

Uncle Kelsey said, "Oh. We don't, uh, have a cat."

"Just as well." She looked at Fon-Rahm. "They're nasty beasts."

She glared at Parker and Theo for a moment before Uncle Kelsey walked her out of the house.

Theo panicked.

"She knows! She knows!"

Parker shrugged with false bravery.

"So what?" He looked to his genie. "There's nothing she can do to us."

Later, back in her office at the university, Professor Ellison dropped her bag on the desk and walked into the back room. She pushed the rack of spears aside, exposing the shimmering wall that had knocked Theo for a loop. She muttered an ancient phrase under her breath and reached out. As she touched the wall, her hands disappeared up to her wrists.

She pulled her hands apart, and the wall parted as if it were a curtain. Behind the wall, floating in midair, were four more metal containers just like the ones that once held Fon-Rahm and Xaru.

Professor Ellison took one of the lamps and turned it over in her hands. She was profoundly worried.

21

PARKER SLID THE MONSTER TRUCK TO a stop.

It was a black-and-silver beast, easily ten feet off the ground. The tires alone were taller than Reese, and the truck had the words SKULL CRUSHER 2 painted on the side. Parker had insisted. He thought that the 2 part was cool because it would make people think that something really disturbing had happened to Skull Crusher 1. This didn't really make a lot of sense. No one else was ever going to see the truck. Since the Porsche incident, Reese and Theo refused to get in any vehicle driven by Parker unless they were positive they wouldn't be seen in public. Hence the Crusher, and the deep backwoods of Cahill.

Reese, Parker, Theo, and Fon-Rahm climbed out of the truck

and jumped to the soggy ground. They were miles from the nearest road, nowhere near anything at all.

Theo said, "Parker, enough. We went hang gliding. We hit the water park. We ate lobster. Can we call it a day, please? My folks will get worried."

"Well, we can't have that," Parker said. "Hey, Rommy, can you give his parents amnesia or something?"

Theo chimed in before Fon-Rahm could answer. "No! I don't want my parents to have amnesia! I'm tired and I want to go home for dinner."

"Could someone please tell me what we're doing in a mud field in the middle of nowhere?" asked Reese.

"Sure," answered Parker. "This is where we're going to put the house."

Theo said, "The house? What house?"

"*Our* house. Right here. Fon-Rahm is going to build us a crib."

"Come on, Parker. Why do we need a house?"

"I want a pool," said Reese. Why not? She worked hard. She got stellar grades. She put up with her mother. She deserved a pool.

Parker threw out his arms.

"Yes! *That's* the attitude I'm looking for. We can have a pool. We can have a pool each, if we want, and an arcade and a climbing wall and a bowling alley. And a submarine dock! I can't believe I almost forgot the submarine dock."

"For God's sake, Parker, what are you going to do with a submarine in the middle of the woods?" Theo asked.

"I don't know. We'll build a canal or something to the ocean. A tributary. It'll be amazing."

Theo sulked. "Well, it sounds stupid."

While Theo and Parker bickered, Fon-Rahm scanned the skies with a worried expression.

"Stop," he said.

Parker ignored him. "Okay, forget the submarine, Theo. Put the submarine out of your mind and just think about the house. It'll be our place. We'll make the rules. No one will be able to tell us what to do."

"Stop," Fon-Rahm said.

"We'll get a bunch of four-wheelers. You *like* four-wheelers." Parker could see Theo wavering. He *did* like four-wheelers. Then Parker added, "We can bring girls out here."

To Reese's surprise, this hit hard. She had no interest, really, in Parker or in Theo. They had been having fun, sure, and maybe you could say they were friends, but it's not like there were any romantic feelings, at least not on her end. So why did this disappoint her so much?

Fon-Rahm exploded with anger. "Stop!" he screamed.

The kids stared at Fon-Rahm.

"I sense something nearby," the genie said. "Something that disturbs the Nexus. I can feel it moving."

Parker dismissed him.

"Get over it, Fon-Rahm. You're always feeling something. I think you should get used to the idea that you're my servant, and the only thing happening is me getting everything I ever wanted."

Theo blanched. "Jeez, Parker. That's a little harsh, don't you think?"

"Stay out of it, Theo. I'm the one who found him, not you."

"It's getting closer," said Fon-Rahm.

Theo got in his cousin's face. "You know what, Parker? I'm getting pretty sick of this. How come we always have to do what you want to do? We're *all* in trouble if we get caught."

"Are you kidding me? If it had been up to you, none of this would even be happening. We would have taken the lamp back to the college."

"Yeah, yeah, you're great and everybody else is an idiot."

"Not everybody, pal; just you. And if you don't want to hang out with Rommy and me, you don't have to." He turned to Reese and added, "Either of you."

Parker knew he had gone too far. He knew he was being a jerk, but once he got started, he found it hard to stop. Theo didn't deserve his abuse and neither did Reese. They were his only friends.

He opened his mouth to apologize, but Reese shushed him. She was far more interested in what Fon-Rahm had to say.

"Wait. What's getting closer? What's coming?"

"Xaru," Fon-Rahm said.

Theo walked away from his cousin. "Xaru?" he said. "What's a Xaru?"

Instead of answering Theo, Fon-Rahm threw his arms into the air. A blue crackle of electricity crawled from his shoulders to his wrists and burst off his fingertips, creating a shimmering, domed force field around himself, Reese, Parker, and Theo that sealed just as the ground around them exploded. The Skull Crusher 2 was blown end over end like a plastic toy. When the rain of trees, debris, and hot rock finally hit the dirt, the area under the dome was the only thing for half a mile in any direction left unscorched. The air reeked of sulfur and charred wood.

The kids huddled together in fear as the force field dissolved. They all followed Fon-Rahm's gaze into the sky.

Xaru, majestic and malevolent in his billowing red robes, floated down until he was just a few feet off the ground, directly in front of Fon-Rahm.

"Hello, brother," he leered, smoke all around him. "It's been ages."

22

WITHOUT A SECOND'S HESITATION, FON-
Rahm sent a bolt of blue lightning at Xaru.

The blast caught the other genie square in the chest and threw him half a mile. Xaru hit the ground feetfirst and launched himself full-strength into Fon-Rahm. Xaru snatched Fon-Rahm from the ground and the two genies smashed into the twisted remains of the truck.

"Now isn't that just like you, to lash out at me before you've even heard what I came to say," said Xaru.

"I can guess what you came to say, and my answer is the same as it always was. No!"

Fon-Rahm freed himself from Xaru's bear hug and punched him in the face. If Xaru was fazed, he didn't show it.

"So stubborn," he said. "After all the time you've had to reflect,

I thought that perhaps you might finally be convinced of the wisdom of my proposition. This new world could be ours, Fon-Rahm! Join me!"

"Never!"

Fon-Rahm took to the sky and set his hands to unleash another storm of lightning.

Parker screamed, "Stop!"

Fon-Rahm halted in midair. Theo and Reese were huddled together on the ground, but Parker stood defiant and unafraid.

"There are *more* of you?" he asked Fon-Rahm.

"You must stay away from this!" Fon-Rahm said. "It is not your concern!"

Parker looked at the barren waste surrounding them. "Anything you do is my concern. I command you to protect us!"

Fon-Rahm had no choice. He directed his energy away from Xaru to create another force field over the kids.

Xaru floated up to him, sadly shaking his head. "You are Fon-Rahm, first of the Jinn, and you take orders from a human child? You and I are gods! We are legends made real!"

Fon-Rahm put himself between Xaru and Parker.

"I do what I am compelled to do," he said.

"You and I have always viewed the rules differently, brother."

Parker said, "Take us out of here, Fon-Rahm! Now!"

Xaru grabbed Fon-Rahm's arm.

"Let me kill this little pest, Fon-Rahm. Then, if you refuse to join me, it will at least be your own decision. I mean, really. It's just too sad."

"I cannot allow you to do that. Stand aside."

Xaru threw up his hands in frustration.

"After what they put you through! After they shoved you in a box and left you to rot for eternity, you still believe that humans are worth saving! You still believe that humans are our betters!" Xaru sighed. "You're as deluded as you ever were."

Fire erupted from Xaru's eyes and went at Fon-Rahm like a hellish blowtorch. Fon-Rahm struggled against it, unable to shield himself or turn away. He was using all of his strength to protect Parker and his friends.

Reese couldn't take it any longer. "He's killing Fon-Rahm! Do something, Parker!"

Parker thought for a moment.

"Fon-Rahm!" he said. "I command you to kick Xaru's ass!"

"Thank you," the genie said.

The force field blinked out of existence as Fon-Rahm turned his energy to fighting Xaru. He pulled back his mighty fist and punched Xaru with enough force to turn a building into rubble. Xaru struck back with a wicked slash to Fon-Rahm's face. The trees shook as the two beings traded blows.

Xaru smiled, enjoying himself immensely. He was, literally, born to fight.

"That's more like it, Fon-Rahm! Your little vacation did wonders for you!"

"Neither of us can win, Xaru. We are too evenly matched. This will always be true."

"Oh, I don't know about that, brother. *Always* is an awfully long time."

Xaru swung up his leg and landed a kick that sent Fon-Rahm flying into the distance.

Reese looked at Parker and gasped. "Parker!"

He was lying on the ground, clutching his head. The sudden distance from Fon-Rahm had brought on massive pain.

In the skies, Xaru reached his genie brother. He saw that Fon-Rahm was struggling and quickly determined what had happened.

"Well, look at that. You're chained to this mortal. Yet another gift from the humans. I must say that is unfortunate."

With all the energy it would take a human to pull up a dandelion, Xaru uprooted a maple tree. He swung it at Fon-Rahm like a Louisville Slugger and connected, knocking Fon-Rahm even farther away from Parker.

Parker's nose gushed blood. Reese cradled his head while Theo watched the action in the air, silently wishing that none of this had ever happened.

Weakened to the point of immobility, Fon-Rahm hung limp in the air, gently turning in the wind. Xaru dropped the tree and approached him with what seemed to be genuine pity.

"I hate to see you like this. I really do. You were the first of us, and I admit that I have always felt a certain . . . tenderness for you." He reached out his hand and gently brushed a speck of dirt off Fon-Rahm's face.

"Then again," he said, "I really, really like to kill things."

With that, Xaru wrapped his hands around Fon-Rahm's throat. As he sucked the life force out of his older brother, Fon-Rahm became more and more gaunt. The genie was dying.

Xaru let a smile of deep satisfaction appear on his lips.

"Sleep well, brother."

He was startled by a voice from below.

"Now, really, you two. Haven't we been through this all before?"

The smile disappeared from Xaru's face as he looked down to see Professor Ellison in the clearing, standing next to a silver BMW SUV.

23

XARU SPIT AT PROFESSOR ELLISON. "You!" he hissed. "Still you live?"

"Still I live," said the professor, serene in the face of the magical destruction that surrounded her.

"Who's that?" asked Reese.

"Um," said Theo. "This lady that works with my dad?"

"I wondered how long it would take one of you to get out," Professor Ellison said, nonchalantly opening the rear door of her truck. "Your capture was a bit of a rush job, I admit, but under the circumstances, I would say I did fairly well."

Xaru kept his hands around Fon-Rahm's neck.

"Do your worst, witch," he sneered. "Without your little metal boxes, you're as helpless as a child."

"Who said I was without them?"

With a flourish, the professor pulled off the sheet covering the cargo bay of her SUV, revealing two metal cylinders just like the ones that once imprisoned Xaru and Fon-Rahm.

Beads of sweat appeared on Xaru's forehead. He released Fon-Rahm as Professor Ellison started to chant in an ancient language of arcane magic. Reese and Theo watched, stunned, as dirt and leaves on the clearing floor kicked up and began to whirl around Professor Ellison. She was creating a tornado that grew steadily in strength and size while her spell took shape.

The containers popped open, ready for new tenants.

"No," said Xaru. "No! Not now! Not again!"

Xaru struggled as the new wind became a vortex pulling him and Fon-Rahm down toward the lamps. Using all of his strength, Xaru managed to break free of the fledgling spell before he was sucked in.

He snarled at Fon-Rahm. "We'll have to continue this another time, brother."

Xaru hurled himself up and away, and in seconds he was gone from sight.

"He's gone!" said Theo, as relieved as he had ever been in his life. He yelled to Professor Ellison to be heard over the gale-force winds. "You can stop now! Xaru's gone!"

"I can see that, dear boy, but that's no reason for me to leave here empty-handed."

She continued her spell, and Theo realized that Fon-Rahm was just floating there in the sky, ripe for the picking. Professor Ellison's chanting grew louder and more intense. The wind was now a cyclone that tore through the clearing, throwing rocks, dirt, and entire trees out of its way as if they were made of paper.

Fon-Rahm hovered in the air, his arms and legs dangling helplessly. He began to circle over Professor Ellison as her spell sucked him in. He whipped around, faster and faster the lower he got.

As Fon-Rahm was pulled closer, Parker sat upright, suddenly recovered. He brushed the blood from his nose and looked up to see a revived Fon-Rahm clawing powerlessly at the sky.

"Parker! She's trying to take him away!" cried Reese.

Parker shook the cobwebs out of his head and stood on legs made of rubber. He sized up the situation and came up with what he considered to be a fairly sophisticated plan of action. He ran at Professor Ellison and tackled her to the ground.

When Professor Ellison's chanting stopped, the tornado stopped with it. The air became abruptly still, and Reese and Theo stopped gawking long enough to shield their heads from falling forest debris.

Parker tried to pin Professor Ellison down. "Will you two stop staring and help me, please?"

Reese and Theo snapped out of their stupor and pounced on the professor. Parker and Theo each held one of her arms while Reese wrapped up her feet and held on for dear life as Ellison kicked furiously.

"Haven't you imbeciles done enough?" she said. "Get off me!"

"Hey, Fon-Rahm, we could use a hand over here!" Parker said.

Fon-Rahm landed next to the tangle of bodies in a heap, exhausted from fighting Ellison's spell and his battle with Xaru.

"Let her be," he said, staggering to his feet.

Parker doubled his efforts as Professor Ellison thrashed. "She was trying to put you back in a lamp!"

"She has her reasons. Let her go."

Parker released Professor Ellison's arm. She kicked Reese away, shoved Theo off her, and stood.

"These pants are ruined, thank you," she said, brushing angrily at her legs. "And these shoes cost more than your father makes in a month."

Parker glared at her.

"All right," he said. "Let's hear it. What's your beef with Fon-Rahm?"

"My beef? With Fon-Rahm. Lovely." She stared down her nose at Parker. "I would tell you, but the day I feel the need to explain myself to you is the day that monkeys fly out of my ears."

Parker shrugged.

"Fon-Rahm, I command you to make monkeys fly out of the professor's ears."

Reese shook her head at Fon-Rahm. The ancient genie was many things, but a guy who got jokes was not one of them.

"Fine," said Professor Ellison. "I'll explain it to you. I'm not saying that you're capable of understanding it, but I can try. Come here."

Parker and his friends hesitated.

"Come here, you stupid children. I'm not going to hurt you."

Parker, Reese, and Theo approached her as warily as if she was a really nasty-looking spider. Professor Ellison waved a hand over them, said two words that didn't sound like they made any sense, and closed her hand into a fist.

Instantly, the knowledge of how Vesiroth created the Jinn was shot into their heads. They saw the desert pit lined with jade and smelled the brimstone burning. They felt Vesiroth's loss when his family was killed, and the triumph he felt when Fon-Rahm stepped forth out of the smoke. They listened as Tarinn's pleas to Vesiroth went unheeded. They were there as Fon-Rahm refused to obey his creator, and they witnessed firsthand the birth of Xaru. They saw Xaru find the Elders' deadly spell and begin to create genies of his own. They stood on a rooftop and watched as Fon-Rahm and Xaru battled over Mesopotamia three thousand years ago. They felt the heat of Xaru's fire and heard the clap of Fon-Rahm's thunder as the genies fought to a standstill in the sky. They knew about the Nexus, and they could feel its power all around them.

They saw the sultan, a man of immense power, reduced to begging Tarinn to save what was left of his city. They were in the room when Tarinn agreed, with the sole condition that the genies would be given to her for safekeeping. They were there as Tarinn climbed the tallest building in the city and used a rare alignment of the planets to trap the Jinn in thirteen metal canisters engraved with magic. They watched as the sultan betrayed Tarinn, throwing her in a dungeon while he sent his men to scatter the lamps across the globe, to mountains in Europe, deserts in Asia, jungles in the Amazon, and a forest in what would one day be called New Hampshire.

The greatest power the world has ever known was divided and spread across the world, never to be collected again. It had simply vanished.

Professor Ellison unclenched her fist. Parker, Reese, and Theo, freed from her spell, fell to the ground. The onrush of new information was almost too much for their minds to bear.

"What happened?" asked Theo.

"We got schooled," Reese answered, rubbing her butt. She had fallen pretty hard.

"There are so many of them," said Parker. "I didn't realize there were so many."

The professor rolled her eyes. "Of course you didn't. You're a child. You're not even a very smart child."

"Well, that's just rude," Parker said.

Theo confronted the professor. "How did you do that to us?"

"It was a simple spell. Anyone with a pulse could master it."

"But why do you know spells? And how come you know about all that stuff, anyway?"

"She knows," said Fon-Rahm, "because she was there."

"You were Vesiroth's apprentice," Parker said. "You trapped all of the genies to start out with. You're Tarinn."

"I'm using Ellison these days. It's simple to spell and it's easy to forget."

Reese couldn't believe it. "Come on. That would mean you're over three thousand years old!"

"Careful," said Professor Ellison.

"This can't be right," said Theo. "It's impossible."

"Really, Theo? After everything that happened to us this week you still think things are impossible?" Parker looked at Professor Ellison with newfound respect. "You're a *wizard*."

"Enchantress, conjurer, necromancer, spellbinder, thaumaturge, alchemist. I have always thought 'sorceress' has a certain panache."

"How did you get out of the dungeons?" asked Reese.

The professor shrugged. "Time moves differently for some of us. Vesiroth had taught me many things, some without even knowing it. One was the secret to a very, very, very long life. I outlived the sultan, and his son, and *his* son, and eventually, I outlived the sultanate itself. There were mobs and lots of exciting riots. The dungeons were cleared and I was free to go on my merry way. I have been hunting for the lamps ever since."

"What happened to Vesiroth?" asked Parker.

"I wish I knew," she said wistfully. Her feelings for Vesiroth were . . . complicated. "I have lived a long time, and I have faced many threats, but the only thing that keeps me up at night is the idea that he's out there somewhere, frozen but alive, waiting to be free once again."

Professor Ellison allowed herself a moment to remember, before she turned her attention back to the matter at hand.

"Now please, children, stand aside." Professor Ellison bored her eyes into the genie in the black suit. "Fon-Rahm and I have unfinished business."

"That we do," the genie said, pointing into the distance. "But perhaps we could discuss it later."

The kids looked where Fon-Rahm was pointing and saw four Jeeps explode through the trees. They were filled with men in black suits carrying machine guns, and they were headed straight for them.

24

"YOU HAVE GOT TO BE KIDDING ME," said Theo.

"It has to be those guys that tried to kill us before," said Parker. "Stop them, Fon-Rahm!"

Fon-Rahm shook his head, spent. "I cannot. I am ... too weak." It was true. After fighting off Professor Ellison's attack, Fon-Rahm could barely stand. It would take time before the Nexus would re-energize him.

The professor calmly assessed the situation.

"Get in my car," she sighed. "If you want to live."

The kids exchanged looks.

"What about Fon-Rahm?" asked Parker.

"Fon-Rahm, too." Professor Ellison looked at the genie with disgust. "I want to keep an eye on him."

Seconds later, they were ripping through the woods in Professor Ellison's BMW. Theo tried to keep his head as low as possible, but the BMW was bouncing around like crazy. It was all he could do to stay off Parker and Reese. Strange, he thought. Just last week his biggest worry was not making the football team. Now he was riding in a car with a genie and a three-thousand-year-old sorceress while men in Jeeps shot at him with machine guns. Professor Ellison and Fon-Rahm, in the front seat, didn't seem overly concerned. They had seen worse, probably, Theo thought.

Definitely.

Ellison gave Fon-Rahm the once-over. "What happened to the robes?" she asked.

"I wear these clothes at my young master's request."

"Always a stickler for the rules. The suit makes you look like a bouncer."

Reese popped her head up long enough to see that one of the Jeeps was right alongside of them.

"They're coming!"

Professor Ellison expertly jerked the wheel. The BMW rammed into the Jeep, which swerved madly before recovering and rejoining the chase.

The first bullets came. They were way off their mark, but the point was made. Ellison stepped on the gas.

More gunfire erupted. This time, a bullet shattered the rear window. Reese shrieked. Professor Ellison made a series of high-speed turns, weaving in between the trees. Metal howled as she clipped off branches with the truck's fender and roof. Professor Ellison let the Jeep come closer, and then aimed the BMW straight at a massive pine tree. She waited until the Jeep was directly behind her, and at the last second, made a brutal turn to the right that took the SUV up on two wheels. The Jeep didn't make the turn and crashed full speed into the tree. It made a gruesome noise. The BMW thudded back on all four wheels and kept going. There were three Jeeps left.

Two Jeeps pulled even with the BMW, one on either side. Professor Ellison slowed the SUV to match their speed and rolled down the rear windows. Theo, Reese, and Parker were terrified. They could see scowling men aiming their guns right at them.

"Heads down, please," said Professor Ellison.

The kids ducked just in time. The Jeeps both fired a steady stream of bullets that shredded through the BMW, went over the kids' heads, and exited straight through the other side. The men in the Jeeps cut each other to ribbons with their own gunfire. Both Jeeps peeled off and crashed, out of the chase for good.

The men in the last Jeep fired at them. They were getting close.

"Take the wheel, please," Professor Ellison told Parker.

Parker wriggled his way into the front seat and took over the BMW as Professor Ellison opened the sunroof. She grabbed her Louis Vuitton bag and stood with her body half out of the SUV.

"Um, Professor Ellison?" said Reese.

The professor was not taking questions. As the men in the Jeep tried to get a bead on her, she calmly rooted through her bag and came up with a small marble-and-glass amulet shaped like a pyramid. She closed her eyes, held the object up, and said a few words under her breath. When she was done, she opened her eyes and pointed the amulet at the Jeep.

One of the men in the Jeep was pointing a rocket launcher directly back at her.

Just as the man in the Jeep fired the rocket, the professor's magic took effect. The Jeep stopped dead in its track and lurched straight into the air. When it came down, the Jeep hit the ground and exploded into flames.

The rocket spiraled wildly into the sky, its trajectory ruined. Everyone in the BMW watched it, hoping it wasn't what they all feared. When it righted itself and plummeted directly at them, their hopes were broken.

"Heat seeker!" cried Theo. He was the veteran of a thousand video game wars, and he knew what he was talking about.

"It will miss us," said Professor Ellison as she climbed back into the truck. She shoved Parker to the backseat so she could take back control of the speeding BMW.

Reese said, "I'm not so sure."

The professor swung the BMW around, trying to shake the rocket, but it was no use. The missile picked up their heat and streaked right at them. Professor Ellison spun the SUV around again and headed back toward the burning Jeep.

The man who had fired the rocket stumbled out of the wreckage, bruised, scorched, but still alive. As the BMW sped at him, he fired his handgun into its windshield. Neither the professor nor Fon-Rahm paid him any attention. The man ran out of ammunition and dropped his gun. He was sure the SUV was going to plow into him, so he hid his head in his hands. When at the last second the BMW turned away, he peeked out. Xaru be praised, he had survived!

Then he saw his own missile blasting toward the blazing Jeep, and he screamed. The missile exploded, leaving a rain of metal, burning dirt, and a crater behind.

25

PROFESSOR ELLISON SLID WHAT WAS left of the SUV to a halt, and everyone got out. Reese gaped at the hole where the Jeep had once been.

"You killed them," she said. "You killed all of them."

"Would you rather that they had killed us?" Professor Ellison asked.

"I would rather that no one got killed at all."

Ellison shrugged. "They're prepared to die," she said. "They call themselves the Path. They're the descendants of a very old and very disciplined religious order that worships the Jinn. It's impressive, really. They recruit members from around the world to renounce their nations and pledge their lives to bring about genie rule."

"They *want* to be ruled by genies?" asked Reese.

"Some people are more comfortable in chains."

"The Path are fanatics and they will stop at nothing to ensure that Xaru succeeds in his mission to control the world," said Fon-Rahm. "They are after the lamps."

"They must have found a way around the tether," Professor Ellison mused. "How do you like that, by the way? It's just a little something extra I threw in when I trapped you, as a precaution."

"I don't understand," said Parker. "If you think the genies are such a threat, why mess around with lamps? Why not just destroy them?"

Fon-Rahm answered, "If one of the Jinn is destroyed, his power will return to Vesiroth. The wizard must not live again. This time he might succeed, and mankind would forever be under Vesiroth's thumb."

"It might be worth it, for a world without war," said Theo.

Reese shook her head. "Yeah, if you want an evil wizard making all your decisions for you."

"Xaru was trying to kill Fon-Rahm. Isn't he worried about Vesiroth?" asked Parker.

Fon-Rahm frowned. "I do not believe he cares. My brother is an embodiment of chaos. Where he goes, madness follows."

"And that's why I have to find the lamps before the Path does," said the professor. "They have already unearthed Xaru. Who knows what else they've found?"

"Okay, fine," said Parker. "There are twelve evil genies out there. So go get 'em. I don't see why you have a problem with Fon-Rahm. He's on our side."

"He shouldn't even exist!"

Professor Ellison realized she was yelling and made an effort to get herself under control. "He isn't human. He doesn't feel the things that we feel. He has no emotions. He doesn't understand what it's like to be a human being. He might talk a good game, but don't be fooled. Fon-Rahm is a weapon. He is too powerful to be free, and he is not to be trusted."

She looked at the genie with nothing but contempt. "He is simply a spell that got out of hand."

Fon-Rahm stared back at her. "I will fight you if I must. This time, I warn you, I will be prepared."

Smoke began to pool around his eyes. He was now rested and ready to go. Professor Ellison stared him down. It was a standoff, and it was getting very tense.

Parker stepped between them.

"Wait! Wait! You both agree that the genies are a threat, right?"

"The others must be trapped, I agree," said Fon-Rahm.

"You *all* must be trapped," countered the professor.

Parker said, "Then the logical thing for us to do is join forces."

"Us?" Professor Ellison huffed. "I hope you're not under the impression that I need *you* for something."

"Yeah, okay, you might not need me, but you could use Fon-Rahm, and he can only do what I tell him to do. We're a package deal."

"I am doing quite well by myself, actually. Why on earth would you think I need Fon-Rahm?"

"Because Fon-Rahm can tell where the other genies are."

Fon-Rahm looked away.

"He can?" Reese asked. "How?"

Parker turned to the genie. "You can feel them, can't you, Rommy? That's why you knew Xaru was here. I think you even knew when Xaru's lamp was opened. You were talking about a disturbance in the Nexus the first night we stashed you in the barn."

Fon-Rahm let a hint of a smile play across his lips.

"I believed you were not paying attention."

"So," said Reese. "Fon-Rahm is the only one who can sense where all the genies are, and Professor Ellison is the only one who can trap them. It's pretty clear that we'll be stronger and more effective if we work together."

The genie and the professor glared at each other. Neither wanted to be the first to back down.

Fon-Rahm broke the silence. "It's agreed, then? We join together to recapture the other twelve?"

Professor Ellison nodded. "Agreed."

"Ha! Yes!" said Parker. "This is going to be so cool!"

"That's one word for it, I guess," said Theo.

Parker, Reese, and Theo walked back to the BMW. The SUV was dented and Swiss-cheesed with bullet holes. The windows were gone. The roof was barely attached. It took Theo three tries to open one of the back doors. He had to brush broken glass off the seat before he got in.

Professor Ellison and Fon-Rahm lagged behind.

"You realize, of course, that when this is all over I'll be coming for you, dear," she told Fon-Rahm.

Fon-Rahm smiled a grim smile. "I would expect no less," he said.

26

THE ARMY BASE WAS ABANDONED. The people of Lithuania, poor but resourceful, had stolen anything of value long ago, leaving nothing behind but rusting metal, weeds, and empty cinder-block buildings that were already crumbling.

Nadir sympathized. He had come from nothing himself, and he had no time or patience for those who didn't help themselves, through legal means or not. The world was a cold place. Nadir's strategy was to embrace its cruelty.

Most people would have regarded Nadir's childhood as a horror. He had been orphaned at a young age and left to scrounge for food in the trash cans and back alleys of Munich, alone and unloved. What he couldn't beg, he stole, and by the time he was nine he had progressed from stealing food to lifting wallets, purses, and whatever else he could lay his hands on. He was good, too, nimble-fingered and quick, and with a mean streak that frightened both competition and companionship away. He might have grown up to be a crime boss, or he might have been jailed as a thief, if he hadn't one day innocently walked off from a teeming restaurant with a nondescript black leather briefcase. He had run around the corner and hid behind a wall before opening it, expecting to find money, or something he could sell, but the only thing in the case was a list of names. Some were crossed out in red ink.

Another child would have thrown the list away and gone back to shoplifting and picking pockets. Nadir, however, was intrigued by the list. It was information, and information was often worth more than watches or rings.

He tracked the owner of the case (not difficult for a child who lived on the streets) and found a lean, dead-eyed Colombian man with odd tattoos and a black suit. Nadir offered to give him back the list in exchange for cash.

The owner of the case had an eye for talent and was impressed both with Nadir's skill and his nerve. He didn't give him money, but he gave him something better. He gave him a home.

That man turned out to be the leader of the Path. He became a father figure to Nadir, and the boy worshipped him. He taught Nadir about the Nexus and the Jinn, and he trained him in the dark arts.

Nadir took to his new calling with enthusiasm. He learned the language of the Path and took a new name to show he had broken completely from his old life. When he learned that the collection of names he had stolen was a list of the Path's enemies targeted for assassination, he snuck away and killed one himself.

He was ten years old.

Nadir missed his father figure, sometimes. Sometimes he even regretted killing him, but it was the smart move. Nadir had taken over leadership of the Path himself, and he had never looked back.

Nadir stood inside the deserted hangar with his men and Xaru.

"I should have known Tarinn would still be alive," said Xaru. "That woman is too annoying to die. Still, I suppose a few snags are to be expected. Worlds do not enslave themselves."

Nadir had still not gotten used to the idea of seeing the genie walking among them. For so long, Nadir had dreamed of the day the Jinn were free, and now that it was happening, he felt uneasy. He had been told that the Path was to be rewarded for its centuries of service, and he hoped to sit at the right hand of Xaru's throne. So far, though, Xaru had said nothing about a job well done. He only issued demands and spilled blood.

A lamp had been discovered nearby, and the Path was already in the middle of the ritual. A brother wore the robes and knelt, his hands on the lamp, ready to sacrifice himself for the cause. He tried to be brave, but he was shaking. Badly.

Xaru sniffed. "This time we will be ready for her. And for Fon-Rahm."

The sacrifice finished his words and twisted the ends of the lamp. The lamp burst open, throwing everyone back. There, rising in the smoke and stink, was the genie Yogoth. Although he was one of the first genies that Xaru created, he had none of his older brother's charm or intelligence. Yogoth was a misshapen brute, with four arms and a twisted version of the face Xaru and Fon-Rahm wore.

Yogoth lacked even the ability to speak. He pointed at the kneeling brother and grunted.

The sacrifice, scared out of his mind, scrambled to his feet and tried to run. Xaru raised his arms to stop him, but there was no need for magic. In one fluid motion, Nadir drew a knife and threw it. The man fell dead at Yogoth's feet.

The four-armed genie seemed confused. Where was he? Who were these strange men? Did they mean to harm him?

Xaru approached him carefully, his arms outstretched.

"It's all right, brother. You're safe, now."

Nadir turned his cold blue eyes away as the two genies embraced. He had never understood the concept of affection.

27

FON-RAHM CLEARED OFF THE
workbench and unfurled an antique map. He weighed down the
corners with old tools and a coffee can filled with washers and nuts.

Reese peered over the genie's shoulder.

"Are you sure we should be using this?" she asked. The map
was hand-painted on some kind of cloth, and the writing was in
florid German script. "It looks like it might be valuable."

"Priceless, really," Professor Ellison told her. She was sitting,
her legs crossed primly, on the broken tractor. "Sixteenth century.
One of a kind." She shrugged. "It's all I have with me."

Fon-Rahm pointed to the map.

"They unearthed Xaru here, in Greenland," he said as Parker
and Theo gathered in close. "That means that there are eleven
more of us out there somewhere."

"Seven," said Professor Ellison.

They all looked at her.

"Well, what exactly do you think I have been doing with my time?"

Parker said, "Fon-Rahm won't be able to find the other genies until they're freed. We'll have to wait until somebody digs up another lamp."

"The Path already has," said Fon-Rahm, pointing to a spot that was once part of Russia. "Last night. Here."

Professor Ellison sighed.

"The realignment of the planets is causing the lamps to reveal themselves. Three thousand years have passed without a single one of the Jinn getting loose, and now three have been freed in one week. We have to stop this before it gets completely out of hand."

"Yes. We must go and confront the Path," said Fon-Rahm.

"Go," said Parker.

"Yes."

"To Russia."

"Near Russia, yes."

"I'm into it. I'll go pack."

"Wait. Wait. Wait," Theo said. He couldn't take it any longer. "You guys have got this, right? I mean, you don't need me. I'm not contributing anything."

"Too true," said Professor Ellison.

"I mean, look, guys, it was fun to have a pet genie for a while. It was great, really! I had a lot of fun! But this is *crazy*. It's just too dangerous."

"Oh, come on, Theo," Parker said. "Don't be such a . . ."

"Theo's right."

Parker was surprised Reese agreed with Theo. Reese was a little surprised herself.

She said, "We're way out of our league."

Theo was relieved to learn he wasn't alone. "So you guys can go to Russia or wherever, and Reese and I will stay here. Everybody wins."

"I don't believe you two," said Parker incredulously. "Stay here? Stay here for what? Reese, are you really going to fall behind if you miss one violin lesson?"

"Viola," she said, her eyes locked on the floor of the barn.

"And, Theo, buddy, I know you're trying, but nobody even knows you're here. If you didn't show up at school for a week, who would even miss you?"

Theo flushed red with anger. Before he could say anything, though, Parker continued.

"And me? Please. My own mother shipped me out of town. It's Thanksgiving on Thursday and she's not even coming. As sad as it sounds, you two are the closest things I have to friends at all."

The barn was still.

"Something is happening. And we're right in the middle of it. This is our chance to be a part of something big. Magic. Adventure. Don't you see what this is?"

Parker laid his hand on the map.

"This is *destiny*."

"I'll go," Reese blurted, almost without thinking. How had Parker won her over so quickly? "I mean, I never get to go anywhere, except for my grandparents' house in Maine and that one time the academic decathlon team went to Rhode Island."

Theo threw up his hands.

"Fine. Whatever. Go to Russia. Get burned to death by a genie. Get shot by a guy in a suit. I'm staying."

"That is out of the question," said Fon-Rahm.

Parker said, "Hey, if he doesn't want to come, he doesn't have to come. Let him stay here and keep his parents company. Who cares?"

"The Path will kill him!"

The force in Fon-Rahm's voice shocked the kids. They stayed silent while the genie spoke.

"Theo has been marked. Parker. Reese. All of you. The Path does not stop. They cannot be reasoned with. They will give up their lives to bring about a new age, ruled by the Jinn. They will die without a thought if they believe it will help their cause. And now that they have Xaru to lead them . . ."

He didn't even want to consider the possibilities.

"Theo must come with us. It is the only way I can protect him."

The kids all looked at one another.

"We're stuck with each other," Parker said.

Professor Ellison slid off the tractor seat.

"Well, that's settled. See how nicely everything is turning out?"

"Well, yeah," said Reese. "But there's one little detail I think we might have overlooked."

"What is that?" asked Fon-Rahm.

"I think maybe my mom and dad might notice if I'm in Russia instead of my bedroom."

They all let this problem sink in.

"Fine," sighed the professor. "I'll see what I can do."

An hour later, Reese, Parker, and Theo stood in the living room of Theo's house and stared back at themselves.

"Problem solved," said Professor Ellison.

Ellison had used her magic to create exact duplicates of the kids. The fake Reese, Parker, and Theo looked, acted, and spoke just like the real things.

Reese said, "This is too weird."

Theo walked up to his twin and gave him a little push, thinking his hand might go right through it. It didn't. The fake Theo stumbled, regained his footing, and pushed the real Theo right back.

"What are they?" Theo asked.

"They're you, basically," Professor Ellison answered. "I created them in your own images."

Reese's jaw dropped with newfound respect.

"You can create human life?" she said, awed at the prospect.

"No, I can't create human life. No one can create human life. They're illusions. They were programmed to do whatever you would do in any given situation."

"So, um, Reese Two will go to my classes?"

"She'll go to your classes and argue with your parents and make inane comments with a vacant look on her face, just like you."

"I don't like this," said Fon-Rahm, his arms folded across his chest. "This kind of magic can easily spin out of control."

"Oh, relax," said the professor. "I barely put anything into them. In two weeks they'll vanish back into the Nexus. It will be like they were never here."

Parker circled his double, a grin on his face.

"This is wild. How do we know they'll pass for us?"

The fake Parker's voice dripped with sarcasm. "Yes, how could we be expected to master the subtle intricacies of minds like these?"

Parker nodded his approval.

"I like him."

"We have to leave," said Fon-Rahm. "Now. We must reach the Path before they move again."

Professor Ellison said, "It's taken care of. We leave tonight."

Reese was once again dazzled by the prospect of real magic.

"On a magic carpet, right?"

"No," Professor Ellison said with a look that might be considered amusement. "I have arranged something a tad more comfortable."

28

PARKER, THEO, REESE, AND FON-RAHM got out of the limo and stepped onto the wet tarmac. They followed Professor Ellison past airport workers carrying fuel and up the stairs that led into a gleaming blue-and-white twin-engined Gulfstream jet.

"Chartered G650," said Parker approvingly. "Fancy."

"It's not chartered, my dear boy. I own it." Professor Ellison shifted her bag. "Anyone who lives more than three thousand years and fails to get rich lacks common sense."

"I've never been on a private plane before," said Reese.

"I've never been on a *plane* before," said Theo. When Reese looked at him, he shrugged. "*My* grandparents live right down the street, and I'm pretty sure I never made the academic decathlon team."

Reese said, "I don't know. You're not so dumb," and Theo practically tripped on the stairs.

Parker didn't know it, but as he was boarding the G650, his mother was wheeling a tattered bag through the very same airport, less than a thousand feet away.

She had flown in from Los Angeles on the cheapest flight she could find, sandwiched between a woman with a tiny yapping dog and an overweight man in sweatpants who had fallen asleep on her shoulder. It was a miserable trip, made even worse by the nervous, gnawing feeling that had settled in her stomach the second she had gotten on the plane. She was in no way sure that Parker would be glad to see her when she arrived. She was going to surprise him for Thanksgiving.

"I still think you should have told him you were coming," Aunt Martha said. She was there to pick her sister up in the rusted Subaru.

Mrs. Quarry was tired from the flight but happy to be on the ground.

"Tell him when? He won't even talk to me on the phone." She shook her head. "You know how he is. Parker never would have forgiven me if I told him I was coming and then something came up and I couldn't. I wanted to wait until I was absolutely positive I could get on that plane."

"Well, he'll be happy to see you, I'm sure. He misses you."

"He's good at hiding it."

She squinted out an airport window and saw the Gulfstream jet. Mrs. Quarry shook her head. Private planes were for a different class of person than she would ever know.

"Must be nice to have money," she said, and then she kept on walking.

The inside of the jet was gorgeous and rich, with soft carpet and polished wood accents. Instead of a million seats jammed together, there were white leather recliners. There was a wide-screen TV and a small vase full of fresh flowers on every table.

Professor Ellison placed her bag beside her and sipped on a martini that was already waiting when she boarded the plane. Theo and Parker ran down the cabin, scoping out seats and pushing buttons.

"It sucks that I can't tell anybody where I'm going," said Reese as she sank into one of the chairs. "This is the most exciting thing that has ever happened to me."

Fon-Rahm nodded gravely. "Yes," he said. "I'm sure it will be . . . exciting for all of us."

He looked out one of the jet's round windows and saw that the flight crew was making their last-minute preparations. He turned away before the plane's copilot stepped onto the stairs. The man had a sinister look in his eye. He also had a curved knife stuck in the waistband of his stolen uniform pants, and orders to kill everyone on board the plane.

29

THE G650 WAS OVER THE ATLANTIC Ocean, flying smoothly through the night sky. The cabin was quiet. Theo, Reese, and Professor Ellison slept in their seats. The only light came from the reading lamp above Parker's seat.

He was too wired to close his eyes, and he was frankly amazed that anyone could sleep at a time like this. They were in a private jet, streaking over the ocean, on their way into the unknown! His mind flashed to the rich kids at his old school and how jealous they would be if they could see him now, and then he realized that they were in his past. His future was happening right *now*, and he was the only one awake to enjoy it.

Well, not the only one. Fon-Rahm sat in a recliner facing him, and Fon-Rahm never slept.

Parker drummed his fingers on the table and contemplated the covered plate in front of him.

"A cheddar cheeseburger, I think," he said. "Medium rare, please, with fries and a slice of raw onion."

Fon-Rahm waved his hand. When Parker lifted the polished metal cover, the food he requested was magically there. Parker dug in. He held the perfect burger to his mouth and then paused. The genie was staring right at him.

"Are you going to watch me the whole time?"

"If you would like me to look away, I will," said Fon-Rahm. "I confess that I have always found the ritual of eating very curious."

"Yeah, well, some people find junk food very calming."

"I would not know."

"You've never had junk food?"

"I have never had any food."

Parker put the burger down. "Never? Like, at all? No chicken fingers or peanut butter cups or Nerds? Jeez, no wonder you're so tense. Here. Try this."

Parker held up a French fry. Fon-Rahm of the Jinn looked at it with disdain.

"Are you commanding me to eat this?"

"I'm not going to command you to eat French fries. You should *want* to eat French fries."

Fon-Rahm just stared. Parker shook his head and went back to his food. "I eat when I'm nervous. Or bored or happy. It's a miracle I'm not a million pounds. You should see me put it away when I go to see my mom at work. My father's the same way."

Fon-Rahm nodded sagely.

"I have much in common with my father, as well."

Parker stopped eating and looked Fon-Rahm dead in the eyes.

"My dad tricked a bunch of senior citizens into trusting him, and then he stole all of their money. Then he abandoned me and my mom when he got sent to prison. Get this straight. My appetite is the only thing I have in common with him."

Fon-Rahm turned his gaze to the darkness outside the jet's window.

"Why did he steal?"

"What's the difference?"

"There are many reasons for men to do wrong. Was he hungry? Was he desperate?"

Parker thought about this for a moment.

"No. He was doing fine. We were doing fine. I mean, we lived in a little apartment and we didn't have fancy cars or anything, but I didn't care. My dad just... He was never happy with what he had. He was always complaining about how he deserved better. He had to be a big shot. He couldn't just..."

Fon-Rahm waited patiently, but Parker didn't continue. He realized that he might as well have been talking about himself.

"All men have two sides," Fon-Rahm said. "My father created me in his own image, yet there are things about him I do not understand. I doubt I ever will." He turned back to Parker. "Vesiroth was not always evil. He was once just a man who made a mistake."

Parker mulled that over. Then he held up one of his remaining fries.

"You sure you don't want one?"

Fon-Rahm just sat.

"Xaru's right," said Parker. "You are stubborn."

The genie was trapped. He took the French fry and, with great care, put it in his mouth. The look of disgust on his face vanished as he chewed.

Parker beamed. "Good, right?"

Fon-Rahm scooped up the rest of the fries from Parker's plate. He smeared them in ketchup and shoved them in his mouth.

"Not bad," he said.

And then the first missile streaked past the window.

30

PARKER JUMPED OUT OF HIS SEAT. "What was that?"

"Trouble," said Fon-Rahm. He rose to get the others, but they were already up and staring out the window.

"That was a missile," said Professor Ellison. "Someone's attacking us."

Reese scanned the sky desperately. "Who? I don't see anyone!"

Then, silhouetted against the full moon, they saw another plane.

"Oh. Oh, wow," said Theo. "That's a MiG-17. It's a Russian fighter jet from the fifties. I have a book about old fighter jets. I have a *couple* of books about old fighter jets."

"It's the Path," Professor Ellison said. "They must have followed us."

The MiG banked and then flew straight at the G650, firing its machine guns.

"Get down!" commanded Fon-Rahm, pushing Parker down to the floor of the cabin. Bullets shredded the wall of the plane, but no one was hit. The Gulfstream banked away and the MiG disappeared back into the clouds.

"A simple flying machine," said Fon-Rahm, gearing up for action. "By your command, I will dispose of it."

"No!" yelled Parker. Everyone in the cabin turned to him, sure he was out of his mind. "No. The Path isn't after *you*. They think Professor Ellison put you back in a lamp. They're just trying to kill *us*."

"So what?" asked Theo. "Either way we're dead!"

Parker blew him off and focused on Fon-Rahm. "You can feel when other genies do magic, right? That's how you knew the Path freed Xaru, and that's how you knew to protect us back in the woods."

"Yes."

"Then that means that Xaru can do the same thing to you. That's how he found you."

"Yes, I suppose so."

Theo blurted, "Parker, who cares? We're under attack here!"

"Look, Fon-Rahm, you haven't done any real magic since you fought Xaru. Nothing big or dramatic, right? Which means that he doesn't know where you are. He thinks you're gone! If he knew you were here, he would be here himself to take you on. If you destroy that jet, he'll feel the burst of power and he'll know you're free and working with the professor. We'll lose the element of surprise."

"Parker's right." The professor was as surprised as anyone to be saying it. "Fon-Rahm should stay out of this. Leave this one to me."

She reached into her bag.

In the cockpit, the pilot was steering the G650 into a cloud bank for cover while trying unsuccessfully to call in a Mayday. He couldn't get a signal at all. Impossible, he thought. The only way the radio wouldn't work is if someone had tampered with it, and the only person that could have done that was the new copilot. The pilot turned to confront him. The last thing he ever saw was the gleam of the copilot's knife as it flashed in the moonlight.

As the professor dug around in her bag for a suitable amulet to destroy the MiG, the G650 suddenly lurched. Everyone in the cabin slid back as the plane headed straight down.

Reese grabbed an armrest to steady herself. "What's happening?"

Then the door to the cockpit burst open and the copilot stepped out, his knife dripping blood. Theo could see the pilot's body slumped over the plane's controls.

"He killed the pilot!" cried Theo.

"Then who's flying the *plane*?" asked Reese. She knew the answer. She just didn't want it to be true. No one was flying the plane.

His knife at the ready, the copilot walked deliberately toward Reese, who suddenly missed her mother. At a time like this, math tutoring and sculpting lessons didn't seem quite so bad.

Fon-Rahm stepped in to intercept the copilot. Without his magic, the genie was no stronger than any human man. "Perhaps," he said, "you would prefer to fight with me."

The copilot slashed at Fon-Rahm but missed. The genie grabbed him. As they fought over the knife, the jet entered a death spiral. Everything in the cabin went flying. Parker snagged onto the door of the cockpit.

"Fon-Rahm, I wish I could fly this plane!" he said. Fon-Rahm paused in his battle with the copilot to nod at him, and Parker felt a stream of information flood into his brain. He learned principles of fluid mechanics, the use of avionics, and the operations of every gauge, button, and lever in a Gulfstream jet in less time than it took him to take a breath.

"Hey, Reese, could you help me out for a second, please?" Parker said as he made his way into the cockpit. Reese didn't have anything better to do besides cowering for her life, so she joined him.

The view out of the plane's windshield was terrifying. The G650 was spinning, plunging lower and lower with every passing second. Parker unbelted the dead pilot's body and pushed it aside before he sat behind the yoke. With new knowledge and skill he flipped switches and checked lights as he leveled out the jet.

"I'm going to need you to watch our altitude and airspeed. These gauges right here," he said. "Reese?"

Reese was staring at the dead pilot.

"Reese. You can do it."

Reese snapped out of it. She stepped over the pilot's body and sat next to Parker.

"Okay, good," said Parker with a determined look on his face. He searched the sky and found the Russian jet. It was heading right at the Gulfstream, its machine guns spitting fire.

"Hang on," said Parker, grinning as he expertly slid the G650 away. "We're going to have a little dogfight."

Parker's maneuver caused havoc in the back of the plane. Fon-Rahm and the copilot, locked in an epic struggle for the knife, smashed into the wall next to Theo. Professor Ellison's bag flew out of her hands. When it landed, its contents were thrown all over the cabin.

The copilot got his knife hand free. He pulled back to stab Fon-Rahm. The genie, for the first time in his existence, felt a flicker of self-doubt.

Theo, thinking fast, groped around for something to hit the copilot with. He came up with a golden statue of a monkey that had fallen out of the professor's bag, and swung it at the copilot's head. The copilot simply ducked out of the way. He sneered at Theo, but then the monkey came to life and sank its metal teeth into the copilot's hand. The copilot let out a yelp and rolled himself and Fon-Rahm away. When Theo dropped the monkey, it hit the floor and became a statue once more.

Making himself useful, Theo helped Professor Ellison gather up the things from her bag. There was a quill pen, a lump of mis-shapen metal, what looked like a voodoo doll, a dried snake, and an assortment of other amulets, talismans, charms, and trinkets.

"What is all this stuff?"

The professor searched the floor. "Just a few things I've

collected over the years. If you see a small glass globe, please hand it to me."

Theo found the globe under a seat and handed it to the professor.

"Thank you," she said, before throwing it against the wall. The globe shattered with a muted pop, blowing a huge hole in the side of the G650. The plane dipped and oxygen masks dropped from the ceiling. Professor Ellison was ready for it, but Theo scrambled just to hold on. He was almost sucked right out of the plane.

"Are you crazy?" he yelled. "I could have been killed!"

"And what would we have done without you?" She looked out the hole. "Now we have someplace to fight them." She caught Theo's eye. "We need to find the Bow of Qartem."

"What's a Bow of Qartem?"

"It's a bow, like an archery bow, but smaller."

Great, thought Theo, looking at the disaster that the cabin had become. That shouldn't be too hard to find at all.

Despite the danger, or maybe *because* of the danger, Parker felt alive and confident. He compensated for the sudden drop in the cabin's pressure with the ease of a seasoned pilot and craned his neck searching for any sign of the MiG-17. He found it, marked starkly against the night sky. The Russian jet banked high, rolled, and made another pass, firing off two more missiles before diving away.

Reese watched the missiles streak toward the G650.

"Parker?"

"Not yet," Parker said, his nerves made of metal.

"Parker?" Reese was getting very nervous now. The missiles were so close.

"Wait for it."

The missiles were right on them. Reese could read the Russian letters on their fins.

"Parker!" she cried, and, at the last second, Parker screamed "Yee-haw!" pushed the stick down, and rolled the Gulfstream away.

Theo was on all fours, searching for the Bow of Qartem. His eyes were drawn to a small object rolling around. He picked it up and saw that it was a small glass vial sealed with red wax. It held some kind of bright green liquid.

"Did you find the bow?" asked Professor Ellison.

"I don't see any bow," he said, holding the vial up. "But I found this."

The professor saw what Theo had and reached out to him.

"Don't touch that!" she yelled.

And then the plane rolled, Theo, Professor Ellison, Fon-Rahm, and the deadly copilot found themselves shoved onto the ceiling of the G650, and the vial slipped out of Theo's hands.

The missiles shot right by and exploded close enough to shake the Gulfstream. Reese was surprised to find herself gripping on to Parker's arm as hard as she could. She let go.

Parker brought the jet out of its roll and watched the MiG speed up and away.

"He's only got one missile left," he said.

When the Gulfstream righted itself, Theo, Fon-Rahm, the co-pilot, and Professor Ellison thudded to the floor of the cabin. Theo stretched out his hand to catch the vial, but it brushed his fingertips, landed with a crash, and broke. On contact with the air, the green liquid started to bubble.

That's probably not good, thought Theo. He was right. Theo was eye level with the carpet, so he got a great view of the tiny flaming skeletons dressed in armor that rose out of the spilled liquid. He tried to stand up, but fell backward as the skeletons grew in size until they were as tall as professional point guards.

The skeletons looked at Theo, their eye sockets empty but for green flame, and raised their burning swords. Theo screamed and buried his head in his hands. No more baseball. No more go-karts. This was it.

The ghostly warriors didn't kill Theo. Instead, they whirled and charged out the hole in the side of the jet in an ill-fated attack on the MiG. It might have worked, too, except for the fact that they couldn't fly. The flaming skeletons just dropped harmlessly into the ocean below.

Professor Ellison kept looking for the bow. "You might want to be careful," she said. "Those are some of the most powerful talismans in history."

Theo agreed. He also noticed that, on top of everything else, the inside of the G650 was now on fire. He watched as a line of flame sped toward Fon-Rahm and the copilot as they wrestled on the floor, locked in their fight to the death. The copilot smiled and forced Fon-Rahm's head to the ground. The fire was racing right toward them.

"Uh-oh."

Parker tugged at the yoke. Something was wrong with the controls. The plane was not responding.

"I don't mean to alarm you," he said, looking out Reese's side window, "but we seem to be having a problem with the starboard wing."

"What kind of problem?" Reese asked.

"Part of it no longer exists."

Reese planted her hands on the glass and looked for herself. Smoke was pouring out of the wing, and a chunk of it was indeed missing. The missiles must have exploded even closer than she had thought.

"Can you still fly the plane?" she said.

"Sure, I can fly it. I can even probably land it, but we're not making any more fancy moves."

He looked out the window and saw the MiG as it looped overhead, preparing to make one more fatal run at the G650.

"It's up to Professor Ellison now."

Theo saw an object by his feet. It was a small bow, maybe four inches long, made out of a knotty twig and strung with a wire of silver. A small metal arrow was already mounted. It looked like a harmless toy.

"Um, I think I found your bow," he told Professor Ellison. He nudged it with his foot, afraid to touch it.

The professor stood at the hole and reached back for the bow.

"Give it to me! Only a sorcerer can wield the Bow of Qartem!"

Theo reached for the bow but stopped. Beyond Professor Ellison he could see the MiG. It was right on them.

"Theo! Throw me the bow!"

Theo couldn't move. He was frozen with fear.

Fon-Rahm knew that they were in trouble. He gathered all the energy he could and flipped the copilot over, pushing his face into the path of the fire. Right before the flames reached the copilot, Fon-Rahm head-butted him and tossed him screaming out of the plane. Fon-Rahm jumped to his feet. Element of surprise or no, he had to act.

"Enough!" he cried. He pushed the professor aside and stood in the middle of the hole, smoke pooling in his eyes, as the MiG headed straight at them in a last-ditch attack. The genie raised his hands, but before he could unleash his terrible magic, the MiG exploded in a burst of bright flame and shattered metal.

Fon-Rahm and Professor Ellison looked behind them to see Theo, holding the Bow of Qartem. It was full-size in his hands, but its arrow was gone. Theo had shot the MiG out of the sky. He lowered the bow, awed at his own ability. When he placed it on the ground, it shrank back down to its toy size.

Professor Ellison attacked the flames with a fire extinguisher. "It appears you have an affinity for magic," she told Theo. "Go figure."

In the cockpit, Parker cleared his throat and grabbed the mic. He grinned at Reese and put on his best Midwestern pilot drawl.

"Ah, attention, passengers. Please fasten your seat belts and put your trays in their upright, locked positions as we make our, ah, final descent. We hope you have had a, ah, pleasant flight, and thank you for flying Parker Air."

Theo collapsed into his seat, as far away from the hole as he could get. Fon-Rahm sat next to Professor Ellison.

"The Path grows more brazen by the hour," he said. "And I will not be able to find Xaru unless he uses his magic. I fear we may be in for a long and fruitless search."

"I know someone who might be able to help us," said the professor.

"Is he human?"

Professor Ellison mulled it over. "Sort of," she said.

31

DESPERATE. THAT'S WHAT ELLISON thought of herself. She could not believe that she had agreed to work alongside the Jinn. She could not believe that her companions were children. It was pathetic. She would only resort to this kind of behavior if she were desperate.

But she couldn't help it. As she led them to their meeting place in one of the seedier parts of Utena, Ellison couldn't stop herself from worrying. Not about the dangers of the city, of course; she could protect herself with any number of simple spells. No, she was worried about herself. Maybe she was slipping. She had *known* that one of the Jinn was hidden near Cahill. That's why she lived there in the first place, so she would be close by. She had *known* that the lamps would start to make themselves more visible. There was nothing she could do about the stars. They were aligned now, just as they had been three thousand years ago, just as they would be in another three thousand years.

Three thousand long years of waiting. Time that moved slowly. Until now.

And she had *known*. She should have been able to do something.

Now two of the Jinn were out, and that meant that two more sources of Vesiroth's power were in play. This was what had made her worry more than anything over the millennia, and now it was happening. No matter how much she had tried, no matter how much she had studied, there was one thing the Nexus refused to divulge: she could never see the future. Ellison could, however, maintain a relatively close control over the present. That is, until the Jinn started to return in number.

All this to say, Professor Ellison was a bit distracted as she walked into one of the least-friendly bars in Lithuania with a genie and three middle-schoolers.

Maksimilian was fat and greasy, with sweat stains under his arms and brown gunk under his fingernails. His eyes were bloodshot. He hadn't shaved in days. He needed a haircut. He needed a shower.

He was at a scarred table in the back of the bar, surrounded by a crowd of cheering, jeering bar patrons, and locked in an epic arm-wrestling match with a shirtless Lithuanian strongman. His fans cheered him on, but Maksimilian was overmatched. His opponent was made entirely of muscle, and it looked like Maks was done for. Just as his arm was going down, however, Maksimilian reached deep inside himself, leaned in, and let out a massive belch into his opponent's face. The he-man, stunned by the evil stench, lost his focus. Maks forced his arm down with a satisfying thud. Victory.

While the strongman complained about what he saw as cheating, Maksimilian stood and acknowledged the cheers of the crowd. He raised one arm to the sky and with the other he drained a glass of cheap vodka.

"He's like a garbage dump brought to life," said Parker, entranced.

Parker, Theo, Reese, Fon-Rahm, and Professor Ellison tried their hardest to fit in. If they weren't standing in the single scariest bar in the world, Parker didn't want to know what was at the top of the list. The place was filled with shady characters with darting eyes and unkind faces. It reeked of body odor and old beer. It was dark and it was nasty. Plus, despite Parker's lies, this was the first time he had ever set foot in a bar. It was maybe not a great place to start.

"He may not look like much now, but Maksimilian was once one of the most powerful magicians alive," Professor Ellison said. "There is not much that happens in this part of the world without him knowing about it."

"Um, do you think it would be okay if I waited outside?" asked Reese as she took a step behind Fon-Rahm. There was a strange man leering at her.

Theo shifted the weight of the bag the professor had given him when they got off the plane. It contained two empty metal canisters.

"I would rather be with everybody in here than outside alone," he said. Reese weighed her options and decided he was right.

When Maksimilian caught sight of Professor Ellison, he broke into a wide grin that showed off one black tooth. "Julia!" he cried, embracing her in a sweaty bear hug. "As beautiful as always."

"It's nice to see you, too, Maks. Keeping busy, I see."

Maks shrugged. "It keeps me in vodka. There is only one reason you could possibly be here. You have finally come to your senses and accepted my proposal of marriage!"

Reese felt a shudder rack her body.

"Long-distance relationships never work, Maks," said the professor. Parker could have sworn he heard a smile in her voice. This is what a three-thousand-year-old woman is like with old friends, he thought.

"I would like you to meet some friends of mine," she said, pointing to Reese, Parker, and Theo. "These are some children. I forget their names."

Theo rolled his eyes.

"And this…" she continued, gesturing to Fon-Rahm.

"Wait. Don't tell me," said Maksimilian, looking Fon-Rahm up and down. "One of the Jinn, isn't he? I never thought I would live long enough to actually see one in the flesh." He peered at Fon-Rahm as if the genie was on display. "Fascinating. He can almost pass, can't he?"

"I would prefer it if you spoke to me directly," said Fon-Rahm.

"Of course, of course," said Maks. Then he turned to the professor. "Touchy, isn't he?"

"We need your help," said Professor Ellison.

"Of course you do! No one ever comes to see me unless they need something. What is it? A rare herb? A map to the hidden treasures of Amenhotep IV? An introduction to some crime boss?" Maks waved his hand. The squalid men that surrounded the area all picked up their drinks and moved to the other side of the bar. "Sit! Sit! Can I get you anything?"

"I'll take a beer," said Parker hopefully.

Everyone ignored him. They all sat. Reese was instantly repulsed by the sticky table.

Professor Ellison said, "We're looking for the Path."

Maks seemed surprised. "Somebody's looking *for* the Path? That's a new one. Usually, people are looking to avoid them."

"Do you know where they are or not?" said Fon-Rahm. His patience was wearing thin. "We have no time for games."

"He's not much on charm, is he?" Maksimilian said, a twinkle in his eye. He poured himself another drink. "I may have heard something about them skulking around. What do you want them for?"

"That is none of your concern," said Fon-Rahm.

"It's my concern if you cause trouble and it comes back to me."

"We're not looking for trouble, Maksimilian," Professor Ellison said. "Just a little information."

"I suppose I owe you, after what happened in Mongolia," the fat magician said.

The professor smiled. "I was too much of a lady to bring it up."

Maksimilian took a dainty sip of vodka. "I have heard—now I don't know this for a fact, mind you, as I have not seen it with my own eyes—but I have heard that some hoodlums who may match the general description of the Path have set up shop nearby. I have also heard that they are not alone."

Parker said, "Xaru is with them."

Maks regarded Parker. "Perhaps. I value my own delicate skin too much to go and make sure."

"Where are they?" asked Fon-Rahm.

"Holed up in a closed museum. It used to be named for Stalin, before the unpleasantness. There's not much left after all the looting, but it's big and it's private. There are worse places to hide."

Professor Ellison rose, and the rest of her party joined her. "Thank you, Maks. I'll consider us even."

Maksimilian kept his seat. "Think about my offer, Julia. None of us is getting any younger. Maybe someday I'll tire of waiting and I'll marry someone else."

"My loss," said Professor Ellison as they walked out of the bar.

Parker looked at the professor with a new sense of who she was.

"Julia? Really?" he said.

"Shut up," said Professor Ellison.

32

"THIS IS A MISTAKE," FON-RAHM SAID.

They were hiding in the dark, crouched behind a low wall overlooking the crippled museum. It was a blocky monstrosity without windows or adornment, an ugly building, dingy, run-down, and sad even by Soviet standards. In its prime it would have been unpleasant. Now it was downright depressing.

"The Path is not to be trifled with. We should proceed with patience."

"We should go now," said Parker. "We don't have time for games."

"There is always time for caution."

Professor Ellison said, "The boy is right. We don't even know if they'll be here in the morning, and if they leave we may not be able to follow them. Tonight we can catch them by surprise."

They ducked lower as a Path guard made his rounds. He passed right by their wall and stopped. Reese held her breath, but the guard only shifted his rifle's strap from one shoulder to the other. Then he picked his nose and went on his way.

"He's the only guard on this side," whispered Parker.

Theo checked his watch. "I've been timing him. He goes the same way over and over. He'll be back here in seventy seconds."

"I have something in here that will turn him to ash," said the professor as she dug into her bag. "That way his family can save money on the cremation."

"No! We don't have to kill him," Reese said. "We can create a diversion and sneak past him." She rooted around in her brain for something to justify her idea. "That's what they did in *A Tale of Two Cities.*"

"One of these days you'll have to get over your squeamishness, my dear."

"Or maybe you can just stop killing everybody that we meet."

While Reese and the professor argued, the guard made his turn and came back to the wall. Theo picked up a baseball-sized rock, took careful aim, and simply beaned the guy in the head with it. The guard folded like a map.

Parker stared, openmouthed, at his cousin.

"What?" said Theo.

They pried off some boards and made their way in through a side door. As bad as the building was from the outside, the inside was worse. The floor was marble and the walls were stained concrete. A few old paintings still hung at weird angles. Broken statues lay on the floor in pieces. It was dark and scary. It smelled like mildew.

Fon-Rahm pointed the way. "I can sense Xaru and one other. They are this way."

They started to walk through the looted museum.

"I can't help feeling we should be armed," said Theo.

"Guns are for simpletons," the professor said. "And they're unnecessary. All we need to do is get within eyesight. I'll cast one spell to trap the genies and another to"—she glanced over at Reese—"*incapacitate* the Path."

Theo said, "Yeah, well, I would still feel better if one of us had an Uzi."

The professor locked eyes with Theo. "You're not wrong to distrust magic, Theo, but I believe you'll find it's sometimes necessary." Ellison paused. "Perhaps I might even teach you a few things. Better you than"—she glanced at Parker—"someone who lacks self-control. Nothing major, of course, but enough to test the extent of your gifts."

"I'm tested enough already, thanks."

"You should give it some thought. It's not an offer I make lightly, and it may not be repeated."

Professor Ellison walked on. Theo stared at the ground and followed behind her.

They crept down a long, soggy hallway and up a curving flight of stairs. As they passed a water-damaged Renaissance painting of a woman, naked except for a strategically placed bedsheet, Parker did a double take. He went in for a closer look and then turned to Professor Ellison.

"Is that *you*?" he asked incredulously.

"I got around," the professor said with a shrug. Reese grabbed Parker by the arm and pulled him away from the painting.

When they got closer to the museum's center, Fon-Rahm motioned for them to be quiet. They all took cover behind a pile of crates and shattered chunks of concrete. They peeked out and saw that they were perched on the edge of a round walkway that looked over a domed atrium. There were holes in the dome, and two stories down, the legs of what was once a giant statue of a Greek athlete stood atop a crumbling pedestal.

They saw Xaru, pacing as he screamed at his minions.

"Find her! Is that too much to ask?" he fumed. "I recognize that you are lower life-forms, but even for humans you are unconscionably stupid. I would have been better off with camels!"

Fon-Rahm spoke in a whisper. "Good. They are distracted." He turned to Professor Ellison. She was pulling the two empty lamps from Theo's bag. The genie regarded her with mistrust. "I have your word that you will not try to trap me."

"I won't. Not yet, at least."

"Fair enough. Do you need anything before you begin?"

"No," she said, "but you might want to get a mop."

"Why?" asked Parker.

"Because when they realize what I'm up to they may very well wet their pants."

The professor made a few last-minute adjustments to the open containers. Then she stood, her arms wide to the sky, and opened her mouth to start the incantation. Before she could get a single word out, Yogoth materialized out of thin air behind her.

They had walked directly into a trap.

33

"PROFESSOR ELLISON!" REESE SCREAMED.

It didn't do any good. The ugly brute Yogoth grabbed the professor with his four arms. He used one hand to bat away her bag of tricks, and another to cover her mouth so she couldn't speak. Fon-Rahm rushed him, but the drooling genie was faster than he looked. He batted Fon-Rahm over the railing, where he landed heavily at Xaru's feet.

Xaru regarded Fon-Rahm with some amusement. "Bring the witch and the children down to me," he said, and three Path members stepped out of the shadows to seize Parker, Theo, and Reese. Two more Path members took control of Professor Ellison from Yogoth. They were careful to keep one hand clamped over her mouth.

On the ground floor, Fon-Rahm shook off Yogoth's hit and reached for Xaru.

"Oh, Yogoth," called Xaru. The four-armed genie leaped from the rail and landed directly on Fon-Rahm, forcing him to back to the ground. Then he grabbed Fon-Rahm by the legs, swung him in a circle, and let him go. Fon-Rahm was thrown through a wall and into the next room. Yogoth followed him through the hole to finish him off.

Reese squirmed in her captor's arms. She knew that Parker would be in pain. She was right. Parker tried not to show it, but his eyes were watering and his teeth were clenched. His head was on fire.

As Fon-Rahm and Yogoth battled in the other room, the Path members hauled the kids and Professor Ellison down to the atrium. Xaru smiled warmly.

"And now we're all together," he said, gently touching Reese's cheek. Theo put all his strength into breaking his captor's grip, but the thug outweighed him by a hundred pounds. He didn't have a chance.

Xaru shook his head. "Humans. Really. It's all too pathetic." Then he raised his voice so he could be heard over the sounds of the brawl in the next room. "You might as well come out now."

Maksimilian stepped into the atrium. Professor Ellison squirmed in the arms of her abductor and stared knives into him. Maks averted his eyes.

"So we're good now?" he said. "You'll call off the Path?"

Xaru stood directly in front of Professor Ellison, enjoying her anger. "Of course. You may go back to your little life, secure in the knowledge that you are a traitor to your own kind."

Maksimilian turned to leave, desperate to be anywhere else.

"I'm sorry, Julia," he said. "May we meet again in happier times."

Maks put his head down and left the museum. Professor Ellison couldn't do anything besides close her eyes and wish that things were different.

There was a mighty crash, and Yogoth was thrown through the wall and into the atrium. He landed near Xaru, bent iron bars pinning his four arms to his sides.

Fon-Rahm, angry, stepped through the hole in the wall. "This is absurd, Xaru. I can defeat any of our brothers, and you and I could fight for centuries without one of us declaring victory."

"How right you are, Fon-Rahm," said Xaru. "Such a flawed plan seems out of character for me. It's almost as if I were only trying to distract you for a few moments."

"Distract me? Distract me from what?"

Fon-Rahm whipped his head around, but he had figured it out too late. Nadir had been training for this moment for years. He was dressed in a robe passed down through generations and covered with arcane runes. His arms were raised, his mind was focused, and he was chanting an ancient spell. Winds whirled around him.

Fon-Rahm's empty lamp was set in front of him, open and waiting to welcome the genie home.

34

THE WIND TOOK FON-RAHM AND SPUN him around the room like a leaf in a hurricane. The genie bounced off the walls and tried desperately to find something, anything to grab on to. It was no use. He was pulled down and, in a haze of fog and brimstone, sucked back into the lamp. Nadir finished his spell and threw his arms to his side. The lamp sealed itself and began to faintly glow. Fon-Rahm was gone.

Parker fell to his knees. There was no hope now. His captor dragged him back to his feet.

If Xaru felt anything at all, it didn't show. "Good," he said. He turned to his prisoners. "Now, then. Tarinn, my old friend, I am well aware that you have, in your possession, one or two other recovered lamps. I have given some thought as to how I might discover where you're hiding them, and I have decided that torturing you until you tell me is probably the most fun."

One of the minions holding the professor pulled out a knife.

"She would rather die than talk!" said Parker. Easy for him to say, thought Reese. No one was threatening to cut his throat.

"Well, let's see!" said Xaru cheerfully. "Start with her left eye and then take her nose," he instructed the Path member. "After that we'll get creative."

Professor Ellison looked truly scared. The goon with the knife pulled back her hair and held the blade inches from her left eye. She locked her mouth shut. She would never talk.

It was Theo who finally broke. "No! Stop! I know where the lamps are!"

Parker said, "Theo, shut up!"

"*You* shut up! They're going to kill her!"

"They'll kill her if you tell them!"

Theo turned to Xaru. "I'll tell you, if you promise to let us go."

Xaru put his hand over where his heart would be, if he had a heart.

"I promise," he said.

"He's lying! Theo!" said Parker.

Theo shut him out. "She has a secret space in the wall at her office at the university. I saw it. It's a hiding place. I bet the lamps are in there."

Parker deflated like an old balloon. He didn't think Theo would really do it.

"Thank you. Now there is a levelheaded boy." Xaru turned to the professor. "And you keep your entire face."

Parker glared at his cousin. Theo looked at the ground.

Xaru walked over to help Yogoth, who was still struggling on the floor. "Now," Xaru said, easily unbending the iron bars that trapped Yogoth's arms. "Nadir. You and I, along with my dear brother Yogoth, of course, will bring Tarinn back to her home, where she will give us the lamps. No doubt she protected it with some kind of a pesky spell. She was always so clever." He picked up Fon-Rahm's lamp and admired the glow. "A mine in Belarus is set to be collapsed tomorrow. It reaches almost five miles into the earth. The rest of you are to place this lamp gingerly at the bottom. When they destroy the mine, poor Fon-Rahm will be buried under millions of tons of rocks and dirt. Let's see how long it takes him to find his way out of *that*."

He caressed the lamp in a cartoonish display of brotherly love.

"We could have shared the world," he whispered to the lamp. Then he spoke to the Path. "Kill the children. Drop their bodies into the mine, as well. No use stirring up trouble."

"But, you said..." said Theo.

"Start with him," said Xaru, nodding at Theo. "No one likes a snitch."

35

PARKER EYED PROFESSOR ELLISON'S
bag. It was plopped down against a wall, kicked aside and ignored
in all the confusion. He didn't know any of the spells that went
with the doodads inside, but he knew the bag was filled with
powerful stuff. If he could reach it, he thought, he'd find some
kind of magical talisman he could use as a weapon. He would
make the guards tell him where they had taken Fon-Rahm's
lamp, and he would figure out a way to stop Xaru from getting
into the secret hiding place in Professor Ellison's office. He would
save the world from genie domination. He would be a hero to
Theo and Reese. His mom would be sorry she had treated him
so badly. His dad would realize that he had made a huge mistake
in being so selfish and abandoning him.

If he could reach the bag.

But he couldn't. Parker was sitting on the floor with Theo and Reese. Their backs were propped up against the base of the statue, and their feet were stretched out in front of them. Their ankles and wrists were tied with rough, itchy nylon rope and, just to make things a little more uncomfortable for them, they were each gagged with a piece of cloth that smelled like sweat and tasted salty. Parker could no more reach the bag than he could swim the Pacific Ocean with a motorcycle strapped to his back.

Xaru, Yogoth, and Nadir had taken the professor and four or five members of the Path back to New Hampshire. Some of the others grabbed Fon-Rahm's lamp and left for the abandoned mine in Belarus. The goons who remained behind were sitting around an old crate, playing cards in the dim light. They were pretty drunk. They goaded and insulted one another in whatever language it was that they spoke. While they were distracted, Parker used a jagged crack in the marble pedestal to saw at his ropes, but he wasn't getting anywhere. He hoped that they would play cards all night.

One of the Path members threw down his cards in frustration and the others laughed. He had lost the game. He protested, but the others waved him off as they got up and collected their gear. One of the goons slapped Parker's face. He said something funny to his comrades and they laughed and staggered out of the atrium. Parker knew that the man they were leaving behind had lost the game and gained a chore. It was his job to kill Parker, Theo, and Reese.

The remaining minion got unsteadily to his feet and carefully folded a map. It took him three tries to find his pocket. Then he weaved his way over to where the children were tied and unsheathed a dagger from his belt.

Parker felt Theo squirming away beside him. Then the Path member pushed Theo's head back and put his knife to Theo's throat. Theo shut his eyes tight.

"MmmmmMMMmM," said Reese through her gag. "MMm-mmmmMMm." She had something to say. The Path member ignored her and turned back to Theo, but Reese was insistent.

"MMMmmMMMMmMMMM!" she said.

Finally, the man with the dagger relented. He leaned over and pulled Reese's gag down.

"Thank you!" said Reese. "That thing was driving me nuts."

The Path member had a quizzical expression on his face as Reese swept his legs out from underneath him with one swift and powerful kick. The dagger flew out of the minion's hand as he fell and smacked his head hard on the marble floor.

Parker followed the path of the dagger as it went up and then came down. He managed to spread his legs just enough so that when the dagger landed tip-down, it clanged off the marble floor instead of imbedding itself in Parker's thigh or someplace even worse.

The Path member was out cold. Parker and Theo looked to Reese, amazed.

"Brazilian jujitsu," she said with a shrug. "My mom made me take a class at the Y."

36

PARKER, REESE, AND THEO FOUND
themselves walking down a desolate country road. It was a beautiful night. The stars were out, and there was a warm breeze blowing. The only noise came from crickets. The whole thing would
have been magical, really, if they were back in New Hampshire.

But they weren't.

"Okay," said Reese, shifting Professor Ellison's bag on her arm.
"So. We don't have any money, none of us speaks the language,
and we have no way to get home. All true. All very real problems.
I'm not saying they don't exist. But still. How many American
kids even get to come to Lithuania?"

Or Latvia, she thought. She wasn't a hundred percent sure
exactly where they were at the moment.

"And not just the tourist sites, either!"

Her attempt to lighten the mood was doomed from the start. They had been walking for hours, and the tension between Theo and Parker was ready to boil over. Parker planted himself in the middle of the road and exploded at his cousin.

"What were you thinking?" he screamed. "Why would you tell them anything? They're trying to enslave the whole human race. Do you really think you can trust them? I mean, we all know that you aren't exactly straight-A material, but are you really that stupid?"

"Parker..." Reese said.

"Yeah, well," said Theo, "I was trying to save all of our lives."

"You betrayed us! You handed the professor to the Path! And plus, also, now they have however-many lamps she had stashed away. Do you realize you might have doomed the whole world?"

Theo stared into his cousin's eyes for a moment. Then, without warning, he hurled himself at Parker and tackled him to the ground. Reese jumped back as the two boys wrestled in the middle of the road.

"Me? Me? I'm the one that doomed the whole world? What about *you*?"

"Parker! Theo! Stop it!" Reese tried to break them up, but they ignored her.

"What *about* me?" said Parker.

"It's your fault Fon-Rahm got captured!" Theo was on top of Parker, as angry as he had ever been in his life. "He warned you! He said to be careful, to plan it all out. But *no*. That's not good enough for Parker Quarry. Why listen to anybody else? There's no fun in that! You have to make all the decisions. It always has to be about you! You don't care about anybody but yourself. It's no wonder your own mother can't stand to be around you!"

Everything came to a halt. Parker stopped fighting back and Theo climbed off him. Parker stayed on his back and looked at the moon.

"You're right," he said.

Theo shook his head and threw up his hands. "I'm sorry, Parker. About what I said about your mother. That was . . . I didn't mean that."

"Well, you're right about the other stuff. Will you help me up, please? Theo?" Theo just glared at him. "Fine." Parker pulled himself up from the road and checked his hands for scrapes. "I should have listened to you and I should have listened to Fon-Rahm. I got cocky. I do that sometimes. I can't do anything about any of that now except apologize and admit I was wrong, and I do. I apologize. I admit I was wrong."

Reese and Theo waited. It was the first time either of them had been on the end of a sincere apology from Parker.

"You're right. It *is* my fault that Fon-Rahm was captured, and it's going to be up to me, or, well, to us, to get him back."

"And how exactly do you plan on doing that?" asked Theo.

"I'm open to ideas."

Reese thought for a moment.

"We have the map we got off the Path," she said. "We have the professor's bag and all of her magic talismans. We have a dagger. We have maybe one or two hours before the sun comes up."

"Right," Parker said. "What we need is some way to intercept the Path before they get to the mine in Belarus."

"Come on, Parker. There's no way we can do that," said Theo.

Parker pointed down the road at a barely manned government roadblock. There was a swing-arm wooden traffic gate painted in fading orange and white. A uniformed guard was sleeping in a chair in what could charitably be called a shack. Parked well behind it was a beaten-down old military truck with a canvas roof.

"It would be a lot easier if we had some kind of a vehicle," Parker said.

37

"SOME GANGBANGERS TAUGHT ME
how to do this in LA," Parker said as he crawled under the truck's
dashboard. After a solid four minutes of bending wires with
nothing to show for it besides bent wire, Parker came up again.

"Okay," he said. "So I didn't know any gangbangers in LA."

Theo rolled his eyes. "Yeah. I kinda figured."

They were being as quiet as they could be, but everything
seemed to make noise. The door of the truck creaked. The seat
groaned. Theo stood outside the truck, watching Parker and
occasionally glancing over to make sure the guard was still asleep
in his shack. Theo might as well have relaxed. Nothing ever
happened at this checkpoint, and the guard had gotten used to a
six-hour nap every night.

"Excuse me," said Reese. Parker moved over so that she could slide under the steering wheel. After a few seconds of tinkering, the truck's engine fired with an impatient rumble.

Parker said, "Let me guess. You took a class at the Y."

"Nope." Reese grinned. "Saw it in a Jason Statham movie."

Parker slid her over and got behind the wheel. He unfolded the map he stole from the Path. Their route was drawn in red pen, and their destination marked with an X.

"All right. So, here's Belarus, and here's us," Parker said. "As far as I can tell, these lines in black are railroads. The Path are planning on taking a train to the mine. If we can cut them off before they get on board, we can steal Fon-Rahm back. We'll have to hurry."

He shut his door. Reese looked for a seat belt, but there wasn't one. She moved over to make room for Theo. Instead of getting into the truck, however, Theo started walking.

"Theo? Where are you going?" asked Parker.

"I'm going home." Theo stopped and turned back to his cousin. "I'm sorry. This stuff is just... It's too much for me."

Parker said, "How are you going to get home? We don't even know..."

"I'll find a phone. Somebody will have a computer. I'll go to the police. I'll stop at a house. Somebody will help me."

"We can't let you go out there alone!" said Reese.

"Somebody has to save Fon-Rahm. It just can't be me," Theo said. "It'll work out. I'll be okay. Really. I'll be okay."

The two cousins looked at each other for a moment.

Theo said, "So, good luck, I guess. I'll see you when you get back. I'll save you some Thanksgiving turkey."

"Yeah," said Parker. "We'll see you then."

Parker put the big truck in gear, gave it some gas, and looped around the guard shack. He tore through the swing arm over the road, startling the guard awake. The guard ran after the truck, screaming in Russian. Parker watched in his rearview mirror as Theo walked away from the roadblock.

"Good luck to you, too," Parker said quietly. He knew he had lost the best friend he had.

38

REESE NAVIGATED WHILE PARKER drove.

"I think we're okay," she said, examining the map. "The problem is that this map is in Russian."

"I'm sort of surprised you can't read Russian," said Parker.

"Well, technically, I guess, you don't read Russian, you read Cyrillic. It's an alphabet that dates back to . . ." Reese knew she was giving Parker more information than he needed, so she stopped. "Anyway, I can't read it."

Parker grinned. "I knew I could find something you couldn't do if I hung out with you long enough."

Reese found herself blushing. The transmission made a horrible grinding sound as Parker shifted gears.

"Parker? Is something wrong with the truck?"

"It's not the truck. Fon-Rahm's spell is wearing off. Pretty soon I won't remember how to drive."

Reese was able to find the train yard, and Parker managed to drive there. They idled on a hill, looking down at the tracks, and they watched as men walked around the back end of an idling freight train.

"Are you sure we're in the right place?" asked Parker, absently playing with the dagger he had taken off the goon in the museum.

"They circled it on the map."

"I don't see them. Do you see them?"

"No, but the train's still here. Maybe they just haven't shown up yet." Reese put her feet on the dashboard, trying to get comfortable. Then she put them down again. "I don't know why you and Theo have to argue all the time," she said. "I would kill to have a cousin or a sister, somebody that has to hang out with me. I feel like I don't have anything in common with any of the girls at school. I guess maybe I'm not the easiest person to be friends with."

Parker seemed genuinely surprised. "Really? I think you're great. You're smart, you're cool. You're happy all the time. You're always excited by things. You're up for adventure."

Reese smiled to herself.

"If I was a girl, I would *absolutely* want to be your friend," said Parker.

Reese's face fell.

"There!" Parker sat up. Three Path members were climbing out of a Mercedes sedan. One of them carried Fon-Rahm's lamp. They all had guns.

"How are we supposed to get it back?" asked Reese.

Parker groped around the truck, never taking his eyes off the lamp. He came up with a dull green hat that he plopped on Reese's head and a ratty scarf that he wrapped around his own face.

"I'm going to drive down there and park right next to their car. You're going to sneak up next to the guy with the lamp and brain him with this." Parker pulled a massive wrench out from underneath the seat and put it next it to Reese.

"This," Reese said, "is a terrible plan."

"There are only three of them, and you know karate!"

"They have guns, Parker."

"We'll be out of there before they even know what happened! Just hit the guy and grab the lamp. I'll have the truck running right next to you."

Reese picked up the wrench. It was so heavy she could barely lift it.

Parker said, "Okay. I'm just going to creep down there real slow. They'll think we're army guys looking for something on the train. Are you ready?"

"No. I'm not doing this."

"Well, do you have any other ideas?"

"Yeah, my idea is we *don't* do your plan."

Parker moved around in his seat and accidentally hit the gearshift. The truck lurched forward and started to roll toward the train tracks.

"Uh-oh," he said, grinding the gears.

"Parker, stop the truck!"

"I'm trying! I don't know how to drive!"

The truck shot down the hill. The Path members dove out of the way right before Parker creamed the truck directly into the Mercedes. When they looked up from the crash, Parker and Reese found themselves once again surrounded by men with guns.

"I told you this was a terrible plan," said Reese.

One of the Path members ordered the others to board the train with the lamp. As they ran off, the leader grabbed Professor Ellison's bag from Reese and pushed Reese and Parker against a wall.

"Parker, I'm scared," said Reese. She was trembling.

The Path member checked his rifle.

Parker was in shock. Everything had gone so wrong, so fast. "This was all supposed to be fun. I just assumed it would all work out. I'm so sorry I dragged you into this, Reese. I really thought we could pull it off."

Parker wished that Fon-Rahm was there to save them, but he wasn't.

Reese took Parker's hand.

"Good-bye, Parker."

The Path member raised his rifle and took aim.

39

JUST AS THE PATH MEMBER PULLED his trigger, the barrel of his gun bent upward, as if being pulled by an invisible force. The minion looked at it, bewildered. It was a good gun. Very reliable. The barrel had never turned to rubber before.

He heard a voice say, "Hey, moron," and he turned around just in time for Theo to crack him in the face with the giant wrench from the truck.

"That's my cousin," Theo said.

Reese was pretty happy to see him. "Theo! How did you..."

Theo shook his head and pointed to his left. Maksimilian was there, his hands raised to the sky. He was the one who cast the spell that saved them.

"I'm a little rusty," Maks admitted, "but I still got it." Then he let out a burp.

"Gross," said Reese.

"The train!" said Parker. The train was moving, with the Path members and Fon-Rahm's lamp on board. Parker snatched Professor Ellison's bag off the ground and took off after it.

"Parker? Where are you going?" said Theo.

Parker was on the move. He thought he might be able to catch the train, but it was picking up speed and moving away from him fast. Parker slung the bag over his shoulder as he ran. He reached for the railing on the back of the train. He missed. He reached again and this time got hold of the railing by his fingertips. He tripped and was dragged along for a moment, but he managed to find his footing and, finally, pull himself on board the train. He tried the door that led into the train's last car. In his first burst of good luck all day, Parker found that it was unlocked.

40

THE TRAIN WAS OLD AND NOISY, AND it pitched from side to side as it sped down the tracks. Parker found himself in a freight car loaded with boxes and equipment piled high and strapped in place. He grabbed what he could to steady himself, and made his way carefully and quietly deeper into the train.

When he heard voices, Parker stopped and ducked behind a stack of crates. He peeked out. Two Path members were sitting on some gear, eating sandwiches and drinking coffee out of paper cups. One of the men had his hand on the glowing metal lamp.

Parker hunted through Professor Ellison's bag. He came up with a jeweled snowflake, which he thought didn't really fit the occasion, and a small porcelain ballerina doll, which he rejected as too girly. Then he found an amulet made of a piece of clear amber attached to a soft golden chain. He held the jewel up to the light. Inside the amber was a tiny, fossilized spider, trapped since prehistoric times in tree sap that later hardened into a gemstone. Parker felt a power flowing through the talisman. He knew instinctively that he didn't need any fancy spell to make the thing work. He just needed to point it and believe.

Parker aimed the amulet at the Path members. He felt the thing start to heat up. Before it could do whatever it was going to do, however, the train hit a stretch of uneven track. The car bumped and bounced, and the jewel went flying out of Parker's hand. It landed in the middle of the car, right where anybody could see it. Anybody, like, say, the thugs armed with machine guns seven feet away.

Parker froze, but the minions kept on eating. They didn't see it. One of them wadded up his coffee cup and threw it to the side. Then he got up and made his way to the front of the car. He slid open the car's huge side door, unzipped his pants, and started to, as Parker's dad would have said, make some yellow snow.

This was Parker's best shot. He grabbed the dagger from his waistband and cut the straps holding the pile of crates in place. Then he scratched the crates with the knife, making an unpleasant sound. The man with the lamp didn't hear it. Parker did it again, louder this time. The Path member grabbed his gun and got up to investigate. Parker waited for him to get close, and then he shoved. The crates fell on top of the minion, knocking him silly.

Parker was pleased with himself. All he had to do now was grab the lamp and set Fon-Rahm free. The second he reached for it, though, the other Path member came storming back, his gun at the ready. Parker had overestimated the amount of coffee the guy drank and how long it would take him to pee.

Parker pulled back his hand and threw himself behind a huge crate just as the goon started blasting with his machine gun. The box was marked in Russian and had a series of holes near the top. It smelled bad, too, but Parker didn't have time to complain. Bullets ripped through the car and knocked the lock off the big crate.

The lamp was just sitting there, right in the open. It was Parker's only chance. He waited for the Path member's ammo to run out. Then, when the minion stopped to reload, Parker jumped out and made a desperate grab at the lamp.

He came up about a foot short. The lamp was out of Parker's reach when the thug clicked the new magazine into place. Parker looked up to meet his doom, but a noise from the crate behind Parker startled him and the Path member. It was a growl, or maybe a roar. The gunman lowered his weapon and leaned forward, peering quizzically at the crate. Then the crate burst open and a polar bear meant for a circus in Poland, and upset at being woken from a deep sleep, leaped at the Path member. The goon screamed and tried to fight the bear off, but it was no use.

When the bear was through with the Path member, it turned to Parker. It didn't know what the metal container in Parker's hands was, and it didn't care. It had faced weapons before. Parker twisted the thing, and the bear found himself thrown back by a sudden explosion of smoke and lightning that cut the train car in half.

When the fog cleared, Fon-Rahm and Parker found themselves in the wreckage of what was once a train car. They were stopped on the tracks while the rest of the train chugged on, towing the other half of the freight car in a trail of sparks. The polar bear had had enough of people and lightning and trains. It was out of the car and running from the tracks on its way to a new life.

Parker scooped the amber amulet off the floor. You never know when something like that might come in handy.

"I missed you, buddy," he told Fon-Rahm.

"Yes," said the genie. "I suppose I missed you, too."

41

"THEY HAD ME OVER A BARREL,"
Maksimilian said. He was, along with Reese, Theo, and Parker,
trying to keep up with Fon-Rahm as the genie rushed through
the train yard, ripping open steel shipping containers. "The truth
is, I got soft. Pip-squeaks like the Path never would have gotten
to me a century ago."

Parker took off the professor's bag and handed it to Reese.
"Will you do me a favor and carry this purse?"

"Why?"

"It's a *purse*," he said.

"Who's going to see you?" Reese asked.

"Nobody. Just, please?"

Reese rolled her eyes and took the bag. Boys.

"When this one," said Maks, pointing to Theo, "came to

me for help, I just couldn't say no. It was a chance to wipe the slate clean and stick it to Nadir. He's a hard man to like. Plus, I couldn't very well pass up the chance to actually see one of the Jinn in action. Legendary."

Maksimilian stopped, winded. "That's enough for me. I believe there is a gallon of vodka with my name on it." He offered his hand to Fon-Rahm. The genie stopped tearing through the metal containers long enough to take it. "I can sense there is something big happening, but I'm in no shape to help. All I can do is wish you luck."

"I'll see you later, Maks," said Theo.

Maks winked at him. "Give my love to Julia. I'm sure she'll forgive me in a thousand years or so!"

Maksimilian walked away, his laughter echoing through the train yard. Fon-Rahm went back to his search.

"Maks is right. Something big is happening. An impending doom descends upon us, and Xaru is one step ahead. There will be a reckoning."

"Where?" Parker asked.

"Your home."

Reese said, "But our families, all our friends…"

"They are all in great danger."

"We have to get back," said Theo.

"How?" said Parker. "The jet's totaled and we're halfway around the world."

Finally, Fon-Rahm found what he was looking for. He tore the doors off a shipping container and stepped inside. When he came out, he unfurled an ornate carpet on the ground. Fon-Rahm looked at the kids and then back to the carpet.

"Not big enough," he said.

He went back to the container and unrolled a massive sheet of linoleum.

"You're kidding, right?" asked Reese.

"We have no time to lose. Climb on and sit down."

The kids stepped onto the center of the linoleum and sat. Fon-Rahm stepped to the front edge. Smoke misted from his eyes.

"You may want to hold on," he said as the linoleum rose into the air.

42

REESE'S MOTHER HAD READ HER
stories from *One Thousand and One Arabian Nights* when she was
a small girl. Reese had found the book too scary, but she did like
one thing: the flying carpet of Prince Houssain. When she was
tucked in bed, Reese had imagined herself flying on her own
magic carpet. She would go to London to see Mary Poppins and
drop by New York City to visit Eloise. She would fly across the
ocean, the wind blowing through her hair. She would smile and
wave at the people below, so far away they looked like ants.

Now that she was actually on a magic carpet (or a magic piece
of linoleum; really, it was pretty close), she had a completely different reaction. She was terrified.

"I'm going to fall off!" she screamed as the linoleum ripped
through the air.

"You will not fall off," said Fon-Rahm.

"How do you know?"

"Because I have made it so."

Reese trusted the genie. She locked her fingers on to the edge of the linoleum and carefully, carefully looked over the side. They were flying over the ocean at unimaginable speed, yet the wind was no worse than as if she were home riding her electric bike. They were so low that they were skimming the water, the linoleum tearing a white wake through the waves. Dolphins were chasing alongside. A whale breached not a hundred feet away.

All of Reese's fear was gone. She was mesmerized by actual, real-life, swear-to-God magic.

"When I was a kid I dreamed of flying," she said, "but this is better than anything I ever imagined."

"I think, you know, I might be sick," Theo said. He was still in the middle of the linoleum, trying his hardest not to yak.

Reese said, "Over the side, please."

Fon-Rahm strode to the front of the makeshift craft, where Parker was staring out toward the future.

"What if we don't get there in time?" Parker asked.

"Better to think of more pleasant things," said Fon-Rahm.

Parker turned to look at his two friends. He had come so far since his days in Los Angeles, and so much had happened. Maybe the most amazing development of all was his new friendships with Theo and Reese.

"Reese and Theo truly care about you." Fon-Rahm spoke as if he could read Parker's thoughts. "I know that it is hard for you to give your trust to anyone, but your new friends have earned it. Perhaps it is time for you to let them in."

"Theo gave up the lamps," Parker said.

"He made a mistake."

"What if he makes another one?"

"He will. As will Reese. As will you."

"But not you."

Fon-Rahm thought for a moment. "I was not sure that you would return for me or that you possessed the courage and the skill necessary to free me again. I underestimated you, and that was a mistake."

"Fon-Rahm, was that a compliment?" Parker looked surprised.

The genie allowed himself a grin. "Let us call it an observation."

"I've been thinking," said Parker, "about what's going to happen when we get home. There's going to be a fight."

"There is going to be a war."

"Then we should use every weapon we have."

"You have something in mind?"

"A little strategy and some insurance," said Parker.

The genie nodded. "We can discuss it on the way." He aimed the linoleum at the sky, and in seconds they were tens of thousands of feet above the sea, so high they could see the curve of the earth.

Fon-Rahm called out to Reese and Theo. "We'll be there in an hour or so. You will need your full strength. You should try to get some rest."

Reese stayed glued to the side, where she watched a 747 fly by underneath them. "That doesn't seem likely," she sighed.

43

PROFESSOR ELLISON HAD KNOWN PAIN.
She had almost drowned once, when her boat was sunk by pirates off the coast of ancient Egypt. She took a Spartan arrow to the shoulder in the Peloponnesian War. She twisted her ankle fleeing from Rome when the emperor Nero set the city on fire, she was tortured on the rack for weeks when she found herself on the wrong side of the Spanish Inquisition, and her hair was singed to a crisp when she was tied to a stake during a particularly nasty witch hunt in Scotland. An artillery shell shattered her leg near Verdun in World War I.

But the worst pain was the hunger she had felt when she was still a girl named Tarinn, poor and begging on the streets. She had gone days without food, and the pain in her empty stomach had been enough to double her over. A slumlord took "pity" on her and made her his property in exchange for a bowl of rice. She cleaned, she cooked, and she slaved. She accepted her regular beatings as part of the price she paid to keep the pain of starving at bay.

It was at the tables of the wealthy, serving food that she herself was forbidden to touch, that she first heard the stories of the dark sorcerer who bent the laws of nature to his own will. A man who could do magic, real magic! A man who never went hungry, who never had to bow to anyone! A man who had conquered pain!

Then she found Vesiroth, and for years, the pain went away. He didn't listen to her, but he didn't thrash her as long as she stayed out of the way, and eventually, grudgingly, he became her teacher.

She learned small things at first. How to read, how to pronounce the arcane language in the texts, how to cast a spell, how one spell combined with another. It was there that her thirst for knowledge of the Nexus became unquenchable. She was enthralled at the feet of her mentor. She learned how to sway emotions. She learned the secret to living for thousands of years.

She also learned a healthy distrust for the power that attracted her to Vesiroth in the first place. She was not surprised to find herself enchanted by him. He was a sorcerer, after all, and the passion that poured from the wizard with every breath was mesmerizing to his young apprentice. He was magnetic, and Tarinn could at times barely force herself to look away. But as she studied the books and legends, she found story after story of wizards who had destroyed themselves in the never-ending quest for power, and story after story of good intentions twisted by the accumulation of might. Power brought ego, and ego brought more ego, and she saw that it was all too easy for someone with a noble goal to become the very thing they hated most. A human being was just a human being, and human beings were creatures of fragile minds and hurt feelings. They lashed out when they felt threatened, and the more power they had, in Tarinn's experience, the more they felt attacked. People with power saw enemies everywhere.

Vesiroth had always been gruff. He had a frightening temper and was quick to lash out. He was also, even after his centuries of solitude and the immense knowledge he had acquired, human. There was a hurt that lay deep inside him and, horrible as it was, it kept him connected to the people he saw age and die all around him.

She could sense a change in Vesiroth after she brought back the last piece of the Elders' spell. When she read the spell on her own (not aloud, of course; she wasn't suicidal), she realized with a sudden certainty that if her mentor used it, he would be corrupted to his soul. The exposure to the power that was the Nexus would be too great. His mind would snap. The Elders knew the spell would bring only suffering. That was why it had been so hard to find.

Tarinn tried to bring Vesiroth back from the edge, but it was far too late. The Nexus called to him. The temptation of power was too strong.

She had to get away. Away from her mentor and away from the frightening power of his vengeance.

Away from the pain.

"This can all be over, witch. Release the spell and give me the lamps."

Xaru was inches away from Professor Ellison's face. She was in Yogoth's grip, his four arms holding her like a straitjacket. Her face was bruised, and she was experiencing the most intense pain of her long life. Xaru and the four members of the Path he had brought with him had not shown her any mercy. They were more than willing to kill her if it meant that they would take possession of the lamps. They were more than willing to kill her even if it didn't.

"No," she said.

They were in her office on the campus of Cahill University. All of her treasures, so carefully cataloged and arranged, were scattered on the floor. Shelves were tipped over. Her clippings were torn from the walls. They had found the shimmering wall, but none of them could breach the magic field she had placed to protect the only things she owned that could not be replaced.

"Don't be a fool, Tarinn. Give me the lamps. Spare yourself hours of torture."

"No."

The professor knew that it would be useless to scream out. There was no one there to help her. Fon-Rahm was buried under tons of rock. The children were probably dead. She was doomed. After thousands of years of life, she was finally going to see what came after.

Xaru grabbed her by the hair. "You are seconds away from becoming a limbless torso. Give me the lamps!"

The professor looked the genie right in the eye and spoke with steely conviction.

She told him, "The next time you see a lamp it will be from the inside, and I will be the one that put you there."

Xaru could take her impertinence no longer. His anger took control. His fist became a flame as he pulled it back to hit her and put a stop to her meddling once and for all. Professor Ellison closed her eyes, ready for the end.

Before the punch was unleashed, Nadir grabbed Xaru's arm.

Xaru paused for a brief moment. "Please," he said, his voice hiding his fury at Nadir. "Please tell me that you did not just grab my arm."

Nadir let go of Xaru's arm. He was calm as he bowed to his master. Then he turned to Professor Ellison. She tried to squirm away, but she was held tight by the drooling genie Yogoth. Nadir placed his hands on her temples and locked his scary blue eyes onto hers. His grip became tighter as his concentration grew more and more intense.

"No," she said. She was shaking, but not with fear or pain. She was shaking as if something were being pulled from her. "No. Stop."

Nadir doubled his efforts. He was reaching deep into her mind, probing her for the spell that would bring the lamps into the open. His hands trembled. His teeth clenched. Finally, the professor screamed and passed out cold in Yogoth's arms.

Nadir turned to the shimmering wall. Then he chanted a few words and reached in his hands. The wall parted at his touch, revealing four metal canisters floating unprotected in a sea of pure energy. Nadir smiled. The lamps were theirs.

44

THE CAMPUS WAS A GHOST TOWN.

That was the first thing Theo noticed when they landed. It was the middle of the day, on a Tuesday, and Cahill University should have been busy and noisy and crowded. There should have been a rush of students changing classes. There should have been professors drinking coffee and marking papers on benches. There should have been Frisbees. There should have been music. There should have been life.

There was nothing. All the students and the faculty and the workers were lying on the grass or on the sidewalks, motionless and silent. The only sound was the chirping of birds.

"We're too late," said Theo. "They're all dead."

Fon-Rahm shook his head. "No. They are not dead. Only sleeping."

Parker knelt by a collapsed student and put his fingers to his neck, looking for a pulse. "He's right. They're all unconscious."

"What happened here?" Reese asked. "It looks like they all just passed out at the same time."

"A trick of Xaru, no doubt. He does not like to be slowed down."

All of a sudden, Parker was frightened. He knew that Xaru was dangerous, but so far the only people that had gotten hurt were a few Path members. This was his first glimpse of what Xaru was capable of on a larger scale. If he could entrance an entire college full of people without breaking a sweat, what was to stop him from doing much, much worse? All the bodies on the ground could easily be dead, and instead of hundreds there could be thousands. Or millions.

"Dad!"

Parker looked up to see Theo running through the quad. Reese and Fon-Rahm were chasing after him.

Theo dropped to his knees. Both of his parents were sprawled unconscious on the sidewalk.

"Dad! Mom! Wake up!"

Theo was slapping his father in the face, trying to get him to snap out of his trance. Parker reached Theo and put his hand on his cousin's shoulder. "Theo. It's okay." Parker's voice trailed off. Lying next to his aunt Martha and uncle Kelsey was Parker's mother.

"Mom?" he said. He held her head in his hands and turned to Fon-Rahm and Reese. "She came! She came for Thanksgiving, and they were giving her a tour. She actually got here." He paused for a moment, and then screamed at Fon-Rahm. "Make her wake up! I command you to make her wake up!"

Fon-Rahm was stone-faced. "I cannot. The only way to wake these people is to stop Xaru."

Parker put a hand to his eyes so that no one could see that he was starting to cry. He pulled himself together and stood. Theo was lying on the ground, one arm around his father and one arm around his mother. Parker gently pulled him away.

"It's okay, Theo. We'll save them."

Theo, stunned, managed to stand.

"We got this," said Parker.

Fon-Rahm zeroed in on Professor Ellison's building. "They are in there."

Reese nodded. "Then let's go get them."

They ran through the archaeology building, down deserted hallways and past empty rooms. When they reached Professor Ellison's office, Fon-Rahm turned to the kids.

"I can take care of Xaru and Yogoth. You must deal with the Path on your own."

The kids nodded. They were outmanned and outgunned, but they knew they had no choice. They would do whatever it took to stop Xaru and the Path.

Fon-Rahm looked at them with something like respect. Then he turned the handle on Professor Ellison's office door, and the wall exploded in front of him.

45

AT FIRST, ALL THAT PARKER COULD see were bright white spots that danced in and out of his vision. As soon as he focused on one, it vanished. Parker couldn't tell if they were really there or not.

Soon, though, his head cleared enough to see what had happened. He had, along with Theo and Reese, been blown backward by an explosion. It didn't take long for Parker to realize what caused it.

"Now really, Fon-Rahm," said Xaru, hovering three feet off the ground in the ruins of Professor Ellison's office. "What took you so long?"

Xaru released a ball of flame that Fon-Rahm easily deflected.

"There is no reason for more innocents to be hurt. Surrender, Xaru!"

"Oh, I don't think so," said Xaru. He gestured to the back of what was left of the professor's office, where the Path members were just completing the ritual to open one of the newly freed lamps.

"No!" Fon-Rahm cried, just as the sacrificial Path member twisted the lamp. Fon-Rahm was too late. The lamp was open.

But nothing happened.

Parker helped Reese and Theo to their feet. They rushed to Fon-Rahm's side.

"Could it be a dud?" Parker asked.

"I fear not," said Fon-Rahm.

Nadir walked over to the kneeling Path member and casually slit the man's throat. The sacrifice slid to the floor without a sound. Nadir peered into the open canister. Then his face turned gray. He leaped for cover just as the lamp detonated, erupting with the fury of a blazing sun. Everyone in the room was tossed away from the blast.

Again, Parker found himself on his butt. He coughed and waved his hand in front of his face to clear away the smoke and dust. When he saw the sky he realized that the roof of the building was gone, obliterated in the explosion.

And then he saw Rath.

The newly freed genie was a horror. He was huge, the size of a building, so massive that he couldn't even fly. He had squirming, squealing rats for hair, attached to his horrifying head by their hairless tails. Any resemblance he had to Fon-Rahm, Xaru, Yogoth, or even Vesiroth was hard to see. He was simply a roaring monster.

Rath wielded two giant, curved scimitars and howled at the heavens.

"Oh, crap," Parker said. "You are a big boy, aren't you?"

The Path members were dumbstruck. They dropped the professor, who collapsed to the floor, and then they fell to their knees in front of the rat genie. Insane with rage that had been building for three millennia, Rath swiped with his twin swords, instantly killing the kneeling thugs. Only Nadir and one other Path member survived.

Fon-Rahm marshaled the kids behind him. "Take cover."

"What are you going to do?" asked Parker.

The genie took to the air.

"I'm going to keep them busy," he said as he flew off to do battle with Xaru, Yogoth, and Rath. The genies sized each other up. There was suddenly a lot of firepower in the airspace over Cahill University.

Reese was searching around the rubble.

Theo asked her, "What are you looking for?"

She pulled out the professor's bag. It was dusty, but intact. "This. There has to be something useful in here."

Parker saw Nadir and the remaining Path member coming for the unconscious professor. "Theo! Can you get to Professor Ellison?"

"Yes."

Parker took the bag and threw it to Theo. "Then take care of her. She's the only one who can trap the genies."

"Got it."

"Good," said Parker before he threw an age-old bowl from

the professor's collection that smashed against the remaining Path member's head, knocking him out cold. Nadir turned away from Professor Ellison, livid, and drew his curved blade. He was getting pretty tired of this meddling seventh grader.

Parker took Reese's hand. "We should probably go."

Reese nodded. "You're probably right."

Parker and Reese ran, with Nadir right behind them.

Fon-Rahm withstood the fire from Xaru, and he held his own against the mindless fists of Yogoth, but Rath was harder to ignore. His swords cut huge arcs through the air, and when one hit Fon-Rahm's arm, it cut him deeply. The wound would heal, but it would sap precious strength from Fon-Rahm just when he needed it most. They were going to wear him down. They were going to punish him for standing against them.

And they were going to enjoy every second of it.

Theo held Professor Ellison's head in his hands. At first he was afraid that the professor was dead. Her face was pale, and she felt almost weightless in his arms. For the first time, Theo saw Professor Ellison for what she was: a very frail, very elderly woman.

Then, with a start, the professor came to. Theo scooted away from her in fright. He rushed back when she made it clear that she was trying to stand.

"Don't try to get up, Professor."

"I have to," her voice was a hoarse croak. "I have to contain them."

"You're too weak!"

"Nonsense! I'm stronger than I have ever been!"

She got to her feet and raised her arms. Before she could cast any kind of a spell, she fell back into Theo's arms. He lowered her gently to the floor and bowed his head, wondering what they would do if she was too far gone.

Parker and Reese ran through the wreckage of the building.

"Do you think we lost him?" Parker asked, looking over his shoulder. A thrown dagger stuck angrily in the wall behind them.

"No," said Reese.

"This way!" Parker pulled Reese with him, but he was too far from Fon-Rahm. He broke down from the searing pain in his head.

"Parker! Get up!" Reese pulled him to his feet, but he could barely move. Nadir kept coming. They were not going to be able to run away.

The battle in the air shifted as Fon-Rahm clutched his head.

"Now! He's weakened!" said Xaru. Yogoth grabbed Fon-Rahm from behind and held him while Rath used his mammoth scimitars to slice hundreds of rats from his own head. Rath couldn't fly, but the rats could. They streamed at Fon-Rahm, their razor-edged teeth dripping venom.

"Now, this should be fun," said Xaru.

Reese saw that Fon-Rahm was struggling and in real trouble. She braced herself and did the last thing in the world that Nadir expected. She dropped Parker and charged him. Nadir made a quick stab with his blade, but with the skill of a martial artist, Reese planted one foot on the ruins of a wall and launched herself at him. His knife missed and Reese punched Nadir as hard as she could in the throat. Nadir went down, gasping for breath, and Reese picked up Parker. She dragged him back to the professor's office and he revived.

"What happened?" he asked.

"Nothing," she said. "Just giving Nadir something to remember me by."

With Parker close, Fon-Rahm recovered instantly. He threw off Yogoth and obliterated the attacking swarm of rats with a burst of blue lightning. Yogoth and Rath charged at him from opposite directions, enraged, but Fon-Rahm flew straight up and out of their way. The two brutish genies smacked into each other, and Fon-Rahm landed on top of them with enough force to leave them both dazed.

"Such heart!" said Xaru with a laugh. "I'll miss you when you're a pile of dust!"

He blasted Fon-Rahm with white-hot flame.

Parker and Reese knew they could only go so far before Parker's tether held them back, and now they were out of options. They were trapped.

Nadir turned the corner and saw them. He held his wounded throat as he walked slowly and deliberately, straight at them.

Parker pointed to the only way out. It was a hallway strewn with rubble. At the other end was a hole that led to the outside.

"Go that way," he said.

"No!"

"I'm the one he wants. Let him chase me."

"I'm not leaving you here alone! He'll kill you!"

"Reese. I have this covered. It'll be okay. I swear. Go."

Reese paused.

"I'll be okay. I promise," said Parker.

She nodded and turned to the hallway. Parker sprinted away and around a corner. Nadir, holding his throat with one hand and his knife with the other, went after him and out of sight. Reese tried to go the other way. She even started to. But in the end, she couldn't help herself. She turned on her heels and followed them.

Theo and Professor Ellison had great seats for the battle of the genies, but Theo would have rather been anyplace else. Even math class, Theo's least favorite thing in the world, was better than this. All he and the professor could do was watch as Fon-Rahm was worn down by the other three genies. Fon-Rahm was powerful, but he was also overmatched. He would block Rath, only to be sucker punched by Xaru or battered by the four fists of Yogoth.

Theo came to the only conclusion he could possibly reach. "Fon-Rahm can't beat them," he said. "He's just not strong enough."

The professor looked to her own useless hands and gritted her teeth.

Nadir was confused. He had followed Parker into a maze of destroyed offices, but somehow lost him among the debris. The Path leader had spent almost his entire life working to make Xaru's rule a reality, but at this moment, blinded by rage, the only thing he wanted was Parker's slow and painful death. Nadir was a man used to suppressing his emotions. He was violent and cruel, yes, but not because he enjoyed it. Everything he did was to advance a goal. This was different. Killing Parker was something he was actively looking forward to. Nadir had never before felt such hatred.

Where had the child gone? Nadir stepped into a destroyed classroom. Two of the walls were completely torn down. He kicked over a desk, expecting to find Parker hiding behind it, but there was nothing there. He huffed in exasperation.

"Looking for me?"

Nadir whirled on the voice behind him and was met with the hard edge of a Bronze Age shield in Parker's hand. It caught Nadir on the chin and knocked him sideways. Parker raised the shield to deliver a harder blow, but Nadir was a trained fighter with instincts to match. He grasped the shield and wrenched it away from the seventh grader. It clanged to the ground, out of the boy's reach.

Parker was defenseless, but not beaten. He charged at Nadir with his fists.

"Come on!" he cried. "Come on, you coward!"

Nadir slipped his punches with ease, and with one blow thrust his blade into Parker's chest.

Reese was watching from the doorway. "Parker?" she said, her hands over her mouth in horror. "Parker!"

Then Nadir pulled the knife from the boy's heart, and smiled as Parker Quarry slid to the floor, dead.

46

NADIR WIPED THE BLOOD FROM HIS blade on Parker's shirt. He had killed many, many men in his life, but this death was by far the sweetest. He would have liked to have savored it for a few moments more, but Reese was standing in the doorway, paralyzed with fear. There was no time for Nadir to contemplate his own successes. The girl needed to be tended to, as well.

He stepped over Parker's lifeless body and walked slowly at Reese. He wanted her to be good and scared when she died.

"Oh, I don't think so."

Nadir froze. He recognized the voice coming from one of the destroyed walls, but he knew that his ears were playing tricks on him. It was impossible.

He turned slowly and saw Parker step over the ruins of the wall and into the room. The seventh grader was with Reese and Theo, but that didn't seem right, either. Theo was with the professor in the other room, and Reese was still standing in the doorway. He could see her.

Nadir looked down at the boy he had just killed and saw that the body was dissolving into sand.

"Don't look so confused, buddy. You're not the only one who knows magic," said Parker, and Nadir knew. Doppelgängers! Magic doubles! Tricks, no doubt conjured up by that wretched witch who Xaru called Tarinn.

Nadir was enraged. He charged at Parker. Fine, he thought. Now I get to kill Parker Quarry twice.

As Nadir took his first lunging steps, Parker—the real Parker—aimed the amber charm from Professor Ellison's bag at him. Heat and vibrations come out of the amulet, and Parker could have sworn he saw the spider inside the amber twitch its legs. Then the jewel fired out a blinding yellow light that hit Nadir in mid-stride. As the magic struck him, Nadir began to rapidly age. His blond hair turned white and his skin wrinkled. His bones grew brittle and his head drooped. Only the hatred in his cold blue eyes remained intact.

Nadir's pace was slowed to a crawl, but he did not back down. He continued to come at Parker, deliberate step by deliberate step. By the time he reached Parker, Nadir was so old that he could no longer hold his knife. It dropped to the floor. With one final lunge at Parker, Nadir collapsed. He was now an old, old man, gasping for air and too weak to move.

Reese hated Nadir, but she couldn't bear watching years being taken away from anybody's life in seconds. "That was horrible," she said.

"I know," said Parker, taking her hand. "But right now we have to go." Reese nodded her head, and with one glance back over her shoulder at Nadir, she and Parker took the fake Reese and Theo and ran to rejoin the fight.

"It's the end for you, brother," said Xaru. Fon-Rahm was being battered by another onslaught of rats sliced from Rath's head. He was swatting them away, one by one, but their accumulated bites, added to the punishment from Yogoth's fists and the fire from Xaru, were taking a toll. Every time Fon-Rahm blocked one attack, two others struck him.

As Fon-Rahm evaded a swipe of Rath's swords, Xaru grabbed him and gave him a nasty head-butt to the face. "You should have joined me when you had the chance."

Professor Ellison had seen enough. She stood on shaky legs, brushing aside Theo's offer of help. "Give me my bag."

Theo did what he was told. Parker and Reese, with the fake Theo and Reese in tow, reached Theo and the professor just as Fon-Rahm kicked Rath through a wall.

"Where did these two come from?" Professor Ellison asked, nodding to the fakes as she searched inside her bag of tricks.

"I had Fon-Rahm summon them on the way here," said Parker.

"Smart," said the professor approvingly. "Maybe I can find something for them to do." She found what she was looking for, something in a soft velvet bag with a pull-string. "If I'm going to capture those genies, I'll have to prepare. Fon-Rahm will have to buy us some time."

Reese looked up at the battle. Rath had returned, hauling his bulk back into the building with a roar of anger. Fon-Rahm threw off Yogoth again. Xaru peppered Fon-Rahm with blasts of fire and laughter.

"That's not going to happen!" cried Reese. "He's getting killed up there!"

"That's true. But that would change if he had more power."

Theo said, "How can he get more power?"

The professor looked Theo dead in the eyes. "I can lend him some of mine," she said. "With your help."

"I can't help you! I don't know anything about magic or spells or any of this!"

"I would have preferred to bring you along more slowly, but we don't have the time and there's too much at stake. I need you to tap into your potential right now and help me."

Theo cast his eyes down. "I don't know how."

"You do; you just don't realize it yet."

Professor Ellison shook a glass prism from its velvet bag. "This spell is a doozy, and I'm too weak to cast it myself. I need you to concentrate on this prism and repeat the words I say. If I'm right about you, and I think I am, a good part of the power I have absorbed through the centuries will flow from me to you, and from you to Fon-Rahm. It's the only way."

"What if you're wrong about me? What if the thing on the plane was just a fluke?"

"Then we all die in an explosion of fire and ash. No pressure, Theo."

Theo didn't have a choice. He took the prism in his hand.

"Okay," he said. "I'm ready."

"You had better be," said Professor Ellison. She pushed Theo's hand up so the prism was between them and the genie fighting above them, and she began to chant words older than history.

Theo repeated the words. Even as the professor's voice wavered from her effort, he could feel raw power flowing through him. It was a strange sensation, like nothing he had ever experienced before. His hair stood out, as if someone was rubbing a balloon on his head, and he tasted metal. Finally, the spell was done, and the power left Theo in a burst of purple mist that enveloped Fon-Rahm.

Professor Ellison fell limp to the floor. Theo hoped against hope that whatever they had done together was enough to save all of their lives.

Fon-Rahm saw the mist close around him. He closed his eyes and took a deep breath, drawing the mist into himself and feeling the professor's years of accumulated power stream into his body. For a moment he thought the wreckage of the building that surrounded them was getting smaller. Then he realized that he was, in fact, growing larger. In seconds he was a giant, a colossus striding through Cahill University. He dwarfed even Rath.

Xaru paled as Fon-Rahm grew and grew. "What . . ."

Fon-Rahm flicked the attacking rats away with the tiniest movements of his fingers. He caught one of Rath's swords in each hand, tearing them away from the rat genie and casting them aside before crushing Yogoth beneath his titanic foot.

Xaru hit him with all of his might, but he barely felt it. Fon-Rahm pulled back his fist and let fly. He caught Xaru in the face and blasted him half a mile.

"You were saying?" he asked.

"You did it!" Reese told Professor Ellison. "He can win!"

"No," the professor said, struggling to her feet. "He has enough power to destroy the others now, but only *I* can trap them, and I only have enough strength left for one good try." She looked around the wreck that was her office. "Theo, all of you. Get me four containers. Jars, bottles, anything that can be sealed."

Parker raised his eyebrows. "Three," he said.

"What?"

"You said four containers. You meant three."

The professor smiled slyly, caught. "Of course. That's what I meant. Three."

With his new power, Fon-Rahm dominated the other genies. He was so huge and scary that Rath turned and lumbered away from the fight. Fon-Rahm grabbed Xaru by the throat. He held him and hit him again and again.

"You're time is up, Xaru. I'm sorry you could never listen to reason."

Xaru smiled through his pain. "That's always been your problem, big brother. You never learned that reason only goes so far. Now!" When Xaru yelled, Rath stopped stumbling and lashed out, not at Fon-Rahm, but at the kids and Professor Ellison. The rat genie knocked them aside and grabbed Parker.

Xaru laughed as Rath pulled Parker away from Fon-Rahm. "You never learned how to be truly vicious. You never learned how to do what it takes to win."

Fon-Rahm reached for Rath, but Yogoth held him back. Rath moved farther and farther away, straining the limits of the tether. Soon both Parker and Fon-Rahm were in searing pain. Parker felt sure his head would explode. He pressed his hands to his temples and screamed.

Xaru told Rath, "Not so quickly, my brother. Let's take a moment to really enjoy this." He floated lazily over to Fon-Rahm. "There's no escape for you this time, Fon-Rahm. This time *I* win. When the world is mine, do you think they'll remember you? Do you think they'll care whose side you were on? Now you have nothing, while every living thing on this world will pray for mercy in my name!"

Xaru slapped Fon-Rahm across the face. Fon-Rahm was helpless to stop him.

"All right, Rath," said Xaru. "We have much to do, and only eternity to do it in. Let's see what happens when we get these two a few miles apart."

Reese's stomach dropped. Parker was going to be killed. Fon-Rahm was going to be destroyed. Xaru was going to win.

47

REESE LOOKED OVER HER SHOULDER
and saw herself.

"The doubles," she said. "We can send the doubles!" She grabbed the fake Reese and the fake Theo and yelled something in their ears. The doubles nodded and started to hunt through the professor's ruined gear.

"What can they do that we can't?" asked Theo as the fakes pulled a long orange extension cord from the debris. They each grabbed an end of the cord and ran at Rath.

"They can *die*," said Reese.

The doubles made a mad dash at Rath, winding underneath his legs in attempt to get the rat genie tangled up.

"That will never work," said Professor Ellison. "That thing is too big. Even if they manage to trip him, he'll still have Parker."

Reese told her, "I didn't tell them to trip him. I told them to make him mad."

Rath was, indeed, getting annoyed. He stomped at the fakes, but they were too fast. He couldn't pin either of them down.

"Ignore them!" commanded Xaru. "Finish the boy!"

Ignoring pests was not in Rath's nature. He kicked at the doubles, and then swung at them with the fists that held Parker. The rat genie was just too slow to make contact. Finally, enraged, he dropped Parker so that he could have full use of his hands. Rath balled up his fists, timed his blow, and crushed the fake Reese and the fake Theo into the ground. Satisfied, the genie lifted his fists. He seemed perplexed to find nothing but sand beneath him.

Theo and Reese were already dragging Parker back to be near Fon-Rahm.

"Are you okay?" said Reese.

"I got the wind knocked out of me."

"And your head almost exploded," said Theo.

"Yeah," Parker admitted. "There was that."

With his head recovered, Fon-Rahm was himself again. He rained blows on Rath and Yogoth until their fight was over, and then turned to Xaru. "It is over, Xaru. It is finally finished."

Xaru, exhausted and bloodied from the battle, took in the scene. His brother genies were spent and useless. The children were out of his reach. The professor was already lining up two old jars and a wine bottle, ready to trap him and the others. His fire, once stronger than a blowtorch, was dying.

"Go quietly," said Fon-Rahm. "Do not make me hurt you anymore."

The professor was ready to begin her chant.

"I won't be trapped again, brother," Xaru said.

"You made your decisions yourself, Xaru."

Xaru stared off into the distance. "There are things I know that you don't, Fon-Rahm. Things Vesiroth thought you would disapprove of. Things he thought you would not understand."

"Stop talking in circles."

"If I can't rule the world, no one can." Xaru closed his eyes and floated into the air. He raised his arms to his side and began to chant to himself.

Fon-Rahm was confused. "What is it? What is he doing?" he asked Professor Ellison.

"It's Vesiroth's spell of destruction. It was designed as a failsafe, one last weapon that would destroy his enemies and leave him standing. I didn't think anyone else knew it. If Xaru finishes, everything surrounding this building will be vaporized."

Yogoth came out of his stupor and joined Xaru in the air.

The professor said, "Make that everything for miles."

Rath pulled himself up and joined his brothers from the ground. Lights started to flash around them.

Fon-Rahm launched a volley of lightning at the chanting genies, but Vesiroth's spell had created a shield around them. The lightning dissipated as it hit.

"I can't reach them through the shield," said Professor Ellison. "Can you bring it down?"

"No. It is too strong. The energy needed to breech will obliterate them as well." Fon-Rahm was stuck. "I cannot stop them without destroying them."

"You know that can't happen," said Professor Ellison.

"I may not have a choice."

The professor was using a Sharpie to draw arcane symbols of containment on her bottles and jars. "I just need a few more minutes."

"There is no time!" said Fon-Rahm. "If I do not stop Xaru now, he will finish his spell!"

"Let him finish, then!" Professor Ellison snapped. The kids were shocked. Ellison pushed Parker aside and spoke directly to Fon-Rahm. "You and I will survive!"

Fon-Rahm could hardly believe what he was hearing. "But the children, the town..."

"There are other children and other towns! There will always be more people. It will be easier to trap Xaru after he finishes the spell. He'll be tired. He'll be weak. Let him do what he wants."

The chanting from the genies was getting louder. Parker could feel the air around him changing. He knew the spell was almost complete.

"Fon-Rahm, don't listen to her!" he said. "I command you to destroy Xaru and protect us!"

Fon-Rahm hesitated.

"You can't do it, can you?" said the professor. "It's because you know I'm right. The greater good takes precedence over your master's whims. That's why you wouldn't obey Vesiroth in the first place. You know that if you destroy Xaru and the others, their power will return to Vesiroth and he will walk again. What is the sacrifice of one pitiful town and three children next to that? Let them die!"

Static electricity filled the air. Lights and smoke swirled around. The end was coming.

Fon-Rahm looked to the genies, and then to Parker.

"This is a decision I cannot make," he said. "You must command me."

48

ONLY WEEKS AGO, PARKER WOULD
have made the decision in an instant. He would have ordered
Fon-Rahm to annihilate the other genies, no matter what the
cost was to anybody else. Now he was torn. He wanted to save
himself and his friends and his mother, who was unconscious less
than five hundred yards away. He wanted to tell Fon-Rahm to
blast Xaru out of the sky, and deal with the consequences later.

But he wasn't sure.

What if he made the wrong decision and the world was condemned because of it? What if he unleashed Vesiroth and more
people died than would die here? The decision was too much for
any seventh grader, so Parker did what any seventh grader might
do. He turned to his friends.

"I don't know what to do," he said, looking to Theo and Reese. "This is bigger than just me. I need your help."

They stood in silence, thinking, for as long as they dared. They knew they didn't have much time.

"We have to let Professor Ellison trap them," said Reese. "We have to save the world, no matter what."

Parker nodded. "Theo?"

Theo said, "No! We can't! You heard the professor! Everything will be wiped out! My parents are here! Your *mother* is here!"

The lights spinning around them grew more intense by the second.

"They're almost finished!" said Professor Ellison.

"Parker, I don't want to die," said Theo.

Parker said, "I don't, either."

Theo, tortured, stared at the floor and nodded. Reese put her arms around him. Parker spoke up to the giant Fon-Rahm. "Let Xaru finish. Even if it means we're destroyed." He looked to his friends. "It's what we decided."

"You would make that sacrifice?" said Fon-Rahm.

Parker took Reese's hand. "We would."

Fon-Rahm nodded. "And that is why humanity deserves to make her own decisions."

With that, Fon-Rahm made the only choice that made any sense to him. He turned his immense power on Xaru and the other genies. Professor Ellison cried out, but he ignored her, concentrating all of his firepower on the shield. The shield buckled and fell, and the genies, powerless, were engulfed in Fon-Rahm's storm of lightning.

Xaru cackled as the Nexus took him. "You were always a fool, Fon-Rahm. This is only the beginning."

Xaru let out one final scream as he, Rath, and Yogoth were vaporized.

49

ALL WAS STILL.

Parker, Reese, and Theo stared at each other. Fon-Rahm knelt down so he could speak to them on their level.

"We're still alive," said Reese.

Parker said, "Why, Fon-Rahm? Why did you do it?"

Fon-Rahm had a gleam in his eye. "I do what I am compelled to do," he said.

Parker smiled at him, and the genie smiled back.

Theo was not interested in anything so touchy-feely. Reese had to hold him back from attacking Professor Ellison. "She would have killed us!" he screamed. "She wanted us dead!"

"Let her be," said Reese, staring daggers at the professor. "She never pretended to care about us."

The professor smirked. "Children. You think you know everything." She held out her prism and craned her neck to talk to Fon-Rahm. "I believe you have something that belongs to me."

"Yes. Yes, of course." Fon-Rahm placed his hand over the prism and closed his eyes. All the power the professor lent him returned to her in a purple fog, and Fon-Rahm shrank to his normal size.

"You should have kept it," said Theo. "It might've come in handy."

"It was never mine to keep."

Parker turned pale, remembering suddenly that his mother was still passed out on the grass. "My mom!"

He started to run out of the building, but Fon-Rahm grabbed him. "She is not hurt. Now that Xaru is gone, she and the others will awaken with no knowledge of what happened here."

"I have to see her!"

"Shouldn't we get our stories straight first?" asked Theo. "I mean, how are we going to explain all of this? We destroyed an entire building."

"I can just have Fon-Rahm put it back the way it was," Parker said.

Reese shook her head. "It won't last. In a day or two it'll be a pile of bricks again. And this time there might be people in it."

Professor Ellison took a step back and looked at what remained of her office. "It was an old building," she said. "And I often smelled gas. I believe that I put a few complaints in writing over the years."

Reese said, "Really?"

"No. But I'm sure I can whip up a convincing forgery or two." She looked at Parker and Theo. "You might as well run along to your parents. No one needs you here."

They didn't have to be told twice. Parker and Theo sprinted across the university campus, leaving Reese, the professor, and Fon-Rahm behind them.

All over Cahill University, students and faculty were waking up. They were groggy and confused, but they were safe and they were alive. An administrator found himself dangling halfway out of his Saab. At first he thought it was strange, but then he forgot all about it, the way you might forget an intense dream the second you wake up. A sophomore wondered in a vague way why she had decided to take a nap facedown in the middle of the quad instead of going to class, but the thought quickly vanished from her head, replaced by more pressing concerns like her GPA and the fact that her roommate kept eating all of her ramen noodles no matter how many times she told her not to. A custodian was only slightly curious as to how it got so late. He would put off cleaning the men's locker room until tomorrow. There was plenty of time.

Theo found his parents on the sidewalk. His father weighed more than two hundred pounds, but Theo hauled him to his feet as if he were a small child. Theo's mother ran her fingers through Theo's hair, and he grinned like it was Christmas.

Parker's mother was coming to on the ground next to a bench. She blinked at the sun as if she had been asleep for weeks instead of hours. Parker wanted to run to her, but he stayed back. He didn't know what to feel.

Then his mom looked at him. She squinted as if she couldn't quite make him out.

"Parker?" she asked.

That was all it took. Parker ran to her and threw himself into her arms. He hugged her as if he hadn't seen her for three thousand years.

His mom hugged him back. "I missed you, too," she said. "I missed you so much."

Professor Ellison and Fon-Rahm watched respectfully, as far as the genie's tether would allow. The professor couldn't stop her eyes from misting over.

"Do not tell me you are going to cry," said Fon-Rahm.

She composed herself with a snort. "I haven't cried since Thomas Jefferson insulted my cooking."

Reese had gone back to the archaeology builing for one last look. She was out of breath when she caught up to them.

"Everyone from the Path is gone," she panted. "All of the bodies and everything. I couldn't even find Nadir. And there's something else. Your lamps are gone!"

Professor Ellison shrugged as if she had been expecting the news. "Well. I suppose I had better get back to work, then." She allowed herself another moment to watch Parker and Theo with their families. "Tell them I said good-bye, please. I'm sure I'll see them around." She turned back to her office and shouted over her shoulder to Fon-Rahm.

"Keep your eyes open. Things are about to get much, much worse."

50

THE MERRITT HOUSE WAS FILLED WITH people and the smell of roasting turkey on Thanksgiving. Uncle Kelsey sneaked a swipe of mashed potatoes before they were ready, and was rewarded with a playful slap from his wife. He was in a great mood. The explosion that destroyed most of the Cahill University Archeology building was chalked up to a gas main rupture, and just by sheer luck, not a single person had gotten hurt. Plus, some secret donor had already pledged enough funds to rebuild the entire structure. There were good people in the world. Reese helped Theo set the table in the other room. Her parents lounged in front of the TV, her dad happily watching football while her mother shook her head and wondered why anyone in their right mind would allow their kids to play a game in which somebody might be seriously hurt.

Parker's mom sat with a smile on her face, happy to be with her family and some new friends. Maybe today was the day that she would tell her son that she had decided to move to New Hampshire. Her original plan was to wait until Parker's dad was out of jail, but he was in for another year at least, and time was too precious to waste. Parker needed a family and, looking around, it seemed to her like he had one here. When he got out they could all move in together. She had already started looking for a job and a place where she and Parker could stay. It was going to be great, she thought, a new start for all of them. And New Hampshire seemed like the perfect place. It was so quiet and peaceful.

Parker stood outside and watched them all through a window. "My mom, Reese's folks, my aunt and uncle. They don't even know that anything happened. Everything seems like it's back to normal, but nothing will ever really be the same again, will it?"

"No," Fon-Rahm said from the shadows nearby.

"I wish my dad could be here."

"Is that a command?"

Parker thought for a moment. "No. I don't think I'm ready for that yet."

"Your mother cares very deeply for you. I would tell my mother how much she meant to me. If I had a mother."

Parker grinned. "You've got me."

"Yes," said the genie. "I suppose I do."

Parker's aunt yelled from inside the house. "Parker! We're eating!"

Parker said, "Let's go inside."

"Very well. I shall make myself unseen."

Before Fon-Rahm could make himself disappear, Parker stopped him. "Maybe we could try it another way," he said.

They were all sitting patiently at the table when Parker came in with Fon-Rahm. At first, Reese and Theo were confused. Why was the genie wearing Dockers and a button-down plaid shirt? The Fon-Rahm they knew was a magical being that performed miracles with a wave of his hand, not a schlub in a cubicle on casual Friday. The bigger issue for the kids, though, was that everyone in the room was looking right at him. Was it possible that they all could...see him?

"Mom, everybody," said Parker. "This is Mr. Rommy. He's our new math teacher at school. I hope you guys don't mind I invited him. It's just that he didn't have any family around to spend Thanksgiving with."

"Oh, it's our pleasure," said Aunt Martha. "It's so nice to have you." She was already back in the kitchen for another plate.

Uncle Kelsey pulled another chair up to the table. "Any friend of Parker's."

Fon-Rahm sat in between Reese and Mrs. Quarry. Reese smiled warmly at the genie. She thought she saw him blush.

"Mr. Rommy, is it?" asked Reese's mother. "That's an unusual name."

"It's very old," he told her. "I believe in the beginning it was..."

Theo and Reese held their breaths, hoping he didn't start talking about ancient Mesopotamia.

"French," said Fon-Rahm. The kids relaxed.

Parker's mom said, "Well, I'm thrilled that Parker has someone to look up to. I'm almost afraid to ask you how he's doing in your class."

Fon-Rahm sized Parker up. "Parker," he said, "is an excellent student."

Parker beamed.

His mom was pleasantly surprised. "Good! That's good to hear!"

Parker took the seat next to his mom. "This is great, Mom. I'm really..." He gave her a genuine smile. "I'm glad you're here."

She took his hand on the table. "Thank you, Parker." She thought she might cry, so she turned her attention back to Parker's new math teacher. "I hope you're hungry, Mr. Rommy."

"I am. Do you have any French fries?"

"Try the mashed potatoes," said Parker.

They all dug in, thankful for many, many reasons.

After dinner, as the adults drank coffee and digested their turkey, Parker, Reese, Theo, and Fon-Rahm stood in the backyard and stared up at the night sky.

"I never really appreciated the stars before I almost got killed a bunch of times," said Theo.

Fon-Rahm said, "You know, it might not be such a bad idea for me to come and teach at your school."

"Excuse me?" said Parker.

"That way we could remain within the tether's limits and we would be ready if we were needed."

"I'm not crazy about this plan."

"Oh, I think you will find that as a teacher I am tough, but fair."

"The whole point of having a genie is to avoid things that are tough but fair."

Fon-Rahm was thoughtful. "I wonder if they would give me my own parking space?"

"Do you really think that Vesiroth will come back, after all these years?" Reese asked Fon-Rahm.

He looked to the moon. "I do not know. It has been a long time, and he has only regained three small parts of his power. It would be difficult, I think, for anyone to endure what he was put through."

Reese was relieved.

"Of course," Fon-Rahm continued, "Vesiroth is the most powerful sorcerer the world has ever known. If anyone could have survived all this time, it would be him. If he has revived, his anger will know no bounds. Even in a weakened state he poses a dire threat. And let us not forget that there are still nine more of the Jinn out there, somewhere."

Fon-Rahm saw that he had worried Reese.

"No," he said, shaking his head. "We will never see Vesiroth. His body was probably destroyed years ago."

"Good," said Parker. "I think we could all use a little downtime."

EPILOGUE

THE CARNIVAL WORKER WALKED WITH a slight limp. He wished that he could say it was from getting bucked off a horse, or maybe that it was an old football injury. It wasn't. His leg just bothered him, that's all. The fact was, he was getting old.

"Now, see, when the ride jams, nine times out of ten it's right here," he said, pointing his flashlight down. "The track is bent."

His trainee furrowed his brow and nodded, all business. That was good, the carny thought. You didn't keep something like the Train of Terror running without knowing your stuff. It was an old ride, built in the sixties and showing her age. The carny could relate.

"I keep asking for replacement parts, but the owners are too cheap. Ah, what do they care about an old ride? I think I'm the only one who'll even notice when it finally stops running."

He had no idea how long that might be, but when it did happen, he knew he was probably out of a job. He had been touring with the carnival for more than forty years, and he had seen it go straight downhill. When he started, the rides were shiny and new. Now, the whole place gave off an air of seediness and disrepair. He wasn't even sure it was worth anyone's time to train the new kid. Still, the trainee wasn't so bad. He wasn't a genius, but if he was, he wouldn't have been there, would he?

It was dark inside the ride, and it smelled like stagnant water and metal. It was supposed to be a train through a haunted mine. The walls were fixed up to look like black rock, but the paint had fallen away in places, and the white stucco underneath poked through. The plastic skeleton on the first turn was missing a foot, and the thing that popped out from behind the dynamite kegs looked more like a mangy dog than a werewolf. Really, what was a werewolf doing in a haunted mine, anyway? A ghost would have made more sense. The carny guessed that it was too late to change it now.

As the carny bent down to look at the tracks, the trainee let out a yelp. He had backed into an iron cage hanging from the ceiling.

"Oh," said the carny. "Have you met Harold?"

The carny aimed his light at the cage. Inside was a mannequin dressed in rags and coated with shiny lacquer and a thick layer of dust. It was in a standing position, with one hand extended, as if he was reaching for something, maybe. The carny let the trainee stare at it for a few moments.

"It's a real body, you know," said the carny slyly.

"Get out of here."

"I swear. It's an Egyptian mummy. It was part of some old traveling exhibit. After they went bust, this thing ended up in here. They call him Harold because, well, I don't know why they call him Harold. He looks like a Harold." He lowered his voice to a whisper. "They say if you're in here by yourself after midnight, you can hear him moving around in there. One time, when I had just started working here, I heard him say something."

The trainee was skeptical. "Yeah? What did he say?"

The carny brought his voice even lower, making the kid lean in to hear him. "He said . . ." Then the carny yelled as loud as he could, "Lemme out!"

The trainee jumped and the old man laughed. "I'm just pulling your leg, you dope. Come on, let's go."

They walked down the tracks and out the exit. The carnival was closed. Workers swept the grounds and closed up booths.

"Ah, man," said the trainee, "I left my crowbar back there."

"Well, you had better go and get it. The last thing we want is for a car to derail because you left something on the tracks."

The trainee jogged back into the murky tunnel. He found the dent in the track and saw his crowbar on the floor. As he reached for it, his flashlight found Harold. The trainee stood up and peeked into the cage for a closer look. It sure was an ugly thing. Harold's face had been painted over so many times it hardly even looked like a face anymore.

The trainee smirked. A real mummy, right. And he was going to play shortstop for the Detroit Tigers next year.

He bent back down to get his crowbar. When the trainee stood, Harold reached out of the cage and grabbed him by his throat.

As he choked the trainee to death, the mannequin's lacquered mask crumbled away. Underneath was a face brutally scarred on one side. It was good to be free, thought Vesiroth as his lips twisted into a grim smile.